From Alice
with Love

From Alice
with Love

Jo
DUTTON

ARENA
ALLEN&UNWIN

This project has been assisted by the Australian
Government through the Australia Council, its
arts funding and advisory body.

Arena Books, an imprint of
Allen & Unwin
83 Alexander Street
Crows Nest NSW 2065
Australia
Phone: (61 2) 8425 0100
Email: info@allenandunwin.com
Web: www.allenandunwin.com

Cataloguing-in-Publication details are available
from the National Library of Australia
www.trove.nla.gov.au

ISBN 978 1 74331 334 3

Set in 11/18 pt Sabon by Midland Typesetters, Australia
Printed and bound in Australia by Griffin Press

10 9 8 7 6 5 4 3 2 1

For Gerard

CHAPTER I

I'd been expecting Mum to call. I'd left her quite a few messages during the week. When my phone rang just as I was going to bed and Michael's number came up I half expected it might be her.

'Alicia,' he said. 'Your Mum is really sick. She's been admitted to the ICU, they think it's acute hepatitis.'

It was impossible to take in.

'Alicia, sweetheart,' Michael said anxiously, 'are you there?' At first I could only nod. I think I was waiting for it not to be true. The seconds stretched. Finally I said, 'Yes. How on earth did that happen?'

I sat down while my stepfather told me what he knew. He'd only got back from a week out bush that afternoon. At home he'd found Mum slumped in the bathroom, vomiting, her skin a jaundiced yellow. When he asked how long she'd been there, she couldn't tell him; in fact, he said, it'd been hard to get any sense out of her. He'd rushed her up to the hospital. That was hours ago. He hadn't wanted to call till he had some idea what was happening. Like me he knew there was no way I could have just grabbed a flight anyway. There was only a morning flight to Alice Springs.

A team of doctors had assessed her. She'd been put on a range of drugs to stabilise her. Antiviral and immunosuppressant. He wasn't sure of all the details and I didn't really care. I just wanted to know she'd be all right. They'd know more by morning he said. They were waiting to see if she responded to the drugs; if not, they might have to transfer her to a liver transplant unit, probably in Adelaide.

That really shook me but I didn't know what to say. He sounded overwhelmed and I felt too far away.

'Is someone else with you?'

'Yeah, the unholy trinity has arrived.'

That would be Frank, Iry and Lucy. Part of my Alice family.

'Good.'

'I better get back upstairs. My phone will be off but I'll check messages regularly.'

'Tell her I'm coming. I'll be up in the morning. And keep me updated. If they look like moving her let me know as soon as you find out.'

'Of course,' Michael said.

'See you tomorrow, tell her I love her, and you of course.'

I rang my ex, Floyd. We'd been together for ten years and though our relationship had ended, the last nine months hadn't been easy for either of us. Leaving my job as a primary school teacher at the same time probably hadn't been the best decision to have made. Financially and emotionally, it had been a difficult time. Just when I thought Floyd wouldn't answer he did. He was in Darwin, getting some background on a story but was coming back to Sydney on the red-eye. He suggested we meet at the airport. His calmness steadied me and I was grateful he was still available to me in a crisis.

It was a warm night and I packed with the fan whirring, aware that·this heat would pale into insignificance when I got to Alice. Everything summery I had went into the case. At the last minute I threw in my bush boots and hiking shoes. Without really thinking about what I was doing I found myself tidying up the flat as though I'd be away for some time. As I was clearing up my desk, I came across my employment folder in the bottom drawer, containing my CV, qualifications, references. For some reason I picked it up and threw it in my suitcase too.

When I'd finished packing, I paced my small balcony, wishing I had a view to calm me. But the ocean was blocked by flats just like mine. Four floors up, I faced the back of other concrete boxes, and the whining of air-conditioning units which had spread like tumours on outside walls, blowing hot air. I couldn't go to bed. Sleeping was impossible. There was no way I could stop worrying about Mum. I felt so useless and scared.

In the end I rang a taxi to take me to the airport.

It was 4 am, still warm, and on the street, I could hear the sea tumbling in the distance, the waves murmuring reassuringly, and for a moment I thought about how it might be all I'd miss.

The airport was dead but at least I felt like I was on my way. I organised myself near Floyd's arrival gate. To pass the time I watched the cleaners run their machines back and forth over the floors as the terminal slowly came awake. The worst-case scenarios about Mum, that she'd die or need a new liver, kept me tightly wound and awake.

Floyd was easy to spot in the disembarking stream, a head above most of the other passengers. He looked tired, but on spotting me his face broke into a warm smile. As he drew up alongside me he swung an arm around my shoulder, steering me through the crowd into a corner booth in a café.

His kindness in spite of everything that had passed between us made it easier to lose it for a few moments. I felt overwhelmed with sadness and found myself crying on his shoulder. He hugged me, his arms strong and reassuring, his stubbled chin resting on my forehead.

'Hey,' he said, passing me a napkin so I could wipe my tears and blow my nose. 'Ros'll be fine.'

'You don't know that,' I replied.

'She's tough. She's the toughest woman I've ever met. Have some faith.'

Floyd was good company, telling funny stories about Territory politicians and generally trying to distract me from spinning into too dark a space. No doubt he had heard from mutual friends how much I'd been struggling lately. My fragility was no secret and he knew I'd been leaning on Mum for support. Times had been hard. I didn't want Floyd back, it wasn't that; I just wasn't confident I'd ever get the family of my own I wanted.

Floyd and I both started when the baby in a nearby pram began crying. Only its small bunched fists were visible, flaying the air. I sighed. Life seemed so unfair. I folded my arms on the table and rested my head on them.

Floyd rubbed his palm in a circle on my back. 'It'll be alright,' he said.

I hoped so. A message had come through from Michael. Mum wouldn't be moved.

'See,' Floyd said, optimistic as ever. 'She's already on the mend.'

On the flight, the fear that Floyd's presence had kept at bay returned, swamping me. My chest was tight and Panadol seemed powerless against my headache. The cold glass of the window provided some relief, though, so I rested my forehead on it for most of the three-hour journey. Descending was an absolute relief; as the familiar landscape moved into focus it calmed me a little, like the presence of an old friend. In steady waves the caterpillar ranges marched away to the west. To the south, ochre claypans were revealed, delicately detailed, indecipherable as ancient maps.

As we swooped lower the white conical roofs of Pine Gap came into view. 'Spooky ears,' my childhood friend Lekisha had dubbed them for the spying the defence base was rumoured to do. For a moment the lime-white road to the Aboriginal Catholic Mission, one of the places Lekisha called home, appeared at the tip of the wing before unfurling eastward like a cowboy's cast rope. The green smudges took form—mulga, corkwood trees, and acacia bushes. And then we'd landed with a bump, and were taxiing towards the terminal.

The heat hit me like a slap as I stepped down onto the tarmac. Outside of the plane, the country seemed more foe than friend. The sky, vast and daunting, stretched before and above me. Distant brown ranges circled, shimmering threateningly, and heat radiated from the black tarmac.

Inside the terminal I waited in a daze for my bags, trying to distract myself from my fear by watching the dance of arrival play out. I saw a couple of people I vaguely knew, including the receptionist at Mum's work, who smiled at me sympathetically.

Wheeling my bags outside, I waited in the stifling heat for Michael.

The last time I'd been here was at Easter. Floyd and I had come up for a holiday. It had rained for two days and the river had flooded. The waterholes had filled. It was a joyful time, watching the country spring to life as opportunistically as the desert did, in a sudden bright burst of colours. Buoyed by the beauty, inspired by these images of hidden possibilities re-emerging, Floyd and I had almost fooled ourselves into thinking we could make it.

Since then there had been barely a drop of rain, not even in January when cyclones often pushed storms inland. The bright colours had long since faded, and the plants did what they could to survive, receding back into a hazy purplish wash over the landscape. At the end of the airport concourse the ghost gum cried tears of sap, leaving sticky amber blotches on the ochre paving. Foreign buffel grass had rampaged through what had been an attractive native garden, reducing it to a scratchy brown patch. Unsettled by how unhealthy everything looked, I hoped it wasn't some kind of sign.

Fortunately, just then Michael pulled up next to me in a Land Cruiser, the legal service emblem emblazoned on its door. I threw my cases in the back and opened the passenger door, grabbing the hand rail and swinging myself up onto the seat. Michael leant over and landed a kiss above my eyebrow before I'd even shut the door. I gave him a clumsy hug over the gearstick.

'I'm glad you're here,' he said.

'How is she going?' I asked, watching his face carefully.

He played with words in his mouth, taking a long time to choose the ones he wanted. 'She's resilient,' he said.

How careful he was with his words made me certain she was no better than last night. She might even be worse. I fidgeted with my bag. I wanted to ask him more but I thought it might be better just to wait and see her for myself. He obviously found talking about her too hard.

Old songs I hadn't heard in a while played on the local radio reminding me of Mum. Everything I saw out the window reminded me of her. The wide sandy river, the red and purple hills, even the buffel grass which she hated. It struck me that if she died I'd never be able to bear coming back here, and I'd lose both her and this country I loved so much.

'She'll make it,' Michael said in the tone he reserved for facts. In his court voice. Which often made them not facts at all but details in a narrative he was trying to sell.

'Am I that obvious?' I asked. 'I thought I was hard to read?'

'Who told you that?'

'Floyd.'

'Well,' he said. 'I suppose it depends on the situation. I think blind Freddy could see how you feel right now.'

He squeezed my hand.

The driver of an oncoming van stuck a black hand out the window, the turn of his palm, thumb and finger cocked. What's up?

'Was that Henry?' I asked, craning my head around to stare after the van. Henry was Lekisha's uncle and I'd always had a soft spot for him. 'Yeah. He's been great. A real leader. Now the new housing has been built at Promised Land everyone's more or less up there all the time and he's getting the kids in and out to school.'

'He's running the kids into school in town?'

'Yeah.'

'That's a big commitment,' I said. And expensive too, given it was a round trip of over two hundred kilometres.

'Ros found some money to help with the costs.'

'Of course she did.' Mum was every funding body's nightmare. If there was a dollar to be found she could sniff it out. She'd shown a natural talent for finding money since starting here over thirty years ago as a volunteer social worker partnered with an Aboriginal mentor, Lekisha's grandmother, Magdalene. It was probably Mum's nose for money that prompted the Aboriginal health organisation to give her and Magdalene some of their earliest paid roles. Later, I'm sure it was this same skill that had her promoted reluctantly into a management position. It couldn't have been her tact: Mum's feisty nature had often landed her in trouble with bureaucracy. It was knowing just how to write a submission that had saved her neck. That and her relationship with Magdalene.

With a pang of fear, I wondered what would save her now.

'They think they might finally get that school up and running there soon,' said Michael, clearly determined to keep talking now he'd started.

'Really?' I said, jolted back. The dream of starting a school for Magdalene's small community at Promised Land was almost as old as I was.

'Yeah, they're pretty confident. I heard there's been a response to the last report they wrote to put up to the department. The one Floyd was lobbying on behalf of.'

'That's good,' I said, too distracted for the conversation. We were nearly at the hospital when Michael, ever the pragmatist, made a quick detour home so I could drop off my gear.

When we pulled in to the driveway, the house and garden looked the same.

The old red gum was still standing. Above the roof line the flame tree was ablaze with tongued red flowers. Fat purple fruit weighed down the mulberry tree so heavily it looked like a weeping variety. At the doorway I nearly tripped over Mum's red Birkenstocks. All by themselves they could have made me cry. I put my head down and tried not to look at her old brown leather work bag on the hat stand as I dumped my suitcase on the floor of the entrance hall.

Coming out I noticed Mr and Mrs Press across the street sitting on their verandah in the same sofa chairs they'd reclined in for as long as I could remember. Mrs Press caught my eye as I was getting into the car. I raised a hand in a wave but her return smile was so loaded with concern and sympathy that I had to look away in case I started crying again.

CHAPTER 2

When we got to the hospital I insisted Michael drop me off in the car park and head on to his office. I saw him waver, his instinct to support me at war with his duty to return to work. Like Mum, he had always been a complete workaholic. He'd been the senior lawyer at the legal aid office in Alice for decades. I knew even this morning's break would be enough to have created a backlog. There was no mercy in his line of work, no let-up.

'Go, see what's happening at work then come back,' I instructed.

'Are you sure?'

'Michael!' I bit my bottom lip and I think he saw then that it wouldn't have mattered if his desk was totally clear: I had to see Mum on my own the first time. I needed space to cope.

He nodded. 'Take care,' he said, giving my hand a squeeze before driving off.

ICU was on the top floor of the hospital near the operating theatres. I made my way through the automatic doors and down the hospital's expansive entrance, the big bright mural painted by women I knew failing to get my attention for the first time. I didn't notice Frank, Iry and Lucy, who were waiting for me near the lifts, until they intercepted me.

'Hey,' I said, realising now why Michael had agreed to leave me.

We hugged in an uncoordinated scramble. Iry's hair was blacker and she was thinner. Frank was getting wider. And Lucy looked as blonde and gorgeous as ever.

'We just wanted to make sure you're okay.'

Lucy held my hand while she spoke.

'Thanks,' I said. ' I just want to go up and see her.'

'You don't want one of us to come?' Iry asked.

'No. I'm right.' They were making me more nervous, not less.

'Call,' said Lucy. 'For anything.'

I promised to and having just missed both lifts, took the stairs at a run.

On the first floor I turned down the corridor towards the theatre recovery room and then passed through some double swing doors. The meeting room where families are given news of patients and where they can just sit together when things are really bad was to the left. The main door to ICU directly in front. I pushed the buzzer and waited. I was just considering whether I should push it again when a nurse answered.

'You must be the daughter,' she said. 'Your dad said you were coming.'

I didn't correct her, only nodded and followed her into the open and falsely cheery light of the space.

'There,' she said, tilting her head and letting me go on ahead.

In spite of all my fears and dark imaginings over the last few hours I was underprepared. The impact of the shock seemed to travel to me in slow motion. It didn't seem possible that the woman in the hospital bed could be Mum. Her face seemed bloated. Her skin was an unnatural shade of yellow and hung off her loosely. She looked as though she'd aged ten years since Christmas. Why did Michael say she was resilient? He should have just told me she looked like she was about to die. Because she did. Mum was on oxygen and had another tube down her nose. Her eyes were taped closed. She was surrounded by machines, boxes that beeped and displayed alarming-looking numbers that flashed red and green like traffic lights. It was hard to know how to get closer to her. Tentatively I chose the side of the bed with the least obstructions and took her hand, bending over to kiss her. I was shocked at how putrid her breath was.

A large bag of clear liquid hung on a stand beside the bed, a drip line feeding into a cannula just above her left wrist. I tried to focus on something small, something I could understand, and attempted to read the label on the bag of liquid, but the letters were as incomprehensible as Mum being in such a bad way.

No wonder the others thought they should have come up with me.

Fear pounded like surf. An undertow threatened to drag me out where I couldn't stay on my feet.

The nurse stopped by to check Mum's drip and she adjusted a valve.

'We're getting on top of it,' she said. 'This sort of acute liver failure is most unusual. But try not to worry, all the indicators tell us she's going well.' She smiled reassuringly and moved on.

How could I not worry? I felt sick with it.

I knew I should have managed to be tougher for Mum's sake. She couldn't bear it when I was upset. But as soon as the nurse turned away I burst into tears. I didn't notice she'd turned back until I felt a comforting hand on my back.

'It's a shock,' she said. 'A big one. Have a cry. It's good.'

I really cried. Nothing, though, like the crying this room would have seen. The raw grief the nurse would have witnessed. The rituals.

'Thanks,' I said, when I'd managed to blow my nose and pull myself together.

'All part of service,' she said, kindly. 'And it's Ali,' she added as she moved away.

'Alicia,' I said.

I took down the rail on Mum's bed and perched carefully next to her, holding her hand tightly, taking in more calmly her ravaged state, her shrunken chest, the worried creases embedded in her face as though, even so heavily sedated, she somehow knew she was in deep trouble.

I wanted to do something, to say something, and I remembered how in books and movies people are instructed to talk to unconscious loved ones—that even if they can't respond, they can hear.

'You'll be right, Mum,' I said. I felt a bit silly talking to an unconscious person aloud but I knew the staff wouldn't think it was odd, even if they heard me. I rubbed Mum's cool hand warm in both of mine as I wondered what story I could tell her that would best show her how much I needed her. There were so many. In the end I chose an old one, from when I was nine years old and Mum would have been thirty-two. Younger than I was now, I thought.

13

'Do you remember the time you took me to the waterhole? It was a Saturday—I know because I had a bye at netball and you were home. And suddenly you said, "Grab your shoes, a hat—we're off." They were always spur-of-the-moment decisions, our trips—at least I thought so, but maybe you planned those adventures. "Girls' business," you'd sing out to Michael, and we'd head off on what you called a one-box adventure. The single swag would be in the boot, and forty litres of water ready and waiting as usual. I always chose the stuff for the food box. I picked biscuits, fruit and some nuts and dried fruit. A stub end of cheese. And at the last minute I grabbed a few eggs and some bread and you laughed.

'We always followed the rules and told Michael where we were going and when we'd be back. We knew he'd give us twenty-four hours leeway before he'd come searching, in case we'd had a minor breakdown or we were having a good time and in no mood to rush. That happened a few times, didn't it?

'On that Saturday we headed north, past the turn-off to Promised Land. Remember, Mum, the protest signs on the roadside, the fight still on for the excisions up there. And that old sister of Magdalene's was sitting there next to the signs like she could have been part of the land. And you said to me, "Can you imagine begging like that for your home what some fella stole?" Of course I couldn't. Still can't.

'That day we went far, up and then off on the Plenty. It was stinking hot, unusual for early August, and the air-conditioning in the car didn't work. Did it ever, or did you buy the beast like that?' I threaded a strand of Mum's hair back behind her ear. She'd always been ridiculously tough.

'We lost our way in the scrub searching for the waterhole you said existed somewhere hidden in the hills. Not lost, lost—we could have always made our way back to the main track and then to the main road, we just didn't want to give up. We were quite methodical, I know that. For years I kept in my diary the coordinates you got me to write. I wish I could remember the final ones—then we could go back there. But maybe we can go without them, find it all over again. When you're better, I mean.

'By dusk we still hadn't managed to find it, and you decided it was too dangerous to keep searching so far off the beaten track in the dark. We saved the rest of the picnic food for lunch the next day and the eggs for breakfast. "Good thinking to bring the eggs," you said, teasing me. "Maybe you planned this." And when I looked like sulking you tickled me and made me laugh.

'We ate the last apple as though it was the most special apple in the world. You cut it into wafer-thin slices and fed them to me one by one. We were sitting up on the wide bonnet of the car and once we'd finished eating we leant back on the windscreen to watch as the stars emerged from the darkness. The famous desert light show. And you told me that the stars were the souls of children waiting to be born. That that was why all my life I'd feel as if I'd been here before and had known you forever. Because before I was born I was waiting up there, looking down.'

I imagined then that her grip tightened in my hand. Clearing my throat, I pressed on with the story. 'As the night grew darker, you made me a bed on the back seat and gave me your sarong to keep the flies and mosquitoes off my face. You camped on the single swag just outside my open door.'

'I remember waking before dawn, when the light was the pink and blue of fairground spun sugar, so soft, so beautiful, before it simply melted away into the yellow heat of the rising sun. I've never seen light change like that anywhere else. In fact, when I think of home it's that image of sunrise which always comes to mind.

'Anyway, I was looking down at you as the first of the sun's rays reached you. Your hair was so long back then, lit up like a crown of wild red sparks. It was the first time I'd ever really looked at you when you were still. You seemed perfect to me—your proud nose, your wide face, your mouth with the dark pink lips—more beautiful than an angel. I knew then I'd seen you from the sky and chosen you to be my mother.'

She'd been a good choice. Not always sweet, but fair and strong. Mum could always look after herself and was pretty capable out bush. Getting slightly off course had been unusual, and in the morning it didn't take us long to find the small pool less than a kilometre from where we'd slept. The break in the escarpment she'd been looking for was hidden around the next bend in the rocky curves of the ranges we'd been following the day before.

Standing in the riverbed with the water at our feet we spent some time looking up at the face of the range, amazed by its beauty. It felt as if someone, a god perhaps, had gone to great trouble to find just the right shape and shade of red rock to make this dramatic setting. I remember feeling as though my heart would burst with love for the place, for my mother, for the life I'd been given.

Overcome with emotions I couldn't voice, I ran straight into the water in my shorts and top. After I'd splashed her enough, Mum followed me in. It was lovely water, cold and brown but clean enough to drink. She told me this was a special place, and that we were lucky Magdalene had given us permission to come.

I'd never understood why she said that when from memory, the water was nowhere near Promised Land. Why would we have needed Magdalene's permission?

We floated for ages in the small pool; when we were cold we got out and lay on the bank and waved our arms to leave angel imprints in the sand. I could have stayed for much longer, but we had to be back before Michael reported us missing. When we left I'm sure Mum promised we would go back sometime, but for some reason we never had. Perhaps, if she got better, we could go there again.

I stood up and stretched. At the central desk the nurse was busy with the duty doctor, studying some data or other on a computer screen. I assumed some of the information from the monitors on Mum were fed there but I had no real idea how the system worked.

I moved a chair closer to Mum's bed so I didn't have to perch on the bedside. It wasn't much more comfortable sitting down. There was a deep indent in the seat and it was hard not to be reminded of all those other people who'd sat here before me. Waiting. Wondering. Hoping like I was that everything would be all right. With so little control it was a terrifying place to be.

I leant my head back, slipped off my sandals, put my feet on the bed and stretched out as comfortably as I could, as close to Mum as possible. 'I'm staying, here at the hospital with you,' I said, trying to sound lighthearted, 'until you at least say hello.'

High above me on the opposite wall was a single window. Anyone with business in this room had no time for views, but I was glad to be afforded a scrap of sky. It was reassuringly blue, with small clouds, white as cotton wool, being chased across it by the wind.

I texted Michael. FYI all fine here, no change. Tell others I be in touch.

Finally the early start and the stress caught up with me, and I closed my eyes, just for a moment.

CHAPTER 3

It wasn't till voices woke me that I realised I'd fallen sleep. I looked up to see two doctors standing at the end of Mum's bed, one of whom I recognised. Embarrassed, I ran a hand over my face trying to look alert.

'So you did end up a doctor,' I said, smiling wearily at Fiona Gordon. 'How long have you been back?' We'd never been close and she'd left for boarding school in grade nine already determined to be a doctor.

'Years,' she said. She introduced her resident to me and then turned back to Mum.

'Ros?' She put a hand on Mum's shoulder as though she was a conscious patient, and informed her politely that she would be checking on her. She seemed to spend a long time palpating the area around her liver and then reading notes on the charts.

The clock on the wall and I kept a tense company while Fiona and her resident joined the other staff at the desk where they all had a long discussion. Every now and again I could see Fiona make the resident change the screen she was looking at. When it looked like she was finished with her discussion the resident left. I assumed she'd come and talk to me but she sat down and used the phone. She had two long telephone conversations. By the time she signalled me over I'd convinced myself the news was bad. I followed her to the meeting room feeling sick with anxiety.

'Are you sure, you shouldn't tell Michael?' If it was bad news he should hear it with me.

'I've already spoken to him. I just thought I'd update you so there's no confusion.'

Fiona pointed out the couch for me to sit on. Her manner was clinical, entirely professional. Results from the antigen tests were positive, as they'd suspected Mum had hepatitis B, nothing worse. But she had been extremely unlucky. Only one per cent of hep B cases were as acute as hers, and she was still not out of the woods. She was suffering from encephalopathy, a state of disorientation caused by liver failure, and the sedation they'd given her to cope with the naso-gastric tube had added to her confusion and sleepiness. She'd stay in ICU while they monitored her to make sure there was no damage to her other organs, especially the kidneys. They were considering dialysing her. She was still waiting on the opinion of a specialist in Adelaide to decide, though she was quick to reassure me if it happened it would just be the once. It didn't mean Mum had renal failure.

I certainly hoped not. It was hard to shake the image of the renal unit which seemed to have expanded every time I came back. In Magdalene's family three people I knew of were on dialysis—Uncle Harry, Auntie Rosie and Big James. It wasn't much of a life being tied to a machine.

Fiona moved on at a clip through Mum's other results. The CT scan was clear, there was no brain damage and her lungs were fine, with no signs of pneumonia. Blood clotting was normalising. What she wanted to make clear to me, and what she hadn't talked to Michael about was that the liver could fix itself. It could regenerate. How fast varied from case to case. But, rest, hydration and a healthy diet would be crucial.

'So read the dietary information the nurses will make sure you get and get organised around her food. That's the best help you'll be able to give her. Good clean food. No fat. No sugar.'

'Sure.' I tried not to let her see I was a little amused she assumed I was the cook. It was Michael she should talk to about food.

'So how long will she be here?' I asked. 'In ICU?'

'It's hard to tell, at the outside a couple of days. She can pick up as quickly as she went down. We'll keep an eye on her bloods and see how she goes. Anything else you want to know?'

'Why does she smell so bad?' I felt a little disloyal mentioning it, but Mum never had bad breath.

'That's part of the disease: we call it fetor. That and the jaundice made it pretty clear what we were looking at, but we had to check a few other possibilities too.'

Fiona was gathering her papers.

'How did you end up back here?' I asked suddenly curious, even though she didn't seem to want to personalise things. She went for the shorthand approach.

'Studied medicine on a rural scholarship, which meant I had to come back for two years. After years of Melbourne winters I loved it, stayed on, and specialised in the liver, which is why I'm attending to your mum. Met and married David, who's a mid-wife—a bit of a role reversal, I suppose. Three kids—two girls, one baby boy—huge mortgage, big house, obligatory water-wasting pool. And you?'

In the spirit of the game I'd foolishly started I forced a lightness I didn't feel. 'Four years art college, Dip Ed—you know what they say, if you can't do, teach, that's me. Live in Sydney, divorced from Floyd who's a journalist, no kids, no mortgage, no job.' If this was a competition, which it always was, clearly I was the loser.

Fiona smiled politely, then paused at the door, head cocked. 'You and your friend—what was her name? Lavisha?'

'Lekisha.'

'Yes, that's right. Do you still see her?'

'Yes.'

'God, what a pair you were,' she said. 'The class clowns. I'll never forget some of your antics. The trouble you got into.'

I smiled. Well, what else do you do when you're thirteen and it just hits you that most of the world hates Aboriginal people and that means they might hate your best friend? You laugh. Make everyone laugh so they leave you alone.

Michael had texted back that he'd come when he could. I could see through the door that the nurse was with Mum so rather than going straight back into the bright cave of ICU, I wandered downstairs. Outside I half hoped I might find Magdalene. Someone would have told her by now. The sun still had a firm grip on the day and coming out from the air-conditioning the heat was a shock. I shielded my eyes with a hand, looking over the lawns. Magdalene, sitting with a group of women in the shade, spotted me first.

'Hey werte,' she said, greeting me in her own language and waving me over.

I sat down next to her and she hugged me tightly. She smelled of fire and bush. Mulga sweet. Gorgeous. She rubbed her hands up and down my arms. Finally, I felt truly home.

'Good girl,' she said. 'Your mum needs you.'

She introduced her relatives from Mission, giving me a quick refresher course on the complicated family relationships. Only when that was done did she offer me her hand so I could help her up.

'Have you been up to see her earlier?' I asked.

'No, that security stopped me. It wasn't visiting time. They real strict these days. I was waiting to catch you. I knew you'd be straight here.'

'You want me to take you up now?'

'Of course.'

We held hands as we walked. She seemed unchanged since I'd last seen her, wrinkled, squinting short-sightedly, walking on legs that looked like two young sticks, and carrying more weight than she should at her waist. I didn't have any memories of Magdalene being young, but she never seemed to get older either. To me she'd always been this age, the age of an elder.

The security officer acknowledged us with a friendly nod as we passed, and in ICU the staff were unfazed by me bringing her in. If Magdalene was scared of being in this place, she concealed it well. Many of Magdalene's friends and family had been patients here over the years, and it was here that Lekisha's mum, Magdalene's daughter, had died. It might be over thirty years ago but I was sure it would still hurt deeply.

Magdalene was a traditional healer, a Ngangkere. With Lekisha I'd often collected plants to be worked as Chinese medicine practitioners or naturopaths would do into various medicinal combinations, however, there was much more to Magdalene's healing than organics. She had a gift. Her work was regarded as powerful, and I knew that anything she offered could only help. I stayed for a few minutes while she looked Mum over, whispering to her in language, until she gave me a look that said my presence wasn't required.

Downstairs in the café I ate a couple of dim sims, the last of the fried food on offer at the end of the day. They were full of fat and sugar. I thought they were delicious, coated in soy sauce, and I would have happily eaten more if there'd been any.

When I went back to the unit Magdalene was gone and I'd wished I'd stayed closer so we could have caught up. Mum seemed to be looking a little more relaxed. She smelled different too. On her face were shiny traces of grease which I presumed to be goanna fat because Magdalene had once told me it helped the good medicine to absorb into the skin.

I held Mum's hand. 'I think you're going to be right.'

I imagined she heard me because she seemed to turn slightly towards me.

'I think you've got quality help here.'

*

It was Magdalene who had called the taxi when Mum went into labour. Mum always said the look on Magdalene's face when she told her that my dad Eddy, not a circle of women, would meet her at the hospital, was absolutely priceless. Once in labour she said she knew exactly why Magdalene had looked at her like she was mad.

I took my time coming into the world. Perhaps I was waiting for Dad to run out of film. Before being born in a white sheen of vernix, I led Mum on a long journey into herself. During those hours, Eddy took literally hundreds of photos. They were never intended for viewing—no doubt they're stored in a box somewhere—but he couldn't have been at my birth without the protection of his camera. When I emerged I had soft light fur all over me. Mum, like every mother before her, thought I was the most beautiful baby in the world. She planned on calling me Alice but Eddy insisted on Alicia.

Eddy and Mum had never married but she thought they were committed to each other. When she'd found out she was pregnant Eddy and her had decided they could cope even though it was not in their plans. But he had grown restless from the moment there could be no backing out. Always packing his bag and following the possibilities of a scoop, the first winter after my birth was no exception. He'd received a tip that a small family of Pintubi people had been sighted out west, beyond the last settlement in the desert. These were Aboriginal people who as yet had not succumbed to rations and settlement, and he wanted to be the first to capture them on film; such a picture, he knew, would be enough to set him up as a photographer, somewhere else. Escape plans dominated Eddy's thoughts. Mum was left alone in their small house, barely coping with my fractious and colicky moods. Before I was born the apparent ease with which the Aboriginal women she'd met managed their babies had stopped her from panicking about being a mother. Unfortunately, I bore little resemblance to the contented babies she'd seen. I hardly slept. I grizzled a lot. Mum's store of energy was rapidly spent. Isolated, she was raw with needs she had lost all confidence of ever having met. Sometimes when I was screaming she knew she couldn't be trusted to pick me up, in case she hurt me.

We don't talk about what might have happened if Mum hadn't bumped into Magdalene on her way past the hospital one day. Magdalene had been visiting her eldest daughter, Faye, who was unwell, and was feeding Lekisha a bottle. Without an invitation, Mum sat down on the grass next to Magdalene. Lekisha fell asleep, while I whinged and fidgeted.

After passing Lekisha to her niece, Magdalene demanded to hold me, and Mum gladly handed me over to have my cheeks squeezed and my white fuzz of hair admired.

I squealed angrily but Magdalene was merely amused. She lifted me up in her strong hands and laughingly spoke to me in language. Before she returned me, she rewrapped me much more tightly in my blanket and told Mum off for not coming to work. Mum was taken aback. She hadn't thought of working so soon after my birth. But she was more surprised by the use of her skin name, Perrurle. It had been given to her when they'd first started working together. The name placed her inside the kinship system as Magdalene's daughter but Mum had previously assumed this was a token gesture. Most of the other activists she'd met in her brief time in Alice Springs had a skin name. Some had two if they knew people from other language groups. Till Magdalene called her by it she'd thought of it as a form of politeness and perhaps expediency. Now she realised the name might be an invitation and she could chose how real their relationship became.

Mum took it up like a lifeline. She knew Magdalene lived between Mission and a shed at a town camp. Hoping to help she offered her the use of our house and its amenities at any time. As Mum pushed me home in my pram that day she knew she'd just stepped into unknown territory, and she felt a rush of pure pleasure at the possibility of what might unfold.

That evening Magdalene came with her niece and Lekisha. They stayed that night and the next. Both nights I slept soundly, and my mother felt safe at last. On the third day they left before we were up. Although Mum pushed me around town most of the morning hoping to catch up with them, she had no luck.

Early the next morning Mum fronted up at the resource centre with me where she resumed her unpaid work. Everyone was glad to see her and to meet me. No-one was fazed with her mixing family and work. In fact she found I gave her a connection with the community she hadn't had before. She was more recognisable as a mother.

At the end of the week Magdalene reappeared and Lekisha was no longer with her. She didn't explain where she'd been and was vague when Mum enquired. Mum left it alone. Although it took her a while to get used to it, she was beginning to understand that some things were none of her business.

It was a blue-sky winter. Life was busy, sunny. Magdalene came and went from our house as she pleased. Mum no longer had to worry about Eddy's complaints as his pile of clothes and books in her room lied about his presence. She no longer had to listen to his Jethro Tull records or his criticisms about her domestic skills, which were endless. Sometimes she could have sworn, despite his flares and tie-dyed t-shirt, he was more 1950s than her father. She relaxed. She loved working, and the resource centre had even started paying her. I had become a happy grub, rolling in the sand and playing with whatever I was given—a spoon, a pair of sunglasses, occasionally a toy. Finally grounded and content, I slept soundly. The only cloud was Faye's poor health, but Mum had little idea just how grave the illness was and neither it seemed did anyone else.

Faye's death rocked Mum. The grief she witnessed being out-poured at the hospital was like nothing she'd seen before. She kept her head down. She was careful. She did as Magdalene told her and took a very small place in a ritual of mourning which had been practised for thousands of years. Sorry business. Serious business.

There were many steps to be taken. Some she witnessed. Some not.

The family house Faye had lived in was abandoned and every-one shifted to sorry camp, which was set up on the edge of the Mission. Mum took all our food and blankets out to camp, buying more bedding from the disposal store on her way. She knew the family wouldn't be able to keep anything Faye might have used: traditionally, Aboriginal people couldn't keep the possessions of the deceased. Nor could they use the person's name or even a name that sounded the same, replacing it with Kumanjay, a generic title. No-one would return to the house either because even though Faye had died in the hospital her spirit remained where she'd lived.

Mum thought she knew all about these cultural traditions, but she had no idea until she got to sorry camp just how shallow her knowledge was. Sorry business was like tumbling over a cliff and falling and falling into dark water, deeper and deeper. The keening pitched her this way and that. Sorry sounded like a strange bird, calling over and over, desperately sad. She had no idea pain had such clear notes, its own song. The notes knotted tightly around her chest, squeezing her. When she thought she could no longer cope she started to cry with such force that she felt her rib bones opening. Grief poured out of her.

She wept not for Faye, whom she'd hardly known, but for her brother killed in Vietnam, her failed relationship with Eddy, all her old hurt. After a time the tears stopped, the darkness lessened, she found speckled light, was propelled to the surface, could breathe again. It felt as though she'd been away and out of her body for a long time.

Magdalene held Mum in her arms that day, rubbing her hands up and down her back, her sides, taking the energy from her body. The healing smoke sent from the fire was soft as a gentle touch. Calming, smooth. I lay in Mum's lap quietly watching. The smoke filtered in my nose, my mouth, settling grey in the creases of my skin.

Mum slept where she was told to in the women's side of the camp. She split wood and cooked food. Every job she was given she took. She could have got up at any time and left and no-one would have held it against her, but she didn't. If our skin name had started as a simple cross-stitch joining us to Magdalene's family, by the time we left sorry camp more complex patterns of belonging had been sewn, patching our different-coloured skins together.

CHAPTER 4

I was glad to see Michael when he turned up again. It had been a long day and I was starting to wonder where he had got to, but my phone had died.

'A bit of a run around,' he said. 'Not quite the day I intended.'

'I wondered where you were.'

'I have come back. I missed you. I saw Magdalene and ran her home and then made the mistake of dropping by the office . . .'

I smiled. 'It's okay. It's been nice to have the afternoon more or less with her to myself.'

'So Lucy didn't come back? Or Frank, Iry?'

'No I told them I'd give them a call and they are clearly being unusually respectful of my wishes. I did talk to the doctor, Fiona, and she said she'd told you pretty much everything she told me.'

'Yes, she said she'd talk to you. It's easier, I think, to get some information direct.'

'Thanks. She left me a swag of information on how to cook for Mum.'

I laughed. My culinary uselessness was well known.

'Hear that?' Michael said, leaning in towards Mum. 'You can wake up soon and start bossing us all around again. And Alicia's doing the cooking.' He shot me a smile.

His fingers stroked Mum's hair affectionately. I gave him my chair.

I sat for a while in the meeting room and thought about what an odd and long day it had been. Incredible as it was I seemed to have adjusted to Mum's crumpled and comatose self. I looked less often at the monitors. Whatever they were saying was good, which was all I needed to know. I didn't even jump anymore when the machines started beeping. Nor was I thinking there was an emergency every-time and madly trying to get the nurses to hurry as I had in the first few hours.

Michael stood up and made a show of stretching when I went back in.

'I'm going to push off soon,' he said. 'Do you want a ride back with me?'

'No, I won't come home tonight. I told Mum I'd stay.'

'It's not that comfortable sleeping here. I did last night.'

It seemed a little unreal that only last night I was in Sydney. It felt as if it were years ago.

I walked Michael to his car, the ground still radiating warmth in the dark. He was perhaps an inch on Floyd. He was similar in many other ways too. A very good cook, calm, good-humoured. Childless, if you didn't count me. Since my break-up with Floyd I'd sometimes wondered about that, whether it was Michael or Mum who didn't want more kids.

'I am an idiot, we should have left your bags in the car,' he said unlocking his car door.

'No problem. I've got what I need in my little backpack.'

'You look wrung out. I hope you get some sleep.'

'You too,' I said. 'And don't worry. She'll be all right, she's got me.'

He put a hand on my head, just as he had when I was a kid, and ran a thumb over my forehead, his eyes gentle. 'You're a good girl.'

I wondered how he could be so certain of that. Did good girls really leave their marriages just because they didn't get their own way?

That night I slept badly and so did Mum. Her eyes were no longer taped shut and occasionally she peered at me as though she didn't know me. Whenever I managed to drift off to sleep, I was woken by the beeping machines or by the nurses moving around the unit.

When I unfolded myself from the chair the next morning I knew Michael hadn't been exaggerating how badly he had slept. He had another six inches on me to curl up. I stroked Mum's forehead and whispered, 'Good morning.' I hoped it would be.

I checked the clock. It was seven and the shift was changing. Ali, the nurse who'd been on duty when I had my meltdown was back and I was glad to see her though I couldn't imagine working such erratic hours.

She helped sort out somewhere I could shower and also told me Fiona made very early rounds on the weekend. I hurried.

In the bathroom mirror I saw my eyes were ringed with dark circles and my face looked thin and tired.

Lines fanned out at the edges of my eyes, which in the fluorescent light looked even worse than usual. I was starting to look old. I ran a brush through my thick hair roughly and told myself off for being so vain.

Upstairs I found Lucy and Michael had arrived. I'd forgotten what early birds they were. Mum was still asleep, a frown on her jaundiced face.

When Lucy saw me she leapt off the bed where she'd been sitting and wrapped me in a strong hug, kissing me on both cheeks. 'Hello, stranger,' she said. 'I just couldn't wait. I rang Michael because you never replied to any of my texts and he said it was okay if I came up.'

'Sorry. I left my charger in the other bag at home.'

Michael held one up.

'And no, Mr Prosecutor, I did not go ferreting through Alicia's bag as she accuses. It was in my box of a million spare chargers.'

'That was a look of surprise. Not accusation,' I protested.

'So like your mother,' he said, teasing me.

'Rubbish.'

I took the charger as Ali and the doctor came to attend to Mum.

'Anywhere I can plug this in?' I asked.

'The meeting room.'

When I came back Mum's naso-gastric tube had been removed.

'Did I miss Fiona?'

'No,' said Lucy, 'They took it out on her instructions. Apparently she's coming in later.'

'Well, Mum must be going well if Fiona can just give orders over the phone.'

Michael must have noticed how I sounded a little peeved, which I was, though I wasn't sure why. Maybe it was just a bad sleep.

'She's a specialist. She hardly needed to do it herself. She'll come in later. Apparently she left instructions for it to come out this morning if there was no downward trend on anything. And there's not, which is good.'

'Good,' I said. It did all sound like Mum was going well. It was just she still looked so bad.

Lucy must have been thinking the same thing.

'Yellow, it's not really her colour, is it?'

'No,' Michael and I said together.

'She hardly looks much better. She looks yellower, if anything.'

'But,' said Michael firmly, 'she's improving. And we don't want to talk negatively around her.'

'No,' said Lucy. 'Sorry.'

Michael took from a basket an assortment of options for breakfast. Food was his way of showing love and he was determined we'd eat. He put out Japanese omelet, cut fruit, boiled eggs and breads onto a small bedside table. 'Is that why you thought I should go home last night, to clean up after you? You've been making a mess for me in the kitchen,' I said, only half joking.

''Course, no other reason,' he said. 'You used to love cleaning up.'

I had too. I'd gone away to boarding school for the senior years, and whenever I came home for holidays I'd clean madly, affronted by the mess of my parents' house. Though I'd never had much time for Eddy or his wife, Kristina, I had liked their stylish, immaculate house in the eastern suburbs. By year twelve the cleaning role in our house was officially mine. Michael cooked. I cleaned. Mum had opinions on both and did neither very often.

Ali brought us over another table and we sat around at Mum's feet. Michael encouraged her and the doctor to get a plate of food too. It was a strange place to have a picnic and I'm not sure it would have been allowed if there had been another patient in the room, but there wasn't.

'Are you staying?' I asked Michael after Lucy had left. 'If you are I might get out for a little while. Go for a walk.'

'Go,' said Michael. 'I expect I'll be here most of the day.'

'My phone should have some charge up, so I'll take it. Text if you need.'

'I'm sure there'll be no need,' he said, and gave my hand a friendly squeeze as I left.

I checked my phone and deleted the text messages from Lucy and read the ones from Frank and Iry. They didn't need responding to. I replied to Floyd's inquiry. Mum was on the up and up I said. I was a bit disappointed there was still no reply to my text two days ago telling Lekisha I was coming and why.

An ugly new building was going up in the main part of town and I thought it would go well with all the other unimaginative buildings that made up the eight blocks the town centre was divided into. The pedestrian mall, once the central strip, was now a neglected no-man's land. I felt sorry for any tourists who might come here expecting a quaint tourist town. Alice wasn't like Broome, which preserved an old quarter like a theme park of living history. In

Alice Springs we'd been completely honest in our hostility towards the past and knocked down almost every reminder of what was once here.

I went to the supermarket in one of the two air-conditioned shopping centres on offer. Thankfully, the layout of Woolies was the same as the supermarket I went to back in Sydney, so finding the deodorant and shampoo I wanted was easy.

I was just getting some Easter eggs, which were already in the shops, when I spotted Lekisha down at the refrigerated section. She was looking at the yoghurts, a mop hanging out the end of her trolley like a blue tail. I was going to sneak up behind her and scare her, an infantile habit we hadn't yet given up, when I saw with shock a tiny baby wrapped in a cocoon of blanket on a pillow in the plastic capsule at the trolley's front. I turned, crazily considering a retreat, but at that moment she turned and saw me.

'Hey, hello, my sis. You right?'

'I'm fine.' I couldn't meet her eyes.

Lekisha gave me a big hug. 'Long time. Sorry, I got no credit. You know I've been thinking of you.'

'No worries.' The baby was such a shock that I felt awkward and fake. Normally when we met, Lekisha and I just took up where we'd left off. Surely, I thought now, she would have told me if she was pregnant? Maybe she was worried about upsetting me, knowing how much I longed for a baby of my own, but she should have known that a surprise like this was by far the worst way of finding out.

The baby smiled up deliciously, her legs bunching in the air. She was a spitter for Lekisha. Same eyes. Same mouth. Same frown in the middle of her eyebrows and a dimple in her chin.

'When did you have this?' I asked, rudely.

Lekisha looked at me as though I was a lunatic. She shook her head and laughed, putting her hand on my arm to try and help me to calm down.

'It's not mine, it's Caleb's. You're mad.'

'You're a grandmother? You never said anything.'

'Didn't know, did I, till a little while ago. The mother just turned up last month, maybe less, on the doorstep, a few weeks to go. Caleb's secret woman from up north.' She laughed again. 'Maxine—she's not a secret now.'

She ran a finger proprietorially under the baby's chin and then took its cheeks and gave them a gentle pinch. The baby was certainly beautiful. Just like Caleb had been. However, I hadn't envied Lekisha at all when she finally let on to everyone at six months that she was pregnant. I'd been barely sixteen and I'd felt sorry for her and stupidly, stupidly certain that people shouldn't have babies until they were older. Not that anyone except Mum and me seemed alarmed by Lekisha's youth or thought she'd ruined her chances of a good life.

Lekisha turned the trolley into the next aisle, and I walked numbly beside her.

'How's your mum?' she asked, her lovely round face soft with concern.

I reached out my hand and placed it on hers. 'She's getting better. Out of ICU tomorrow, hopefully.'

'That's good,' she said gravely. 'It's real good you still got her.'

Her thoughtfulness made me ashamed of my own selfishness.

'Yes, it is,' I said, 'thankyou.'

The baby made a cry which sounded like the mewing of a cat. While not very loud it was persistent and urgent. I put my finger out to her and she grabbed it and held it between two chubby fists. Caught like this it was hard to take my eyes off her.

'What's she called?' I asked.

'Rosia.'

'Rosia?'

'Yeah. We put together the beginning of your mum's name and the end of yours.' Lekisha beamed at me.

'That's great—but didn't the mother mind you naming the baby?'

'Oh no, she had no ideas. So I helped her out.'

I felt a small wave of sympathy for Lekisha's daughter-in-law. Lekisha was well intentioned and generous, but she could also be quite the bossy one.

Rosia was trying to suck on my fingers and managed to get one to her mouth where she gulped on it desperately. I wasn't sure it was a good idea, and though Lekisha didn't seem fussed, I tried to uncurl Rosia's tiny fingers from mine. Her grip, to my surprise, was incredibly strong. Before I succeeded she worked out that she was not getting what she wanted from me and started to howl. It was a desperate, heartbreaking sound.

'Look, she's starving. I thought Maxine had fed her,' Lekisha said, reaching into the capsule and picking Rosia up. It calmed her down only a fraction, despite her jiggling her up and down soothingly. 'I'll have to get her home for Maxine to feed and bring your mum's car back after.'

'I didn't know you had it.'

'Michael let me take it from the mechanics to go to Promised Land.'

'Did he? Well, if you don't bring it back before I need it I'll come chasing you.'

'Okay.' She grinned at me over the baby's head. I doubted she would care if I had to chase her all over town for the car. She needed that car and I didn't.

Rosia. The name grew on me with every passing minute and I found I didn't mind the idea that as she was Lekisha's grand-child—or 'granny'—I'd be seeing a lot more of her.

CHAPTER 5

When I came into the ICU, Michael was working on a crossword. Looking relieved I'd returned, he folded up the paper. I told him I'd bumped into Lekisha and seen the granny. He agreed that Rosia was gorgeous but he didn't shed any light on why neither he or Ros had mentioned her and I didn't feel like now was the time to ask.

I did ask about the reduction in equipment and monitors around Mum. I'd missed Fiona, it seemed, who'd decided Mum didn't need quite the support she'd been receiving. New blood results had come in, and with them more good news. Mum's enzyme count was dropping and her blood glucose heading higher. No-one was overly worried about her drowsiness; now that she was less agitated Fiona felt she was simply getting on with resting, which was what she needed most.

Frank had also come when I was out. He'd brought a bag of apricots.

They were absolutely delicious.

'From Warakata,' Michael said.

It was right out in the western desert.

'The last few trees from Frank's time out there. Some old fellows look after what's left of the orchard. He tends to make a few visits at this time of year.'

'Nothing to do with the fruit, just his important work, I suppose,' I said facetiously. Frank was a community development consultant these days. He'd been a social economist. An advisor. A patrol officer. He'd been around.

'Oh very important work,' said Michael. 'Pass me a couple, would you.'

They were about the best apricots I'd ever eaten.

In the late afternoon the nurses suddenly decided to move Mum, even though when Michael had left the word had been that she was staying one more night in ICU.

I didn't really want to watch Mum being moved and the resident had said there was an airlift coming in from a car accident on the road to Uluru. I certainly didn't want to see anyone who'd been involved in an accident. Just when I was wondering where I might go while she was shifted, Iry turned up. She saw Mum briefly and then met me downstairs.

Of everyone I knew, Iry was the most like Mum. She was very tough. She worked as a senior policy officer in the department of children and families. We never talked work. Michael respected her, Mum loved her, Lucy was loyal and Frank was entirely over her. They'd been divorced a decade before when their boys were young.

We went outside and lay on the grass in the long shade of the building. It was one of those rare days the summer would occasionally offer up to stop you going mad. It wasn't too hot and I lay on my back and admired the sky. The wide blue sky was one of the first aspects newcomers found to love about the desert. It made you feel good. It was so expansive. Having grown up with it, it wasn't until I moved to the city that I really appreciated it.

Iry had brought chicken and chips for an early dinner.

'Sorry, it's just takeaway.'

'Don't be,' I said. 'I have a taste for food like this. It's perfect.'

Iry had a theory to explain this new craving I had for fat and sugar. Like Mum she had a theory on everything. It was fairly simple. The brain, she said, goes into a certain fight response whenever we're told we can't have something. Even if you didn't particularly crave it before you were denied it. If it was something you did desire, when denied it, the reaction was stronger. Her theory might have had no basis in fact but I thought it made plenty of sense. Floyd's opposition to a child had certainly made me want one even more.

I wished Iry could have stayed longer. She was good company. But the hospital lawns were hardly relaxing for her. There were too many clients about. I followed her to her car to get some books she'd brought for me.

'Trashy,' she said. 'Crime.'

I gave her a hug. I loved crime.

Back inside the hospital, the receptionist told me where to find Mum in the general ward. She'd been lucky enough to get a room of her own. Unlike ICU the room had a large window with an expansive view of the ranges. The nurses were prepared to give me a mattress on the floor next to Mum's bed. I put it under the window but out of the way. It was luxury compared to the previous night and I lay on my bed and read. Mum stirred occasionally but she never showed any signs of waking. Having got used to the bustle in ICU, sharing Mum's single room in the ward was like staying in a highway motel. I could hear everything through the paper-thin walls but after a while it faded into background noise and not even the nurses coming in and out during the night really disturbed me. I read late and slept well.

When I woke Mum was turned on her side looking at me.

'Hey, I'm glad you're awake,' I said.

'I've been watching you,' she said.

'You've got a good view out there,' I said, pointing out the window as I got up.

'I'd rather watch you.'

'I love you.'

'I know. You chose me,' she said. I hugged her tightly. I was rather amazed she had actually heard me telling the story.

'So how do you feel?'

'Like I've been run over by a truck. My head's full of stories and events I'm not sure are real.'

'It was a yellow truck,' I said, lightly. 'It left its paint all over you.' She attempted a smile and I kept hold of her hand. I wanted to keep her to myself for a little longer before I had to share her.

I rang Michael and handed her the phone. To give her space I took myself for a walk up and down the corridor for a while, very pleased to have Mum back.

When I returned to her room, not more than fifteen minutes later, I found her asleep with the phone on the bed next to her.

I phoned Michael and met him in the lobby where we couldn't stop smiling at each other, before hugging, the embrace awash with our relief.

'She's on her way back slowly,' I said. 'I'll just stall Lucy from coming in.' Michael gave my cheek a kiss, then I watched as he strode keenly towards the ward and Mum.

Lucy and I sat on one of the benches downstairs. It appeared she had been planning for Mum's recovery while I'd been reading the detective novel I'd got from Iry. Her organisation made me feel guilty I hadn't done more. Lucy estimated there were about forty people we could put on a care meal roster. I liked the use of the royal we. She'd already compiled the list of contact numbers and distributed an electronic version of the dietary notes we had been given. She showed me the set-up on her laptop.

I was concerned that it was perhaps too much to expect of other people but she was sure it wasn't.

'It's Alice,' Lucy said. 'We like to show our love. And cooking for Ros is the easiest way people can do this. And they want to. So don't try and stop me.'

'As if,' I said. 'I suppose Michael knows about this.'

'Of course,' said Lucy, tucking her long curls behind her ears. 'Not the details just the theory.'

'Well, I'll buy a cookbook,' I said, 'a liver-friendly one. You can add me to your roster.'

'Don't worry,' Lucy said, 'it's not a competition.'

I suppressed a smile. Who was she kidding? I'd seen this mob in action.

*

News Ros was awake spread fast. I left Michael to play the gate-keeper at the hospital and Lucy with my blessing to do whatever she wanted about organising help.

I was intent on getting out of the hospital for a while.

On the short trip home in a taxi, I felt a little like a prisoner set free. Although I was grateful for the care Mum was receiving and how well she was doing, hospitals were unhealthy places to hang around in too long. The sooner she got better the sooner she would come home. Hopefully with the usual pressure on beds and the amount of support she'd have at home she'd be high on the list for early release.

As the taxi pulled up in front of the house I thought for a moment that Lekisha had actually dropped Mum's troopy back, but then I noticed that the vehicle had government plates. When I'd paid the driver and rounded the front of the house I was met by a bloke with longish dark hair, walking purposefully.

It was Patrick, Michael's friend who was also into botany. Gardening. Plants in general.

'How you travelling?' he asked.

'Okay,' I said.

'Can you tell Michael I left the papers for him in the kitchen?' he said. 'I didn't want them getting lost with all that stuff on the hall table. Actually, I was half hoping to catch him. I suppose he's at the hospital?'

'Yes, he is. Mum's awake.' Just saying it made me feel delighted.

Patrick seemed equally pleased. He gave me a lovely smile. 'Hey, that's great news. It sounded so bizarre, how sick she got and so quickly too.'

'Apparently only one per cent of people get that complication from hep.'

'Poor thing. What bad luck.'

'Yes, it was.'

'Well, let's hope it's all good from here. Did Magdalene see her?'

'She did.'

'Good.'

He slapped the bonnet of the car in what seemed a nervous gesture and swung into the driver's seat. 'Right, then, I'll be seeing you around,' he said through the open window.

I hoped so. He seemed much cheerier than I remembered. Younger. Not that I'd ever talked to him much. That was probably our longest conversation.

As he made a U-turn and drove past I flicked my hand up in a wave.

The house was a mess. Although I'd seen it in a worse state before.

I started with the washing, putting on the first load from a pile of sheets and towels, no doubt from when Ros was quite sick. They stank. But washing was no drama in this heat. Generally, one load was dry by the time another finished. The kitchen was its usual untidy self. Half a loaf of bread left in full sunlight had turned into stone, and tomato seeds, salami skin and the end of a block of cheese littered a cutting board. The floor needed a mop, the windows were dirty and the deep wooden windowsills wore a thick coat of dust. It was incredible how little neglect a house needed up here before the dust tried to bury it.

While I was having a quick squiz around the rest of the place, my eye was caught as always by the large photograph of Mum on the back wall of her bedroom. Whenever I looked at it I felt such a strong connection to her; it seemed to encapsulate something essential to her spirit. Taken in the early seventies, the black and white image shows her moments after her arrest at the anti-apartheid demonstration during the Springboks' tour. Her lips are bruised and swollen, her skin split open above one eye, and a trickle of blood runs down her face, which appears far younger than her twenty-two years. The photo captures the conflict between an old corrupt and racist power and a younger generation's call for equality. It helped to gain the anti-apartheid movement support in new quarters in Australia but I always thought of it as the photo that launched Eddy's career as a photographic journalist. The paradox was that while a camera might have brought my parents together, it also provided Eddy with his escape too.

My father liked to say he fell in love with Ros when that image came into being in his darkroom. It was the only thing he ever said about their brief relationship that I find plausible. The photo is shocking. Not because of Mum's injuries but because far from looking beaten there's a confidence in her eyes, a steadiness in her gaze. She's defiantly sure of her position as the right one. It's a look I've seen a hundred times. It's classic Mum and it always makes me feel really protective because being so righteous makes her extremely vulnerable to attack.

There were very few cleaning products in the cupboards, and they were wussy environmentally friendly brands I wasn't confident would be up to the job. I needed to buy some proper, lethal products to make the job easier, then hide the evidence to avoid a lecture from the very eco-friendly Michael.

As I left the house to walk to the local corner shop Mr Press was out in his front garden in spite of the heat, watering his flowers. He waved me over to his side of the street.

'Hello, Mr Press,' I said, still unable to bring myself to use his Christian name. Lots of things had changed since I was a kid but that wasn't one of them.

'Hi, Alicia, welcome back. We hear your mum's awake now. That's good. We feel real bad that we didn't realise she was sick. With the car not there Gloria and I thought she was away.'

'It's not your fault,' I said, although I had wondered why a woman with so many friends could get as sick as Mum had without anyone noticing.

Mr Press and I talked about his family and how things had changed, especially with the young people, before he declared it too hot to stand about yarning and sent me on my way. When I looked back I wasn't surprised to see he hadn't stopped gardening at all. Some weeds had caught his eye. No-one worked much harder than Mr Press. Much of his life he had laboured on a road crew; his free time was spent volunteering with local sports clubs, particularly with the Magpies Football Club, where his eldest son Tommy jnr had been the star before he went on to play for the SAFL Port Adelaide club and eventually returned to Alice, married up, with kids.

I had a lot of respect for Mr and Mrs Press. They were from a generation that had been ordered about by various government policies. Childhood sweethearts, married young, they had been moved into their public housing home nearly half a century before, after passing through a welfare program which forced them to first pass an independent living test. How crudely they'd been compulsorily managed I hated to think. I imagined I'd have been very bitter if it had happened to me. If they were bitter I'd never seen any sign of it. The home where they'd brought up every one of their six kids, not to mention the children they'd fostered, was always a favourite for the neighbourhood kids and I'd played there a lot as a youngster.

Further down the street I passed a group of young men lounging about on the recently landscaped verge. These were just the sort of young people Mr Press had been alluding to, and they responded to my greeting cautiously, treating me with the same suspicion they did the world.

The local shop was unchanged, still crowded with trinkets and food that was about twice the price it would be at my deli down south. I paid using Floyd's credit card—again. I'd used it to pay for my flight too. Hopefully the financial settlement, the last part of our divorce to be resolved, would happen soon and I'd be able to pay him back, although I knew he didn't mind. Money was one thing he really didn't care about, and even now it held the strange honour of being the only subject we'd never argued over.

Taking a different route back home, I passed the service station with an alcohol licence. When Floyd first visited Alice with me he couldn't believe you could buy grog and petrol in one transaction. It was the first time I'd seen him shocked, but I knew it was just the first of many times he'd be surprised by the world I came from. As it turned out, of course, I was the person who got the biggest surprise during the ten years we were together, when it finally dawned, just as he'd insisted all along, that he really didn't want any children. Not then. Not now. Not ever.

A friend had introduced me to Floyd in a bar one Friday night. She liked journalists, so we were in a pub they were known to frequent. I'd met Eddy there from time to time. It wasn't my cup of tea but I had nothing better to do so I went along.

Floyd was onto my journalistic connections straightaway. 'Are you related to Eddy Davey?' he asked.

It was a long bow to pull. My surname was pretty common, so I don't know how he made the association. Maybe it was a hunch.

'Yes,' I admitted. 'His daughter.'

Floyd's friend Robert laughed at him. 'You're like a bloodhound. That must be why you're such a good journalist and I'm just a sports hack.' He turned his bulky frame towards me. 'Eddy's a legend. Those Springbok demo shots—they are top drawer photos. Especially that one of the woman with her face smashed open above her eye.'

Floyd studied me with a raw interest. I could see he was putting the pieces together. 'The woman was your mother?'

'Yes, he met her there.'

'You don't look much like her,' said Robert. 'Perhaps it's just that you're not black and blue.'

'He's amazing,' Floyd said. 'In a class of his own.'

I winced at his adulation. Eddy was revered by many people. I just wasn't one of them.

'It must be incredible to grow up with a man like that for your father.'

I decided to stop him there.

'He didn't bring me up. I knew him but he's never been hands-on, and I didn't think he was a legend, then or now. I just thought it was a bit sad that work was the most important thing to him.'

'Better than a dickhead for a father,' Floyd said, trying to sound flippant, but I thought I caught a sharp edge in his voice. 'Drink?'

'Vodka and lime,' I said.

'Scotch, double,' said Robert, 'if you're buying.'

I stood with Robert while Floyd went to the bar. I couldn't see my friend anywhere in the crowd, so I planned to have the one drink and go. Spotting a free table, Robert steered me to it, neatly cutting off a group of blokes who also wanted it. Seating was at a premium. I was pleased to get out of the crush.

Robert lit a cigarette and used it as a baton, conducting his flow of words. He was entertaining, full of stories about football players in compromising situations and gambling jockeys dropping races. When Floyd returned with our drinks the conversation continued to flow easily. I stayed, had another drink. Usually people's admiration of my father put me right off, but I found myself intrigued by Floyd. He was handsome, there was no doubt, and he knew it. He was also smart and funny. And despite his obvious interest in my father he showed little in me, which presented a challenge.

Suddenly Robert looked at his watch. 'Shit, I've missed seeing Sophie before she goes down. I'm going to be killed. Nice to meet you,' he said to me, then: 'See you Monday, Floyd.'

Floyd put up a hand in farewell. We watched Robert shoulder his way through the crowd.

'Poor guy,' he said. 'I wouldn't want to be in his shoes.'

'How old is his daughter?'

'Six months, I think. He's meant to be home in time to put her to bed. Every night.' He rolled his eyes.

'It's nice he does that.'

'I don't know about that. Seems like a terrible trap.'

I looked at Floyd curiously. 'Someday you'll want kids.'

'Never.'

I laughed. I was sure he'd change his mind. I guessed I was only a year or so older than Floyd but I already knew that never was a word only young people used.

'Another drink?' he asked.

That would make it three. More than I usually drank. I studied him as I considered my options. He had slightly sharp features, softened by brown eyes. His mouth was generous. Definitely kissable.

'Actually I'm a bit hungry. I might push off.' It was a safe way to see if he did have some interest in me but was playing it expertly cool.

'I'm a bit hungry myself,' he said, suddenly showing his hand. 'Why don't I come with you? I know some good places around here.'

'So do I,' I said competitively, 'I'll show you my favourite.'

Of course he knew the Japanese noodle bar I took him to. It was small and narrow. Intimate. We drank warm sake and ate fat udon noodles. Floyd was nearly as adept with his chopsticks as Eddy, who'd introduced me to this place. By the time we left it was late and we'd drunk too much. It was only sensible to share a cab. It went from there.

I took the last bucket of rinse water out and ditched it on the garden as Michael had trained me to, relieved the cleaning was over. His fabulous garden was the main reason we'd never moved to a bigger house on the Eastside where most of their friends lived. It had nothing to do with making a political statement, which people tended to assume was behind them remaining in this less popular area, dominated as it was by housing department stock, small blocks and plenty of people on the breadline trying to get by. Standing under the umbrella of the mango tree, out of reach of the battering direct sunlight, it was easy to understand their decision.

I'd often thought about how Michael used what he knew about plants to help us grow together as a family.

When I was growing up I always thought of myself as having four families—my little one with Michael and Mum, the one with Mum's friends, the one with our Aboriginal family, and the one with Eddy, his wife Kristina and their two boys. I thought of each family like Russian dolls sitting inside the other. I'd never dreamt I wouldn't have added to this family myself by now. And sometimes my biological clock seemed to be ticking so loudly it would drive me insane.

I put the cleaning gear away. Thinking like this was fruitless. Things could be a lot worse I told myself sternly. I could have been here for a funeral.

CHAPTER 6

I had a shower and obeyed the water-saving timer, feeling guilty I hadn't got back to the hospital yet. I was just running up the hall looking for the sarong I'd dropped when Lucy arrived, calling out as she came in. No-one knocked and waited outside this house. They just waltzed in. If you were out of practice and naked like Lucy found me it could be a little confronting. Embarrassed as I was, I could console myself it could have been worse; it could have been Patrick.

'Alicia,' Lucy said, taking a step back to the kitchen but not perturbed. 'I just dropped in to report Ros ate a little of the food Frank brought in. She's still quite out of it. And I brought you lunch.'

'Well serve it! I'm famished.'

When I came back, dressed in wide-legged linen pants and a t-shirt she had quite a spread out. Homemade pasta with salmon, salad and some small ricotta cheesecakes. And she thought I shouldn't think of cooking as competitive!

'I meant to ask, are you still managing teacher training?'

'Yep, with Darwin still in charge, of course. I'm part of the furniture these days.'

'And Lekisha's still going well?

'Very well.'

She scooped some pasta into her bowl. 'I heard Floyd's off overseas?'

'He's off to London soon, which will be good for him. A fresh start. And you?'

'I'm fine and before you ask, still a single woman like yourself.'

Younger than Mum, Lucy was like a big sister and she was easy to talk to. The conversation meandered all over the place before we fell into our old favourite: Aboriginal education. Why the hell were things going so badly? Not everywhere, just most places. Lekisha was going well according to Lucy because she was well educated. Because it had been assumed she could learn. The next generation had been let down by poor teaching and low expectations. Lucy raved on. I managed to get in a few long points myself. On and on we went, getting ourselves into a great lather and then ended, as we always did, laughing at having pretended to be experts. Our laughter was hard and long and aimed at ourselves. Talk was cheap and we knew it.

After Lucy left I made a quick trip to the hospital, whizzing up on the new scooter Michael had bought himself for Christmas. We teased him about it being his mid-life crisis present to himself. Other men bought Harley-Davidsons, he splashed out on a postie bike.

Windswept and hot from the ride, I found Iry had taken over Michael's job protecting Mum from too many visitors. She was a good choice. She'd enlisted the nurses to intercept visitors at the desk. I was challenged and had to explain I was Ros's daughter before the nurse let me go on.

Mum was dozing, reluctant to wake when I tried to engage her. Iry gave us a bit of space but Mum was clearly tired and I didn't stay very long. There was plenty to get on with at home and keeping active was easier than watching Mum so lethargic.

I left Iry sitting reading a book, grateful she was generous enough to stay for hours to entertain Mum for the very brief periods she wasn't dozing. Iry was perpetually busy and I knew it was a big thing she was doing for Mum. I told her to tell Mum if she woke I would be back in the evening when Michael was there.

I wanted to research some recipes and get a bit more organised so I could do my share of the cooking.

Mum's cubbyhole of an office used to be the laundry when I was a kid and it was well set up. Her computer was new and to my delight the internet service was as fast as was available in Alice.

I Googled 'hepatitis' and was shocked when I got over eighteen million hits. There were many more types of hepatitis than I'd thought. C seemed to have its own story and then there were all the non-specific types as well as the various strains in each category. The articles shook the new feeling of confidence that I was on top of things and made it evident Mum's recovery could be a longer process than I'd anticipated.

I looked for diets for people with liver problems and that was a bit cheerier. The recipes didn't seem very complicated at all. I'd just need the right food. I spent far too long on the computer and by the time I realised how much time I'd squandered it was late.

I rang Michael to check on Mum and when he said she was still obviously needing sleep I decided not to go to the hospital. I could do with an early night.

I was annoyed to discover I'd left my novel at the hospital. I only had two chapters to go and in crime that's where the answers were. I didn't like being left having to think about it, which I'd started doing. Crime got to me like that. I was getting a drink of water to take with me to bed when I saw Patrick's papers. Needing a distraction I picked them up. If his writing was confidential I figured he should have put it in an envelope. In bed I turned on the reading light. 'Aboriginal Thinking about Healing' the first chapter announced. It was well written and interesting but I was too tired and didn't get much further than the first few pages.

It was still early enough that the light was predawn white when I got up. Even Michael was still asleep as I began getting the pantry sorted for the new eating regime Mum, and I assumed Michael and I, would loosely follow. Mum's habits wouldn't be easy to change. She drank five cups of coffee a day and liked her cheese French, soft, about a hundred per cent pure fat and three thousand calories a wedge. She was thin but only because she burnt much energy quickly and ate erratically. If Michael wasn't home she went back to being the laziest cook, eating toast and eggs or cereal when she was hungry and I wondered how she was going to handle this new diet she needed to follow.

I had a box to throw all the unsuitable food into. I thought I could give it to Lekisha. She had plenty of people to feed. Later

I'd go shopping for new basics: Adzuki beans, garlic, turmeric and walnuts. I was confident I could buy everything on my list locally, including powdered barley grass, olive leaf extract and dandelion coffee. There was an Asian grocer and an organic one now where I could get fresh vegetables regularly. Both supermarkets had smartened up their act too. It had been a while since we'd been obliged to stuff our suitcases full of food products every time we returned from down south, carrying back the exotics to restock Michael's pantry.

I put Patrick's manuscript back on the bench for Michael before I left for the hospital. I hadn't seen him yet but his work car was in the driveway. I figured he must have stayed late with Mum and was sleeping in. His postie bike was also there. But not Mum's car. I'd forgotten about her car. I texted Lekisha to bring it back. I put a happy face at the end hoping but not really believing it would be enough to have her hurry up. If she didn't have it back by the afternoon I'd send her a few unhappy faces and then start trying to pin her down.

Reluctantly I rode the postie bike and in the early morning cool I discovered its attraction. It was almost cold with the wind on my skin. It was also a load of fun now I had the hang of riding it better and I felt like a teenager.

Mum was awake. She was pleased to see me but a bit flat. I was relieved she thought the food roster was a good idea. I wasn't sure how she'd take to being organised. She said she'd tried to stop it but Lucy and Michael had reminded her of all the times she'd organised food rosters for people in need: women who'd had babies, families with a member who was sick or who'd died and so on. They'd told her she had no choice but to take her own medicine.

I wasn't sure if I was tiring her because her mood didn't pick up and I didn't stay long. The only spark I got was as I went to pick up my book, which was on her sidetable. She grabbed it before I could.

'I'm reading it.'

'I've only got two chapters left.'

'Bad luck. I'm sick.'

'I need to know what happened.'

She held the book to her chest and made an exaggerated sad face. I conceded defeat and blew her kisses from the doorway.

'See you later.'

When the shops opened I got everything on my list except for the milk thistle, a tincture which I'd have to get from a naturopath. I'd just finished putting the groceries away and my new cookbook, *Love Your Liver*, on the shelf when I heard a car pull up.

Seconds later Lekisha appeared.

'I got that car back. You busy?'

'No, not at all. You're good,' I said.

'Tired. Everyone just wants a lift. Bloody troppy, there's too much room. I've been running everyone around.'

'Cup of tea?' I asked. I was pleased she hadn't made me play the old game of running around after her.

She nodded agreeably at the suggestion of tea before wondering out loud if Michael had made the dark fruit cake she liked. I pulled it out of the cake tin and we sat it on the bench. I had considered putting it in the unwanted foods box but it was one of my favourites too.

'You want a thick slice?'

She nodded and I cut her a generous serve. I dunked the tea bags into the cups and filled them from the kettle. Lekisha put two fingers up, her mouth full. I put in another tea bag, drowning it with a spoon and pushing it towards her with the sugar bowl.

'Not for me. I'm diabetic.'

'No,' I said, 'true?'

'True story. Just type two. Early one.'

I looked at the box of food I'd put aside, full of sugar and the overly processed, wondering if it was a good idea to offer it to her.

'That cake's got plenty of sugar,' I warned her.

She didn't care. She sliced off another piece of cake and tucked into it. I decided then if she wouldn't help herself I'd boss her. If she hadn't wanted me to help she should have kept the information to herself. I quickly culled the food box I was planning on giving her of the most sugary items. Like the large packets of family assorted biscuits we strangely seemed to have quite a few of.

'How is your Mum?' she asked.

'Sleepy. Mostly she sleeps.'

'Nana says she's yellow, real bright.'

'Yeah. She was bright, glowing.'

'Like yellow cake. Dangerous.'

'I suppose,' I said, amused by the comparison.

'I was thinking we should take her to that protest and stick her there. That would put people off.'

'Where?' She'd lost me.

'At the protest. You know, about stopping that dump from coming here.'

'What dump?'

'The uranium rubbish dump. Don't you read the news now you finished with Floyd?'

I laughed. It was kind of true he had been my news desk, and without his interest in the world mine had certainly waned.

'Someone's been sleeping there all the time. One traditional owner. T.O. for that country. She says they may as well kill her there if they going to make a dump and kill all her family anyway.'

'Good on her.'

'Yeah. All the hippy mob been helping her. Nanna reckons some of them look like your Mum did in the old days.'

I'd have to tell Mum. She wouldn't find the comparison flattering. She didn't think of the young ferals as being like her at all. I liked to tease her about how she and her friends fancied themselves as the quality generation of protestors, the true peace warriors.

'You in town then or at the block?'

'Town and there. But I can't get any sleep in my house here. Too many drunks. Too much humbug.'

I thought it had been like that for a while and perhaps my lack of response showed I didn't think this was exactly a new problem.

'Worse. It is worse, Alicia. But I got my course in town some days and then up in Darwin. So I have to hang on to this house here too. But it's lovely up at Promised Land. Quiet.'

We talked about going bush and made a plan for the morning. Then she pushed her cup away, a sure sign she was leaving, although I wasn't sure where she was going or how. On her way out I offered her the best of the food boxes but she insisted on taking everything I'd packed, clearly not wanting my interference.

She brushed off my concerns for her health and bluntly reminded me how many kids she fed.

I picked up the car keys presuming I'd drive her home but she told me not to worry. Curious, I saw her out, certain she wasn't walking with those boxes.

Out the front a blue Falcon was waiting on the street under the big tree, a reggae song by the mission band blaring, a man behind the wheel.

'Has he been waiting?'

She nodded like it was no big deal.

I shook my head. Poor bastard, he'd be practically baked by now.

'He's too shame to come in.'

'Who's that? Your boyfriend.'

'You are mad. That's my uncle.'

She didn't introduce me, though, or explain how he was related, so I didn't believe her. She'd always kept her private life private. I didn't even know who Caleb's father was.

It wasn't possible to make it bush the next morning or the one after. By the time I finished making Mum's lunch, after insisting I was on the roster, it was already too hot to venture outside, although it was really her depression that stopped me feeling like I could leave her. While she was awake, she was quite down, and it was hard to take. Mum was always up. She was a big believer in getting on with things. Now she couldn't use action she didn't seem to have an alternative coping strategy. Michael, I assumed, was as worried as I was but he handled her better, simply being with her, doing his crosswords or reading. Just keeping her company. I couldn't help myself and tried to engage her, which tended to leave me feeling disheartened. When Lucy told me to be patient and that I could hardly expect one or two meals from my cookbook to do the trick, I got quite mad with her. And we had a sisterly and safe fight. All my anxiety came out and I took it out on her, calling her an up-herself, bossy bitch. She called me a self-focused sook. The fight was like a grassfire. It flared, never got too hot and was soon out.

Lucy and I apologised to each other quickly but when I left her in the hospital courtyard I knew I needed a change of scene: a break from the house, the hospital and a nagging irritation I hadn't seen Patrick again, whom I'd half expected to pop in to see Michael sometime.

I texted Lekisha. *Go bush morning*. She texted back. *K*. That night I went to bed early, looking forward to getting out.

Chapter 7

Lekisha's house was on one of the bigger town camps, East camp, but as I'd explained to friends down south, it wasn't a camp as they might understand one. There weren't tents and caravans and people on holiday. The camp wasn't on her traditional country. It was an Aboriginal town lease. When the camps first started they were each based on family groups. Not many of the camps had held their original shape. Mostly all the different languages and families were mixed up. There were sixteen other leases like hers all under the control of an Aboriginal umbrella organisation. All the houses were overcrowded. There just weren't enough beds and the visitors were endless. No new houses had been built for a long time which compounded the overcrowding.

Lekisha's family didn't get land under the federal act in 1976, only rights to a place on one of the old station stock routes. Promised Land, their living area excision, was only begrudgingly handed over by the pastoralists after a hard fight over nearly twenty years. Little wonder Lekisha was excited by the new houses and finally a chance to live there.

I ignored the trespass signs at the camp's entrance and took the first speed hump slowly where a pack of mangy and mottled dogs flew at my car. Really stupid-looking dogs you only ever seemed to find in Aboriginal communities. Like the Great Dane crossed with a Jack Russell trying to eat the tyre and a Dalmatian-poodle barking like a mad thing alongside it.

Lekisha was right. The camp did look worse than last time I'd been here, although it had often been fairly littered. I'd never quite got the rubbish thing. If I had a dollar for every person who asked: why is there all this rubbish? I would have been rich. The Community Development Employment Program (CDEP) employed most people involved in working on the camp, a way of keeping people off the dole statistics, a cynic might say. Clearly there were issues because the crews didn't seem to be doing much of a job running even basic council services. Some people, like Frank, had been saying for years that the lack of incentive for CDEP workers to work hard was the problem. It was the same pay for being slack or energetic. If you believed Frank, people had got slacker. Why not? I wasn't here for an inspection or looking for something or someone to blame. I was just a bit shocked by the wine bladders and green cans scattered about despite the camp being a grog-free zone. The plastic shopping bags were snarled everywhere on the wire fences. Graffitied rocks told random shorthand stories. *Okay Sluts rule. Big Hole you Mandy B. S.S and T.S 4ever.*

Broken bikes and shattered prams spoke volumes. The new playground installed the year before with much fanfare had been burnt. The slippery dip was a melted mess and the climbing frame holed by fire. Both swings were broken. One hung by a single chain, its black seat strap still attached uselessly like a dirty Band-Aid.

As I drew up at Lekisha's house their dogs came charging out to warn off the others, a huge white dog with a pit bull head leading the charge. I went to beep, the slack way of knocking, until I saw Lekisha was waiting out the front with her bag over her shoulder, ready to go.

'Don't ever get out here,' she warned, smartly getting in the car, kicking the dog as she did. 'That's Lucky, Magdalene's dog. He's real racist and he's arerte.'

He did look mad, just the way the old lady liked them.

'I find that hard to believe,' I said sarcastically, but she didn't bite back. I'd never been sure if she didn't understand when I was being sarcastic; if it ever transcended the language gap, or if she just never chose to respond to it.

Really she wouldn't have been too worried about me getting out here since I hardly did ever since I'd been attacked that time years ago when a dog I'd been running from had come straight through the window after me and bitten me on the shoulder. Mum had to punch it off. True story. I still had the scar. Lucky lunged, snarling and scratching at my door. I did my window up as quick as I could.

As if she could read my mind Lekisha laughed. 'That dog passed on years ago. Poor thing.'

'"Poor thing" my arse. Anyway that one looks like its son.'

And while she hardly needed any encouragement I graciously invited her to keep laughing.

Lekisha had me head north then east. Off the bitumen the red dirt road jiggled and wavered like it might not quite be real. But we were on it all right, moving not too fast, not too slow over the corrugations, a screen of dust in the rear.

'How far?' I asked.

She pouted with her lips. That way. 'Not far,' she said.

I smiled to myself. How long's a piece of string? Why I still bothered asking such questions was more of a mystery.

It wasn't more than another thirty kilometres when she told me to slow down as she sat forward in her chair, her eyes scanning for whatever sign she needed to see. I watched where she watched but I didn't see like she did. My eyes were trained for short-length vision. She could see for miles.

'What are we looking for?' I asked.

'Follow that track,' she instructed without answering my question. 'That one.'

I couldn't really see what she meant but not wanting to appear myall I steered in the direction she indicated.

'Where you going?' she asked. 'That way. See that track?'

'No, I don't see any track. I see a lot of bare patches, all of which could be tracks.'

I was starting to feel annoyed and stupid. When she offered to drive I couldn't hop out quick enough.

Lekisha moved the chair back as if she was taller than me. She drove leaning forward peering over the wheel at the path she managed to track easily. We drove on slowly and up, till we were on a bit of a rise. You didn't have to be very high at all in Alice to get a panoramic view. Before us, blue in the heat were the eastern ranges, following the line of the sandy rivers out. We took a sharp turn south and the view dropped out of sight as we came back into the folds of the scrub.

'There,' Lekisha said, 'see where we are now.'

I looked. The place was vaguely familiar. It was a bit of a wide bowl. There was a lone corkwood, battered and not yet rid of old burn scars I felt I'd seen before.

'See, over there,' she said, giving me another hint. I saw. The scrubby acacia bushes, the onslaught of buffel, the crouching purple soft-leafed bushes. Raisins.

'Your berry garden,' I said, pleased to have remembered.

Lekisha pointed her finger at me sternly like the teacher she was in training to be. 'Now how do you tell if the bush is raisin or nightshade? How do you tell a good one from a poisonous one?'

I felt the tickle of an old joke. I'd heard it had been started by some botanist. 'Ask an Aboriginal person,' I said.

'Wrong. Not just any Aboriginal person, an Aboriginal person who likes you,' Lekisha said, her brown eyes sparkling with amusement. Her laugh was loud and throaty. Infectious.

As we got out I took her by the arm, still giggling. 'I hope you like me.'

Lekisha picked a raisin berry from the small tight clump under the leaves and offered them to me on the flat of her hand.

'Only one way to find out.'

I went to take one but she snapped her hand closed around them and then shoved the lot in her mouth.

'Pick your own,' she said. I wasn't fussed. I turned to look for another bush, my hand shielding my eyes from the sun.

'From here,' she said.

I didn't really like bush raisins. They were okay dried but like bush orange I could take them or leave them. Bush banana I loved when they were small and green toasted on coals but Mulga apples were my favourite fruit. Actually they were made by a parasite that lived in the tree and weren't really a fruit at all. Tiny, no bigger than a macadamia and about as hard, they tasted sweet and a bit like an apple if you hadn't eaten a good one for a while. Neither of my favourites was in season. It was surprising to see raisins still but sometimes when the weather got too dry fruit could come late or not at all.

I wandered around while Lekisha picked, moving carefully through the bush, conserving her energy by never making unnecessary movement, taking and leaving fruit judiciously.

The landscape was scrubby, rocky under a layer of sand. I took the cap off my camera, a new SLR Floyd had bought me. I liked this type of country, the surprising beauty one could find in small details: a rock swirled and patterned by time, the delicate bark on a bush, a pale snail shell on a twig. It was beautiful in its hard way. But it was not the land of plenty.

Lekisha stopped to take leaves from an entirely different plant. It looked like some sort of eramophila to me but wasn't that what most of the plants were?

'Get your Mum to put this under her pillow,' she instructed handing me a bunch of the leaves.

'What is it?'

'Medicine.'

We drove back with a full bag of raisins to take to Magdalene and the other old people—if Lekisha didn't eat them all on the way back. Frustrated watching her scoff them like they were something easily got, lollies from a shop, I took the bag and tied it up.

'You're still proper bossy,' Lekisha commented, without seeming to mind.

'I am I suppose.' There wasn't much point denying it.

'Like your Mum, that's good.'

'I'm not really like her,' I said, defensively.

'You are. You're sad but you're strong.'

I looked away. She was so frank sometimes it was hard to take.

The road swept alongside the riverbank near town. There were plenty of drunks about in the shadows waiting to intercept anyone leaving the takeaway for a can or two. Lekisha scanned the small groups to see who she knew. Jonas, one of her cousins, shouted out cheerfully as we passed.

'He's always happy at two o'clock,' she said, referring to when the takeaways opened. 'Some people got nothing better to do. Even if they got kids they should be worrying for.'

I doubted it was just him she was talking about. There was plenty of it in town. Half of bush came in to party, adding to the chaos.

I'd been expecting her to go back to the camp but she threaded her way through the many circle streets of the western suburbs until she pulled up at a house I didn't know. The front yard was full of people I didn't recognise, although one of the men looked to me like the driver of the blue car.

I handed over the bag of raisins I'd been protecting. Disinterested she waved them away telling me not to forget to put the leaves in a pillowcase under Ros's pillow.

It was only as I was driving to the hospital that it hit me. The raisins weren't why we'd gone bush. We'd gone to get medicine for Mum. The fruit was a bonus.

CHAPTER 8

As he had been each day after his visit, the next morning Michael rang from work to tell me Ros seemed a little better. I suspected the work Lekisha and her grandmother were doing was really helping. I'd popped the plants up and in her pillowcase the night before. When I called up later to see her with lunch, I had to agree with Michael's assessment. She did seem better. Far less jaundiced, and more interested in talking. I would have liked some time alone with her but this was impossible with Lucy and Frank both there. Frank was being his usual totally droll self, dominating the conversation, amusing us all with his stories about the latest drama at work and flirting with the staff. Whatever lunchbreak they were on seemed limitless and my comments about wasting organisational time and money seemed to provoke absolutely no response. In the end, slightly frustrated, I gave them all a big squeeze and left.

Michael and I ate our dull dinner of adzuki bean soup late after he'd dropped in some to Mum. When I complained about feeling a little like there was hardly any room to see Mum on her own he was sympathetic. She'd had two friends up when he'd taken in the soup. He suggested I try visiting very early in the morning like he did, because few of her friends had much time then. Either they were busy taking advantage of the quiet time at work when they could get things done, out exercising or still sleeping. Whatever they were up to it wasn't visiting. Michael proposed we alternate breakfasts. I emailed Lucy to change me on the roster. From now on I'd do breakfast and hopefully get to see a bit of Mum.

Early the next morning I took up to the hospital fruit for my breakfast, not nearly as elegantly set out as Michael would have done it, some porridge for Mum and the two thermos flasks, of tea, a nettle and a dandelion variety, only to find she was being discharged.

'They've decided they need the bed,' she said. 'I'm surprised they didn't send me home almost immediately. I'm not critical.'

'I don't know,' I said. 'You still don't look great.'

Mum seemed still far too sick for me to care for and I thought she was hoping to be discharged rather than that it would actually happen, but it did. The young resident who managed the discharge assured me everything would be fine and notified us there would be a follow-up appointment with the specialist at outpatients in the next week. It wasn't Fiona, which made me wonder if she was happy enough to avoid us as I hadn't seen her since the first days of Mum's admission. When I asked about the change in specialist he said she'd gone on leave and, thinking I was questioning the level of service, he assured me I'd find the visiting specialist just as capable. It was reiterated that all I had to do was make sure Mum rested, and her body would do what it needed to heal. 'The human body is extraordinary,' he said, 'how cleverly it can repair itself as long as it's given a chance.' And the heart I thought, what are its chances?

I took the river road home and on the way we passed the site of the old squat Mum had lived in briefly before I was born. It was now a brand-new office building. The Australian, Territory and Aboriginal flags flew side by side above the shiny cyclone-wire fence. Red, yellow, black, blue, white, all flapping in an unseasonal southerly wind. I noticed her turn and look.

'Who are they?' I asked. I hadn't quite managed to read the name on the building.

'ITS, Indigenous Training Solutions.'

I craned my head back at the old building. It was certainly flash.

'Better known as, Itinerant Terrorist Psychos.'

'Psychos starts with a P,' I said, laughing. 'So how come you hate them?'

'I don't hate anyone. Thirty years on it seems the only jobs are still for trainers.'

She closed her eyes and sighed. 'It's exhausting,' she mumbled.

'What is?' I leant towards her to catch her reply.

'Being hopeful. I think I'm just about out of puff.'

I couldn't think of anything to say in response. I'd just been bemoaning not having enough time with her and now I was wondering how I would cope being trapped in the house alone with her while Michael had his office to escape to.

*

Mum had always thought baths were for kids and a waste of water but when I suggested she have one she agreed. Maybe she could smell it too, the bitter stench on her skin, part hospital, part illness.

She sat on the toilet lid while I ran the water and I opened a bottle of pure lavender oil, intending to tip it in the water, only to have her moan that the scent made her nauseous and insist I take it well away.

It was confronting to be her carer, although who found it hardest was probably a toss-up. Mum was still a mess. Skin sagged off her bones and she was pitifully skinny. She turned her cat eyes up at me and fixed me with a gaze that demanded I didn't feel sorry for her. I could only try. Taking my arm to steady herself, she lowered herself in the water, as exhausted as if she had just run a marathon, resting her head back on the towel I'd fashioned into a pillow.

By the time I put her to bed she was shivering and I had to reassure her several times the air-conditioner was set on low. Although she wanted it off, I knew the house would be stifling without it and refused. I lay down with her for a minute to keep her warm, noticing she still had the old blue blankets folded up for summer on top of her wardrobe. Mum's given lots and lots of bedding away over the years but she'd never hand over those blankets Michael bought them for their first winter together. Even if she abandoned the whole house she'd keep the blankets. They were a possession she allowed an attachment to. Everything else only had a purpose. I had a chair like that. Lekisha had painted it for me years ago. A wedding present. The chair had wooden arms and a vinyl back and seat she'd painted a desert scene on in a naïve style. In the centre a goanna was curled on a clutch of white eggs. Thinking of babies just like you, she'd teased at the time.

'I've been meaning to ask, how come you didn't answer the phone when you were sick? Lucy said she'd rung here a heap. Frank said the same. And you didn't pick up to me or Michael. Not once.'

For a minute I thought she wouldn't answer and I'd already decided not to make an issue of it when she spoke.

'I was scared. I knew I was unwell. I'd been feeling terrible for ages. I kept needing to spit and my mouth tasted rank. Everything smelt and tasted bad. I hadn't felt so nauseous since I was pregnant and I knew it couldn't be that. To tell you the truth I was terrified. I thought I'd try and ride it out. If it wasn't serious I figured I'd get better.'

'You work in health, that's a ridiculous attitude.'

'I know. I really thought I had been immunised against hep, so I thought it must be something else.' She closed her eyes but kept on talking. 'Michael had enough on his plate. I didn't want to worry him. He was up lobbying about the release of that report.'

'The alleged pedophile stuff, the kid thing, sacred children or something?' Floyd had been going on about it. I thought that's why he'd been in Darwin, sniffing the dirt. He thought the NT government was a bad joke and needed exposing at every turn.

'Yeah that. I don't ask about things he can't talk about.'

'Fair enough. But how about when you got really sick?'

'Oh it happened so fast I hardly knew what was happening. I was just trying to get through the moments. One at a time.'

'Lucky Michael came back when he did.'

'Michael's always arrived at the right time.'

So he had. I kissed her forehead. She was lucky. We both were.

As I left the room I glanced at the photo on the wall and it was pretty clear to me we would all have to get some new image of her, one that didn't rely on her being a warrior.

In the morning I woke up and for a moment forgot where I was. Magdalene's painting, a dotted abstract of her dreaming, reminded me. I lay in bed, in no hurry to get up.

It was country noisy. A dog barked. Birds were chatting and singing. Outside my window came the babbling of the bowerbirds as they skipped over the ground hunting for their nests. Lincoln parrots sat clicking their tongues in my tree, the large flame tree. At this time of year the ground beneath its steady branches was blanketed in red flowers. When the tree was small Mum'd planted it with my placenta at its roots, never knowing how large it would become. She'd done it with me watching from my bassinet. I didn't remember it, of course. It was a story, but an important one because every time I looked at it it reassured me, regardless of what other ceremonies Mum went to, whatever else she did, I was her most important creation.

I tried not to make the leap to the next thought, the wish that one day I might recreate the same sense of attachment with my own child, but I went there anyway. These days the thought almost automatically appeared like an alarm on my biological clock.

By the time I was up and about Michael had Mum on the verandah, sat up a like a queen on the chaise longue. It was still pleasant outside, early enough that the heat hadn't hardened into the obstacle it would become. Sprinklers sent soft showers of water onto the lipia lawn, and the automatic drippers hissed conservative measures of water onto the kitchen garden where tiny tomatoes like jewels hid among the green of summer leaf vegetables.

Michael served me wedges of red pawpaw with lime slices, both home grown, while Mum looked on longingly, but cool foods like this weren't on her list. The warm semolina porridge lay barely touched in a bowl on her lap. We all pretended to enjoy the dandelion coffee he had brewed, and Mum seemed happy enough making digs about how many more minutes it would be before Michael made an excuse to get to work and make a real coffee. She didn't have to wait long before he'd collected his work satchel from his study and was ready to leave. He promised her he'd have a latte with his macchiato just for her. She poked her tongue out at his back and pleased by her good mood, I stayed sitting with her. The conversation shifted around until it found family.

'How come you never told me Caleb had a baby?'

'Didn't I?' she said innocently. 'Well I'm surprised Lekisha didn't tell you when she found out, she certainly got a bit of a shock. Haven't you been talking?'

'A bit. But you know how it is. She tends to ring when she needs to.'

'You mean when she needs something.'

I didn't care for her making out Lekisha only stayed in touch for stuff. If she wanted to go down that rocky road she'd have to admit every relationship she had with family, starting with Magdalene, was just about access to 'stuff'. And knowledge like the kind she'd got from Magdalene was the most important stuff of all.

'Sorry,' Mum said, 'I didn't mean that like it sounded.'

I was fairly sure she did, though I shrugged, unwilling to fight.

'It's my bitterness,' she said. 'That's what Lucy would say. The liver is where you store anger and regret, according to her. And all mine is coming up. That's for sure.'

To my horror she started crying. My mother I'd only ever seen cry when someone died or when she was overwhelmed by some big occasion. Like when they gave the deeds to Promised Land to Magdalene and the family or when I won an art prize. She didn't cry like this. I didn't know how to respond.

'Oh come on,' I said, desperately, 'you got a virus. Wrong place, wrong time. That's all.'

She shook her head. 'No. You get what you make.'

In those nightmarish days in ICU, with her thoughts tumbling about chaotically, Mum said she'd realised despite all her talk, all her social working, she'd never dealt properly with lots of things. Perhaps foremost, the death of her baby at twenty-five weeks. My younger sister. She'd simply tried to get on with things after the miscarriage, forever hopeful of having another child but never talking about it. I was gobsmacked. I'd always assumed Mum didn't want more kids or Michael didn't want any. And I'd always been under the impression she could talk about anything. She'd never struck me as being unable to express herself, although on reflection it was true she was much more likely to talk about issues which weren't personal. Other people's emotions were easier for her. This revelation, this admission of a long-dead sister, was what Floyd would have called breaking news.

FROM ALICE *WITH* LOVE

As we sat there stewing in our own thoughts the sun scaled the fence and made its claim on the backyard. I took my mother's hand, wondering why now of all times she'd told me. Why not when my own baby died? Although it wasn't born like my sister clearly was, without a heartbeat or a breath, yet complete. A baby to hold, rock and grieve for—although as Mum told it she never had taken the opportunity to do these things. Instead she walked out of the hospital pretending she could simply go on and try again without looking back, and I wondered why she'd denied herself the chance to grieve when she knew how healing it could be.

My baby died so early I never knew its gender and a small sucking implement was efficiently inserted inside me under local anaesthetic, the 'failed product' scraped out. That was ten years ago, early on in the piece. The pregnancy had been an accident only I had been very happy about. I wept for days when I lost it. I consoled myself with the idea there would be other chances. Floyd insisted it might well have been meant to be. He used it to validate his position as unsuitable father material. It didn't matter how often I tried to convince him otherwise, he believed he would fail as his own father had done. Nothing I could say would persuade him. Despite loving him, in the end I knew I had to leave and I might not have found the courage to go if Floyd had been a different type of man, but he loved me enough to make divorce look like the best idea so I could have a chance to find someone else.

I gave Mum's hand a squeeze. There was nothing much to be done about the past. We both knew that. Although her confession would have been more useful if she'd told me at the time, it was a comfort to know she really would understand how I felt about

79

being childless, something I never credited her with getting. I saw now her sudden visit to Sydney to see me then, in a different light. I thought she'd come to brush over what had happened but she'd come because she wanted to share and she had understood what I was going through even if she couldn't talk about it.

We gave in to the heat, to the lack of available words to heal old hurt and headed back inside. Her to her room, me to the kitchen.

When Lekisha rang just after I'd put some beans in a pot to soak I was glad of the excuse to get out. She told me she was minding Rosia and needed a lift. Mum told me to go. She was reading my book and made a fair attempt to appear cheerful. 'I'll try and hurry up and finish this for you.'

'Don't worry, I'm into another one. Just don't tell me what happened when you do.'

'Of course not.'

I smiled. When I was about sixteen I was reading *Anna Karenina*. I was only three quarters of the way through.

Oh *Anna Karenina*, Mum had said, catching sight of the cover. It's a great book. It's really sad, isn't it, when she throws herself on the railway track and kills herself.

I took months to forgive her for spoiling the ending.

'Happy reading, I won't be too long,' I said, hoping the murder mystery would keep her mind off her own troubles.

CHAPTER 9

I was a bit worried about not having a baby seat in Mum's car, but Lekisha didn't sound concerned when I rang her back and told her. She wanted me to come anyway.

At the entrance to the camp a hot wind picked up a selection of plastic bags, swirling them about in an ugly whirly across my path. When I was a kid, Lekisha had taught me never to let a whirly come near, because they were bad spirits. I hoped now that it wasn't a sign, given I'd just agreed to cart a baby around illegally.

Lekisha wanted to take Rosia to the clinic. I assumed she meant Congress, where Mum worked, but it turned out she wanted to go to a health department clinic, right over on the other side of town.

'How come you're going there?' I asked.

'I don't like Congress.'

I didn't ask why and she didn't tell me. In any case, it wasn't something I'd be telling Mum. The idea that the locally run health service she'd worked in all her life was being rejected by the very people it was established for would add weight to her bag of regrets.

At the clinic there was quite the crowd of mothers and babies. Small children were playing in a safe area with ample toys. Lekisha took a seat next to a young white woman, who looked over at Rosia and smiled.

'What a beautiful little girl,' the woman said.

'Thank you,' Lekisha said, pleased. 'Is that your boy?'

The woman nodded proudly. He was a small boy of about two, a spitter for his mum, happily smashing a plastic truck into a pile of Lego.

'They got good toys here.'

'Yes they do. The facilities are good.' Congress didn't have toys, just tired health magazines. Here they provided a small place to make a tea or coffee while we waited. Lekisha had tea. It was only like this on mother and baby mornings, she told me.

As far as medical places went it was doing its best to be friendly.

'You want to come in?' she asked when her name got called.

'It's a check-up?'

'She's getting the needles.'

'No thanks.'

When Rosia started screaming in the next room I tried not to listen. I was glad I wasn't there to see the press of the needle into her small upper arm or her round pretty face screwed up in pain, her eyes filled with disbelief that anyone she loved would subject her to such cruel treatment.

When she emerged, Lekisha offered Rosia to me with her bottle. She was still sobbing breathlessly, a sound I found frightening.

'Where you going?' I asked, panicked.

'Just to see if I can make a dentist appointment.'

I hadn't fed a baby for years. I held the teat uncertainly at Rosia's lips, but fortunately she was smart enough to help me out and soon stopped her crying, feeding steadily. Lekisha took her time but I didn't mind because in the time it took Rosia to finish the bottle I fell deeply in love with her. I couldn't take my eyes off her for a moment, watching her fall asleep in the crook of my arm. It was a miracle, the adoration a baby could demand.

Lekisha had something to do on the way home, which turned into five things, but I was in such a good mood that it didn't annoy me as it might have on another day. When we stopped at the supermarket for nappies I bought a small brightly coloured cloth rattle for Rosia.

Lekisha shook the rattle when I gave it to her. 'What's inside it?'

'I don't know.'

'It's good, not too loud for her.'

I was pleased my choice met with her approval.

When I dropped them off at the camp, Caleb was sitting on the verandah.

'Where're the dogs?' I asked, surprised not to see them.

'They all inside under the air-conditioner. Once they in, they cry if we chuck them out in the heat.'

I found it hard to believe Lucky couldn't tough it out, but it wasn't hard to believe Lekisha was soft on her dogs.

'If you're not busy, we'll go this week to Promised Land, okay?'

'Sure, I'd like that. If Mum's a bit better it should be fine. Text me.'

She had Rosia in her arms and her hand on the door handle when she paused. 'You loved being a teacher, didn't you,' she said. The comment seemed to come completely out of left field, but it happened to be true.

'Yes, I did.' Though it felt like a lifetime since I'd done it. I'd enjoyed my year twos. I loved all my relationships with the kids I'd taught over the years. They were so trusting. They assumed I'd love them and take care of them, that I'd mind every little thing on their behalf. From a cut finger to a mistake in their work. Sometimes I thought Mum was right and I had given it up as part of punishing myself for wanting my own child more than my husband. 'It was good. Hard work but rewarding,' I added.

'I thought you missed it,' she said, looking pleased.

'I do.'

'I like it. I can't wait to finish.'

'Lucy said you were going well, just one year left. That's great. Remember how Ros was always going on about you being a teacher and you'd have those fights?'

'We didn't fight. Just arguments.' One or two times I thought Mum had been lucky Lekisha didn't get really wild. She could go on once she'd formed an opinion and she didn't like being disagreed with.

'How come you changed your mind like you did? I never asked. Something happen?'

'Nothing happened, that was the whole problem. I was bored. I was sick of Centrelink. Lucy said the main work is health or education. And I decided a teacher pays more and I can't stand sick people. That's why.'

I laughed. I took it she meant she couldn't stand doctors and nurses, because she helped Magdalene out with plenty of sick people. Even Mum. Then again, perhaps the possibility of being managed by Ros had put Lekisha off being a health worker.

'Are you planning to teach in the Promised Land school if they ever get the go-ahead?' I asked.

'It depends,' she said. 'See you soon. Magdalene wants to talk to you. She's got news. We'll go early tomorrow or the next one.'

'The next.'

'Okay, I'll tell her. You get some food. Some tails. Maybe cake. Nanna's still got the sweet tooth.'

'No problem.'

Lekisha turned and waved out the window at Caleb, who was sitting on the verandah, to come and help her.

'Where's Maxine?' I asked. I'd never sighted her.

'She's gone,' said Lekisha. I didn't ask her for details.

'Caleb,' she shouted. She called again and still he didn't move an inch. When I went to get out, she stopped me. 'I'm right, you stay there. That dog will come outside for you.' She swung Rosia confidently into one arm and picked up the shopping from the floor with her free hand.

I was annoyed with Caleb's laziness while his mother struggled to carry the baby and the shopping. 'Hey, you going to help your mother?' I shouted out the window. After all, it was his baby she was caring for, their house she shopped for. But Lekisha was nearly at the verandah steps before he moved lazily to assist her. 'Not just women who eat,' I said, loud enough for them both to hear.

Lekisha shot me a look that said, *Hey girl, you want to get yourself killed?* But she was pleased with my spunk, I could tell.

When I arrived home that afternoon, Michael was just leaving. I frowned, wondering why Magdalene was in the car with him when Lekisha had just told me she was at Promised Land.

Mum was resting on the couch and I tucked a bit of her straggly red hair back behind her ears as I tried to gauge her mood.

'I thought I just saw Magdalene leave with Michael,' I said.

'Yeah, she came here to see him. They were talking. But I drift, you know.'

'You finish the book, want to tell me who done it?'

She gave me a slap on my arm and a silly grin. Her mood was okay.

I was looking forward to going bush. Maybe if it wasn't too hot we'd even go hunting. I looked in the fridge to see what to cook. It was still crowded with other people's meals and I could have started up a takeaway if there was a market for bland vegetarian food. I'd have to talk to Lucy and remind people to stop the meals. We'd found Michael and I could easily handle it between us now Mum was home. She hardly ate much and even I was a not-half-bad cook when it came to this liver-loving style.

I was pounding garlic and turmeric for a cauliflower soup when Michael came in. Seemingly happy to let me keep on preparing the dinner, he started reading. I expected him to offer me some cooking tips but I had the soup on the stove before he even looked up from his article.

'Floyd's written a good piece in this,' he said, holding up the cover of his journal.

'On here?'

'Sort of. Top-end story.'

'He's a good writer,' I said. Since we'd split up I could appreciate this aspect of Floyd more. During our relationship it had become something I'd resented. Being a good journalist took a lot of time. It was the sort of job that could occupy a dedicated person twenty-four hours a day. And Floyd was such a person.

'What do you think you might do?' Michael asked. I knew he was referring to my abandoned career, my stalled life in Sydney, and while the question was not intrusive, it was unusual for Michael to want to engage me like this.

'I don't know. I'm not exactly doing anything for Mum, but I'm in no rush to leave.'

'You are helping, you're cooking.'

'Well, there's not much need. The care meals mob can't seem to be stopped.'

'Perhaps we just need to wean them off their duties. If we just stop it there'll be a protest, you know what they're like.'

I did.

'And a couple a week we could do with. I think Ros is going to take a while really to get better and it will take any pressure off us. I told her earlier today I'm going to take some leave and hang around for a while.'

'Did that scare her?'

'A bit, but I promised her I'd spend a lot of time in my office out the back. I might even start that book I've been thinking of writing.'

'That one you've claimed to have been writing out there all these years?' I said.

'That's the one. And don't be so disrespectful. It's hard to fit in writing when constant training is required so my ninety-year-old mother can't beat me at internet scrabble,' he said amusingly.

'You're a living legend,' I said.

'Yes, in my own small lunch box.'

We laughed. It was good medicine, happiness.

The next day the temperature was predicted to only be in the high thirties. I'd made plans to meet Lucy at the town pool for lunch but she texted at breakfast that she'd had a work crisis and would have to cancel. I felt more crushed than I should have. I'd been looking forward to seeing her. I was relying on her to help me meet more people. Other than Lekisha, the few good friends I'd once had in town had left a long time ago. Like me, once they'd left for school, or university down south, coming back didn't seem like an option. We were expected to stay away. Nobody acknowledged it out loud but coming back was seen as failure. It meant you couldn't cut it outside, in the important big world of 'down south'. It was a strange and rather contradictory expectation, because for the most part our parents would never have contemplated living anywhere else but in Alice.

There were exceptions, of course, like Fiona, but I couldn't think of many others. One old friend, Alison, had been back for a few years after her divorce but she'd left again last year with a visiting academic she'd met. While I didn't consider it a problem that my friends were all Mum's and Michael's, it was a problem that they all worked. And now that Mum didn't need much help, I was getting bored without work or much in the way of company. I wondered if I should start thinking about going back south myself even if I really didn't feel like it. I could leave Mum and Michael to their own devices. They were surrounded by willing helpers should they need anything.

I wouldn't decide in a hurry. There might be few reasons to stay but there were fewer really to leave for.

I was glad when Lekisha texted and confirmed that the trip to Promised Land was still on for the next day. So there was one thing to look forward to.

When Mum appeared in the kitchen, still in her Japanese cotton dressing gown, Michael handed her a large bottle from his satchel that said Coke but clearly wasn't. It was yellow, for a start.

'Bathe in it, Magdalene says.'

'Utnerrenge?'

'I didn't ask,' Michael said.

It looked like piss. Many of the plants turned a yellow colour when they were boiled up. Obediently Mum took her present to the bathroom. We heard the taps running to fill the bath. Michael and I pulled a face at each other, clearly thinking the same thing. She was still too easy to boss. Which was good for us but what did it say about where her head was at?

After dinner I drove down to the local shop to pick up some kangaroo tails. I was only going to get a few but I ended up doing a deal on a whole box of frozen tails. I figured I'd tell people they were from Floyd since he'd paid for them. When I got home I stored the tails in the back fridge. I didn't dare take them inside. Mum hated the smell, even when she was well. Not that they smelled strongly until they were cooked, but Mum had always complained she could smell them even uncooked and in plastic! The tail was the only part of the kangaroo that traditionally could be cut off, to be eaten separately, and its gelatinous fat and stringy meat was considered delicious. I loved it, but it was one of those foods like durian—people either loved it or hated it; no-one stayed impartial. I knew Magdalene would be very pleased I'd gone to the trouble. I was planning to go to the supermarket but decided it would be better to do it in the morning, with such little room left in either fridge. I made a list. Since I'd arrived I'd done more grocery shopping than I had in years and I was feeling like I was on the verge of being efficient.

It took a while to get to sleep that night. I was excited about the trip and looking forward to going, as early as I could manage.

CHAPTER 10

It was early when I beeped the horn outside Lekisha's place. When she didn't come out I beeped again. She was scowling when she emerged, a large pannikin in one hand, her trusty handbag over her shoulder, which I'd never known her not to be carrying since buying it years ago on one of her holidays in Sydney with me and Floyd. Lekisha didn't go anywhere without it.

'I didn't finish my breakfast,' she complained as she jumped in without spilling a drop of tea.

'You said come early, so I did.'

'I said day, not night.'

'You get grumpy now in the mornings?'

'No sleep. Baby, drunks, dogs carrying on. Someone must have been doing something to those puppy dogs.'

There were plenty of dog dreaming sites around and if they were disturbed all the dogs went off. That's what I'd heard as a kid when I was getting a lecture on which way to walk around town and which way not to.

'You get everything?'

'Nah,' I said, exaggerating the word like a joking teenager. 'Where's Rosia, isn't she coming?' I added, trying not to sound too desperate to see her. Michael had lent me a baby seat in case she was coming with us as I'd hoped she would be.

'She went up last night with Henry and Treasure.'

'Caleb?'

Lekisha didn't answer. She turned her gaze out the window, screeching at her dogs to go back. I reversed out and took the wrong turn, heading up the cul-de-sac to house nine. She cackled her jokey laugh. 'You want me to drive, sis? Must be you forgot the way.'

'Get over,' I said. 'As if!'

I'd never forget how to get to Promised Land, but it had been a long time. If I visited Alice at Christmas it was just too hot. And if the weather didn't restrict us, business often did as roads were closed to protect the law men and the initiates. When we were kids, Lekisha used to go out with Magdalene to join the other women when it was time for the men to come back. Sometimes, depending on cultural expectations, she might not start the school year with me.

Everybody, including Magdalene, wanted kids to read and write, to go to school. There might be compromises but they weren't going to sacrifice everything they believed in for it. It made me wonder how they were going with their attempts to get the school started out there. If they ever got it they planned to eventually be able to shift the terms around to fit in with their business. But I had no idea how it was progressing. The topic hadn't come up since the day I'd arrived.

Magdalene and Mum had been campaigning for the school for

years, beginning back when Promised Land was an illegal camp with no services; water used to be carted in weekly, in forty-four-gallon drums. There was no electricity, no refrigeration, no buildings except for the tin-sheeted wiltjas cobbled together. People had nothing except the land, which they were prepared to sacrifice everything else to hold onto. On one of our visits two years ago, Mum had even roped Floyd into helping with the campaign for the school, asking him to write some articles and get the message into the media. He'd enthusiastically got on board, and also enlisted Robert, now a sports writer in Melbourne. He wrote a great article about the young guys who were good enough to get drafted in the AFL who couldn't even go to school in their own country. While I absolutely agreed with the dream, I knew the reality. There hadn't been a new bush school on an outstation since I'd left Alice a decade before. That's how entrenched the lack of support for remote communities was, and much as I hoped it would happen I didn't think they had a prayer.

We reached the edge of Alice in silence. Like lots of small rural towns, it just got scrappier on the edges until it was no longer there. We cruised past the last of the town's many car yards, the holiday motorhome centre, the wreckers, the truck stop and the motor rego. The only buildings left were those in a northern town camp, which stood in all its shabbiness for all to see and some to be ashamed by, just off the main road.

Outside the camp fenceline at the no-grog sign two people sat in a white Falcon with a knocked-out windscreen. It took me a moment to properly process the image and realise the car was sitting on blocks without one wheel to its name. The driver and his passenger were going nowhere, just watching the traffic flowing in and out of town on the highway.

'See that,' I said to Lekisha, thinking it looked rather sad.

She glanced over and laughed. 'That's Lexie Crane, must have his carton in there.'

'Who?'

'Lexie—you know, he used to be with Clemmy. Old Raymond's son, Malcolm's brother, Caleb's nephew on that other side.'

I nodded blankly, wondering as I had a million times before how she could possibly keep track of all her relatives. But for her, knowing who was who, was essential. Kinship and relationships defined the basis of all other business which kept people connected and culture alive. It was a complicated system and I was always impressed by how much she knew, though not as much as Magdalene. What she knew could fill a genealogical guidebook.

I put my foot down and we roared up the hill. Mum's old car had no real grunt but for a minute we were flying upwards and town quickly fell two gullies behind. I loved this drive; these hills, their height, the pockets and folds that revealed themselves in the orange rock. In good years they'd be a chain of pools running through the centre of the valley which descended in folds of rock down the river course into town.

To our right the old highway crumbled into not much more than potted holes worn by past traffic and flash floods. Looking ahead, the sky was momentarily cut down to city size by the edges of the hills. On the north side of the range the sky once again became far greater than the sum of everything else and it was good to feel town slip away behind us.

To the left of the roadside the silver tracks of the railway line joining us to Darwin and Adelaide slipped in and out of view. A red bank supported a spine of grey concrete girders laid evenly in straight rows under the tracks, the orderly repetition mesmerising. Uneven hills of dirt where the graders had pushed the country aside told the displacement story the railway caused.

The car shook as it crossed a cattle grid. At the last metal bar, crown land had become pastoral lease. The stationowners whose land we were now crossing weren't known for friendliness. Even firewood gathering was frowned upon; every stick, the pastoralists liked to remind whoever might dispute it, belonged to them, was theirs and theirs alone. When I'd first got my licence, in a bolshy teenage protest I'd go to this place to cut firewood, ready to have a big fight. But disappointingly I'd never been caught.

A curve in the road swept us on and up on a bridge arching in smooth concrete sections over the gleaming train tracks. It was a majestic meeting of curves in this country of straight lines. I wished a train would appear so we could see its silver carriages, its cargo boxes glistening and rippling like a magic silver caterpillar beneath us.

Lekisha must have had the same thought. 'Ah, no train,' she complained. She pointed towards a wide unofficial parking bay. 'Remember when they first made it how we used to wait over there for one to come, then drive up on top and watch it pass under.'

I did. Floyd had thought it was a lot of fuss about nothing. It's a train, he'd said. So what.

His sneering had never dampened my excitement. This was a connection linking us with the south and the north.

'Did that compensation ever get sorted for the access to land?'

'A little bit of pay. Enough for a packet of smokes each,' she said.

'Well, you can save your money since you don't smoke. Get rich.'

We laughed in a spluttery way, both of us a little unsure how funny it really was that my people had been up to their old tricks of offering bibs and bobs in return for her people's country so recently.

I hadn't seen the plains so dry in a long time. When we were kids they were good years. The country had provided us with many feasts. Lekisha, an excellent hunter, could always find something to eat. We'd eaten bush apple from the mulgas, dug tyape, killed goannas, roasted alangkwe, made corkwood flower cordial, spat seeds from atwakeye. The kangaroos the men shot were fat, our belly's mostly full of good bush tucker. But looking at the withered country now, I thought even someone as clever as Lekisha would struggle out here without shop food.

The track into Promised Land was its usual unfriendly self, full of difficulties: patches of bulldust, rocky creek crossings that had been washed out years ago. There were cracks wider than my tyres, and the odd dead tree had fallen over the route, although none so recent that an alternative track hadn't already been created, and we made slow progress the last few kilometres. It seemed to me Henry deserved a medal—and a wage—for doing this every day.

Finally we hit the grid at the Promised Land boundary. Cattle hadn't been run on the excision since it had been returned, so the land wasn't nearly as degraded. Of course, no-one minded the odd one wandering through a fence. If I'd bothered to look I knew I'd spot a rope or two hanging from the gum trees where a cow had been slaughtered quickly and shared out.

I took the last few creek crossings too fast and Lekisha growled at me for dangerous driving. I laughed and went faster. I always drove the last bit recklessly and Lekisha always told me off. It was how it had always been.

As we passed through the home gate I could see the old tin sheds were still there. The first slabs of concrete, the bough shelter. The fire pit surrounded by flat red stones blackened from use. Rocks I'd helped haul, years ago. Promised Land seemed just as I remembered, until I took the bend and saw what had grown behind the original settlement. There were a number of solid-looking new houses made out of fresh grey Besser blocks, too new to be stained with red dirt. As yet undulled corrugated-iron roofs shone on top. The houses were placed in an arc, all facing north, with some space between them but near enough to be clearly together. A big family of houses.

I didn't know where to pull up. I knew from experience that sometimes areas that looked to be bare patches of dirt were actually as private as lounge rooms and I didn't want to bowl offensively into the wrong space. Only when Lekisha pointed where to go did I move forward and park the car in the place she indicated.

CHAPTER 11

I stood a little awkwardly, my back to the car door as some of the family gathered around us. Magdalene was among them. Henry smiled and tipped the brim of his hat my way.

'Hey! Long time,' he said.

'Long time,' I agreed.

I went up to Magdalene slowly, suddenly feeling overwhelmed. Some of the dogs stretched their limbs and came to check us out. Lucky didn't bother. He just growled from the step. Lekisha waved her hand threateningly and the dogs backed off, except for Lucky, who stayed in his top-dog position, sneering at me until Henry sent him off.

Magdalene took me by both arms. 'Hey, good girl. Good to see you back here.' She gave me a big hug and ran her hands all down my sides, checking again. Making sure I was all right. It wasn't that she couldn't see me—there was nothing wrong with her eyes. It was another way of looking, a deeper inspection. After she'd finished she turned me over to the others.

Treasure and Henry's kids and grandkids were out in force. I hugged Treasure and kissed little Declan, her granny, who was

sitting on her hip. Marjory's big boy Preston said a shy hello and
I recognised Sammy, Priscilla's lad, hanging back behind her. There
were more faces to recognise than I could process and I felt a little
ashamed I couldn't place everyone. But the family here was bigger
than those I knew well. Wider and deeper than the few I thought of
as the Henderson family.

'Mum's much better,' I said feeling an air of expectation, 'tired
but fine.'

'Good,' said Magdalene and I knew whatever was going on, whatever people seemed to be waiting for, it wasn't news about Mum.

'How are you all?' I said in language, and got a laugh for my
slight mispronunciation. An encouraging hello or two came back
from a few of the bolder kids.

'So,' said Magdalene, 'you came to see all our changes.'

'Yes. They're pretty impressive.'

'We'll show you soon,' she said with an inflection I knew well.
It was her 'wait and see' voice. I was used to doing what she said.
I'd wait.

Henry helped unload the things I'd brought. There was quite a
bit. If I was visiting friends for dinner in the city I'd normally take
expensive flowers, wine and chocolates or cheese. Here I brought
staple supplies: eggs and flour, tins of meat and vegetables, instant
noodles. For lunch, I'd brought bags of fruit, juice, bread, some
fresh meat and cooked chickens. And the box of tails.

'Good on you,' said Henry, 'looking after your uncle.'

''Course. And myself.' I grinned.

Lekisha and Treasure sorted through the shopping, taking it into
the house I assumed Magdalene shared with Lekisha. The chaos

inside was too much for me and after a quick scout for Rosia, who I couldn't see, I wandered back outside. It wasn't too hot, only in the low thirties. Magdalene had gone to the house next door and reappeared fairly shortly pushing her older wheelchair-bound sister Esther. An old whiskered man in a jaunty cowboy shirt walked slowly behind, his legs those of someone who'd spent a long time in the saddle. He graciously took my arm as I went to help him up the steps and into the house. I didn't know him but he seemed to know me and I assumed he must be one of Lekisha's numerous grandfathers.

Soon there was quite a gathering at the small house, with many people spilling outside on the verandah with me. Lekisha had kindly taken Lucky to a neighbouring yard for me and shut him there, which I was grateful for but surprised by. Perhaps he actually was as mad as she'd said he was and couldn't be trusted at all, or it might be because we were all going to eat, though food didn't seem to be immediately on the agenda. Magdalene was talking in language to the old people and Henry, but I couldn't make much sense of their conversation. Unlike Mum, I'd never learnt language. Lazily, I'd relied on Lekisha's English. I only had what people called 'baby talk'.

Magdalene spoke for what seemed like a very long time while I tried to follow the thread. I heard 'teacher' and 'contract' and 'school', and it suddenly dawned on me that the approval for the school must have finally come through. Though if that was the occasion, I wondered why no-one had mentioned it before or why we hadn't asked Mum to come.

Magdalene turned towards me and switched to English. 'This is the right place for you, Alicia,' she said. 'You miss teaching. You can do the job. You're a number-one teacher. We know. Michael been telling us. And that good man of yours helped us get this school. Now he's let you come here to be the teacher, we can start this school.'

I had a physical reaction as her words thudded into me. She was crazy. Did she really think Floyd and I were divorced so I could work at Promised Land? Did she think I came back to do this?

My mind went into overdrive. There was no way I could make a commitment to teaching here. I'd like to help. I did like teaching. But it was out of the question. I'd come back to Alice for Mum, that was all.

'I was hoping you'd back us up. And you are,' said Magdalene, smiling.

How confident she was, I thought. I'd only ever seen her this excited once before, when I was a kid and they'd put up the first bough structure at Promised Land, the first thing that said, *We are staying*. It was crazy but her enthusiasm was infectious.

'Now the department agree. Sixteen kids, they said. We got them. We had them now for a while.' She gripped my hands with delight and shook them up and down as though we'd done a deal. 'I already signed.'

'Signed with who?' I asked. I was giddy with the speed of events and I could feel myself hurtling madly towards agreeing. I hung on to a verandah post trying to get steady.

'That boss for them. Mr Abrahams. He always said if we got sixteen living here then we can get a school. Have a teacher. And we did.'

'It's only a piece of paper,' Lekisha said, somewhat dismissively.

I wasn't sure if she was expressing scepticism that an agreement had finally been brokered or trying to loosen the knot of obligation she'd helped Magdalene tie me up in.

'They can't go back on their word,' said Magdalene firmly. 'It's on the paper. All signed. Lots of copies of them papers, whitefella way. And we got the classroom.' Henry nodded in enthusiastic support. 'It's just a teacher's missing. Mr Abrahams says he can't get one for here. But I told him don't worry. I'll get a good one myself for the next term.' She smiled at me. It was a powerful smile. An embrace.

I urged myself to properly consider the offer. I took a moment to walk away from the gathering and down the side steps, looking towards the northern ranges. In the distance, a pair of hills rose in the otherwise flat landscape. Sacred hills, they were detached from the ranges running behind them. In the heat they were a deep purple, gorgeous against the burnt yellow of the dry ground.

Looking up at the enormous blue sky, I saw an eagle, its wings stretched wide, circling in the currents above. I watched, fascinated, as a smaller bird came and rode on its wings, resting on its strength. It seemed a sign. This place could help me heal and I could be useful at last, use my skills, like Mum was always going on about, and make a difference.

And there was nothing stopping me. I was entirely unencumbered.

Feeling surprisingly strong and light, I turned and walked back. Even the milling dogs didn't worry me. 'Okay,' I said. 'I'll start up the school if that's what you want.'

People looked up and past me as though my words had shot fireworks prettily into the sky. The kids I knew best, Preston and Sammy, paused in their marble game and turned to check me out. Magdalene threw her arms open and I embraced her. Over her shoulder was Lekisha's stunned face.

'Good on you, girl,' said Henry, his smile wide and generous.

'Okay,' Magdalene said, as if there had never been any doubt in her mind. 'We got ourselves a good teacher.'

'You better get out of the sun,' Lekisha suggested gently. 'You're very red.'

She shepherded me to the garden tap. I splashed water on my face and stood in the straggly shade trying to cool down and collect myself.

'I'll need a big hat to live here,' I said.

If Lekisha usually thought of me as mad, now she thought I might have really lost the plot. She and I both knew it was more than a hat I'd need.

Before lunch, Magdalene ordered Lekisha to take me over to look at the new buildings and the demountable, which was the schoolroom, not a community centre as I'd thought. I took a more self-interested look at the housing improvements as we made our way around. The houses were better built than I'd expected, but they still made housing commission in Sydney look flash. I wondered where I'd be living. All the houses already looked well occupied, overcrowded in most cases. I didn't think I'd last long if I had to swag it on a verandah and share a bathroom; I'd hardly coped sharing a bathroom with Floyd. And there was no way I could live at Lekisha and Magdalene's. It couldn't be done. We weren't even in the same book when it came to our ideas on domestic life, let alone the same page.

As if she could read my mind Lekisha was quick to reassure me I'd have a house of my own. 'They moving the old silver bullet from Kilka for you. Blokes here got the contracts through the out-station mob. Patrick, the teacher there, is coming to help and give them a hand to make a verandah for it.'

How many Patricks could there be? 'Not Patrick with the curly black hair? Is he the teacher?' I couldn't hide my surprise. I'd never asked what he did for a living. Over the years I'd assumed that he was a linguist who specialised in botany. The papers he'd left for Michael, which I'd read a few pages of, had seemed to confirm that impression.

'Yeah, over Kilka way. They let him stay.'

'Michael's friend, Patrick?' I checked again. For heaven's sake. Kilka was only sixty kilometres away. We were probably both managed by the school at Red Bore, which was the biggest community near here.

'Yes. He's good to Aboriginal people. Patrick, the plant man.'

The plant man. For some reason the idea of working closely with him put me in a flap. God knows why. I hardly knew him.

Lekisha was watching me nervously, as though trying to figure out what was going on. 'He's a good builder,' she said warily. 'Don't worry about the verandah—it'll be all right. We got a contract to do it. He's helping us.'

'I'm sure it will be right,' I said quickly, glad she thought it was just the donga that was troubling me. 'Anything will do.'

'You need your own place,' she added.

Of course I did. I smiled and took her arm. As far as Lekisha was concerned, I was a clean freak and a nag.

'Does Kilka go with us, with Red Bore, is that the set-up?'

'Yes. Red Bore have the principal, Annie.'

'Right. And how many kids do you reckon Kilka's got?'

'Twenty? More. Maybe less. They lost a teacher, that's why we got their old teacher house.'

'So it's only got one teacher and one assistant. Everyday? Twenty? Are you sure?'

'I don't know. I don't live there,' she said, irritated with my questions. She didn't like to talk for places she wasn't from.

I let it go. No doubt all of these details could be checked with the department when I went there to see just how far along the permission for the school was. And if I really could just have the job. There'd have to be some interview at the very least. Magdalene's strength was her positiveness but it could have its drawbacks. Like she hadn't heard any of the thousand possible conditions placed on the go-ahead.

Lekisha led me across the dusty ground talking about seeding an oval and other grand plans. I was trying to take it one step at a time and hardly listened. I was wondering if they had the internet out here. I bet they didn't. There wasn't even a TV aerial to be spotted.

The new building would be a squeeze if there really were sixteen kids every day, but I suspected the numbers were soft. The thinly clad shell had a wide verandah and slab attached. It was basic but workable. I looked around and made a list of everything that was glaringly missing, like decent floor coverings and whiteboards while Lekisha followed close behind me, copying my notes.

'Don't you trust me?' I asked.

'Of course,' she said. 'I'm just helping. I'll be the assistant, you know.'

I grinned at her wackiness. How could I have known? Until a few minutes ago I'd had no idea they were planning this for me.

'I've only got this year to go. With you helping I'll be right.'

I made a noncommittal tilt of my head to show I'd heard, and kept working steadily on my action list. I couldn't start thinking about Lekisha's expectations yet. I was just beginning to realise how much work this would involve: I'd have to tackle one thing at a time and keep a hand up to stop other demands or I'd be quickly overwhelmed by what I'd taken on and last a term at most.

By the time we left the schoolroom we had quite a list. So far we only had a shell. The department would have to put their skates on if we were going to get the school up soon. But it wouldn't be impossible. The first thing I needed to do was meet with the relevant people and see the details of the proposal. Lekisha could come with me. But right now she seemed much more interested in getting me back to Magdalene's and having lunch.

On the way she pointed out Henry and Treasure's new house; it differed from the standard design in having four bedrooms instead of two. Even with double the space it was still too small for their large family. None of the verandahs on any of the houses was as deep as I would have designed them. There was some lovely detail on the cement pavers I wouldn't have expected, and Lekisha explained how each family had designed a unique pattern that had been stamped into the concrete pavers they'd made in town.

Treasure and Henry came out of the house to meet up with us and I fell behind, watching them. I admired the way they walked as if the dirt and heat were nothing. I was red and sweaty, struggling in the baking sun, while they seemed to move effortlessly. Treasure, unlike Lekisha, still had the figure she'd had when she was a teenager, particularly impressive when you knew she'd had six children. Henry too was looking good for a man his age. Esther's son, he was a mix of uncle, big brother and dad to us all when we were kids and I hung out bush a lot.

When I got back to Magdalene's house I was surprised to see that no-one had started eating. A table had been set with a cloth, and fly nets protected piled plates of food. It was much more than the offerings I'd brought and it became crystal clear the day's events had been carefully planned.

Henry headed straight to the far corner of the yard were he had already got the tails cooking in hot coals of mulga wood. Using a long handled shovel to manage the heat, he'd ensure they cooked up nicely. Sometimes when the heat was uneven they'd twitch up out of the fire and Henry would adjust the coals accordingly if this happened. I was glad to see he was in charge. He was a good cook of all kere and I loved tail.

'You sit here,' Treasure instructed me, pointing next to Magdalene. There were only about five chairs at hand and I was embarrassed to be shown such preferential treatment.

'No need to fuss. She's nothing special,' said Lekisha, winking at me.

'She's your boss now,' Treasure said, and I laughed at the alarm that flashed across Lekisha's face.

'Yes, you better watch out,' I said. 'It might be payback time for all those horrible things you've done to me over the years.'

'What?'

'I'm just joking,' I said. 'Although there was that time you told Mum I'd been down the river and I got grounded for a month.'

I'd gone down the flooded waters in a tyre tube, dodging debris, thrilled by my first whitewater experience. I'd floated right through the Gap, down the usually dry wide river almost to the old winery. Mum had been furious when she caught up with me.

'Well, I was right. You could have drowned.' She made a face I knew well, the long-suffering expression that implied it was always her looking out for me, always being the responsible one. As if. I could remember plenty of times she encouraged quite the opposite.

I looked about at the melee over the food. Some things didn't change. Men were standing back, kids were pushing forward, while the women tried to instil some order and then gave up.

Lekisha pushed a huge plate of food my way and I thanked her, although I was really waiting for a piece of tail. 'Nearly ready,' she said. We could smell them from where we were. I didn't eat too much so I didn't fill up before they were done.

Treasure, seeing I wasn't interested in eating, gave me Declan, her daughter Tissianna's boy, so she could eat in peace. Declan would have been almost a year old but he was strong and solid as a bullock. Keeping him from climbing down took some effort, and eventually Preston, who was twelve and had the longest eyelashes of any kid I'd ever known, was called to get him.

Lekisha reminded me Preston was the middle child of Marjory, Henry's sister. I might have forgotten who lots of the kids belonged to but not him. He was born the same year I graduated from art school. Marjory had asked me to take his baby photos and I still had copies in my portfolio, unable to ever discard them despite the fact they were composed with little creativity and were in many ways poor examples of what I could do. But they were pictures of a very beautiful baby, and while I'd gone to bin them a few times, a sense I would be hurting him stopped me. Even though I knew it was irrational.

The food disappeared and the chaos slowly settled. Treasure brought me Rosia. She was sleepy and hot. She fitted into my lap as if she belonged. Preston brought me her bottle and I fed her. From time to time the thought that this was where I was going to be for a while jumped into my mind, unsettling and exciting at the same time. I reminded myself if it didn't work out I could always leave. Nothing was permanent. While the work was daunting it was a good challenge and Lekisha and I would finally fulfil a childhood fantasy of working together. When we were kids, though, we were going to be hairdressers, then air hostesses, then in a leap of expectation we were going to be judges. Being teachers was all right and being teachers here was great. I liked the idea we'd get out into the bush. I'd get to go hunting and revive friendships across the family. I'd have a whole cohort of kids in my world again and when the year was done Lekisha could step up like she should have a long time ago and take over.

Rosia, who'd come to the end of her bottle, started fretting, and Sammy was told to take her to Lekisha.

Treasure introduced me to Uncle Steven, who was delivering chopped tail. He was holding a heaped plastic tray above the kids' heads and sharing it out to the adults before letting the kids go for it. The two sections I got handed were large and fat, and I happily tucked in, salting the meat, pulling the skin off with my teeth. The rich veins of glutinous fat and meat unravelled through the cylindrical bone. I loved it and gobbled it down greedily. I was about to start on my second piece when I caught Preston's longing look. He had what we used to call the mouse's tail, the tiny end of the tail bone. He managed to look so desperate I handed my piece over, at which point his face broke into a grin and he skipped away in case I changed my mind.

Treasure smiled approvingly. Giving in to children was important.

While I'd been busy eating, the men had slipped away. It wasn't unusual for men and women to congregate separately and I didn't mind. It freed certain conversations up. Now the food was all gone the kids scattered too, and the women gathered more tightly around me in the shrinking shade. Politely they mixed English liberally into their conversations so I could follow the thread. I heard many things, including that Tissianna was on the grog a lot with the same drinking company as her cousin Caleb and a group of cousins from the north. Maxine and Caleb weren't getting on and might be finished and she was running with her own crew of drinking and party-loving women. Lekisha's face told me what everyone thought about that: not much. I hoped my own expression was less easy to read because I found the idea that anyone would rather get drunk regularly than look after a child, verging on criminal.

Slowly the conversations swirled into wide-ranging family business about family I barely knew, matters I knew nothing of. The women dropped the english words and I was left more and more on the outer. I realised this was how living here would be and discovered I didn't mind. There was something deeply companionable in being on the fringes of this large family. In town I'd already experienced how difficult it could be finding company to entertain myself. Out here I'd have enough to do running the school and there wouldn't be time or space to be lonely.

I gazed into the distance out at the two sacred hills. One was for men, the other for women. As a woman, I wasn't even allowed to say the name of the men's one, and I certainly couldn't climb it. But there was no harm in me looking. My short-sighted whitefella eyes couldn't see a thing. Even if I could have seen that far I wouldn't know what I was looking at. I'd been to the women's mountain. It had a split in its rocky eastern face where there were sacred paintings. Traditionally, pre-pubescent girls weren't permitted to raise their eyes to the ochre designs, and if they broke this rule I'd been told they were punished with large heavy breasts, which might explain why Tissianna was so top-heavy. It was an unkind thought but I resented Tissianna. I was jealous of her. She had a baby at fifteen. The same year I was realising I'd never have one with Floyd.

It might have been the shock of the morning's events, the heat, or too much food, but I was tired and only Magdalene calling out loudly prompted me to sit up and act more alert. I could hear she was excited. Patrick was coming around the corner of the house with Henry's hand on his shoulder. He greeted everyone by name, a wide smile making his handsome face even more attractive. Flustered, I wished I still had a baby on my lap as a distraction.

The man had some effect on me I couldn't credit with anything rational.

Patrick stood next to me, facing the women but not directly looking at them as he spoke to them in language, completely fluent. I remembered now I'd seen him once at Magdalene's talking to Henry in the yard. He was clearly a favourite and there was plenty of friendly teasing going on. When my name came into the conversation I didn't need language to know they were telling him I would be the new teacher. Something shifted in his demeanour. I could have been wrong but it seemed like unexpected news to him, though he immediately congratulated me warmly. He said he'd heard the department were actually moving the donga next weekend and the verandah would go up soon after. That is, he said, slapping a friendly arm around Henry who'd reappeared, if the old fellow did his bit. Henry gave him the thumbs-up and they switched back into language and moved to the front area again. I would have liked to have joined them but there was no invitation to and it would have been impolite to tag along unless there was.

Making tea, though, was a polite and acceptable way of getting about so when a billy was ready I went and offered to take it to the men.

Lekisha, who came with me, took the billy from my hand before I could pour the tea, swinging it around and around to settle the tea leaves in a big show. That was when I realised Patrick was just one of those men, the one everyone wanted to show off for and please. It was clearly safe to behave like this around him because no-one seemed even the slightest put out or jealous of the attention he attracted, which made me feel better about my own reaction to him, and the situation immediately became easier for me once I realised this.

I took my tea black and strong, refusing all offers of powdered milk. I didn't put cold water in either. Patrick did. As did plenty of the others, and I was able to waylay him on his way back from the tap.

'Hi there,' I said, 'I had no idea you were a teacher, and at Kilka. I thought you were a linguist.'

Patrick pulled at his hat brim as if slightly embarrassed.

'Do I come across like that?'

'Like what?'

Linguists had a reputation for stepping on all sorts of toes.

Patrick's tongue played in his mouth, reminding me of Michael as he searched for the word he wanted.

'Serious.'

We both understood there were other adjectives he could have used. I didn't confirm or deny his assessment. Instead, I smiled as if we were sharing a joke. In return I got a delightful look of amusement.

'So you like it at Kilka?'

'I do. I love it. We'll work together a bit. That is if you are going to live and work here?'

I wondered why he was questioning it.

I was a bit cagey in response. 'Yes. That's the story. If everything goes smoothly with the department. A true story.'

'I was a bit surprised.'

'So was I when Magdalene asked.'

'It's just I thought you lived in Sydney. I remember once Ros told me you weren't into working here. That she'd tried to get you back here to teach numerous times but you'd said you'd never work here.'

I could have pointed out that Ros had been really ill which had shifted everything, but I didn't.

'Things change,' I said. It was unexpected to hear how sad I sounded, although I guessed it probably was less to do with Mum than Floyd.

Patrick's green eyes searched my face for clues and he put a hand briefly on my forearm. A gesture of kindness.

'They do,' he said, as if he really understood how your world could be turned upside down. 'You're right. Sorry.'

We both wrapped our hands around our now empty tin cups, having drunk the tea as we talked.

'You finished?' I put out my hand.

'I'll take it back,' he said. That's how we came to be walking back together and I noticed our hips were almost at an equal height and our strides evenly paced as if we were well matched.

Patrick pushed off before we did, but not before promising to catch up with me in town soon. I looked forward to it. Not long after he'd gone Lekisha and I decided to leave too. She wanted to take Rosia back and I was glad. After lengthy goodbyes and promises to go to the Education Department the next day, we set off. Caleb came with us and sat in the back with Rosia. He'd strapped her into the special seat and was a little anxious on my insistence that she stay in it when she cried. Luckily she didn't object for long and fell asleep when we were only a short way down the track, the car's bumpy movement settling her.

Once we were off the noisy corrugations and onto the bitumen Lekisha came out with the question I suspected she'd been dying to ask all afternoon. 'So, you really going to do it?'

I nodded. If I'd had any doubts, the last had gone after my conversation with Patrick. It had laid down a challenge and piqued my interest in him. Mum hardly needed another live-in carer, I didn't want to live in her place for too much longer and I wasn't keen to go back to Sydney. The job itself was a little scary but that was no reason not to do it, and I'd certainly have my work cut out for me. The teaching wouldn't be easy. Nothing would be. Out bush there wasn't going to be any hiding from myself: country forced reflection. But now was as good a time as any to have a hard look at myself and where I was going with my life.

'Yes, I'm going to do it. I'll meet you at the office first thing tomorrow. Okay?'

Lekisha stuck out her right pinkie finger. I curled my left little finger around it and we tugged. We hadn't sealed a promise like this for years.

'Only for this year, though,' I added. 'What will it be, maybe three terms by the time we start?'

'Don't worry, I'll take over when you go,' she said as if she had a choice.

'You better,' I said. 'Or Magdalene will kill you. You heard what she said. It's time for you young ones to step up.'

Lekisha knew. She'd been taking her time but now she was ready.

'And you know Patrick?' she asked, all innocent. In the rearview mirror I noticed Caleb looking at me curiously. 'Well, he's got no woman.'

She and Caleb played it straight-faced, both looking casually out their windows as if my reaction was of no interest to them. I kept my own face as stony as I could. Inside me there could be no denying a new singing in my spirit, the hum of new possibilities.

CHAPTER 12

It was dark by the time I got home. Mum and Michael were sitting on the couch in the lounge. I joined them and told them about the job excitedly, straightaway. Mum thought I'd lost my mind.

'You don't have to do it,' she said. 'They'll understand you made a mistake, you were overcome. You couldn't shame Magdalene in public. Whatever. You tell them straight tomorrow.'

I looked at her in disbelief. Was this my mother? I couldn't believe her response. I'd thought she'd be pleased for me. I thought she and Michael had been part of the conspiracy to get me into the job.

'Why are you being like this about it?' I asked. 'You've spent your whole life working with Aboriginal people, particularly with Magdalene's family. Our family, you taught me. And you spent years agitating to get the school up—you even roped Floyd in to help. How can you now think it's such a bad idea if I work with them?'

'It's hard work supporting someone else's dreams,' she said. I found this patronising in the extreme.

'Oh really?' I said sarcastically. 'Don't you think I'm up to it? Is that it? What, I'm too city? Too soft?'

'I doubt that's what she means,' said Michael.

I glared at him. 'So what does she mean? Maybe you should translate?'

Michael looked away. He knew it was dangerous to get between Mum and me when we were arguing.

'You've had a rough time lately,' Mum said calmly.

'So? Everyone here has had a rough time. My rough time would be a fairytale come true for a lot of people round here.'

'Do you really think it's the best place for you to be?' she asked.

'Yes, I do.' I was confused and hurt by her reaction, but still confident about my decision. I looked to Michael for help. 'The other day you said it was good I came back.'

'It is,' he agreed. 'I think it's good.'

'What about the job? What do you think about it?'

Michael paused and looked warily from me to Mum. 'I actually disagree with Ros. I think it's a win-win situation. They get a good teacher, you get a job, and we get you back close by.'

Mum turned on him. 'You didn't tell Magdalene this?'

'I did.'

'Did she tell you I'd already told her I thought being a teacher at Promised Land was not what Alicia needed?' Her eyes sparked with anger.

'She did.'

When I was growing up, Michael hardly ever disagreed with Mum on anything to do with my upbringing, so this was a bit of a turn-around in itself. Even more confronting was how they continued to bicker over the top of my head about what I should do as if I was a child.

'What were her reasons to disregard my opinion like that?' Mum demanded.

'Magdalene? She said she thought it was the sickness talking, not you.'

'And that suited you, so you agreed?'

'No. I just told her what I thought.'

I jumped in before either of them could speak again. 'Mum, calm down. I think I can carry the school. It's just for the rest of the year. Seven months, that's all, and then Lekisha will be trained up and ready to take over. It will be a good challenge for me, and I'm up for one. Michael's right, it's a win-win proposition—it means I can stay close to you two. Help out.' Talking calmly and directly seemed to take the sting out of the air. Mum at least let me finish though she didn't seem entirely convinced.

'And I need a job,' I added. 'I can't live on Floyd's credit card forever. He's going to cut it up eventually.'

Her expression didn't change. She knew Floyd never worried about money. And Michael and her had already offered to help me financially if I needed it.

Michael got up to put the kettle on for tea, a standard conciliatory act. I took the opportunity to give Mum a hug.

'It's all good,' I said. 'Stop worrying.'

'I'm your mother,' she said wearily. 'It's my job to worry.'

*

As we'd arranged, at eight-twenty the next morning Lekisha was waiting for me on the small square of lawn outside the office of the Northern Territory Department of Education. I knew then that she was serious about taking on the role her elders had been urging her into for years.

We went inside and approached the front desk. 'I've come about the new job at the proposed school at Irrarnte,' I said to the receptionist, using Promised Land's proper name. It was named after the red-tailed cockatoos.

She turned away dismissively and busied herself making a call. Almost immediately, an efficient young woman came out from an adjoining room and shook my hand briskly. Ignoring Lekisha, she launched into a monologue, explaining that the position at Promised Land was newly created and it wasn't really up to Magdalene to employ me. I had to understand that it was the department, not the community, who were the employer, though of course they would take community views into account. I would need to submit all my qualifications and complete the teacher registration forms for consideration. An interview would be scheduled. Only if they thought I was suitable would the offer be formalised and the start-up funding agreement signed off by Red Bore, the central supervising school in the cluster. If all went well, I'd be contracted from that date, but the school wouldn't be operational until the beginning of second term.

'Sure,' I said slowly, a bit overwhelmed by her rapid-fire speech.

She gave me a smile so token it must have been her spare, handed me a sheaf of forms and disappeared back into her office before I could ask her even one question.

Slightly stunned, I sat down at the stained veneer desk in the lobby and followed her instructions. There were multiple forms to fill in and I had to provide several documents to prove my identity. Lekisha kept me company while I filled in the neat rows and boxes with my details.

Once I went back to the front desk, my academic records and references were fed into a photocopier. When all the papers appeared to be in order the receptionist thrust yet another form at me to sign. It was an agreement to attend an orientation called 'Working and Living in the Territory' at the beginning of second term, should my position at Promised Land be confirmed.

'I don't need to do this,' I said. 'I grew up here. I've spent a lot of my life out at Irrarnte.'

'The position will be subject to the successful applicant completing the orientation. Non-compliance will result in the offer being revoked,' she read from her computer screen.

I took a deep breath. There was a lot to be annoyed by in any bureaucracy, but I knew that if I complained things would only get worse. 'Thanks,' I said, then signed the agreement to attend the pointless workshop.

Once it was over, Lekisha and I went out to breakfast to celebrate. 'Magdalene wants us to go to Iltja with everyone,' she said.

'Where?' I asked.

'Iltja,' she repeated, as if I should know what she was talking about.

'Well, wherever it is, we won't go the first week,' I said, laughing. 'The department would skin us alive.'

'Not the first week,' she said, as if I was myall. 'Later on. After winter maybe. I don't know. She'll tell you.'

'Of course,' I said. 'Whenever she tells me. What's at this Iltja?'

'Water,' she said.

Water, I thought, what a lovely idea. For the first time since I'd arrived I missed water: the ocean, the green river at Eddy's country place, even rain. I missed it all with a distinct pang.

At dinner that night Mum ate all of the adzuki bean and pumpkin casserole I made her. She ate with a dogged determination to finish every last bit of food I'd put on her plate. She went so far as to make the claim that my food was better than Michael's. I didn't believe her but I was touched that she was clearly trying to make up over our fight about the job.

In the morning I woke and I could tell it was going to be a scorcher. The heat was already snapping at the glass and sucking on the water spraying across Michael's vegetable garden. On the radio the announcer said the temperature was already thirty-two. In less than four months it would rarely get above four at this time of day. This place, this country of extremes, was my home again and I was contented to find that my overwhelming emotion was one of happiness. Not everyone gets invited to help make a difference and I felt a warm sense of gratitude for the opportunity. The community would get a teacher and I'd get a chance to make something of a new start.

*

Lucy and Frank were invited for dinner on Friday night. I was glad they were coming and was looking forward to discussing the school with them. I became a little more apprehensive when I found out that Michael had invited Patrick too at the last minute.

'Is that okay?' Michael asked.

'Fine,' I said wondering what he'd read in my face. Dinner would be good. Patrick was not really in the same crowd as Lucy and Frank so he'd add a dimension to what could be a fairly predictable event. I was interested in him and it would be good to see how I found him in what was really a very safe setting for me. On the most practical level Patrick coming to dinner gave me a chance to pump him for information about the job. He would have already established programs for multilevel classes and he'd be able to brief me on what to expect from the kids and the department.

Lucy arrived first. She padded in through the back door in bare feet with her distinctive dancer-like gait. Soon after there was a banging on the front door; I opened it to Frank, who hugged me like the bear of a man he was before I could ask why he hadn't just walked around to the back as usual. It was only when he let me go I saw Patrick standing behind him.

'Look who I found loitering on your porch,' Frank bellowed, a hand on Patrick's shoulder. 'Young Patrick Mathews. Funny fella isn't he, going to the front door so formally?'

'Yes,' I said, relieved to see that Patrick looked as humiliated as I felt by Frank playing the big joking uncle. I let Frank past to go ahead to the kitchen where he could take up his favourite position at Michael's right shoulder offering unneeded advice on whatever it was he was cooking.

'Come in,' I said to Patrick, who seemed a little reluctant. 'How are you?'

'Long week.'

He did look rather done in and I imagined that would be me once I started work.

Mum had made the effort to stay up until everyone had arrived but she wasn't up for a night of socialising and Frank was already in full flight. I followed her to her room to check she was okay. She was sitting on her bed looking a little defeated. I threw her her nightie off the chair.

'The smell of that curry was making me feel nauseous. And Frank—does he always talk so much?'

'Of course he does,' I said, opening the windows and switching on the fan. 'I'll close the kitchen door to cut down on the noise.'

These were strange days, I thought as I shut her bedroom door— Mum going to bed first, not last, and me, freshly divorced and navigating my first gathering in my home town as a single woman.

The others were all laughing at one of Frank's stories as I found a seat at the dining table next to Lucy. He hardly drew breath before launching into another tale, this one about a consultant from Melbourne who'd gone six hundred k's out of his way to a meeting because he'd misunderstood the directions from the old Aboriginal man he was driving with. When he realised his mistake he angrily demanded the old man explain why he hadn't corrected him before they'd gone so far out of their way.

'. . . And you know what the Tjilpi says?' said Frank, looking at me.

'What?'

'He says he hasn't been on that back road for a while and he really enjoyed seeing the country out that way again. It made him really happy.'

We all smiled, as each of us understood the mix of sweet and sour in this story: the frustration of the consultant contrasted with the joy the trip gave the old man. And all of us would have our own similar stories like this and I expected I'd add a few more to my collection before the year was up at Promised Land.

Mum might well have found the smell of duck curry hard going but when Michael served it up it was delicious. It was very rich, though, after the austere diet I'd been sharing with Mum, and I only ate a little. Since she'd been home I hadn't let myself eat a 'bad' thing or anything spicy even.

We'd finished the meal before I mentioned my new job. Lucy and Frank thought it was exciting and good news.

'You do know your new boss is my old girlfriend?' said Lucy.

I didn't.

'Annie? She's that Annie?'

'The very one,' said Lucy.

'How small can this place get? Is there anyone who isn't connected?'

'Yes,' said Lucy. 'There's a new teacher at Red Bore, Blossie. She's really good by all accounts. She's only been there five minutes. I don't know more than that.'

'She on her own?'

'I heard she brought her own man with her,' said Lucy, laughing, 'but Patrick would know more than me.'

'I doubt it. You got to gossip yourself to get any back,' he said as he rose from the table to help me clear the plates.

'Good point,' said Frank.

'It is a small world here if you're looking for someone,' said Lucy a little offended at the way Patrick had shut the conversation down.

'I think there's a little more opportunity on your side of the fence,' said Frank.

'Ha! At fifty there's barely anyone my side at all,' said Lucy without any rancour. 'It's easy for men your age, women are queuing up.'

'Bullshit,' he said.

'Bullshit nothing. Women outnumber men in this town at about five to one. If you can't pull anyone then I'd say you've got a serious problem.'

Patrick and I dealt with the dishes while they kept arguing in a friendly fashion. I was confident Michael would swing the conversation back to something else soon.

'Are they always like that?' Patrick asked.

'They can be heaps worse if they've had a few more.'

The dishwasher was stacked. The sink clear. There was nothing else to keep us away from the others except now they were having a fight about the Howard government.

Patrick cocked his head at the screen door. I grabbed a bottle of wine and two glasses. I followed him out. He dragged two chairs out onto the patch of grass where it was cooler. I poured the wine. I didn't mind how Patrick seemed to like a bit of quiet. There was plenty to look at. A million or more stars danced overhead. Satellites imitated the falling stars. More planes than one would have credited needed to pass this way flew high up, noiseless, their red lights blinking. To the south the ranges made a solid silhouette, except where they had split apart. The Gap.

I pointed up at the left side of the gap.

'See up there that cairn?'

'Near the tree?'

'Yes. Lekisha and I made that when we were kids.'

'You two go way back.'

'We do.' I sipped my wine, not sure how honest I should be. 'I'm a bit worried about working together. Excited but worried. I don't want to have a falling out.'

'It will be right.'

'You want to give me any tips, inside information?'

'Sure. If I can.'

We talked a lot about the school but there were plenty of other conversations we fitted in before the others eventually joined us.

After Frank and Patrick left I sat up with Lucy for a while but it was already later than I'd stayed up in a long time.

As she was leaving she offered me a room at her place if I wanted. I said I'd think about it but it seemed like a good idea to have a town base which wasn't here. And I'd need somewhere to escape to from Promised Land. I wasn't naïve, no matter what my mother might think. I knew I'd hardly want to spend all my time there.

I went to go to bed inside and then changed my mind. I dragged a swag out on the lawn and lay out there. The stars were still dancing. I found Venus low on the horizon, nearly done for the night. I wondered if Patrick might be replaying our conversation, sifting for clues as I found myself doing.

There was no need to rush. No need to panic. Tomorrow the stars would be out again and there was plenty of time to let things unfold naturally.

CHAPTER 13

With surprising efficiency the department set up an interview within a fortnight. It was fairly straightforward as I was the only applicant. Within days I was sent notification I had the job, subject to 'conditions' as stated in the contract. I was allocated a car and given instructions on where to pick it up. The fleet conditions I signed despite knowing I would break them. As if I'd be telling Lekisha she couldn't drive the car. I could try. I was just on a hiding to nothing and I wondered why bureaucracies always made rules they knew would have to be broken.

Mum watched from the front verandah as I packed all my stuff into the troop carrier.

'It's not exactly a new car,' she commented.

'I can see that.'

'They must have misspent your vehicle allocation. Or else one of the boss's mates has got the new one for their school.'

'Probably.'

'If you let them get away with things like this at the start they'll be ripping you off forever. They'll never stop. Your budget will evaporate.'

'Thanks, Mum. But I might just do this my own way,' I said, wishing she'd go inside and leave me to it. I hadn't taken up Lucy's offer of a room, thinking I'd make the transitions all at once but there had been plenty of times in the last few weeks I'd regretted holding off. Mum seemed to have regained enough strength to revert to her bossy ways. Or perhaps it was just that she was still annoyed I'd taken the job that she seemed to be giving me all sorts of gratuitous advice.

Michael came out to join us. I hoped his presence would silence her. It didn't.

'I'd put the boxes at the front of the rack. It's more aerodynamic,' she advised, 'and if you don't tape those boxes they'll be filled with dust by the time you get there. Try getting that fine red sand out of papers and clothes.'

'Anything else?' I asked, climbing the ladder to the roof rack.

'Not for now,' she said.

'You are so bloody bossy,' I said, rearranging the boxes as she'd suggested. 'I have absolutely no idea how you ever survived working with Magdalene and all that mob. Surely someone wanted to kill you.'

'A few times,' said Michael.

'Rubbish. I was a slave,' said Mum.

'More like a slave driver,' I muttered under my breath.

'I heard that,' she said. 'You'll soon find out it's not as easy being a good girl as you think. Especially not in these times.'

Michael went to get the new king-sized swag he'd bought me to put in the donga I'd live in. I seriously hoped they'd managed to get it there before I arrived. Lekisha had mentioned some problem with transport which had made me a little nervous. More than once I'd gone to ring Patrick to check with him on the donga's progress only to change my mind. Partly because I thought I should practise trust and partly because I'd half hoped he might call after the dinner party. When he hadn't my rationale for not just making contact myself became convoluted. It went like this: Because I wanted him to get in touch I thought if I rang I would look like I'd made up an excuse to get in touch. It was all a bit stupid of me but it had been years since I was last single and I found it quite a different world.

Michael came out with the swag balanced on his head. Standing on the ladder I hauled it up onto the roof racks. It was huge and had sheepskin lining, which would be good in the heat and even better when it got really cold. I was also bringing my old light and very portable single swag for when I went camping, as I planned to do when it cooled down a bit more.

After I'd packed the roof and tied it off Michael gave me some produce to take. He'd packed eggs, a loaf of his homemade sourdough and veggies from his garden. I put it in on the floor with the other goodies I'd bought to distribute to people—my welcome-to-country presents.

As I came back around the side of the house with a jerry can of tank water, Mum patted the seat next to her. I loaded the water before sitting down where she wanted.

'Don't forget to look after yourself,' she said. 'You can't care for others if you're not well.'

'You just don't do self-reflection, do you?' I said, hugging her. 'Go rest, Mum. I don't want to come in on the weekend and find you worn out because you can't rest unless supervised.'

'I promise I'll be good if you come back and see me often.'

'Of course.'

She placed one of her fine, thin hands gently on my cheek. She was suddenly very serious. 'I wouldn't have made it if you hadn't come.'

'Of course you would have,' I said.

'I'm not sure. I was so tired.'

'Mum, please don't talk like this.'

Luckily Michael reappeared and Mum made an effort to brighten.

'Go on,' she said. 'Have a go at being a good girl. We can compare marks.'

'I'll do my best,' I said, grateful to her for effort at lightness.

'I know you will,' she said softly.

I drove off waving and tooting. Across the road Mr and Mrs Press waved from their lounge chairs. Their grandchildren took a short a break from running under the sprinkler screaming at each other to shout out raucous goodbyes at me. You'd have thought I was going on an epic journey of discovery, perhaps an exploration to a distant land, not just up the road to Promised Land.

As I was driving in the boundary gate Lekisha was driving out. She was on her way to her training course in Darwin. It was half here and half there for her study blocks. We stopped our cars on the narrow truck. I got out and leant in the blue Falcon's window.

'He lets you drive his car? Must like you.'

Lekisha ignored my comments.

'So they give us an old car?'

I shrugged. 'Not that old. It goes all right, only done 100,000.'

She changed the subject but clearly she thought I was gullible like Mum did. 'You right then.'

'Should be,' I said, hoping I was.

Usually if I was coming here alone Lekisha met me at the boundary gates to bring me into the family's country.

'Don't forget to come back,' I said, trying not to sound as panicky as I felt at the thought of starting here without her.

She gave her exaggerated joking laugh and I flipped her the finger, which only made her laugh more. Within a couple of minutes she had disappeared into a screen of dust.

Getting back into my own car, I felt disconcerted, and for the first time since Henry and Michael had taught me to drive I drove very slowly into Promised Land.

When Henry saw me arriving he came out and directed me past his house. As soon as I saw the small donga I'd be living in my anxiety eased. I'd been half expecting to have to camp in the schoolroom for a while, so it seemed nothing short of a miracle that it was already organised and waiting for me.

From the moment I got out of the car I felt at home. It was as if the vast sky and everyone at Promised Land were stretching their arms around me.

My house was essentially an old government-issue caravan with long narrow windows. From the inside they would frame the country like a landscape painting. Off to one side was an attractive deck Henry and Patrick had fashioned from the old wooden pallets that had been used to transport the Besser blocks for everyone's housing. They'd even put up a tin roof over the deck. I wished I'd brought something special for Henry and Patrick to thank them for making sure it happened in time.

I hadn't even made it inside my donga before I heard the gang of kids running my way, screaming my name as if I was a rock star as they overtook Magdalene and Treasure, who were also heading in a more sedate manner in my direction.

I laughed and braced myself for the onslaught, a tangle of hands at my waist. I gave Preston a rub on the head and he smiled. Little Declan was dropped to the ground by Sammy and he cleverly used my legs to pull himself up. Before I could reach down for him Preston already had him as Magdalene took my arm to lead me to the deck.

'You can see everything here,' she said proudly, indicating the view.

'I'm impressed how fast this place came together. I can hardly believe it.'

'They did a really good job for you,' added Treasure. 'They even kept the generator on at night till they ran out of fuel. All for you.' For a moment I wondered if Treasure wasn't a bit jealous but then I saw she was beaming. I was being paranoid. She, too, was proud of what the men, her husband, especially, had achieved.

'It's going to be really good, now you're here,' said Magdalene, patting my arm. I only then noticed she was sporting new silver-rimmed reading glasses. She put her fingers up to the frames. 'They're so I can help with any work you might want me to do,' she explained.

'Good,' I said. 'I'm going to need all the help I can get.'

I gave away nearly all the fruit and veggies and bread I'd brought. Magdalene was clearly pleased when I presented her with avocadoes and pineapples—her favourites. There were Tim Tams for the kids and litres and litres of fresh milk to share out. I already knew that every drive to town would mean a trip to the supermarket to pick up supplies. It was obvious I'd have to give up my basket and get the hang of pushing one of those big trolleys around, but I was ready for that challenge and all the others coming my way.

Long after everyone else had gone back to whatever they were doing before my arrival, Preston was still hanging around. The boy had hollow legs. He sat up with me on the deck and, in spite of my reservations, steadily ate the remaining half packet of Tim Tams by himself. None of the scary stories about diabetes I told him slowed him down, or threats about holes in his teeth.

He smiled a perfect white teeth smile at me.

'Well you'll get fat,' I said.

He was skinny as a rake. Clearly I wasn't convincing him because his grin just grew wider.

Preston had always been a favourite. It wouldn't be long before he was a young man but he still had a young cute face and while he could be bold he was never rude. Not to me. I was going to have to watch out I didn't give him preferential treatment in class. A teacher shouldn't have favourites but I'd been teaching long enough to know there always was one.

He watched as I carefully unpacked the rest of my belongings. I didn't have much. Three plates and two bowls, an odd collection of cutlery. One saucepan, a frypan, a large cast-iron pot, which was for cooking on the fire outside. I had two wooden spoons, an egg flip, and a lemon squeeze Preston asked to play with. I spent a while arranging my things in the long narrow room, using sarongs as curtains and tablecloths. Every time I looked up I expected Preston would have left. But he stayed and stayed. In the end I asked him what he wanted.

'Tim Tams.'

I gave him the last packet and he ran.

Michael had given me his old green card table and two folding camp chairs, which I set up on the deck with one of the chairs. The rattly old air-conditioner was sucking up the power and I turned it off so I could keep the door open without feeling guilty about using more than my share of electricity. My gaze drifted east. To Kilka. Over the plains which were mauve in the heat lived Patrick. I played indulgently with the possibilities longer than I should have. Since my divorce my friends in Sydney had tried to set me up with all sorts of their single men friends. There was usually a reason why they were single that made them clearly unsuitable for me, even if I had liked any of them. Patrick was the first I'd had some spark with and I wondered what the catch would be, because there was bound to be one, otherwise what would he be doing at Kilka alone.

The next morning I woke up early and realising where I was I leapt up keen to start. By seven I was in the schoolroom writing out my material list in the order book. The fax I'd plugged in the night before started whirring with a message. It was from Annie, inviting me over to Red Bore School for a meeting. She'd said at the end of my interview, which she'd joined by phone link-up, she'd be in touch, though I thought she might give me a few days to settle. Her idea was that while I was waiting for Promised Land's materials to arrive I could spend some time at Red Bore to see how the group worked and to get some help with the programming. Mine would have to fit Red Bore and Kilka's scope and sequence plan. This is not inner-west Sydney, the note read. It offended me at first then I decided not to leap to conclusions. It could be a joke. I decided notes sent by fax might be like emails. Humour could be hard pressed to always work. And she knew I'd grown up in Alice because we'd met a few times when she was Lucy's girlfriend.

I was a little disappointed that she didn't suggest I visit Kilka. I didn't question her though. I might not have worked out bush before but I did know that challenging the boss's judgement wasn't the smart way to start any new job. I faxed back that I'd get up to Red Bore the next morning around eleven. It was about 120 kilometres from memory. Maybe a bit more.

After a day of busy and boring organisation which required ringing the department several times, I realised that I must have inherited some of my mother's impatience when it came to bureaucracy. I told myself to relax. I had plenty of time to pull things together, which was lucky because I was hardly run over with help. In fact only Magdalene had called in first up but I hadn't seen her or another adult since. Preston had popped in looking for biscuits, but it was a fairly solitary day. Not at all what I'd expected.

Later in the evening I saw a woman I thought might be Maxine pushing Rosia in a pram. The thin girlish-looking woman looked like the same woman Lekisha had pointed out in town once, which was as close as I thought I was going to get to an introduction.

Maxine was followed by Caleb, Preston and Sammy fooling around with a football as they made their way down the track in the direction of the dam. I nearly called out to ask if there was any water left there for swimming and could I come with them. But I hung back. I wasn't going to push myself forward. I'd have to wait to be included in people's lives.

Before leaving for Red Bore in the morning I stuck a note on the door of the donga and the school so everyone would know where I'd gone. On an impulse I took the back way not the highway, which was longer in distance but quicker because it was mostly sealed. I felt somewhat daring to be venturing out alone into the desert in late summer rather than taking the bitumen. I was pottering along congratulating myself for being brave, out alone in this country where anything could happen, when a loaded-up old car came towards me brimming with people who smiled and waved as they passed. My inflated sense of self-importance was well and truly pricked. Who was I kidding? This country was remote, sparse and could harshly treat strangers to its ways. At the same time I should remember it was occupied and frequently traversed by its owners.

Though I'd been to Red Bore before, the community had grown much larger than I remembered. I passed the airstrip on the way with its wind sock hanging limply. Further into town, looking tatty and run-down were the Commonwealth Development Employment Program offices. Its scruffy appearance gave an impression of an organisation that was only just limping along. According to Mum, less than ten per cent of the forty real jobs in Red Bore community were held by Aboriginal people. At Promised Land I'd be the only person on a wage until Lekisha began teaching and doubled the numbers. We'd be the only ones in the entire community not answerable to Centrelink, which was the boss for almost everyone out bush. It also meant we'd have more money and would be called upon to share, though Lekisha more than me.

It was only then I remembered I should have brought food. I'd brought nothing except some fruit I'd eaten already. I cursed my disorganisation. I had so much good stuff at home. To avoid turning up empty-handed I decided I'd better go to the shop but I knew it was going to be a disappointment and I was only really looking for a token contribution to lunch. On the verandah outside the shop an old woman was sitting on the concrete slab with paper bags of shopping piled up around her like a barricade. Five dogs prowled nearby. None as rough looking as Magdalene's Lucky but intimidating all the same. Noticing my hesitation, the old woman threatened her dogs with a stone, scattering them momentarily.

'You're right,' she said as I ventured past.

The fresh food inside the store was worse than I'd anticipated and the pastry and fried chicken offerings in the pie warmer looked dried-out and ancient. In the end I settled for a block of cheese and two sad-looking tomatoes. At the counter I handed ten dollars over to a woman with mouse-brown hair, a pale wrinkled face and an expression that said *get me out of here*. I was appalled to find ten dollars wasn't enough and scrabbled round in my pocket for some coins.

'How long have you lived here?' I asked as I gave her the rest of the money, trying to be friendly and not concern myself with what a disgraceful rip off the shop was.

'I'm just temporary while the manager has his holiday,' she said, as if she might be announcing she just got ten years in jail. 'I should have been gone today but he extended his holiday another fortnight.' She sighed.

God, I thought, now we have fly-in and fly-out shopkeepers. What next? I eventually found the Education Department's housing, which was a small excision near the police compound. Three houses rose out of brown emptiness in the slow burn of the morning's heat. Their flapping shade blinds and strange radial arrangement, all with their backs to each other, reminded me of western wagons, under attack. Not exactly an encouraging image.

But Annie wasn't defensive at all. She was friendly and warm, hugging me as though we were old friends. 'Welcome,' she said. 'The Hendersons must be chuffed to have you. Magdalene is so strong. She's fought hard for that school for a long, long time. It seems so right you've got the gig.'

'It feels good to me too,' I said, pleased by her enthusiasm.

'Grab a pew. I'll get our food and put the kettle on,' she said, absently sweeping her long black hair back off her neck. Apologetically I gave her my bag of manky shop food which she politely thanked me for.

She returned from the kitchen with an array of salads, beans and bread, and no sign of the food I'd brought.

'Sorry there's no meat. I'm a vegetarian. It's a bit of a struggle, I have a small garden but Patrick helps out with plenty of fresh stuff.'

'It looks great,' I said, hoping he shared his produce widely.

*

Annie had lots of advice and I spent the day going through pro-grams and looking at samples of assessments she'd brought home for me. I needed some idea of the level students were at in each year. It was all helpful but exhausting. At the end of the day, after a simple meal, I turned down the offer of a room and spent the night in a swag on her lawn. It was rather too hot but I liked it out-side. The sky was huge and moonless, the stars bright, the evening cooling to the point where a sheet was needed. It was splendid to be out in it again, and I spent ages reacquainting myself with the constellations. Red Bore wasn't much further north but enough to make it take me a while to find Orion and the others I had been able to identify with Patrick that night, which was feeling like a long time ago. I slept as I always did outside in the desert, on and off, getting a vague idea of how much time had passed by the revolving parade of the stars. Eventually a yellow carpet of light rolled out before the sun and then it rose, godlike, to claim the day as its own.

By the time I'd showered, the heat had risen out of the ground, come to challenge our resilience again. Hot, Annie and I said to each other and smiled. It did for a morning greeting and we ate breakfast with the sprinklers spraying where my swag had been, coaxing the couch grass into liveliness. We threw crumbs from our toast to the parrots, who dived through the spray, happy to wash a few feathers until the butcher birds with their grey faces claimed a dominance, singing brightly as they dived this way and that through the rainbow-infused droplets of water.

Annie decided I'd start in the classes with the lovely Blossie in the early childhood room at Red Bore school. Blossie was in her first year of teaching and a complete gem. The kids couldn't get their tongues around the l in her name and called her 'Bossy', which was ironic because she was one of the most easygoing people I'd ever met. As Lucy had said, she had a boyfriend, Todd, who was working in a bigger community south west on a young men's health project.

She laughed a lot as she talked, a mannerism Lucy had which made me warm more towards her. 'Last year when I was living in Melbourne I thought Collingwood to St Kilda was a long way. Now I drive three hundred kilometres and back every second weekend so I can see Todd. Crazy, hey?' Her blue eyes sparkled. 'It's a different world up here, for sure. On my second day I put all my short skirts in a bag marked Melbourne, and by the beginning of the second week I'd ditched my make-up. My straightening iron was next, and by the third weekend I'd cut my hair short. The bore water here is so hard it was totally wrecked. It used to be down to here,' she said, gesturing to her waist. 'I'm still not used to how light I feel with it gone. The trouble was, even though I did a course called "Living in the Territory" with the department, no-one had told me people cut their hair when they're grieving. Poor Annie, she had to go around and explain to everyone I hadn't had any bad luck. Just a lousy and very desperate haircut.' She ran a hand over her head. 'The kids call me Emu now, for my sticky-up hairstyle.'

I smiled. I liked her spunk, and how willing she was to fit in to her new environment.

I had a great few days with Blossie and Annie. Like Patrick I found them both easy and good company. And until I met the other teachers it was possible to think that everyone was pleasant around these parts.The other two teachers were much less appealing. Pete and Andrea were an elderly dour couple, not entirely competent but self-sufficient. From Victoria, they'd come out of retirement to take this job. An opportunity they called it. Annie had some other words to describe their contribution but she was fairly sanguine about the situation. It was the luck of the draw the teams one worked with in remote communities. Annie had no choice and the Aboriginal people had even less about who came into their community, which was why we all felt so lucky at Promised Land. I could only hope the Hendersons' faith in me was warranted.

When I left, I asked Annie if I should go to Kilka next time. 'I just thought it would make sense. It's a one-teacher school like Promised Land. And he's got some middle-school kids too, like me.'

To my disappointment, she shook her head. 'No. Come here again. It's not a good time,' she said, without elaborating. 'Soon, but not now you can go to Kilka. He'll probably pop in your way sometime.'

I hoped so myself. It was inevitable I'd see him at some stage. For now I'd have to be patient.

CHAPTER 14

The school would open in early April after Easter at the start of second term. I had three weeks off to get organised and I bit back my impatience or irritation at all the red tape, of which there seemed to be enough to wrap around the whole country several times over. Dealing with it, I tried to avoid getting the same reputation as my mother. It was true she was well respected but there was also a fair amount of agreement she could be a complete pain in the arse if she didn't get her own way.

I took some of the kids along on my second trip to Red Bore. They were all boys, which we had more of, and selected by Magdalene to avoid me being seen to prefer some kids over others. The other kids were meant to go in and out to school in town as normal. That at least was the theory. It was fairly obvious most kids, if not all of them and their parents, considered school optional until their own was up. Who could blame them? It was a long drive and they were on the edge in the town schools. How little they learnt under these conditions was something Lucy and I could discuss for hours.

Preston and Sammy sat in the front with me on the drive. I was constantly amazed by the vast distances they could see, pointing out kangaroos and birds which even with their help I often didn't see at all. They chatted in a friendly fashion, telling me many things about the country. I was impressed by their knowledge, and began to worry about how I could value what they knew once we were shut up together in a class. I had one of my panicky moments, about not being up to the job and failing entirely, which were becoming more frequent as the start date neared.

After the day in Annie's class I was feeling more confident. There were plenty of ways to engage kids. They just all took an enormous effort. Annie started the day with English, using an approach she called accelerated literacy. It wasn't rocket science. It was just a very clear way of using narrative and the rich text it offered to scaffold learning English. In lots of ways it was old fashioned. Very teacher directed. But the kids responded well. And I could see how links could be made to support lessons in other subjects. Her maths classes were good too. She used a lot of movement to reinforce fundamental concepts. Outside in groups the kids jumped and skipped their way through the times tables. She had plenty of fun methods but they were all extremely exhausting. I was a wreck at the end of the day and I was glad Henry and Magdalene had insisted I stay the night in Red Bore, farming the kids out to other family. In the morning we got in another lesson before driving home. My pile of photocopied lesson plans and programs was growing higher on my new desk in the classroom at Promised Land and hopefully I'd be up to implementing them when the time came.

Much to my surprise, I didn't want to rush into Alice at the end of the first fortnight, and decided to stay out bush for the weekend instead. It was pay week at Centrelink so most of the family went into town to shop, leaving me virtually alone.

It was a strange new feeling to be so alone out there. In the city when I felt lonely I just had to step outside my door to be swallowed up in the beach-going crowds. Or I could head to the cinema. There were no distractions here. I didn't even have a telly, and I could feel myself settling into my own company in a way I hadn't for years. I got out my camera and took myself off into the country, taking close-ups of plants I didn't know, prompted by an incident at Red Bore. In the last lesson we'd shared with Annie's English class the focus was on the words same and different. She had the kids run around collecting samples of the plants near the school. The kids then had to group their samples and explain their decisions. Annie assumed because I grew up in the desert I'd know my plants and put me on the spot when she asked me why Preston had put two leaves together which looked quite different. I had no idea they were actually from the same family and couldn't answer. It was one of those humiliating moments which taught me two fundamental lessons I'd do well not to forget. One, it reminded me of how kids suffer when they are put on the spot and clueless. Two, that I knew nothing much about plants and should know more. I should be able to recognise and understand the world around me better. Maybe too, I was well aware Patrick would be able to help me and it might be a good way of getting to know him.

On the Monday I headed into town to try and get in the faces of the builders who kept promising they were coming to complete the flooring but who failed to ever show. I called in at Mum's when

I'd done that, feeling I had been victorious, but how successful my pleading had been only time would tell.

At home I found Mum lying in a hammock under the generous canopy of the mulberry tree. Bending down to kiss her head I thought she looked more rested and relaxed than last time. I made us some hot water with lemon juice, not unpleasant and very good for the liver, and dragged a chair under the shade to sit beside her where we stayed chatting about my work. I noticed she had several diaries nestled in the hammock with her.

'You still reminiscing?' I asked.

'I don't know what you'd call it,' she said sadly.

'You don't think it's too maudlin?'

'It is a bit. But memory is a funny thing. I'm just having a look back at how I saw some things at the time—strange how different it is from how I remember them now.'

'What sort of things?'

'Oh, everything. The life here, the work. What I did or didn't do for you.' She reached out a hand and I squeezed her fingers.

'You did good for me. Now you've even let me take the baton and run out on the track for you, fight the good fight, do the good work and all that.' I was half joking but she wasn't amused.

'That's exactly what worries me,' she said.

I spat a lemon pip on the ground and changed the subject. Why I chose a more difficult one I didn't quite know. 'Do you think there's something wrong with us that stops us having babies?'

'Well, I did have you.'

'So you did, but I wonder sometimes why I lost that baby.'

'It's common. Many women lose their first, often more. It's

just not much talked about, that's all. Even now I think its still taboo.'

Just then, Michael walked around the side of the house. 'What's taboo?'

I was about to tell him, none of his business, when I caught sight of Patrick behind him.

'Nothing,' I said. 'Cup of tea anyone?'

I couldn't get out of there and inside fast enough.

For weeks I'd been expecting to see Patrick again, half hoping he'd drive through Promised Land on the back way to Kilka and then when I least expected it, he appeared.

I was reaching for the cups on the top shelf in the kitchen when he came in. No taller than me, he reached up for the cups as if I needed help, his body briefly brushing mine.

'That enough?' he asked. He'd got four.

'Too many, Ros doesn't need one,' I said and took the cup from him. I deliberately turned away to put the cup back before I asked him where he'd been. I didn't want him seeing my face in case I gave away too much interest.

'Haven't seen you for dust. Where you been?'

'Yes. Sorry. It's been crazy. I've been flat out.'

I faced him now, curious because the impression Annie had given me was far from Patrick being flat out at Kilka, the opposite might be true.

'With what?'

He stuck his hands in his pockets and leant back on the bench looking at his boots while I worried I'd been far too obvious about not really believing him. Really I told myself, for someone who didn't like being put on the spot I had no right to do it to someone else. Especially someone I hardly knew but liked.

I busied myself in the rather uncomfortable silence getting the makings for tea. Patrick followed me around the table to the bench and came to stand next to me with his hands on the edge of the bench. He had long fingers, attractive hands. He must have been bending his knees because he made himself smaller than me to look up at me. It seemed a nervous stance.

'Actually I've been away.'

'Where?' It seemed a bit odd for the start of the year and in school time.

'I'd rather not talk about it. It's a bit boring.'

It clearly wasn't boring at all because he was forcing the light tone. I didn't know him well but I'd been doing it myself a while and had developed an instinct for when people were faking things were okay. 'Good, don't talk about it' I said, putting the plates and cake with the tea on the tray, 'because I want to pick your brains for some specifics now, about how I might organise and run the multi-levels. The room is so small. And at Red Bore it seemed hard enough even with bigger numbers and more space.'

'Sure,' he said, straightening up and taking the tray I gave him. 'I've got some videos of me teaching I can give you too.'

'No thanks,' I said, assuming now he was trying to make a joke.

'They are the English lessons. The narrative specialists tape them. Annie would have a heap. That's a multi-level lesson.'

'Oh, she did mention them. I think I might be getting some training.'

'Hopefully, you will.'

Patrick pushed the back door open with his foot and held it

there as I followed him and his load out as I'd somehow managed to only have the teapot left to carry.

I couldn't say I was disappointed to find Ros and Michael had disappeared. I suspected they were in the studio since they hadn't come in, and Patrick, despite arriving with Michael, didn't seem to find it odd enough to even comment on. We settled on the verandah at the table and I got a notebook in case any of Patrick's answers to my many questions were worth writing down.

By the time he left I had heaps of notes. They wouldn't have made much sense if I hadn't seen the classes at Red Bore but they were a real help.

I mulled over our conversation once he'd left, not to revise the teaching notes but to check I'd read his interest right. He was interested I decided. But an affair out bush was always a risk. No matter how discreet you thought you were, every person for hundreds of kilometres around would know and have a version of the romance to share. To try to initiate an affair before there was enough evidence it would come off was a greater folly. I'd be the laughing stock of the whole Alice Springs circle. Poor man-starved Alicia, they'd all be whispering. Even the thought of that happening was scary.

On the last night of my visit to town Iry came over with a meal. We'd stopped the care meals but Iry wasn't one to take much notice of directions she didn't want to follow. I noticed she had a glass of wine, which she rarely did, and although her conversation was as entertaining as it usually was, I had a feeling something was not quite right. I was clearing the dishes when I heard her ask Mum if she'd seen it.

'Of course I did.' Mum didn't sound pleased.

'Seen what?' I asked.

'The report from the northwest.'

I didn't catch the community's name.

'Sixteen men, charged,' said Iry, 'in a community of about four hundred people.'

'Yes it's terrible,' Mum agreed. 'Sickening.' At that moment her phone rang and after answering she put her hand over the receiver. 'Michael,' she explained, excusing herself.

I hadn't heard the story. Now I lived at Promised Land and wasn't with Floyd I could avoid as much news as I wanted. This sounded terrible.

'Charged with what?'

'Sexual abuse.' Iry's face crumpled and she put her head in her hands, which was fairly shocking all by itself. If Mum was made of iron, Iry was diamond, tough and cutting. Never cut.

I didn't know what to say. There were lots of rumours about bad stuff happening in Aboriginal communities. Not just about sexual abuse. Now I thought about it, over the last few years there'd been a lot of conversations like this. Not so specific to an event but around the lack of services and the level of abuse, mostly in large, remote locations. I'd always tried not to have an opinion, never having felt I knew much or wanting to look like some expert, which I certainly wasn't.

I didn't say anything now. I would listen to Iry.

'I feel so guilty all the time,' she said. 'We all know what a mess it is out there. Somehow we have to get on top of things. It's a fucking disgrace. I just have no idea what to do beyond doing my job, which is just about as useless as recommending taking Band-aids to the war in Congo.' She forced a laugh and I gave her hand a squeeze.

'I'm tired,' she said, 'I better go. I think tonight if I let myself have another glass of wine I could drink the bottle and then some.'

I didn't try and persuade her otherwise and as I kissed her good-night I noticed how she'd aged. The skin on her cheek was soft and finely wrinkled. She'd lost weight too.

'Good luck with the job,' she said. 'You got to back up people where you can. But take care of yourself.'

What was it with Mum and her? Did they never take their own advice?

I drove back to Promised Land on Thursday. Lekisha arrived back soon after and I was thrilled to see her. It felt as though we were about to really get started.

The next day a huge truck arrived with all our supplies: desks, boards, books. The guts of a school. Unfortunately Henry and Caleb had gone out kangaroo shooting the night before and were too tired to be of any help in off-loading. No other men could be found. I was relieved when Treasure came to help Lekisha and me. She turned out to be quite the worker. She organised most of the kids to give a hand and we managed to get everything into the schoolroom without too much chaos or complaining. I paid Treasure some money for her help, figuring if I couldn't get it back from the department, I wasn't Ros's daughter. Though it hardly mattered. I could afford to pay her out of my wage. Besides food, and petrol, there was very little to spend my money on as my donga was free, so was the power, and I used the department's petrol going in and out to town.

Late that afternoon, Magdalene came over to the schoolroom where we were busy unpacking boxes and unceremoniously dumped Rosia on Lekisha.

'Aren't her parents here?' I asked. Despite living in such a small community I often didn't know if people were at home or in town.

'No,' said Lekisha tightly, passing Rosia on to Sammy, who didn't mind giving her a few pecks on the cheek but as I suspected he didn't want to hold her for long. The new footballs and basket-balls had just been discovered in one of the boxes and there was a hunt on for a pump to inflate them. He was keen not to miss out.

'I'll take her,' I said to him, reaching for Rosia. I was due a break from unpacking. Her nappy was swollen with urine so I changed her. I put her down when she had a dry bottom and she stayed lying on a rug near us, happily entertaining herself like the perfect child she seemed to be.

Over the next few days Magdalene took to bringing a chair over to the demountable and watching us as we got the schoolroom sorted. Of course, she wasn't content just to watch; she made Mum look like an amateur in the bossiness stakes. Tiring as it was, I felt a growing sense of satisfaction as we slowly sorted through the chaos and a real classroom finally began to emerge. I was also enjoying having Rosia in my orbit, continuing to find her a total delight.

Just having her on the periphery made me happy in a way I hadn't been for ages.

We'd been unpacking and sorting for nearly a week when I woke up one morning to a ferocious sun. It had slowly been getting cooler over the last month but now it seemed the sun was back for one last hurrah. It must have been in the thirties when I first got up, the heat radiating off the tin on the verandah, and I would have given anything to turn the air-conditioner up high and go back to bed but I knew I couldn't or at least wouldn't while there was still too much to be done.

Lekisha was already at work standing on a stool covering the pin boards in loud primary-coloured paper when I arrived in the schoolroom.

'Hot one,' I said.

She didn't answer. I knew she found the way I stated the obvious annoying. It was just part of how I was, not deliberate. I busied myself in the corner sorting the paper supplies into the cupboards. As the morning wore on and the day heated up the kids kept poking their heads in the door and nagging at Lekisha to take them for a swim.

'Town pool,' they suggested.

'No car,' I heard her say as she shooed them away. She sounded cranky, and as we seemed to be without Rosia I assumed that Caleb must have taken her to town, borrowing Lekisha's car. While she wanted her son to be more responsible for his daughter, I had a feeling she wasn't impressed he'd taken her. At the moment he seemed to only come to Promised Land on no-money days and as soon as he was paid he was gone, which might account for her mood.

'Dam,' the kids suggested.

'No water.'

'Town pool then.'

'No car.' The bickering went on and I tried to ignore it.

Preston came and sat on the floor. 'What about the school car?' he said, looking at me straight up.

I shrugged.

Lekisha resolutely persisted with trying to hang the paper straight as if she hadn't heard him. Her staple gun jammed and she muttered to herself as she tried to fix it.

'Give it here,' I offered.

'No.'

'I can sort it. Don't worry about it.'

She put the gun down. 'The kids are driving me mad.'

'Well, why don't we go swimming? To the dam.'

'It won't be any good,' she said, 'it's all dried up. We could go to the tank.'

As kids we were never allowed to go there. I looked over to check she meant it, and she tipped her head and pouted in that direction-giving way of hers. I didn't have to gather the kids. Lekisha yelled at Preston to get some towels and by the time I came back with my bathers on underneath my dress the kids were piled into the back of the troopy.

'You sure?' I asked.

'Yes.'

I put my foot down and pulled the wheel hard right, to the west.

'You're the boss,' I said.

'I wish,' she said and threw her head back and laughed.

The tank was high on a stand, its tin sides steep and dangerous. All the bigger kids who could paddle a bit and float jumped in. The little ones we dunked and then put safely on the ground below the large tank, on a tarp out of the sun. Everyone swam in the dark water in their clothes except me. I had my swimmers on and bike shorts over the top for modesty's sake.

The kids wanted to play their favourite game, Marco Polo. I could soon see why. Somehow, despite the cramped conditions, everyone managed to avoid me while I was in but any of them could catch me within seconds.

'You mob are too deadly,' I said. 'I think I might sit this next round out.'

Preston looked around to check who might hear him before he dobbed. 'They cheating, they got their eyes half open like Chinese.'

'Say like cat, or just half open, not Chinese,' I said. 'It's a bit racist.'

'I just telling you they are cheating, that's all,' he said, indignant at me for telling him off when he'd been doing me a favour.

'You're right,' I said, ruffling his curly hair, but he ducked off and swam away. I'd discovered that the kids were mostly kind and friendly. Without exception, though, they could all be quite feisty too. From the moment these kids could walk they seemed to make their own plans. Every toddler and baby was as angelic-looking as Declan, and as cantankerous, with an inbuilt ability to entertain themselves for hours. There was definitely none of the constant supervision from adults I'd come to expect from parents in the city. Eddy's young wife, Kristina, refused to push five-year-old Angus high on a swing in case he fell, and she didn't allow either of the kids to ride a pushbike without a helmet under any circumstances. She would have died of shock here. Not that I didn't struggle sometimes with aspects of the kids' lives. But it seemed to me the kids were doing okay. We weren't a mess, that was for sure.

And the kids were always fun. Just then Preston dived from the edge, doing a dangerous backflip into the water, and came up grinning. I pointed a finger, warning him it was a one-off. He swam away, pleased, his anger from earlier evaporated. I took in the scene from a watchful spot on the edge. It was wet and cool in the heat of the desert, the sky vast, the country preciously poised like a beautiful stage. Every bush, every tree, every rise of rock gave the impression it had been placed with great care. I felt happier than I'd been in a long time. I loved the country and being here with this gang.

CHAPTER 15

The opening ceremony was scheduled for the first day after the Easter break. Promised Land school was less than a week away from opening. The floor covering was actually down. The colourful rugs which we'd use to define space were delivered but still rolled up until we'd finished making a mess.

The change-of-season wind was up, blustering around the buildings. The metal pole we'd raised for the Aboriginal and obligatory Territory flags sang all day. We were just about finished our work for the day when the kids started screaming outside. Henry was the first to move, dropping his drill onto the step with a clatter. For a big man he moved fast and he was out the door before Lekisha dumped the corkboard they'd been putting up and raced out after him. I followed.

We soon saw what all the yelling was about. It was a snake. Long and brown. Lekisha roughly corralled the kids onto the school's verandah until it moved off. We followed from a safe distance, watching as it made its way towards my donga, its sinuous movement repellent but spellbinding.

Don't go into my house, I was praying. If it hid under my floor I'd have to move out. I'd never be able to sleep there again. The school would lose its teacher before we'd even started.

Henry stepped out from the side of the deck, the long-handled shovel in his hands, poised to strike. As the snake advanced up the first step to my house he brought down the blade and took the head cleanly. The rest of the snake's long brown body writhed on the ground. Some of the older kids wanted to pick it up and I wrenched them back.

'Never take a snake in the middle or from the front,' said Henry. 'You don't want it to rise up at you and bite.' He mimicked the strike of a snake and the little kids and me jumped back. We all laughed at our own fear. 'If you cut it in the middle it can still move to bite you,' he added.

I'd once seen a python we'd all thought was dead come back to life. It was my last summer in Alice before I went to boarding school. Lekisha and I were digging a hole looking for a goanna when the python came out from a side tunnel. Black and thick, it almost slid into Lekisha's hand. I remember its power as it pushed past us. I'd reacted first, jumping to my feet. But that was as far as I got, scared into a rigid passivity. It was Lekisha who shoved me out of the way and got the shovel. She beat it until we thought it was dead, and then bravely threw it in the back of the troopy to take it home to Magdalene. It wasn't her totem and it was good eating, not to be wasted. It lay in the car for hours while we drove to other hunting sites. On our return to Promised Land we threw it out at the little kids as a joke. To our horror it began to wriggle away, while the kids screamed and cried. Magdalene told us off, proper roughly for being so stupid. When I'd told Floyd this story, he'd actually believed it—unlike many of the others I'd regaled him with over the years. He said that if you gave a snake enough time it could realign its spine and off it would go, and if he was here he would have agreed with Henry: the only way to make sure a snake was dead was to cut off its head.

As I made my way back to the school's verandah I noticed dust rising along the track, coming in from the north. A car was approaching, perhaps from Red Bore or Kilka. As I stood on the steps watching I caught myself hoping it was Patrick.

When the car pulled up, Lekisha elbowed me and said, 'Look who's here.' I swatted her back and casually walked to the tap as if I tidied my hair and washed my face before every visitor. Not that we'd had any other ones except the odd delivery bloke.

As soon as he got out of the car Patrick was dragged off to see the snake. I grabbed my camera and followed along with the group to take some photos. The Western Brown was much bigger than I'd thought; it was no consolation to know that the smaller ones were more lethal, their bites often ten times more venomous. It was the big ones that scared me, with their sassy slither and flicking tongues. Patrick was suitably impressed, listening keenly to the kids' re-run of the events until Henry told me to take him back to the classroom and show him how it was looking so he could get on with burying the snake.

The air-conditioner was on but the room was deserted when we returned; Lekisha had clearly made herself scarce. Patrick walked in and whistled, commenting approvingly at the set-up. I'd been unsure how best to arrange the room for the different levels but he thought the layout was good, keeping the little kids nearest the door where they could get up and go for all the bathroom breaks they needed without disturbing the others. I hadn't done it for that reason but I took that compliment and others with real pleasure. It was generous of Lekisha to leave. She could have done with some of his praise.

Before I could ask Patrick if he wanted tea or something he said he had to get going and I followed him out to his car, disappointed his visit was so short. I figured every eye would be keeping watch even though I couldn't see a soul.

'Here,' he said, reaching into the car and handing me a large paper bag. Whatever was in it was heavy.

'What is it?'

'Bread,' he said. 'Life's most basic pleasure.' His eyes didn't leave my face. 'Sorry, it might be a little crusty after sitting in the car. I've been practising my baking for Lucy's Easter Sunday lunch. I'm a bit nervous. I've never gone before. Though she tells me its not a competition. You'll be there?'

'Of course,' I said, 'but I won't cook. I'll leave it to the A-team.'

He smiled at me.

The wind kicked up at us and we ducked the dust. When the gust had passed he brushed a strand of hair from the corner of my mouth where the wind had blown it. The gesture seemed more parental than flirtatious.

'Ciao,' he said.

I held the bread against my chest.

'See you then,' I said, not noticing Lekisha's arrival.

See you then, mimicked Lekisha as we sat on my deck drinking tea. See you then she repeated, in the silly high-pitched voice which had come out of my mouth. She said it over and over, getting sillier and sillier, eventually forcing me to I laugh at just how simpering and girlish I'd sounded.

I was thinking about Easter as I went to bed. A celebration of another chance. Life, where previously there had been death. I wasn't a believer but to me it seemed like a good sign all the same.

Maunday Thursday dawned colourless and grey. When I looked outside there were clouds high in the sky.

I was having my morning cup of tea on the deck as I'd taken to doing when Lekisha walked past. 'Looks like rain,' I said. 'Good eh?'

She ignored me and I was immediately cross with myself. I had been in the city too long. In cities commenting on the weather passed for a greeting. Here talking about rain wasn't encouraged. It could send it away. And sure enough, by the late morning when I was ready to leave for Alice the clouds had cleared, though I doubted it was down to me.

It seemed almost everyone at Promised Land was heading to Mission as I'd expected them to. They'd be plenty of baptisms. I would have gone if Rosia was being baptised but there seemed some delay with that. I'd heard the problem was Maxine being Lutheran. She wanted her baptised in that church and there was a stand-off. When it was settled I was to be a godmother. So the story went. I thought I'd wait and see if it was actually what Caleb wanted, if and when it happened at all.

Lekisha and Treasure were busy loading things around the kids, who were waiting to go and had keenly bagsed their spots in the cars. There wasn't enough for everyone. Treasure's little old Datsun, which I knew had no registration, was being packed up too.

'You can't take that,' I said to Lekisha. 'It's got no rego.'

'Don't worry,' she said. 'We'll go the back way where there won't be any police.'

'How about if I take some people before I head back to town? We can still go the back way. I haven't been on that road for years. I'd like the drive.'

I wasn't just being polite. The back road curved east and then south, circumventing town. It took longer but it was worth it, and not just for avoiding cops. It was pretty country, more interesting than the highway route, even in this time of drought. Lekisha sang out the news and Magdalene immediately got herself in my front seat. When I stepped into the driver's seat she asked if I was going to stay at Mission and come to the Sunday mass. I told her I wasn't, that I was just dropping them off, and she gave me one of her broad smiles as if she knew better, but I had a good excuse up my sleeve: Mum. She was looking forward to seeing me, and no matter what Magdalene might think she wasn't up to the big party Easter at Mission always turned into—as big as Christmas, with all the families coming together. And I had Lucy's party to get to.

We drove east along a wide road that ran between two low ranges that peeked occasionally above the scrub like soft fuzzy heads. Magdalene only told me off once for going too fast, which I thought must be some kind of record. It wasn't personal, I knew: she told everyone off for their driving. Mum was always in trouble for going too slow. While Magdalene had never learnt to drive her-self, it hadn't prevented her being the expert.

We soon arrived at the rise above Mission. Often at this time of year rain would have already fallen and there would be purple and white flowers carpeting the valley, but not this time.

At the end of the white lime road were the community houses. The small white 'bag-washed' church perched on the side of the hill above them, dominating the landscape.

When I was a kid, Kumanjay, Magdalene's father's brother, had told Lekisha and me about the move to Mission in the old days. People had come there from the settlement at Arltunga. Arltunga was bad sick country. People had originally been trucked out there from town 'for their own safety', while the Americans ran Alice Springs during the war. They were also told to look out for the invading Japanese and to report any they saw to the authorities.

It was an ill-conceived plan. Out east the Arltunga site was entirely unsuitable. The groundwater was poisoned by cyanide from the old works. Like others, Kumanjay lost family, a brother and two sisters, because no bores went deep enough to draw clean water. It was a hell of a time. People were very scared when they were told they would be moved again. It took days to travel to what was now Mission. When they got there the old fellow told us, they felt blessed when they first saw the valley, brimming with life. It resonated with one of the bible stories they'd been taught. That of Abraham leading his people into the promised land.

I'd loved this story because it was such a joyous way of looking at what was a hard life, where personal choice was limited and the living conditions almost intolerable. Culture gave people another strong reason to be pleased to find themselves at the Mission site. Since time immemorial it had been important country, more ceremony than the church was ever going to offer had been stamped into the ground.

Magdalene's family's land was first promised at a land rights meeting on Mission. Its nickname, the Promised Land, was given not because it appeared to be a place of salvation, like Mission, but because for so many years all people had were promises.

Once I arrived at Mission, I actually contemplated coming back for the Easter Sunday service. But as soon as the thought crossed my mind, I knew I wouldn't. I was just being sentimental about seeing everyone dressed up. If I'd come for mass I would have teased Preston, dressed in his white shirt and black pants, his wild and woolly hair slicked back against his will.

Magdalene directed me to her sister Doreen's place. 'I'll pray for you,' she said as she eased herself out of the passenger seat.

I smiled at her uncertainly. Did she think I'd sinned in some way?

'Pray God looks after you and our school,' she went on.

On my own in the car, I drove much faster. I was tired of driving by now and keen to get to town. The width of the road seduced me into assuming it was safe. Really, it looked as though it had been well fixed up since I was young, when it had a reputation as one of the most dangerous roads about. The stereo blared as I scooted along, a screen of dust obscuring my rear vision, the road in front empty. I made good time. I had a clear head. I pushed it just a little more and then I took one of the long slow bends far too fast. For a moment I was tipping. I shifted in my seat as I might have on a horse, to try to regain my balance, feeling the empty space under the tyres, for far too long. I expected the roll to come and tuck me under the weight of the car's metal. Experience told me there was nothing I could do at this point to change the trajectory of events. Now it was up to fate.

One thought came as the sky moved nearer: I might die without having a child.

Somehow the car banged itself back upright. I was fishtailing badly, but with four wheels down. Thank god I hadn't rolled. Thank the lord. Thank you, Magdalene, for putting in a good word for me.

CHAPTER 16

I called in to Mum's on my way to Lucy's. On the verge was an unfamiliar car with a Hertz sticker on its back window. This was always a busy time of year for visitors and I thought little of it. I took off my boots on the back verandah and went straight into the kitchen where I was pulled up by the sight of Floyd sitting at the table with Michael. They were calmly stringing beans.

'Alicia!' Michael got up, flustered as though he'd been caught doing something against the law. He knocked the bowl with his elbow, sending it flying. Floyd managed to catch it before it hit the floor.

'How's that?' he said, pleased with himself.

'I thought you were on your way to London,' I said.

'I am. I just came via here,' he said, as if it was perfectly reasonable.

I made my way past the pair to the tap to get a glass of water. Not because I was thirsty. I needed a few seconds at least to adjust to Floyd's most unexpected presence.

'Why are you here?'

'I wanted to see how everyone was. How Ros is going. And you.'

I turned away from him and put the glass on the sink. He'd called a couple of times since I'd been in Alice, mainly to discuss the business of our financial settlement. A phone call or two was one thing, but this face-to-face visit was disturbing. It made it harder to feel he was in my past quite as firmly as lately I'd been able to manage.

'I'm filthy,' I said hastily. 'I'll have a shower.'

As I went up the hall I saw Mum in her little study, typing on the computer, and went in.

'You see Floyd?' she said. 'He just arrived this morning. He was on his way to Promised Land but we knew you were coming in so we told him to wait.'

'You could have warned me he was here. I'm not much into surprises.'

'I know. We left a message at the school and Michael's been texting you.'

I reached into my pocket. The phone was so infrequently in range I'd not bothered to turn it on. I powered it up and a few minutes later it beeped noisily. Three messages from Michael, one from Floyd.

I read the one from Floyd: *Hey, hope you don't feel crowded but my departure date's changed and I've decided to come up for opening after all. Be nice to see your folks before I leave x*

'He's come for the opening?'

'It looks like it. I assume Magdalene put him on the list.'

'She didn't mention it.'

Mum smiled at me patronisingly. 'And when was the last time Magdalene told you something she thought was none of your business?'

I gave a snort of mirth. 'I might use your shower. Then I'll take Floyd to Lucy's if you want.'

'Do whatever suits you.'

After my shower I found myself fussing about what to wear. Even if we didn't want to be together anymore it still seemed to matter that he found me attractive. I knew he felt the same way. Why else would he be wearing a shirt of his I'd always told him he looked good in?

In the kitchen Michael was nowhere to be seen and I paused to take in Floyd for a moment before he sensed I was there. His hair was longer, soft wisps of blond down his neck. I tried not to notice the deep indent at his nape, the soft skin I'd kissed a thousand times before. I walked around and leant on a chair in front of him. I'd pinned my hair up the way he liked it and I knew he'd notice even if he said nothing.

'Do you want to go out? We could go to Lucy's, she'll be half expecting me, or for a drink?'

I waited out the back as he pulled on his hiking boots. 'You're not expecting to go anywhere in a hurry,' I said, poking a face at the elaborate laces. 'Cattle would be long gone before you were ready to chase.'

Floyd laughed. 'I never had much of the country about me.'

'No,' I agreed. He hadn't. I'd liked that about him. And yet when he came to Alice, he didn't seem out of place. He had an uncanny ability to fit in wherever he was.

'I'd rather not go to Lucy's,' he said. 'There'll hundreds of people, won't there?'

'There will be. In fact, she's probably forgotten she gave me a room.'

One of the reasons Lucy justified having such a large house and living alone was that she could provide a bed for her many visitors. Most weeks she had someone staying. Easter was totally crazy. It was one of her busiest times as people came from south to escape the beginning of winter and enjoy our perfect weather.

'Have you stayed there at all?'

'No, I haven't actually got there yet although I will. Mum's can get a little . . .' I struggled to find the right word.

'Claustrophobic?' Floyd suggested.

'Like that.' Was it disloyal to smile the way we did?

We walked up towards town.

'Ros seems to be going all right. She looks better than I'd expected.'

'Yes, she's getting better. And despite all her moaning I think she's really enjoying having Michael around so much. After thirty years there's this whole new dynamic.'

'So relationships can change, can they?'

I shot Floyd a sideways glance. I hoped he wasn't being sentimental about ours.

It seemed a bit late for that.

We turned onto the main street that ran up through town. Even at the south end of it there were any number of bottle shops, a pub and two backpacker bars.

'Where shall we go?' I asked.

'How about that pub down the corner?'

'No way. We'll go to the bar at the backpackers.'

'Alicia! Why ask if you know what you want to do?'

'It wasn't like that. I just can't imagine why you'd want to go to that pub. It's horrible.'

'It's okay outside. It's nice.'

He was right about that, but we went to the backpackers anyway. I didn't want to sit out and contemplate the view, like we often had done on our visits. It would be too much like reminiscing.

Floyd sat in the courtyard while I ordered our drinks from the bar. I liked the crowd at the backpackers, listening to the different accents. It was one of the few places in Alice which seemed multicultural, rather than divided into black, or white.

'So,' I said when I sat down with our drinks. 'What's going on?'

'Not much. Everything's sorted. I put what I wanted to keep in storage and gave the rest to St Vincent's like you asked.'

So it was done. Our house was sold, there was no garden, no deck furniture, no old king-sized bed or worn leather couches anymore. We'd rid ourselves of all our shared possessions and it felt as if I should feel more as if it was a big moment, but I didn't.

'My chair, what happened to that?' When I'd moved out of our house I'd damaged the only thing I'd wanted, the chair Lekisha had given us. I'd dropped it on the stairs and Floyd had said he'd get it fixed.

'It's still with the repairer. I'll have to text you his details,' he said. 'The solicitor's handling distributing our shares. It might take a little while to get to you. I'm not doing a runner with your money.'

'So, fresh starts. Cheers.' I raised my glass.

He kept his schooner down. 'You know, sometimes I can't believe it, that you're not with me. That I'm not just going away for work but I'll come back to you.'

I wasn't expecting this candid response to my flipness and it floored me. Especially when he tried to cover up his unhappiness with a smile.

'Don't.' I covered my face with my hands. 'Don't smile at me like that. You'll make me cry.'

We drank too much and hardly ate. We told stories about each other, proving some kind of weird point about how well we knew the other. There were lots of stories that represented the fun and good times we'd had together. And some not so cheery we left unworked.

By the time we managed to get up and find a taxi, we'd stirred up so much of the past that everything felt fuzzy, and not just with the alcohol. The cab dropped him at his hotel first and he kissed me as he was slowly getting out. For a brief moment we knew there were places we could take that goodbye gesture.

''Night,' I said with more conviction than I felt. Floyd closed the passenger door and waved. I knew I wouldn't go on to Lucy's. She would probably still be up and there would be a crowd to navigate. Instead I directed the taxi to Mum's. I crept into my room, keen not to disturb her and Michael, and let the strangeness of the night slowly unwind till I could sleep and hopefully forget all it had stirred up.

I slept heavily and for a long time. When I woke I was surprised by how late it was, but I guessed I must have needed it. Didn't people say that when you finished a big emotional episode you needed sleep?

Mum and Michael were out and I was relieved to have missed them, and any questions they'd ask. I escaped over to Lucy's house before they came back. Her place was proper flash and I liked it. It sat up high on a hill and a large verandah wrapped three quarters of the way around. From there you felt as though you could reach out and touch the ranges. Inside, the walls were decorated with vibrant early western desert paintings, so no matter where you were there was one or another version of country.

I walked in through the side door to find Lucy resting on the couch, a dressing-gown slung on over her nightie, a hand to her head. She groaned at my entrance and I laughed, though not unkindly, at her hung-over state. Throwing down my bag, I fetched her a glass of water and told her I'd get some coffee together and a bacon and egg sandwich.

'Good girl,' she said, and closed her eyes while I got to work clearing the bottles off the bench and into the recycling bins out the back. When the bench was clear I busied myself with breakfast, frying eggs, cutting bread—which looked like either a loaf of Patrick's or Michael's—packing the coffee pot and grilling the bacon. I gave Lucy her sandwich then poured two cups of coffee and took a seat next to her.

'Lifesaver,' she mumbled around the sandwich.

'My pleasure. Looks like you had a bit of a crowd last night. Did you give away my room?'

''Course there was a crowd. I think people are out shopping now, but I didn't let anyone have your room. I was expecting you.'

She put on a sulky voice, but I knew she wasn't really offended.

'Sorry. Floyd turned up.'

'He did?'

'Yes. Apparently Magdalene invited him to the opening of the school.'

'Catholics,' Lucy said. 'So fucked up. She must want you to get back with him.'

I doubted it. Lucy didn't believe it either, she was just stirring. Maybe Floyd had wanted to check how he really felt before he left, but it seemed an even bet he was probably here because he liked a big event. As did Magdalene. Between them they would wring the opening celebration for every bit of good spin they could get. And while he might have also had some processing to do, hopefully last night would be the last of what he needed to do with me.

Leaving Lucy with another coffee I took my bag to my room. It was big and light, sparsely decorated with modern wooden furniture. Lucy had even laid out a towel for me. I took some clean clothes out of my bag and headed to the bathroom. It had been remodelled recently, and now had a large spa bath under the window with a glorious view. The low-set windows opened out. I stuck the plug down and opened the taps.

Floyd stayed holed up in his hotel working while I spent Friday and Saturday drifting between Lucy's and Michael's kitchens, helping them prepare for the Easter feast. There was salmon to salt and vegetables to chargrill. Fruit to soak in alcohol. Limes and oranges to peel carefully without pith for sauces. Lemons to squeeze. I took to walking the long distances between the two houses. Even though it took about forty-five minutes I was happy to be outside during the turn of the season. The sky bright and blue, the temperature mild.

On Sunday, once the final preparations were done, Lucy and I took a morning aperitif onto the verandah, dressed in what she called our glad rags. We savoured the view and the sense we were completely ready for the guests who would soon descend. Frank came with Iry, who made it clear she'd only brought him so he didn't drive home over the limit. Their two teenage boys, both at that awkward stage of perpetual teenage embarrassment, muttered incoherently and went straight out the back and down the side steps to the den under the house.

Martha arrived soon after, Lucy's old girlfriend from when I was a kid, with her new partner Jude. Mum and Michael were close behind, arriving with a group I knew, including Annie, who I was happy to see. I liked the fact that the town was too small to expunge people from circles even when relationships disintegrated. Old lovers and their friends stayed included. It certainly hadn't been my experience in the city. Almost all of Floyd's friends had disappeared out of my life since we'd broken up, with the exception of Robert. Floyd had run our social life. Brought people like presents home for me and never invited them again if I didn't like them. I'd taken the social world he created for granted and I'd been so lazy I only had a few friends of mine left by the time we split.

Within about half an hour the large front room was full, the side garden and front verandah teeming with guests. As yet there was no sign of Patrick, and I did my best to ignore my disappointment, telling myself that at least it made things simpler.

I was on the couch chatting with Annie when Floyd arrived. He waved at me across the crowd. I was glad to see I was right and nobody appeared to treat him any differently to the way they had when we'd been together. He was warmly welcomed.

'So Floyd's here?' Annie said.

'Yes.' He had his back towards us, talking to Frank. His shirt was one of his new ones. I didn't like any he'd bought from that brand. Personally I thought they were a bit young for Floyd. The good thing was I could probably read it as a signal he was no longer feeling very sentimental.

'You are not thinking of getting back together? I don't want to have to replace you.'

I was taken aback by her directness. 'No. What makes you say that?'

'He's here. You're here. I saw him look at you.'

'Don't be stupid. Do you think I'd go out with a man who wears a shirt like that?'

Annie glanced at his floral shirt. 'It's not that bad.'

'Don't worry, I'm not going anywhere until Lekisha takes over.'

'Won't that be great? A real first.'

'Surely not a first?'

'Just about. By the way, I want you to know I only asked about your personal life because of the school.'

'That's okay. You can tell me why you left Lucy if you want. We'll trade break-up stories.'

'I didn't leave her,' she said, unamused.

'Sorry.'

'It's okay. I'm sure Lucy likes that story. That's the beauty of gossip—it's mostly just someone's preferred reality.'

I scanned the room. It would be fair enough to suspect mine and Floyd's separation would have a few new stories added to the rumours by the end of the party, and some, no doubt, would be as Annie had assumed, that we were reconciling.

I was beating cream when Patrick arrived. I saw him standing with a box under one arm at the open doors to the deck. Iry stopped him there, going on tiptoes to kiss him, which made me realise how short she was. It was something you forgot about her because she was so imposing. It was unusual to see her so warmly affectionate, and Patrick was in a very small privileged club if he had Iry on his side. I noticed Frank notice and the wry smile. I think part of him would have liked Iry to like him still, though I didn't think he'd ever admit it, even if he was tortured. A young new pretty lawyer took Frank's hand and introduced him to the young men she was with. Frank started telling them something, gesturing effusively, back in his comfort zone as the admired old comrade of the struggle and the great orator.

I could see Patrick scanning the crowd as he made his way in but it wasn't easy now the party was in full swing. There would have been at least thirty people inside and as many again on the deck and on the side terrace lawn. Failing to turn off the beaters I kept a watchful eye on him, hoping it was me he was looking for. He didn't bother disguising how pleased he was to have finally spotted me, and I blushed. Still beating, the cream was a curdled mess.

I was scraping it into the bin when Floyd came up, looking like he was a bit drunk.

'Why does anyone let you in a kitchen?' he asked, trying to take the bowl. 'I'll do this.'

'I'm okay,' I protested, managing to keep the spoon. He got the bowl just as Patrick made it around the island bench and into the clear space of the kitchen's small work area.

'I've just got to whip up some more cream,' I said and held out my hand for the bowl to Floyd. 'Floyd this is Patrick, he teaches at Kilka.'

Floyd was forced to give me the bowl to shake his hand.

'Nice to meet you again, we've met, yes?'

'Yes at Ros and Michael's briefly, years ago.'

'I thought you were a linguist,' he said, and I winced inwardly. 'But I never forget a face, professional training.' He winked. Luckily just then Annie put a hand on Floyd's arm.

'Hey, Annie,' he said, throwing an arm around her like they were the oldest of mates, and I knew for sure then he'd drunk too much. It was now quite crowded in the kitchen and the noise level of the party had risen, voices and music bouncing off the wooden floor.

'Come with me, Floyd, I can't bear kitchens. You always get a job or trapped with someone you don't like. We can talk politics and I'll give you my two cents' worth on why the government's suppressing that report on kids' welfare you're so interested in and you can tell me about your new job in London. I used to live there, you know.'

I didn't mind being left alone with Patrick and the noise gave us an excuse to stand closer while we talked for as long as food preparation provided an easy excuse.

The party was good fun. While I met some new people and caught up with old family friends I couldn't help noticing Patrick and I managed to find ourselves near each other quite often and I didn't think it could just be me contriving it. Thanks to Annie, Floyd found plenty of other people to talk to him about politics, and I didn't see him to talk to again over the afternoon. I was relieved he was happily engaged and off my case.

It was sundown and I was lying on the lawn hiding from the enthusiasts who thought we should all be dancing when Floyd came and plonked himself next to me, seemingly much more relaxed and sober.

'You coming to hide too?'

Not that he would be. He'd fancied himself a good dancer.

'No, I've just done my exhibition piece. I came to say goodbye.'

'You tired of the party?'

'No, I've got some work. I want to go and interview Ted Breen the ex-ATSIC commissioner here about how things are going on remote communities now ATSIC's been disbanded.'

'I could tell you what they think and save you the drive. They think it's one more penalty for wanting to live on their land, and almost impossible to get up anything community-driven. We're back to not even pretending decisions are anything but top down. They'll tell you there were problems before but it's more of a problem having no say at all in their own affairs.'

Floyd smiled. 'That's quite a speech for you. You sound more and more like your mother.'

'Do I? That's a bit scary. Maybe it's just being here. Seeing the way power is always being manipulated away from people. But you're right. It's not for me to tell you what other people think.'

'I didn't mean to judge you,' he said.

'It's okay. I know that. Where are you staying tonight—the same hotel? If not, I'm sure Lucy will find you a bed if you want.'

'No, I don't think I should cramp your style.' He tipped his chin at Patrick.

'You won't,' I said.

'Actually, I thought I'd camp out on the Finke,' he said.

'There's not much water, what's there will be pretty skanky.'

'I don't mind about the water. I never really came up here for the swimming. Anyway, I'll be remembering how it was. How beautiful it was at our spot.'

My heart tightened. Our special spot on the riverside was always gorgeous, nestled under the trees where the river pooled in a dark watery hole, reflecting the sky and nearby rock face. Last Easter we'd spent a perfect evening there, discussing our future together with renewed hope. Now I wasn't sure if he was being sentimental or jealous. I had no way of knowing and it was pointless to try to guess his motive. We could act as if everything was sorted between us, even feel it, but there were always going to be triggers for both of us. Hopefully, not at the same time.

'Enjoy, and if you change your plans let us know so we don't have to embarrass you with a search and rescue helicopter,' I said lightly.

I stayed put until he'd finished saying a long round of farewells. When I got up to see him off I could feel Patrick watching as we walked out. Floyd had parked a way down the street and when he stopped it was at Mum's car, which he'd obviously borrowed. I knew as soon as I spotted the swag on the back seat and an esky on the floor that the trip was well planned. It wasn't a reaction to Patrick's presence at all and I was glad I hadn't accused him of being jealous and looked really stupid.

'I hope things work out for you, Alicia,' said Floyd, kissing me on the head in a fatherly fashion. 'It looks like being here is good for you.' He gestured towards Lucy's house and then to the country in general.

It was two in the morning when Patrick and I loaded the dishwasher with the last of the dishes. Lucy had long since gone to bed and Frank was snoring on the couch. Iry had given up waiting for him a few hours earlier and driven home, knowing that without his car he wouldn't be driving tonight. His snoring was legendary, and in a funny way it stopped me feeling as though I was alone with Patrick, which I wasn't quite sure I was ready for.

We talked as we cleared up, mostly about the school and the opening, but every now and then we gave up some small personal detail. I told him that Floyd and I had met in Sydney. And that I loved the sea. So did Patrick, he said. My divorce I claimed had been amicable. Why I laughed when I used the word I don't know, but Patrick only smiled. He had never married. There was an ex. That was the most we gave up. He was staying at a friend's place in town that night, and when he finally made a move to go I didn't do or say anything to try to persuade him otherwise. It had been so long since I'd picked someone up that I wasn't even sure what one did, and I wasn't confident now was the best moment to try. We were both tired and I still felt a little drunk despite only drinking water for hours.

I walked him to the door. He paused at the open doorway while the cooling winds of autumn blew change about. Turning to look at me, he put a hand out to cup one of my cheeks then kissed the other. If it wasn't for the way he stroked his thumb up and down my cheek it could have been nothing more than a friendly good-night. On an impulse I took his hand and opened out his palm, kissing it once before letting it go. I looked up to meet his gaze, catching his surprise and pleasure. I felt desire and fear race to claim me and took a step away from him. Patrick nodded as if responding to my cue.

'Goodnight,' he said as he ran quickly down the stairs.

Leaning over the balustrade I watched him saunter slowly down the street. When he glanced back I waved.

CHAPTER 17

On Monday I got up late, cooked breakfast for Frank and then sent him home. It had a certain practised efficiency to it.

'Thanks, love,' he said, getting into the cab.

'No worries,' I said. Being good to Frank was my way of being good to Eddy. They were old mates and pretty much the same type of ego, but I'd never be so dutiful towards Eddy.

Lucy and I spent the day watching cheesy videos and eating leftovers for lunch and dinner. She teased me a little about Patrick, but I didn't bite and she soon got bored and gave up. Her place was perfect for lounging around and recuperating. The couches were big and comfortable, and the big glass windows let the outside in; between movies I simply watched the light playing across the ranges with as much pleasure as I would get from watching the ocean.

The next day I had to get up early for the compulsory orientation on 'Working and Living in the Territory'. I rushed to get there on time and was furious when it started half an hour late. Clearly we were in Territory time now. With a brazen disregard for self-reflection, time management was the first subject the CEO raised after his brief welcome. No teacher, it was emphasised, should allow themselves to take on an elastic and Aboriginal approach to time. Exactly 5.4 hours of teaching must be conducted each day, including an hour and a half of literacy work. All instruction had to be in English. These were the rules and there was to be no deviation from them. Sure, I thought, sure.

According to the program, the afternoon offered an insight into 'Community Life'. When the session started after a long and tedious morning, a very large white woman with the unlikely name of Tiffany Jewel introduced herself as the Indigenous section head. She had the least precious of faces, jowly, ruddy and marked by sun.

Tiffany started with a rhetorical question: Do you know who you are? Then she told us the answer. We were professionals. Teaching professionals, in the employ of the government. Under no circumstances were we to forget who we were or our own culture. It was not appropriate, she lectured, for anyone to take on Aboriginal culture.

'You have your own,' she bellowed. 'Be proud of it. What you bring to the communities you will teach in are the tools the students will need to operate in our wider society. Your job is to maintain a professional standard at all times and ensure the Territory Education Department retains its position as a provider of best practice in education.'

I kept my expression as neutral as possible throughout her speech though I doubted her claim.

Without pause, Tiffany went on to introduce the guest

cross-cultural experts. Two women advanced towards the podium. An energetic white woman led the way and took to the stage as though she owned it, plugging her laptop into the data projector and introducing herself as Beryl Lane. After some indecision the Aboriginal woman moved to stand next to her and introduced herself.

I already knew her. It was Mrs Press, my personal hero when it came to fighting for a good education. I'd never told Mum about the beatings we got from our grade four teacher, Mr Sherman; I'd been afraid her reaction would be over the top, and there was also the code we had as kids to never dob. But Mr Sherman was testing our resolve on this sorely.

It was Tommy jnr who copped it the worst, from beatings to regular humiliations, like being taken off the football team despite being the best player, and one day he must have finally cracked unbeknownst to us and told his parents.

It was the morning session and we were doing mental maths, which meant answering Mr Sherman's rapid-fire sums. Tommy jnr, Fred, Michael, Liam, Lekisha and I were all in the back row. Sweet shy Veronica Brown was standing in the tin rubbish bin at the front of the class; Mr Sherman had sent her there for insolence, a word that we didn't understand. We all sat hunched down in our seats with our hands safely tucked under our thighs so that if Mr Sherman was in a mood to swing around and give someone a swipe with his ruler he would have to give it to us on the back where it didn't hurt so much.

When Mr Press arrived he sounded like he'd been running. No-one came uninvited to our class, and Mr Sherman looked very angry at the interruption. As Mr and Mrs Press filled the doorway we sensed something very unusual was about to happen. Collectively we held our breath. I was as anxious as I was excited. Mr Press walked straight past Mr Sherman and lifted Veronica out of the bin. He took the dunce cap from her head and told her kindly she was a good bright girl and to resume her seat. Mrs Press smiled at Veronica encouragingly as she passed, smoothing her hair in a gesture that to this day I think of as the kindest type of touch one human can give another.

Mr Sherman had gone quiet, and watched with a worried frown. It was the first time we'd seen this look on his face. With another man in the room we could see he wasn't very tall, and a nervous twitch pulled at his left eye. I scrunched up my hands so tightly with the tension in the room that when I finally opened them they were blotchy red.

Mr Press turned to Mr Sherman. 'You might not know this,' he said, 'but Aboriginal people have feelings too.' His voice was quiet but stern, just like the time he caught Lekisha and me chucking bush plums at his cheeky dog. 'We don't like to be hit. Or treated like animals. You're not allowed to belt the kids every time you like. You got to tell the principal if the kid's done the wrong thing. He's the one who's going to sort it out. He's got to talk to the parents too. I got a letter, says I'm right.' He drew an envelope out of his top pocket and unfolded an official-looking letter, waving it like a flag over Mr Sherman's head. 'Any one of these kids, the Chinese grocer's boy, my sons, that little white girl, my nephews, my nieces, none of these kids, you can't hit them. Never. That's what the Minister for Education says in my letter.'

Mrs Press took the letter from her husband. She folded it up carefully, returned it to its envelope and secured it in her handbag, snapping shut the big silver clasp. Our eyes were glued on her every move as she walked boldly towards Mr Sherman's desk. Ordinarily, his desk was like an altar. No-one went near it. But Mrs Press simply reached around Mr Sherman and took his beloved cane from where it rested on the dark desktop.

She handed the cane to her husband and then addressed Mr Sherman very slowly, as though speaking to someone dim-witted. 'We're not stealing this cane, we're taking it to the principal. Like my husband explained, only the principal can hit the kids and only in particular situations.'

As she and her husband left, Mrs Press gave us kids a wink. My whole body fizzed with happiness. I felt bubbles of power tingling down my arms, up my legs. There was a stunned second of silence before Tommy jnr whistled loudly and his brother Michael began stamping with his feet, and soon everyone was hammering their shoes on the wooden floor, banging their desk lids up and down. It was like the day the Magpies won the grand final, it was that good.

Sitting on my hard chair in the conference room, I couldn't work out why Mrs Press, the toughest, the straightest-talking woman from the Gap, was playing such a subservient role to this so-called 'expert'. Mrs Press simply sat in a chair to the side while Beryl clicked through her PowerPoint presentation on bush life. The new recruit to my left was diligently taking notes, failing to see what was happening right before his eyes. It wasn't cross-culture being taught. It was boss culture.

Finally the screen flashed blue and then black and the presentation was over. After a small reminder about filling in the attendance sheet we were free to go.

I almost stumbled outside and then walked quickly to the edge of the grounds before I paused. I needed to think about what I'd just witnessed. When had the feisty Mrs Press become so oppressed, so downtrodden? Was Mum right—had nothing really changed?

Feeling a little sad, I stopped in the shade and was playing with the blotchy pink bark of the gum when I heard Mrs Press's distinctive soft voice behind me. 'So you are taking that job at Irrarnte, not just helping out?'

I turned to look at her. 'Yes, I'm staying. I took the contract.'

'And your husband, he's going with you?'

'No.'

'Oh,' she said, confused. 'He's just on holiday then?'

'Yeah. He's come for the opening of the school tomorrow morning. And you're coming?'

'I'll be there even if I get the sack,' she said determinedly, sounding more like the Mrs Press I knew. 'So Floyd's not working for the paper, his place has gone.'

'Did you read his piece?' The last few years he did a round-up on Canberra column, as well as his feature articles.

'Always. We were really happy he helped us out. His articles were real good. We liked the one on the little footy stars the best.'

'Yeah. Our friend Robert actually helped out there. It was a good piece.'

'It was. Magdalene must be glad you're back. She's wanted that school for years and years.'

'Yeah, she's happy and so am I. I'm just staying this year, though.'

'That old lady is really strong,' she warned.

'I know, but I already told her I'm going at the end of the year.'

'You're not like your mother.'

I wasn't sure if it was a question or statement. 'No. No, I'm not.' I wasn't giving my life to Promised Land.

I was about to make a move to leave, but then I decided I might as well ask Mrs Press straight out about what was troubling me. Like she said, I wasn't my mother, who would never have risked offending her like I was about to.

'You were pretty quiet in there,' I said. 'I thought you might have talked more. There were a lot of myall people you could have educated.'

To my relief, Mrs Press wasn't offended at all. 'I'm going to retire soon. That mob have been driving me mad for years. No point me talking when Beryl knows everything.' A mischievous smile played around her mouth.

'Probably not,' I said.

'Nothing she don't know . . .'

I raised my eyebrows. The punchline was coming.

'. . . except how to shut up.' Gloria gave a snort of laughter. I started giggling. In the end we were laughing so hard I think we would have fallen over if it wasn't for that tree.

When I left I took a piece of bark with me and put it on the dash of my car. It could be a totem, I figured, something to remind me not to be a bossy whitefella.

*

I drove straight to the supermarket where I picked up all the food for our opening day morning tea. I didn't arrive back at Promised Land till well after dark and to my surprise, Lekisha and Magdalene were waiting for me at the communal central fire pit. Rosia was in her grandmother's lap. I wasn't sure if they were worried I was late or curious about how the weekend had turned out. A bit of both, I suspected, since Lekisha no doubt also knew about Floyd's invitation and the likelihood I had seen him already.

Once I put away my shopping I joined them, close enough to be illuminated by the low flames. Lucky growled at me until Lekisha punched him once to shut him up and while he put his head down as if he was chastened I didn't trust him an inch. When he slunk back towards their place I was glad.

It wasn't a very cold night, but the fire was still welcome. Lekisha handed me a sleeping Rosia. Her breathing was fast and she twitched from time to time with a dream, her little lips scrunching up, a frown worrying her face. I smoothed it gently with my thumb and kept up the rocking she seemed to like so much.

The women asked polite indirect questions about Floyd's well-being and I gave brief replies. I knew they were keen for a gossip but I decided they could make it up themselves and I didn't give away anything.

'There's plenty of room in your house for Floyd to stay?' Magdalene asked, pointing with her lips to my donga.

'Floyd's not staying,' I said firmly. 'He's just up for the opening ceremony. But he's going to write an article on it and see if he can get it placed in his old paper.'

Magdalene nodded agreeably. 'He can take lots of photos,' she said. I was pretty sure this was an instruction not an invitation.

Lekisha threw tea in the boiling water, followed by a quantity of sugar she measured in her palm. She took the water off the boil and banged the billy on the ground to settle the leaves to the bottom. I noted there was none of the flashy swinging she'd got into when Patrick was around. A pannikin was duly poured for me. Rosia fell deeper asleep, her head tucked into the crook of my arm, and I sat there happily, marvelling at the strong feeling of uncomplicated love that holding a warm little baby elicited in me. It was only when Lekisha started to talk about the baby needing another blanket that I gave her back and returned to my donga. I should have slept badly, given I had the worry about the opening on my mind, but I slept like a log.

CHAPTER 18

At daylight Lekisha padded barefoot over from her house.
'Big day,' she said, beaming, putting my kettle back onto
the gas ring and finding herself a cup.

'There's coffee made,' I said. I was on my third cup after waking
ridiculously early in my nervousness.

She wrinkled up her nose in distaste and attacked the loaf of
bread on my bench. The knife made slow going of it. It was the
loaf Patrick had given me, which needed throwing out. She made
jokes about hard bread and hard men while she foraged around
looking for an alternative for her breakfast. She settled for a slice
of cake.

When she was ready we headed off to the schoolroom. It was
still way too early to get out the food but we set up some tables
and chairs outside and then surveyed the classroom, everything
ready and waiting after weeks of work. I looked around at the
bright boards with pictures of the ecosystem, and at the glossy lam-
inated number sequences and illustrated alphabet we had strung
up. There were pictures of local animals with clear identification

labels in language and English. A large family tree hung on the wall, the branches waiting for the kids to put their names against their photos. On shelves were jars of sharpened pencils, rows of pens, rulers standing stiffly in a jam tin. Our desks were neat and orderly, fresh new daybooks opened, and the older kids' desks and chairs were arranged in a horseshoe shape. The little kids' corner, with its bright cushions and shared work areas, was colourful and inviting. The whole space looked perfect to me.

I watched while Lekisha moved pillows around in the small carpeted square surrounded by a shelf of books which we'd made for a reading area.

'Stop fussing,' I said. 'We're right. It's just great.'

'Well, I'm making it greater.' She threw a pillow at me and left to prepare herself for the dancing.

At eight o'clock the guest cars began to roll in. Mrs Press arrived first with Greg Abrahams, the head of the education department, in a brand-new Land Cruiser. As she got out of his passenger seat she gave me a look that said no cheeky comments, although we both knew I wouldn't have dared. Mum and Michael arrived just after them; I noticed that Abrahams moved away as soon as Mum sat down near him. I'd have to ask her sometime what fight she'd had with him, or more precisely, which fight he hadn't forgiven her for. Not now though.

Beryl, the cross-cultural expert, had sent apologies; a minor staffer whose name I didn't catch attended instead. He didn't seem to think the chairs were clean enough for him to sit down on and stood nervously against a verandah pole. A group of dogs wandered over sniffing out food. Lucky wasn't with them so I went and shut the gate on our small yard. Floyd pulled up in his hire car, looking slightly rattled.

'You right?' I asked.

'Road needs a grader over it,' he said.

'You're not meant to take hire cars on the dirt,' I said.

'You're not meant to do lots of things, Alicia. It's not good to follow all the rules. Bad for the soul.' He kissed my cheek. 'Any water about?'

I pointed it out to him. In the meantime the dust rose thicker as more and more cars rolled in. We'd got quite a crowd. Annie and Blossie came with some of the kids who were connected to Promised Land and some who weren't. Family arrived from town and Kilka. Patrick brought his class. He held himself back in the group of men and I was glad of the etiquette that kept us apart. It made it easier to get on with what I needed to do. This was Promised Land's day, their big moment. I had to show people every respect and make sure I did everything in my role to help the morning's celebrations go well.

By nine everyone except the local member, Bob Rowan, had arrived and all the old people in charge of the welcome were waiting. A big fire had been lit to burn down some coals and a pile of leaves to make the ceremonial smoke was near the ladies. Lekisha, Treasure and the other women were already painted up to perform an important dance.

For some inexplicable reason the day was hotter than it had been for weeks, and old Father Peter from mission in his long black cassock was suffering perhaps more than anyone else. He was sitting next to Magdalene in the front row in full sun. The pair went back years and like us all she had him wrapped around her finger.

He hadn't been allowed to officially bless the building, although I assumed he had covertly done so at Magdalene's request. Like the ceremony of traditional dance and customs that the community were about to perform, a Christian blessing would help make our little demountable a safe place for learning, and I knew Magdalene well enough to know she'd have convinced him to bless it, even if it couldn't have been done officially and witnessed.

Bob Rowan finally turned up. He'd blocked the school at every turn. A typical politician, he was now prepared to share in the ownership of our success. Everyone waited politely while he took the seat we'd set aside for him next to Father Peter. As soon as he was seated, the clapping sticks and singing started, led by Esther, who sat on her bent crippled legs in the dirt. The older women began the dance, coming in from the left, shuffling and stamping rhythmically. The younger women followed, more shyly but still proud. The dancing looked deceptively simple. The women moved forward and back, repetitively. Song was sung. And each woman, each dancer and singer was completely present. I could hardly keep my eyes off Tissianna. She who I'd only ever seen with her head down was dancing, becoming more confident as the dance wore on. As the women danced and sang the welcome it was impossible not to be moved, not to feel like this dance was part of a bigger dance. A link. It joined people together. Today it brought the past to the present. I could have cried with joy.

The dance ended in the same understated way it had started.

Henry and Caleb carried the fire drum into the centre of the vacated stage area on two long-handled shovels, and Magdalene rose from her chair to take her place. Using her leaves, she called the clean smoke out of the drum until she was almost enveloped. The important people went first. The elders. Men and women. Lekisha then ushered the rest of the community forward into the proceedings, keeping the children close to her. I joined them, and then the guests from town followed, imitating the washing movement of the children. Even Father Peter got up and joined in, entering the line at the space Patrick made in front of himself, as Kilka moved forward and then Red Bore.

Floyd's flash blinded me as I passed around and through the smoke. It was a bit invasive but it was better his camera stayed on faces he had clear permission to capture. I'd left my own camera on the table and I would be picking it up as soon as the formalities were over. When I came out the other side of the circle I passed Mum, still in her seat. She was crying, her head bent. Michael had his hand on her back and looked bemused, though I couldn't understand why. He knew as well as me that she always cried at big events and this as far as her life went was a huge moment of success.

Once everyone had found their seats again, there was a few minutes of silence. Amazingly the kids were sitting quietly back in their places, still and respectful.

The last of the smoke drifted away from the fire drum, and I could feel a strange contentment settle. Mum finally raised her head. In spite of the tears her face was glorious, her expression joyful. I clicked off a round of shots.

Bob Rowan took the gap in proceedings to be an invitation to speak and gave the community a clap and himself and his party a standing ovation. Mercifully he was brief. A smattering of hasty applause greeted his closing remarks. Formalities over, the mad dive for the morning tea began, the kids acting as if they hadn't eaten for weeks while their mothers, aunts and grandmothers tried to hold them back without success.

Floyd didn't join the fight for the buns or cakes. After a brief chat with the minister he was taking photos of the community, general shots of people. I went over to join him, and we stood, cameras like shields in our hands, ready to raise them if necessary.

'Do you think I've taken enough shots for Magdalene?'

'I don't know. It was so much easier when you just knew how many rolls of film you'd used.'

'Yes the good old days.'

I didn't know what to say. The mood was sombre between us. We both knew he'd be leaving very soon to head off to his new life in London, and it would really be goodbye. He shifted the strap of his camera and put the lens cap on.

Although he said he'd better get going, that he was on the afternoon plane to Darwin, he didn't move. We took a minute or two to feel the space around us, the physical vastness of the desert and the possibilities which were opening up for us, before I turned back to the throng of people so he could make his goodbyes.

He did a good job, carefully and politely acknowledging everyone he needed to, shaking hands formally. Michael stood up and hugged him. When Floyd kissed Mum goodbye she put a hand on his cheek for a moment and I could see that she was struggling too. It might have been when she first realised the fact that he was leaving our family. Floyd had never been a son-in-law. He'd been like a son to her and she'd miss him.

I followed him to his car and we hugged each other, my cheek to his chest for what felt like the last time. I felt the strength of his body's deep pull on me. After years together there was some kind of cellular imprint that had nothing to do with my head, or even my heart. It was hard not to respond and I held onto him longer than I should have.

'Be safe,' I said to him, finally pushing him away.

'I'll send the photos,' he said.

'And some of London. So I can picture where you are.'

'Sure.'

He got into the car and I watched him drive out the boundary gate, a hollow feeling opening up in my stomach. I remembered a car sticker Mum had once had that said: Remember to keep breathing. I did just that, as I found myself a seat near Lekisha and watched the gathering unfold.

I looked out past the Kilka troopy to the hills, staring until I found a message in their muted purple profiles, so solid in the flat and open vista. Be still they said. So I sat while the complicated and conflicting feelings churned inside me. I sat until I felt a sense of calm and it became obvious that if life was a cycle, endings could come before beginnings. I'd be all right.

Patrick was rounding up his kids and as they were passing he stopped briefly.

'We got to go but I'll call in on Friday,' he said to the both of us. It didn't seem personal.

'No worries,' Lekisha said.

She touched my arm. 'Come on,' she said. 'It's time.'

After thirty years of dreaming, Promised Land school was up and running.

CHAPTER 19

By the end of the day I was a wreck. It was one thing to help in a class, run to someone else's program, like I'd been doing at Red Bore, and quite another to bear the weight of responsibility. Who could have thought such a small class could be so exhausting? About half the size of my class in Sydney, it wasn't half the work, more like double. Too tired to face making dinner, I had just lain down for a nap when there was a knock at the door.

'Come in,' I sang out, assuming it was Lekisha. But the knocking continued until I got up and flung the door open.

It was Caleb who stepped back from my angry face. Rosia was in his arms and he held her out to me like a peace offering. I accepted, curious as to what might have provoked this surprise visit and a bit regretful it had started with me so obviously irritated. His nervousness was understandable, so while Rosia fiddled with my bead necklace I waited for him to tell me what he wanted. I made sure I was quite polite and did not try to make any eye contact.

'We should get a football team,' he said.

'A what?'

'A school football team. If Kilka and Promised Land join together there should be enough players for an under-fifteen team.'

'Really?' I said doubtfully. I did a rough calculation. A team needed eighteen on the field and most of the boys in my class were under thirteen—they'd be too small and slight for an under-fifteen team. Kilka was a larger school, but even combined I didn't think there would be enough boys.

'Yeah, Preston and Sammy can play. They good.'

'They're too young.'

'No rule about that.'

'Really?' I said again, uncertainly. I did have three older boys but they were family from Western Australia who I thought Magdalene might let go back to their father's country now the school was up.

But it was clearly important to him. Important enough to approach me. If we could get the numbers it seemed like a good idea.

'The comp starts next week, I think.'

'Next week!'

'Maybe,' he said backing down, not wanting me to panic.

I wanted to stall him. 'Well, we need to check that and I'm still not convinced of the numbers.'

'We'll get the rest. Don't worry. Plenty of family about, here sometimes and in town lots of young fellas. You just get the uniforms.'

'We could buy some singlets from Kmart and get numbers put on.' We had no budget for football jerseys.

Caleb frowned, unimpressed with my cheapskate attitude. 'Proper uniforms, we need.'

'Proper uniforms cost lots of money. We don't have any money.'
That was true.

'Just get it. From the government.'

If only things were that simple. Caleb had put me in a bit of a fix. Cultural etiquette precluded a straight-out no to him. Not unless I wanted to cause offence. But there wasn't any money. Unless I paid for the uniforms, which seemed a bit patronising. While we stood there, Rosia wriggling in my arms, Preston rode past, dinking one of the little girls, Mary, I thought it was, on his cross-bar. Sammy chased after them; catching up, he hopped onto the stunt pegs on the back and balanced himself with his hands on Preston's shoulders. The bike swerved and then righted. Anyone could see that most of the kids here were exceptionally physically capable and football was a great game for them. And a team needed supporters, which would help us all come together.

'Okay, I'll think about how we can do it. First we need to see if Kilka want to be involved.'

'They want to.'

I was sure he was right but we still needed to ask. 'Let's talk to Patrick, eh, on Friday?'

'He wants to,' Caleb said. 'I asked him this morning.'

Of course he did, I thought. Men first, women second. All right then, I told myself, the uniform problem could also be his first concern.

Having finished his business with me, Caleb reached out to take Rosia. I didn't want to give her back just yet, and suggested I keep her a bit longer and then bring her over to his house. When I saw him hesitate I reassured him I wouldn't keep her long. Despite his frequent absences he was a surprisingly cautious and doting parent when he was around. I knew it was selfish, but part of me preferred it when he was away drinking, because it meant Rosia was left with Treasure, and Lekisha and I got to see her a whole lot more.

I took Rosia outside, onto the small scrap of couch grass I'd managed to coax up in front of my donga, and rubbed at her bare feet. Her toes were like tiny fat buttons. She couldn't sit up by herself yet and I sat her in my lap. I showed her how to clap and played tickling games, making her laugh. When I carried her home half an hour later she wrapped her arms around my neck, burying her face in the hollow of my collarbone, and I fancied she was letting me know she'd miss me. It was hard walking back to my little donga alone after I'd given her back. Sometimes the smallness of the community highlighted how alone I was, though thankfully not too often. Then I remembered Patrick was coming on Friday. I hoped he did. If not I'd go to town after school.

Foolishly I had imagined each day would get easier and it didn't happen. The work was relentless and devoured all my energy at a rate I wasn't used to. I'd come home every night and just crash. I was so thankful the first week was a short one. I counted the days down as they rolled out unevenly. My neat pattern of English, maths, science and sport got loose, my plans unravelling. Preston, who'd been sweet as pie at Red Bore and while we were working to set up the room, was the real wild card. He hardly listened, rarely sat still and I must have used his name a hundred times in the one day. I had no idea what I'd do with him and he was hardly the only problem I had on my plate.

Pitching the class at so many levels was a constant challenge. The younger kids were totally unprepared for school. I didn't mean materially, lacking bags or pens. They had no encoding, no contextual background for the lessons. It was as though they were stepping onto another planet when they came through the door. I had to constantly be careful how to explain things without discouraging or shaming them. I didn't want to waste their time either with what Annie had called 'busy work'. She had a group school rule that banned colouring-in for longer than ten minutes a day which I knew I'd find hard to stick to. While I would have been lost completely without the planning time with Red Bore and Patrick's help, I still felt like I was drowning. I absolutely depended on Lekisha's help to mediate a strong and safe bridge between my learning goals and the kids. She translated all my instructions into language, and tried to stop things getting too tense as they invariably did much more often than I'd anticipated.

They were the longest four working days of my life.

Patrick arrived in the afternoon when we were trying to restore some order to the room. He jumped in to help and Lekisha sat down.

'The football's a good idea,' he said.

'Caleb's idea.' For a moment the tiredness on her face was replaced by a flash of fierce pride. 'He's really strong,' she said. 'But me, I'm fucked. I'm going now.'

'See you then,' I said, and Lekisha laughed, remembering before me the last time I'd used that phrase.

Although I'd been almost delirious with tiredness I soon perked up. As Patrick helped to sweep the floor, wipe the desks and sort the reading area, he and I brushed past one another in a sort of dance. The room felt charged with our awareness of each others' bodies.

We discussed my week and Caleb's idea for a school football team. Patrick thought it was a great idea, and believed we had the numbers, given there were often visting boys at Kilka too, and Caleb would have no trouble getting more in town. It would just add to the organisational chaos. Football would be seen as men's business according to Patrick and I'd have to do very little. Hurray for that, I thought.

'Football will give you a big carrot and stick to use. With Preston. And the others. It's a stroke of genius on Caleb's part.'

He was right. That advantage hadn't occurred to me.

Patrick followed me out and waited while I locked up. He seemed in no hurry to leave and followed me home, accepting the offer of a cup of tea.

If he felt as awkward as I did, he didn't show it. He took his tea black, like me. A fact I remembered only after I'd asked. We took our cups out onto the verandah, watching the red sky fade into darkness while the noise of the children playing in the distance nearby floated over us and a wind fussed the ground. A grey butcherbird came calling, his song sweet. Patrick told me how he loved the song of the butcherbird. I agreed it was sweet but what I liked about them was how their offspring always waited a season to help with new chicks before leaving. He claimed not to know this and I doubted he didn't. The man knew both the scientific and language names for the species. But I didn't mind if he was pretending I knew something he didn't. Floyd was always a bit keen on letting me know he always knew more.

Patrick was easy to talk to. He lacked the competitive edge I was more used to and he didn't mind a conversation which wandered. And wander widely it did. After a while I saw what we were doing. We were looking for safe yet common interests and storing up the information for next time, to build a connection.

Before he left he invited me to come over to Kilka and drew me a mud map to show me how to get there. I hadn't been there since I was a kid, and I watched him draw it as if it might be complicated, rather than two simple tracks and one turn. I noted the neatness of his handwriting, so different from mine. At the door we paused. I wondered what he would do, whether he would kiss my cheek again, or whether I was brave enough to make the first move. But then, somehow, we hugged as if it wasn't a big deal. Our bodies briefly lined up against each other and as I waved him off I knew I'd go to Kilka sooner rather than later.

We made another week by the skin of our teeth and it was finally Friday afternoon. Unexpectedly Lekisha turned up as I was packing for a weekend away.

'You busy now?' Lekisha asked, sitting down. This was her usual way of letting me know she had something to say.

I just hoped this would be a short conversation as I was on my way to Kilka. I'd faxed Patrick to say I'd come and visit. To see the school, of course.

'No,' I said.

I didn't have much time if I was going to get there and then into town. As it was I'd be driving in the dark at least part of the way, but I made sure I didn't appear to be hurrying her. It always slowed things down if I tried to rush her, so I sat down, which was just as well as what she had to say came as a shock and totally without preamble.

'Patrick can be your boyfriend. Or your husband if you want. Your skin is right. You know this?'

Of course I didn't know his skin name. Or that she was such a matchmaker. In fact I had no idea why she'd be so bold.

'Our skin is right?'

'Yes it is.'

'Only because you made it right. Like you did for Floyd.'

'How could we? We knew you a long time before him and we didn't name him. Another family did.' Lekisha dramatised outrage at my insinuation the kinship system had been faked up for a bit of matchmaking, but she also knew better than me that these days it was no longer so rigidly controlling of personal relationships. Accommodations were always being made.

'Okay. Don't get sooky. I believe you. What do I need a husband for? I just got rid of one.'

'A baby.'

She was looking at me seriously. She wanted me to get what I wanted.

'I just met him,' I said, 'Kele.' I picked up my bag. There wasn't much more I needed and I'd closed the subject.

'Kele,' Lekisha agreed. For now.

CHAPTER 20

The road wasn't too bad and I made Kilka in good time, having mulled over the curious and brief chat with Lekisha long enough to be finished with it. For now. Kilka had been a past winner of a tidy town award and it showed. Very neat it was, and I was impressed to note the even covering of grass on the small community oval. No doubt this was what Lekisha wanted for Promised Land. Usually ovals went to dust even if they'd been seeded, and I wondered if this was an example of Patrick's green thumb which I'd heard about from Michael.

He was waiting for me at the school. It was hard not to be jealous. His room was about double the size of ours and they had a great mural on the outside. The yard wasn't just a patch of dirt either. They had play equipment. Some lawn. A basketball ring. I felt extremely ripped off.

'It's taken a long time to build up,' Patrick said, putting a hand on my arm, 'and we lost kids anyhow, so it's not just about what you've got.'

I'd heard that. It was just very easy to be jealous.

'Yeah I know. But really I'm going to put the hard word onto the department to put a bit more infrastructure in. Seeing this school I wonder if they are just thinking of us as temporary.'

'I don't think so. I think they just haven't got a clue. There is a contract out on the grounds for you.'

'Is there?'

'Yes. It just got stalled because I helped Henry object to the winning tender because the work didn't come to their team like the house did. And it should have. The outstation mob oversee. It's just rude to give the contract to someone else.'

Patrick showed me around inside. I looked in the kids' books and felt a bit better. They weren't so outstanding. We could get good work out of kids even in our less flash school. He gave me a free hand to look around. He didn't seem to mind me even inspecting his day book and seeing his roll. His students' attendance was erratic. I wondered what that was about. It looked like the football wouldn't be bad for Kilka as a carrot and stick.

When we'd finished I followed in my car to his house. It was on the far side of the community, hidden behind a high iron fence, surrounded by trees. When he opened the gate I was as surprised as I had been by the school. This was no dry country garden. It was another world. Patrick shut the gate. I reached out to stroke the thick glossy green leaves of a small avocado tree in a large pot.

He came up behind me. 'No fruit yet I'm afraid. Maybe next year.'

'Wow. I never expected to see a garden as good as Michael's anywhere up here. This might even be better.'

'Years of nothing better to do.'

I found his understatement attractive. 'You must love plants,' I said, stupidly stating the obvious again. Lekisha would have rolled her eyes.

Patrick didn't seem to mind. 'Look around,' he said warmly. 'It'll give me time to get the notes I've made about how we might get a football team funded and in the comp. Caleb's rung every five minutes to check we're onto it. I need to get him off our back.'

I had no argument with that, secretly pleased he was being humbugged not me.

In the sheltered southern corner of the yard I discovered more tropical plants: mangoes, star fruit, a tamarind. A few degrees north of Promised Land, Kilka was clearly beyond the frost line, and Patrick had cleverly used his geographical advantage to build up a tropical oasis. He had a small orchard of citrus—three oranges, a lime, a lemon and a mandarin. The trees were just beginning to fruit or were flowering still.

Close to the stumped house which was a full two rooms bigger than mine was a well-organised vegetable patch. The silverbeet waved like a green sea near the back deck. Local plants screened the low front of the house. I didn't recognise them all but some were bush medicine plants. Looking around, I could see why Michael was so impressed with the man. It would have taken a great deal of time, energy and dedication to put together this beautiful garden.

I wandered around to the back again. Patrick had some bread and cheese on the kitchen table, a pot of tea ready. Nice cups, I noticed. He had good taste.

'Any idea where we're going to get the money for football?' I asked as he poured the tea.

He made some enquiries. As I'd expected, the department wouldn't give us a cent. None of the businesses he'd contacted saw any value in sponsoring a bunch of bush kids whose communities did no trade with them. 'And charity,' he said cynically, 'begins and ends with Centrelink these days.'

'Why don't we try letters, send some cute photos of the kids?'

'They don't think they're cute. They think they're little criminals who smash their windows and steal their cars.'

'That's their cousins,' I said flippantly. 'Bored townies.'

Patrick made no reaction to my non-PC comment. 'I thought we should try out of town. Go for the big companies.'

He had a list of corporations and their addresses. As we divided the list between us I saw street names I recognised. Streets that until less than a year ago I walked everyday as I commuted through the city. I didn't miss them at all.

'We don't have much time,' he went on. 'We'll miss the first game at least. I think we should get started as soon as possible, even if we don't have uniforms at first. Caleb suggested the boys could train one week here, one week at Promised Land, to make it fair. And before games if needed, so any ring-ins can get an idea of where they fit in. Caleb's hoping the team will just fill up with some of the older ones who tend to hang about here at Kilka sometimes but see school as a babies' place.'

There had obviously been lots of discussion I hadn't been in on. He continued talking about ways to organise the team and I didn't really concentrate on what he was saying. I was more interested in observing him. He sat with his hands still and clasped without any of the gesturing I was used to with Floyd. I liked his accent, the steady, calm way he spoke. Outside the open doors the sun had dropped behind the fence. Soon it would set. The light softened into dusk pastels. It was beautiful and I said so, interrupting him. He went silent and then leant over and kissed me tentatively.

It was easier than I'd expected to slip out of my clothes and find myself skin on skin with a man who wasn't Floyd. The difference was far more exciting than strange. For all its intensity it wasn't without a certain light-heartedness, especially when the only condoms he had were from the local clinic. The black on white was quite a bold sight.

I didn't think I'd ever had such a good time with someone the first time, though it was a little scary how everything about Patrick seemed right. I kissed his mouth hard so I didn't ruin things by starting to analyse the situation straight away.

It was well dark by the time we got up. I sat in the kitchen, wearing one of the t-shirts I'd taken from a pile on his shelf. Part of me was marvelling at how effortless our transition to lovers had been, with none of the awkwardness I'd feared might creep in. While Patrick prepared some fish I cut up salad vegetables he'd gathered from his garden.

The youngest of three kids, he came from the river country of northern New South Wales and had gone to a boarding school in Sydney on scholarship. Far posher than the one I'd been to, though I understood his discussion about what it had afforded him as an escape. School had definitely done that for me. Becoming a teacher and then working out here was a source of friction with his family. Though his mother had been a teacher she expected more from her last and brightest son. He'd been expected to do great things with his advantage.

'I told them the other day I'd met someone who thought I was a linguist,' he said. 'They were so proud.'

I froze. Surely he hadn't mentioned me to his parents. Catching the look I must have had on my face he swung a reassuring arm around me and kissed me.

'Oh no it's not what you are thinking. I said it was a man. A senior man. My parents very much value the male view.'

I let my body rest on his. His parents sounded terrifyingly conservative but I liked him more and more.

I liked his dry humour and how he was smart enough to not want to talk about our school days in Sydney. All places were small, even big cities, once you started to play that game.

It was lovely watching him finish making our dinner, knowing that his body and mine would find each other again. I told him I'd read some of the book he'd left for Michael; I could tell he was pleased, though he quickly added it was all a draft. I let him know I'd read so little he needn't worry about any criticisms. From Michael he'd heard I was bit of a photographer. I had been but I hadn't done much of it for a while. Getting it out for the school opening had been the first time in a while. He wondered if I'd take some photos for him, if I had time or any interest.

'Yes,' I said. 'Sure.' I liked the idea of sharing in his project.

He searched for the paper he was looking for. It was a list of plants to be photographed. This was even better than what I'd hoped might happen when I started a month back taking my photos of plants. Perhaps I'd show him those sometime.

'Only if you want,' he repeated holding out the paper.

'Yes. I want to,' I said trying to take the paper from him. We wrangled teasingly. It wasn't like he won. I let him take his t-shirt back from me.

It was too late to go anywhere by the time we ended up getting up again and finishing making and eating dinner.

I woke early. Patrick was already up. I could hear the water running in the shower. I put the kettle on and while I was waiting for it to boil I looked around. I studied the framed photos on the shelf. One of a woman and a small boy intrigued me. I figured they had to be related to Patrick. Same noses and eyes. When he came out of the bathroom I was glad to find it still felt really easy and good between us. He kissed me, his wet hair dripping. I looked back at the photo, comparing.

'You're a spitter for that fellow,' I said.

'That's my son, Tom,' he said, 'with my sister, Gillian. I don't have a picture of his mother, Linda, I don't think. You want a coffee?'

'No, I'm having tea.' I was bit gobsmacked. I sat where I could watch him on the couch and hugged my knees to my chest.

'It's a long story,' he said.

'I got time.'

Tom was six, he told me, and lived with Linda in Sydney. They'd been together a couple of years before going up north to the Islands when Tom was four months old. She was a nurse. While Patrick looked after Tom, she ran the clinic. But she didn't like the physical environment: The flies, heat, mosquitoes or crocodiles. She couldn't stand the smallness of the community, the people, the responsibility or, as it turned out, Patrick. At the end of the year she told him she'd been having an affair with the visiting doctor, Paul. She moved back to Sydney with him and took Tom with her. He took the job in Kilka. It seemed less far away and it didn't remind him all the time of her and his son.

When they first split Tom was still so little and needed his mother. He saw that. He'd tried to accept his role as a father without primary responsibility. In community he'd seen how Aboriginal men all had different fathering roles. Being blood was only one part of the job. The trouble was Linda didn't want him to have any role. Every deal they made she reneged on. Paul had plenty of money and connections. It was a nightmare trying to organise even some access. She was dead against their son visiting Kilka, even Alice. She said they were dangerous and damaging places for a child.

'Really?' I asked.

'Really. She told me to pick up a paper and see what sort of dysfunction I was living in. It's her biggest stick. The fact I live here. Even though now Tom's at school and we could meet anywhere in the holidays. But she's so unreasonable. In fact she's been such a horror I decided last week to up the ante and go for primary custody.'

I watched him carefully. He was trying to swallow down his anger. I could understand why Michael hadn't told me. He never talked about other people's personal business. Ever. But I didn't understand why Patrick hadn't mentioned it earlier.

'Why didn't you tell me?' I said. 'You know, like, Alicia, I've got a kid.'

'Because,' he said, 'I don't know. It didn't come up.'

I wasn't sure that was good enough. And my silence said that.

'Look it wasn't something I could just mention. Oh by the way. If I'd said anything about him you would have asked where he was. And you'd see what you can see now. One fucked up fella, boiling with rage.'

I thought he would cry.

'It doesn't seem at all fucked up to want to be a father to your son,' I said. 'In fact, it seems the most beautiful thing a man could want.'

He put his head on my shoulder. 'Thanks.'

I left late in the afternoon. As I started the car, Patrick slapped the bonnet as though it was a horse needing encouragement. He leant in the window and kissed me.

'Ring me,' he said.

I thought about my own childhood on the drive in to town. It was Michael who I considered my father. There'd been no big fights about where or how I lived. Eddy had been my Father Christmas. He'd never wanted custody as far as I knew. He liked being free Ros used to say. Perhaps it suited her, that line. I didn't know. Anyway, it was all in the past and couldn't be undone. Patrick was not Eddy either, not in any way I had seen. Eddy had so much ego. When I was a kid I think he only remembered I existed on the few occasions I visited. We didn't really know each other at all till I was in boarding school. Then when he got with Kristina I found him a bit embarrassing again. She was only five years older than me and our relationship had gone back to its token ways. Birthdays. Christmases, rare crises like Mum being ill.

I rang Patrick so he'd know I'd made it safely to town. I left a message when he didn't pick up. For the first time I went straight to Lucy's. Excited, I was thinking of talking to her about my feelings for Patrick.

I had a quick shower and made some tea. Lucy found the left-over of some whiskey cake she'd served the night before. She had three cups out.

'Who's coming?'

'Ros, she rang to speak to you when you were in the shower.'

I wondered how Mum knew I might be here. She joined us on the deck where we'd decided to sit in the sun. It was funny. Up here you spent half the year avoiding it, the rest chasing it.

'I called the pay phone and Lekisha said you were coming in. I knew you'd come here if not home.'

'Today you called?'

'Yes, a few hours ago.'

I had to hide my smile. Either Lekisha had developed special powers or someone from Kilka had seen me leaving and passed on the news. Mum was keen to settle in for a long catch-up, which made me feel guilty. I'd been so busy thinking about work and Patrick that I hadn't even phoned her since the school opening day. Lucy offered Mum a drink but she held up a thermos of nettle tea she'd brought. She even had some of her own healthy snacks. I was glad to see how well she was doing looking after herself or at least better at taking Michael's help.

It was only then I noticed the chair sitting at the other end of the deck, covered with clear bubble wrap. I must have walked straight past it on the way in.

'When did this get here?' I asked, pulling at the plastic, popping the bubbles.

'Yesterday,' Lucy said.

'It just came?'

'It was here when I got home from work.'

How strange that it was here to mark the first day of what I hoped would be a new relationship.

The repairer had done a good job; it was impossible to see where it had cracked. Once all the bubble wrap was off I sat in it. Right on top of where the goanna eggs were nesting, white and glossy as they had been years ago when Lekisha had painted them. I traced a finger over the dappled orange skin of the lizards. The chair had come with a card congratulating us on our wedding, not that it actually happened for another year but in Lekisha's mind, moving in together made us husband and wife. We'd been grateful for the comfort and beauty the chair brought our small home. So many times I'd sat in it envisaging my future, the children I would have. The chance of that happening seemed to be evaporating at a frightening rate until now, although I sternly warned myself against getting so far ahead of where things actually were.

The view I looked out to of the country was achingly, sparsely beautiful. It could take your breath away no matter how many times you'd seen it.

'So,' Mum said, 'you're finding it a bit tough.'

'What makes you say that?'

'You look exhausted.'

I tried not to smile at why that was.

'It is harder than I thought it would be, the teaching.'

I was still debriefing, telling them about the kids, my lesson plans, the football team, when Michael came to pick Mum up. I felt like I hadn't shut up for hours though I hadn't said a word about Patrick. I was glad now Mum had stopped me being able to even talk to Lucy about him. It was better to keep him secret until I had a clearer picture.

'Call,' Mum said, 'use me to unload onto.'

'Thanks,' I said. She'd forgiven me, I thought, for taking the job.

'And me,' said Lucy. It was a good idea. If I moaned to them I wouldn't have to talk to Patrick about work. It wasn't the way I wanted to have a relationship if, in fact, that's what the last twenty-four hours were the beginning of.

CHAPTER 21

At the weekend's end I unloaded my shopping and Lekisha helped me with the chair. She was bemused that I'd chosen to bring this back with me and not my leather couch, which she thought was comfortable and flash. Many times when she'd visited she'd preferred it to the spare bed. When I told her the chair was actually the one piece of furniture Floyd and I had argued over, both of us wanting to keep it, she was even more confounded. Shaking her head, she reminded me she'd got the chair from the dump. Although she had to agree it did look grand in the small room—like a piece of art, the nesting goanna seeming to shiver with life.

'You see Patrick?' she asked.

I tut-tutted like a teacher. 'You know I did.'

'He's a good man, like Floyd,' she said, in that way she had of making a statement sound like a question. I fussed with repositioning the chair a bit more. 'You tell stories? He tell you his?'

'Yes,' I said, 'he did.'

I didn't encourage her questions. I didn't know what she knew and I didn't really need to find out. The less said the better while I didn't know where Patrick and I were going.

It was only when she left that I thought about how discrete Lekisha had been to actually leave me alone about Patrick. I imagined there was only one reason for that—she must want it to work out and would let us announce any relationship.

On Monday I wrote a letter to send to the companies we were asking to sponsor the football team. Caleb came in and helped the kids make cards to send out. The children took turns writing a simple line in each card, asking for assistance.

'The more personal our approach the more chance we have,' I explained.

Caleb wasn't convinced. 'We could send a class picture instead.'

'It's good for them to see the kids can write.'

'They should see the kids play footy,' Caleb said. 'Then they'd back us.'

'Some people worry more for writing than footy,' I pointed out.

'Not me,' he said. I laughed. Definitely not him.

'We got training tomorrow,' he said. 'Patrick's coming this way.'

I knew. There'd been a message on the phone this morning. It was entirely impersonal. I told myself it had to be and not to read anything into it but I'd listened to it about five times anyhow.

Football training started when Patrick arrived with his Kilka kids.

Caleb ran the show. Coward that I was, I took my camera with me for protection. In case things weren't as good with Patrick as I was hoping, I'd have a shield.

Out in the dust, Caleb had the young blokes in a complicated training drill. Patrick was helping, and he lifted a hand in greeting at my arrival. I stood a bit away, leaning on his car. I tried not to watch him as he walked over and stood just inches away from me.

'I've missed you,' he said.

'You too.'

It was easier not to look at him but it was tense enough standing next to each other. He gave the hand I had next to his leg a surreptitious squeeze.

I could feel Lekisha's eyes on us. 'I better take some photos,' I said.

To my unprofessional eye the boys' handpassing and kicking looked magnificent and I used my fancy sport setting to collect some rapid-fire shots. I managed to snap a great series of Preston taking an impressive speccy before Caleb told him off. No marks could be taken where an opponent's body was used like a ladder.

Preston was unrepentant. 'That's a shit rule.'

Caleb gave him twenty push-ups for talking back. I shook my head. He was tough. None of the parents watching seemed to mind if he told off their kid. It was as if a football coach was the only young person with genuine authority over others.

I took a few photos of Patrick when he wasn't looking. I felt a bit like a thief. But everything would be sneaky unless we decided to be public and I could hardly work that out by myself. In the meantime I shot hundreds and hundreds of photos of the training session until Caleb admonished me for distracting his boys. Obediently I put the camera away. I felt a little vulnerable without it and when I saw Patrick was caught up with Henry in deep discussion I went to the school room.

As I watched the download of photos I noticed that eight kids and Caleb were dressed in stripey Geelong jumpers. It was the same team I'd always supported, as did Magdalene, Henry and Lekisha.

On an impulse I picked up the phone and rang Robert. He seemed genuinely pleased to hear from me and more than happy to put in a good word with Geelong for us, promising to take care of it as soon as possible. We chatted for a while and I told him about my new job. Just before he rang off he said, quickly, that it was good to know not all the communities up here were totally dysfunctional.

As I hung up I wondered where that comment had come from. I wondered briefly if the government's report on children's health in remote communities was finally out and whether the content was as damning as rumour had it. Sometime soon I'd have to get my head out of the small bubble I lived in and read the papers, see what was going on. Right now, though, I had a letter to write to the Geelong Football Club.

By the time I'd finished and printed off the letter it was late and the community seemed asleep. I had enough on my mind and decided not to wait till the next day. I drove into town and posted the express bag I'd filled with my letter and photos of the kids.

Once that was done the tiredness hit me, and I couldn't face the drive back to Promised Land. Lucy's house was in darkness but the key was where it always was. I treated myself to a long shower, letting the jets pound me in a way the weak dribble of a shower at Promised Land was incapable of doing. I set my alarm for five and was asleep almost instantly.

I was putting one of her thermoses in my bag full of coffee with some fruit I'd pinched when Lucy came in looking exhausted.

'Hey, morning, good one? An all-nighter?'

'With Iry,' she said. 'Not much fun. The government's released some of the report's findings. She's trying to rev things up more. She says there'll be a revolution in service delivery. It's all too fucked according to her.'

I bit into my apple. I knew I should have been more political. I just wasn't. We were doing all right at Promised Land and I had a class to get back to.

'I got to go,' I said, 'or I'll be late.'

'How's Patrick?' she asked, following me out.

'Fine,' I said.

'Lekisha told me,' she announced to my back. I was halfway down the stairs.

I turned around hoping my surprise was well hidden. 'I know you mob don't gossip, so I don't expect any commentary.'

Lucy laughed. 'Michael and your Mum don't gossip. The only ones.'

I shook my head and smiled. 'At least they are on my team.'

The sun was well up as I turned in to the boundary gate. To my surprise, someone was standing there, waiting. It was Henry. I couldn't imagine him being there unless there was bad news. My stomach dropped as I slowed right down before drawing level.

'You the only one up?' I asked.

'No. Everyone's up, wondering where the teacher goes in the middle of the night. Running off!'

I laughed, my stomach righting itself. 'I went to town. To post a letter.'

'Oh,' he said, his face softening with relief. 'We thought you might have had bad luck. With your Mum.'

Bad luck. I loved the way the phrase managed to be patently clear and entirely ambiguous at the same time.

'Must be one important letter,' he said.

'Yeah, it was.'

'I'm not your boss, Alicia, but if you got to go town in the middle of the night, you tell someone, eh. Everyone's too worried for you.'

'I didn't want to disturb anyone,' I explained.

'We not deaf. Or blind.'

'Sorry.' How dumb was I? I really had thought I'd managed to sneak out undetected.

'You right,' Henry said. 'Now you can give me a lift. I'm a bit stiff from all this standing. Feel like this old post.' He laughed, his smoker's throat catching.

'Get in, you old man,' I said.

He climbed in the passenger side. 'It's only a short drive, not too risky.'

'I'm a good driver now.' He'd given me some of my first lessons. Taught me to always let the dirt do the talking, always have loose hands. Things I'd never forgotten.

'You're a crazy driver like all that city mob.'

Just to rattle him I took off fast and fishtailed in the dust.

'Come over to the school later,' I sung out happily as I dropped him off, 'and I'll show you the letter I had to send.'

CHAPTER 22

The Geelong Football Club didn't seem to even think about it. The speed of their reply was so fast I thought they must have agreed almost the day they got our letter. They would sponsor the combined Promised Land and Kilka football team. The cost of uniforms would be met in its entirety and there would be a contribution to playing costs. When the full agreement arrived by fax two minutes later I couldn't believe it: we had enough for uniforms, food and petrol for the whole season. The only condition was that we had to include Cats in the name. I ran over to tell Lekisha and Caleb, who said we'd have to have a meeting for the name.

I rang Annie and then Patrick last so I could talk. He wasn't as thrilled as I'd thought he would be with our success.

'Sorry,' he said, 'it is good. I'm a bit distracted. They released some of those findings you know, finally.'

I had heard. I couldn't see how it would affect him.

'My lawyer faxed me today with bad news. Linda's going to use the findings to back up her argument. He says if this stuff gets any bigger, if the media really go for it and the federal government step into service delivery through their funding agreements, my chances of getting Tom except for supervised visits are a snowball's chance in hell.'

'Lawyers always exaggerate. Think of Michael. He can be very dramatic about a case.' It was all I could think of to cheer him up.

'I don't know. Maybe he is just chipping away at my expectations so he doesn't look bad if I lose.'

He sounded really flat and I would have liked to have helped. I just didn't think I could or that it was any of my business to start giving him advice.

'On a cheerier subject, we are having a meeting about the name of the team. You want it here or there?'

'Here. Your turn to drive.'

I didn't expect Annie would want to be involved but she said she'd come along to help keep things peaceable. Just because people in the two communities were related didn't mean they weren't competitive, she reminded me.

Choosing a name wasn't easy. We'd been arguing for about half an hour and had no agreement. I didn't know why we'd bothered to do it this way, which had been Caleb's idea, and I could only presume it was a way to make sure we all had a say face to face. I liked Bush Cats, but Lekisha said it would be hard for the kids to get their tongues around the B, and they'd say Push instead. Caleb suggested Promised Land Cats, at which, Patrick proposed the Kilka Cats. He thought the alliteration worked well. Caleb didn't know what alliteration was, but he wasn't going to let Kilka take all the glory.

'What about Promised Kilka Cats?' Annie proposed but Patrick's teaching assistant Jeanie pursed her lips firmly against. She objected to their name coming second as much as Caleb had opposed ours being last. Lekisha thought it sounded like we were making a bad joke about promised marriages.

'What about a language name? What's the word for cat?' Annie asked.

'There's no word for cat,' I said. 'There isn't a native cat.'

'There is,' Lekisha contradicted me. 'It's not exactly a cat, it's like a cat but it's a marsupial.' She told us the word was alwepaye. I was surprised; I'd never heard of it before. I saw Patrick raise an eyebrow her way, but he didn't actually challenge her and the name was agreed to with no more debate.

On the way home Caleb didn't come back because we planned to go hunting for tyape and he thought of it as women's work. Which it was.

Between Kilka and Promised Land we stopped off the road in a thicket of witchetty bushes Lekisha knew to be a good spot for getting the grubs. It was pleasant sitting on the dirt and digging the roots where the tyape lived. I was a fairly ineffectual digger. I was a bit dreamy too about Patrick. He'd been cheerier when we'd arrived after a talk with Michael, who'd told him more or less what I had. He was waiting he said for the next instalment. Taking a chance when we were out of sight in the school's little kitchen I'd kissed him. It was brief but passionate and I hadn't minded the thrill of it being clandestine either.

'Hey,' said Lekisha. 'Come over here and help me if you can't dig.'

I was pleased to put the heavy crow bar down. A lovely purple light was bringing the dusk on, creating an illusion everything was soft. Lekisha made it look easy, but there was nothing easy about digging this hard ground or splitting the roots the tyape lived in. We worked quietly. Noise would send the tyape away.

'Scoop the dirt,' she said. Repetitively she banged the crowbar in to loosen the soil as I scooped the earth away.

We got four grubs in one tree. In the next we got three in one root and two in another. My arms were tired from scooping but Lekisha needed to get some more because she'd have to share. We got lucky and found six in the next tree.

The country had been generous to her, which put her in a good mood because it was widely understood country gave only to those who were respectful. On the way back, Lekisha, by far the better night driver, drove as dark was falling quickly, singing one of the country music songs she was so fond of. I minded the pieces of root which had the grubs in them. I didn't want one to crawl out and be lost. They were totally delicious and I hoped I'd get one at least. They tasted a bit like almond paste to me, though some people said they tasted like egg and I liked them cooked on coals, not raw.

'Hey,' I said, 'I never heard of that animal you named the team for. I can hardly say it. What is it, it's not a cat, is it?'

'You're right. Of course there's nothing like a cat around here. I was just sick of all the arguing. I wanted to get tyape.'

'So what does the word actually mean?'

'It's for that little hopping mouse only the old people seen. Caleb and Jeanie they got to learn. Our language and culture is going to disappear if everyone gets as lazy as those two. Animals they don't know. Words they don't know. Whole dictionaries!'

It was a worry. And there was the immediate worry about the arguing about the name, which would start again.

'Just tell everyone,' said Lekisha, 'We call the team Cats. Plain and simple. Even you can say it,' she said with a cheeky dig at me.

The local organisers made sure we were in the draw and kindly allocated us a bye. It was what I'd call a good outcome. We'd missed the start of the season but technically only two games.

Caleb volunteered to pick up the jumpers when they were ready. It was the first time he'd gone to town for a while and I was worried he'd find trouble, but he came back on time, as fresh as the new uniforms. The word CATS looked good in square black lettering on the back of the jerseys. Most of the kids had such slight frames that a longer name wouldn't have fit. I liked it, a feral animal name. And the joke was that it would be the town kids who went feral when they started to get knocked over by our deadly team, week after week. That was the dream, anyhow.

In my class, where the boys outnumbered girls three to one, the behavioural issues we'd been having were much tempered by the forming of the team. We told them no school, no play, so their attendance was perfect from then on. Once we had the uniforms dangling like prizes on coathangers in the room, their behaviour became so good I longed for a department boss to come and see the miracle of order I presided over, which even I knew would only be temporary. Preston had turned from ratbag into a leader.

I rang Patrick to find out if it was just our special miracle. It wasn't. According to him things were totally sweet there too. And he was looking forward to seeing me. Soon.

'You seem well,' Mum said when I popped in on the weekend. 'Hard work clearly suits you.'

'And you look better too. I think you've finally found your forte.'

'Lounging and bossing,' said Michael boldly. 'I've suspected a latent talent for some time.' We laughed together and Mum threw a cushion at us from her cane lounge.

'We've got our little football team in the competition,' I said proudly. 'We start next week.'

'Well done you,' Michael said.

'There's a lot to do.'

'Always,' Mum said.

I got up and pulled on a pair of gardening gloves, then followed Michael around his garden doing what I was told. I hauled manure, I layered straw, I shovelled sand. I halved the artichoke plants and picked the last of the small egg aubergines.

'What do you think's going to happen now they've released some of those findings?'

'Unlikely sort of question from you?' he said, as he pushed his hat back a bit to look at me. 'What's the interest?'

'Nothing much.' I hoped this was one of those times he couldn't read my expression.

'Well, I'm not sure. There's a lot of noises coming from Canberra, but I'm not confident I know enough to even comment. It would be good if Floyd was around. I'm sure he would have a better idea. I suspect we'll be the last to know. But there is a big shake-up rumoured.'

'What do you think, Mum?' I asked, interrupting her reading. Another crime novel, I noticed, by the same author of my book which she'd never given me back.

'I think I don't want to talk about it.'

The subject was closed. Michael and I put the last of the autumn vegetables we'd harvested in a small box.

'You can take these. I don't suppose you growing anything out there yet?'

'You've got to be kidding. Sometimes I'm not sure we'll get enough water out of the bores for basic amenities. I don't know how Patrick does it.'

'So you've been there?'

I nodded and he gave me a very neutral look. I had no idea what he might know, if anything, from Patrick but it seemed a good idea not to volunteer any information and I kept the topic to water.

'We're in the queue for a water assessment. We're also chasing the contracts on the ground works for the school. If we get any-thing done in the landscaping we could put a school garden in. But since the school started up more people have been drifting back into the community and we use a ton more water. Quite a lot of family have come down.'

'They must have heard how good the school is going,' Mum said.

'Sure,' I said facetiously, 'they moved for school.'

'They might have.'

'Maybe it's just the chance to coach football. The men are suddenly all champions! There's a few very senior fellows camped there. I'm not sure why they've stayed so long. Usually movement's north this time of year but I'd be the last to know if it's anything more than a catch-up with family.'

'I remember. It was a lifetime of not knowing,' she said.

There was something self-pitying in her tone which surprised me. I'd always thought Mum was a hundred and ten per cent sure of why she was here and what her role was. She never seemed to be out of the loop either.

Michael must have thought the same thing as he put his arm around her and said, 'Come on, love, you're sounding like one of the revisionists now: "Self-determination was a mistake. We were wrong. Should have kept the missions." All that rubbishing talk.'

Mum leant into him, her red hair drifting out of its clasp. 'Steady on. I was just saying you don't always get told everything. I think you're getting carried away.'

'I'm just pointing out it's two ways, the lack of understanding. No matter how you look at things it's always going to be that way. The trick is respect.'

Respect. His favourite word. A good one.

I was about to leave when Mrs Press came over to see if Michael had a bike pump. One of the grannies had a tyre that needed pumping up.

'I saw Magdalene the other day. Up town,' she said, while Michael searched the likely drawers for one. 'She said you were going to Iltja.'

'Yeah. I did hear that from Lekisha. She hasn't mentioned it to me.'

Mum gave Michael a look that said, You see I was right.

'I'm sure she will,' said Mrs Press. 'She wants the biggest mob to go.'

She took the pump Michael offered. 'Thanks,' she said as she left.

'You never mentioned a bush trip to Iltja,' Mum said, as if I should have.

'Like I just told Gloria, Lekisha mentioned it to me once and it's entirely dropped off the radar. You ask her if you want to know. My plan is to say nothing, keep working and keep just on top of it.'

'Are you right?'

'Yes, I'm tired. And you know things are often a bit tricky,' I said. I was thinking of Patrick, really, not the school. 'So don't give me a hard time.'

'I wasn't.'

'Mum!'

She put her arms out and I hugged her. Michael put the veggies on the back seat. I was no wiser about what might politically unfold and affect Patrick, which I'd been hoping to get some clarity on. I wanted Patrick to get what he wanted with his court action, in fact I needed him to succeed because it didn't take much perception to see my own aspirations for our relationship were linked to the outcome.

*

I pulled in just before dark to find Lekisha waiting at my little house. 'What do you reckon we get Caleb a job in the school?' she asked, rolling my artichokes back and forth across the table.

I frowned. 'Don't wreck them.'

'I don't know why you like them. Just a big prickle.' She kept playing with them, so I took them off her.

'You can talk, some of the stuff you eat, like sweet bread.'

They were sheep glands, absolutely disgusting. But Lekisha just licked her lips at my insult.

'Milk gut,' I said. Tripe. Revolting.

'You got some of my favourites from the butcher then?'

I made a face at her that told her no way.

She took an apple out of the box and fixed me with a serious look. Joking was done with.

'Caleb's got to stay at Promised Land, not go to town anymore. And he's good with the kids. With the football.'

I could see where this was coming from. Caleb was good at the moment but if I was his mother I'd be worrying too about his aimlessness and lack of purpose other than when it came to the football team. She knew it wouldn't take much for him to go back to the drinking world Maxine had lost herself in. I too could see it was getting harder and harder for young men like Caleb to feel as if their role in a community had much value. There was lots of pressure from radio, TV, movies, newspapers, just plain old talk that they were being short-changed staying out bush. The message was clear. Whitefella places were where status and success were to be found. It was quite a change from my teenage days when the outstation movement was strong and men felt it was their role to lead families back to country. Now if you encouraged people to stay out bush there was an implication you were ripping people off. Denying them a suburban dreaming: a house, car, job. Certainly very little infrastructure ever went into remote settlements.

Lekisha took up fiddling with the salt shaker. I had a feeling she might have a proposal for countering his aimlessness.

'He needs a job at the school.'

'A job with us?'

'Only place there's work.'

'Right.' That was certainly true, unless the contract for landscaping ever came through.

'Caleb,' she said firmly, 'he's clever. A proper man.' She was telling me he wasn't just initiated but had proved himself exceptionally capable. 'Ask Henry,' she said, knowing full well it was a cultural impossibility.

'I don't need to ask Henry. I'll think about it. There might be a way to employ him, at least a bit.'

I didn't want to promise anything, but I'd never seen Lekisha so obvious about how much something meant to her. She was a good poker player usually. I wanted to help if I could. And if he could stay off the grog it would be good for everyone, especially his daughter. I could already think of some funding possibilities. The school was owed a cleaner and possibly some individual support assistance for kids like Sammy, who had problems with his hearing. I'd talk to someone in the office and see if I could get some help.

'He got his school certificate, from St Luke's,' Lekisha added.

I knew he'd only finished year ten but that was probably high enough.

'I'll do my best,' I said. I tried not to sound hopeful but Lekisha's face brightened, as if a deal had been struck. I heard her humming as she left. For all our sakes I hoped it worked out.

It turned out it wasn't as hard as I thought it might have been to employ Caleb. I found a sympathetic special education teacher who collected the assessments that had been done at other schools on some of our kids. It turned out three others had issues which qualified for learning support. Little Mary, who I had been wondering about, had foetal alcohol syndrome, which explained a lot about her inability to learn much. It was actually a useful exercise finding out this information which I hadn't known about, and there was certainly enough evidence for Caleb to be employed on a part-time basis. By the Thursday I had him signed on as a tutor and cleaner. He brought a new energy to the school, a masculine roughness. Even his nervous swagger into the room gave the day a new edge, for the kids, for us.

Lekisha couldn't boss her son and I couldn't step in over her either. These factors made supervision a little tricky, so after the first day I called a meeting with Henry and Magdalene to establish them as the bosses and to work out a policy. I provided biscuits and cake to make the meeting more attractive and I put myself in charge of scribing the minutes on a whiteboard.

'Because we all know each other, we got to be clear on what our roles are,' I began. 'So the kids get the best education.'

Caleb nodded agreeably. 'So Promised Land is the best school?'

'Yes.'

'Better than Red Bore, Kilka?'

'Yeah.' I was impressed with his competitive spirit.

'We got to be the best,' Lekisha said, not wanting to be left out of talking ourselves up. Promised Land mob resented how long they'd waited for their own school. Now it was up and running there was a point to be proved.

'Don't worry about that other mob,' Magdalene said, steady as usual. 'We got to worry about here. Caleb, you got to do what Alicia tells you. She'll teach you the right way to do things.'

'At school,' Henry said.

'At school,' Lekisha reiterated.

I took the lead and wrote our job titles on the board with our names next to them. While my back was turned, Henry and Magdalene decided their presence was no longer required and left. I shrugged. Hopefully the point had been made: school had its own laws.

'We've got to write down what each person should do,' I said. 'So we don't make one person's job too much, or give them all the boring jobs. Like sharpening pencils.'

'I can sharpen pencils. If I can use the electric one,' Caleb offered enthusiastically. The electric sharpener was only to be used by adults, because the kids would happily spend all day sharpening and our allocated pencil stock would be nothing but shavings in no time.

'Of course you can use it,' I said. 'You're staff. But I think with the jobs like that, the ones that can get a bit boring, we should swap them around.'

Lekisha gave me one of her 'you make me tired' looks. No doubt she thought I was being too bossy and over-organised but

I wasn't going to be put off. It was better for me to risk irritating her now than allow a situation where Lekisha and Caleb got jack of the tedious jobs in the classroom and left me to pick up the lot.

'You give me a headache,' Lekisha complained as we stacked up the chairs.

I smiled. I knew this was most likely to be my only victorious moment. Getting everyone to follow the guidelines we'd set up would be a headache for sure, and I was certain it wouldn't be Lekisha's. While I didn't mind being expected to do the bulk of the work as I got paid well to take the responsibility, the school had to rely on more than me if it was to survive after I was gone.

That evening as we headed across the raked bare earth to our homes, a flock of the red-tailed black cockatoos this land had been named for lifted off from the far gumtree. Their tailfeathers fanned out in flight, revealing their bright red stripe. They were absolutely beautiful and I wished I could look for some but only men could collect them. Stirred to wanting some decoration, I picked some grass and shrub leaves from nearby.

The foliage at least brought colour to my place.

I settled on my bed and re-read the fax from Patrick I'd managed to hide from Lekisha. I didn't really have to think about it. My answer was yes.

CHAPTER 23

On Saturday there was a crush of people into every available car to get to our first football game.

We weren't far down the narrow dirt road when the cops from Red Bore unexpectedly appeared from the opposite direction. Constable Brett was at the wheel. Paranoid, I wondered if Caleb, who was driving the school car, really did have a licence as he claimed. Constable Brett had been out at Red Bore two years and was respected, but in the passenger seat was another cop who I'd never seen before. We drew level awkwardly on the narrow track, tipping into each other on the slope with our outer wheels resting up the steep graded edges. There were more people than belts, which wasn't exactly illegal unless the cops deemed it unsafe, according to Patrick, who had just given me this handy bit of information on the phone when I'd been freaking out about transport. Lekisha, more practised in dealing with police attention, calmly looked straight ahead.

Constable Brett's offsider looked studiously in the opposite direction while he gave us a good look over.

'Fab uniforms,' he said to the boys. 'And go the mighty Cats!' he said, as he gave us a thumbs-up and drove off around us, tooting.

Everyone was at the oval. Mum, Michael, the Presses, Lucy and Frank had all turned up. Not Iry. She hated sport. Not even for me, her god-daughter, would she turn up. It was great to see the amount of support we did have and you might have thought we were top of the AFL league, not playing our first game in a boys' comp.

Patrick turned up late. He'd been sent to the town camp to get some boys at Caleb's instruction. The boys he drove in circles looking for, chasing every flakey lead he was given, had in the meantime made it to the grounds themselves on foot. By the time he arrived all our little camps were made and he sat down with the blokes, which suited me fine. Mum would spot in minutes we were together, and while Michael might suspect, I knew I could rely on his habit of prudent discretion to not look to have the matter either confirmed or denied.

The boys played well, and we never lost the lead from the third quarter. We hardly had to use our town boys at all but Caleb, with a good sense of keeping them on side, made sure everyone got a turn.

At the final siren, Lekisha hugged me and lifted me off the ground. 'Champions!' You would have thought we'd won the flag.

The score was 65 to 46. It was a dream start to our season.

Preston came running off the pitch and high-fived me exuberantly then grabbed me around the neck as if he might kiss me, before stepping away, embarrassed.

'We did good,' he said, trying to look cool and poised.

'You sure did, you did brilliant,' I said, surveying all of the shining faces lit up with the thrill of winning. They were so vibrant, so alive and I couldn't ignore the power the game gave the kids, their families and supporters.

'See,' I said, provocatively to Mum, 'football is more than a game.'

'I never said it wasn't.'

'Oh, you used to sneer about sport when I was young.'

'Did I? Are you sure you're not thinking of Iry?'

'No, you too. You said it limited what people expected of Aboriginal people. That people didn't mind them being sporty as long as they knew their place.'

'I said that?'

'Something like that.'

'I'm not sure I'm going to rely on your memory, Alicia.'

'Don't then,' I said, amused by her stubbornness. I gave a thumbs-up to the Kilka boys as they passed in an excited bunch.

'We always came to the games. We were Magpies fans. I don't believe we ever missed a game Tommy jnr played,' Mum went on defensively.

'You're right, we didn't,' I said. I didn't want a fight.

'But if you mean that it annoys me when people are shocked when a kid from up here gets into medicine but not that he gets picked in the AFL draft, then yes, you're right.'

I was pleased to see Mum's old self-righteousness returned.

Lucy made sure she had my attention before she looked over at Patrick then back at me and winked. I made a sour face to discourage her, relieved that if she had been spreading the word at least everyone else was more discreet. Unperturbed she blew me a kiss and then hurried off to catch up to Frank. Over at the car park Patrick was looking a bit harassed, sorting out kids and cars. It would be no easy job and he was going to be tied up for a while. I felt a bit smug. I'd given Lekisha the troopy and she had responsibility for the kids who weren't with parents, so I was already well free of work responsibility.

The cold grass was getting to Mum and I helped her up. We wandered over to meet Michael, who was coming back from the canteen carrying a big box of takeaway. A mob of kids jumped up and down around him, like pesky pups. It was funny watching him try to control handing out the food fairly and in the end he had to concede defeat. He handed the box to Lekisha, who took the only sensible course of action. She grabbed a pie, put the box down and let the kids sort it out themselves.

I walked to the hotel thinking about how it had been a very long time since I'd been to one to stay. Floyd hated them. They reminded him of work. When we holidayed it was always to friends' shacks or to Eddy's weekender. Or camping down the coast. In fact I couldn't think of one time I'd ever slept with him in a hotel.

I liked this. The idea of doing something new with a new person. With Patrick.

CHAPTER 24

On Monday I stood on the schoolroom steps with Lekisha as Caleb organised the kids into lines. Since the weekend, football was all the kids were talking about. But the adults had clearly found other topics to discuss; even Treasure gave me a cheeky look when she came over with the grandkids. Foolishly I thought I'd been very discreet. I'd borrowed Mum's car to come back rather than have Patrick drop me off, and as far as I knew no one saw us together but I'd been wrong. Lekisha obviously thought we'd come out as a couple and I was now fair game.

'So it was good?' she asked as the kids filed in and took their place on the mat.

'What?'

'He's good?' She made a none-too-subtle gesture with her hips.

'Get out of here,' I said, swatting her one, trying not to smile.

'No hitting,' Preston said, pointing to the class rules next to the board.

'I didn't hit her,' I said.

'I didn't hit Sammy when you did keep me in.'

'What happens for hitting?' Caleb asked the children, a big grin on his face. A chorus of voices shouted out, 'No play, one day.' Caleb wrote my name in the time-out section of the board.

'And say sorry, and shake hands,' Sammy called out.

I shook Lekisha's hand. 'Sorry,' I said, finding it all as funny as she did. She was laughing so hard she had to clamp her hands to her mouth and dash for the door. On the listening mat the kids waited with their legs and arms crossed for me to start reading. There was an unusual quiet. They might have been wondering if the shaking of my hands didn't mean I was crying because when they got teased they all cried. Even the big kids.

'I'm right,' I said, recovering my composure. 'Let's get on with some learning.'

The weeks soon fell into a pattern: work, football and Patrick. Work was the hardest by far. Football went up and down. We discovered we could be losers as easily as winners. Being champions was no sure thing and the kids would have to work hard at it. Being with Patrick was getting easier all the time, especially once the teasing began to die down. Mum said only one thing to me about the relationship. As long as you're happy. It was her stock standard response for anything I did she wasn't completely in favour of and I chose not to explore what her reservations might be.

I used getting photographs for Patrick as an excuse to venture further and further away from the community until Magdalene pulled me up. She didn't like me going places alone. When I told her what I was doing she dropped her hard-line stand to ban me. Instead she decided she'd show me where to go. When I told Patrick about this interaction he was not impressed I'd tried to look on my own.

'I just assumed you'd know to go with someone. She's not too offended is she?'

'No, she just thinks I'm a bit stupid. Nothing new.'

Patrick was relieved I hadn't created any issues for his work. The book, it had become obvious, was his special project. It was the thing that he used to justify sticking it out at Kilka, not moving and making life easier for himself with his ex. The book, in acknowledging Aboriginal people's knowledge as important, implicitly implied his life, his time recording this information, also mattered.

It was good going out with Magdalene. She took me places and pointed out what grew where. Sometimes she'd give me permission to go back again. Not always, and she rarely chose to share her reasoning with me.

I enjoyed my trips with her and those I took alone. They were different but both forced me to look closely at the land. Slowly my eyes adjusted to see more than the dry surface, the smudging of colours in the scrub. There was still plenty of life if you looked closely. There were seeds and straggly ground cover just waiting for the right conditions to leap up and grow. It made me wonder about other things. Patrick and I rarely talked about what was happening with his court case. It wasn't something I wanted to press him about, but when it was over I hoped we might talk about a future, one he'd hopefully be prepared to bring new kids into. Lucy might have thought I had another ten years before I had to panic. But it was easy for her to say. She'd never wanted a baby herself. Frank indiscreetly shared this information with me when I asked if he knew why she'd split up with Annie. Apparently Annie, who was older than me and did want a family, had given Lucy an ultimatum and lost. I found it intriguing I didn't know this about Lucy and though it meant I had to confess to gossiping about her, I asked her if it was true. Apparently it was. She was candid about her reasons. 'I'm with Floyd, on the subject of babies. I don't have the gene to be a parent. I'm selfish and self focused. I like order and I like holidays. I've never even looked after a pet.'

I was glad she'd waited till now to share this. I'm not sure I could have coped knowing how closely she lined up with Floyd before this.

Seven weeks into term, I had to run into town to replace the order book. We couldn't function without one. Lekisha was not worried as I'd expected but thrilled to be left in charge when I told her I'd have a town day. Her obvious pleasure at getting rid of me was a bit of a revelation. It gave me a rather a swift reminder that part of mentoring was about letting go.

I left so early I had time to call in at Mum's for breakfast. She was in the kitchen stirring a vegetable dish on the cook top, dressed in her old Japanese kimono.

'Hey,' I said, kissing her. 'You should get that winter one of yours on. It's a bit cool now.'

'I'm right.'

'What's going on anyway?' I joked. 'What if Michael comes back and catches you wrecking his pots?'

I put on the kettle to make us tea.

'He'll say, I'm looking after myself at last.'

'Well, you seem to be.'

'Poached eggs?'

'Lovely.'

Within minutes she had our eggs ready.

'You know I never realised cooking could be relaxing. When Michael said it helps him unwind I always thought it was just a line, a way of letting me off the hook. But this way I know I'm eating all the right things. And I find it quite contemplative.'

'Contemplative, that's not you.'

Her blue eyes bored into mine. 'Is it that hard to understand? Have I been that manic?'

'Pretty much. Except when you were ill. In fact, I don't think I can remember ever having breakfast with you as a kid.'

'Really?'

'Really. Michael was here sometimes, but not you. You were always gone.'

'There was a lot to do.'

'Yeah. There still is.'

'I'm not sure it was all that helpful making lists of things that needed achieving, developing policy, sending people out. A continuous stream of energy that was chewed up and spat out. The help required out there is endless.'

'Come on. Some things have got better.'

Mum's bony shoulders rose and fell in a shrug of resignation. 'I should have spent more time with you.'

'Mum, you did. It just wasn't here. It was out bush. I loved it.'

'But it wasn't ever about you and me. It was always work. I made you muck in too hard. How many swags do you reckon I had you roll, how many cups of teas have you made for old ladies?'

'It wasn't Alcatraz. And you were kind to me. Remember how you let me have the front seat to myself when I was asleep? And sometimes if we were leaving early I'd pretend to be asleep and you'd go along with it so I didn't have to squash up in the back of the troopy with everyone else. And if someone spotted porcupine you'd never stop because I loved my kere but I couldn't bear seeing porcupines killed because they cry tears, just like us.'

'Did I?'

'Yes you did. Even if people got cranky with you. You put me first.'

Mum's face was long with grief. I couldn't understand it. The last few times, admittedly only at the footy, she'd seemed her old self.

'Mum, I had a fine time growing up with Michael and you,' I said, nursing my tea and waiting with little enthusiasm for what dark thing she would say next.

'I don't know, Alicia. Maybe I've got too much time on my hands. I do find myself thinking about the past more than might be healthy. I think of all that time, all that effort. Stupidly putting you second to work. And what's changed?'

'I didn't feel like you ignored me.'

'You did. When you left I remember you said, "Mum, you won't even notice I'm gone, you never even know if I'm here."'

'I was sixteen. I was a teenager. You say whatever gets you the most advantage.'

'You had a point.'

She lay her head on the table. I stroked her soft hair. Freshly hennaed it was deep red. Perhaps her liver wasn't going as well as I'd thought it was. Poor function made for depression—that was the standout fact I'd memorised from the reams of information I'd read.

'Get better so you can go back to work,' I said. 'Clearly the job's not done.'

'No way. I think I'm over the helping professions,' she said lifting her gaze.

'Study then. Do a doctorate.'

'What, become an expert in some aspect of Indigenous health practice? I'd rather eat my own arm.'

'All right, do that,' I said, sighing, putting my plate in the sink. 'Or if that's not to your taste go away somewhere and do a cooking course.'

Mum managed a polite smile and I kissed the top of her head.

'You always said, "Be kind to yourself,"' I reminded her. 'Now you need to practise what you preached. I've got to go.'

Running around town getting what I needed I was far too busy to think about Mum until I was on the drive home. I found her regret painful to witness. It was one thing to regret her personal journey, the child she never had. It was something else to find her regretting her life's work, to suggest that the lifestyle she'd insisted on living might have been the wrong one. That I'd been right to leave, to abandon her at what she'd always said was the face of contact history, the one place where colonisation had not neatly run its wheels of change over people. And if she thought her lifetime's work had contributed nothing, it made me doubt I could make an ounce of difference in a few months in a little bush school.

For now there was nothing I could do except try to forget the conversation. I turned on the radio. It was on the news. The report the government had been holding on to was now out. The contents were absolutely appalling. According to the breathless reporter it contained things which all decent Australians should hang their heads in shame for ignoring.

As soon as I got back I rang Patrick. He was distracted as I'd thought he would be but not overwhelmed like I'd feared. He'd had some lead time since the first part of the report was released and had been busy getting his own case together so wasn't so freaked out. He'd spoken to his lawyer, who was fairly circumspect. The report was just more of the same. Sure it was getting more noise, but essentially it just expanded on what the report had hinted at. Linda had already mounted a case assuming the report would back her and the only change was that this was now confirmed. The report said abuse was rife and current services were failing kids especially, but essentially everyone on community. From Patrick's side, the report, damning as it was, was not a development. I was glad to hear him so calm.

'No need to freak out twice,' he said. 'It's done now and I have managed to get a good barrister for the court. Hopefully the hearing date, when it's set, suits. He's one of the best according to my lawyer and I hope so. He earns an hour my daily rate! The keep breathing thing is not bad advice,' he said. 'So thanks.'

I laughed. That car sticker of Mum's had come in handy plenty of times before as gratuitous advice.

The last weeks of term we were all trying to be courageous. To be better human beings. I knew there was a storm about the report. But it howled and raged in Canberra, in places of power and we could easily ignore it. And not having telly or ever buying the paper, except the local one for the lawn sale ads, made it easier.

Gently I let go of the class a bit more. Lekisha stepped up and started to take three sessions a week alone and I'd go home. The space helped her find her feet. It also let her fall over without me there to watch. Each Wednesday there was football training and every second week I'd see Patrick when he brought the boys over for training. Sometimes we managed to see each other in between.

Winter now had a firmer grip on us. It was bitterly dry and the days warmed up late. The kids didn't seem to notice the cold at night and kept up playing outside in shorts, often without jumpers. A few got bad chests. Kane was admitted to hospital with pneumonia. In the second-last week of term I drove in and out of town in an exhausted fashion, rotating family members to stay with him.

The week before the Cats' last game of the term, Caleb came down with the flu. I assumed Henry would take the boys to Kilka for training on the Wednesday, but he was nowhere to be found. I considered cancelling but I couldn't bear to think of the boys' disappointment. They were waiting patiently, blowing on their hands to keep warm, huddled next to the classroom. Taking pity on them, I volunteered to go.

When I arrived I was irritated to find that Henry was already there, talking to Patrick in the cabin of the Kilka school Toyota.

Slamming my car door I went up to Henry's window. 'What're you doing here?' I asked.

'I come to train the team. It's the Kilka week. Last one.'

I knew all that. What I couldn't understand was why he thought there was nothing odd about going there alone instead of taking the boys. 'You going to coach then or just sit here?' I snapped, stepping away.

He mumbled something I didn't catch and nimbly alighted from the car, clearly keen to get away from my bad temper. I watched him call the boys into a starting running drill. I was still seething at the casual way he'd wasted my time without so much as an explanation.

'What's with you? Don't you want to see me?' Patrick said, kissing my neck indiscreetly.

'I'm fucking busy,' I said. 'Reports, acquittals, you name it, and I'm behind. I don't have time to be here and it's frustrating that I can't get openly cranky with anyone.'

Patrick smiled. 'I don't think you hid your mood that well.'

'Didn't I? Oh.'

'You shamed him talking rough. I don't think he'll hold onto it for long, though. He's used to cranky whitefellas. And you especially.'

'Gee, thanks.' I punched him on the arm.

'Exactly what I meant,' he said, laughing.

For the rest of the training session I sat in the car and wrote reports. I didn't feel comfortable about going to Patrick's place with him while Henry trained the boys—it didn't seem like a good look, though I would have liked to. At the end of the session Patrick returned and I was glad to see him. I got out to see what he was unloading that all the kids were so excited about and discovered it was hot chocolate and warm bread.

'You already win the all-round good bloke award and I might add the amazing gardener and language speaker awards,' I said. 'Just how many points do you want?'

'How many do I need to get for you to stay tonight? You're already here.'

'Get out of it,' I said. 'No chance! I'm going for the teaching award and going home.'

He grinned and I pinched his bum as he turned to go.

Henry drove me and the boys back to Promised Land in the school troopy. How he'd got to Kilka in the first place remained one of the many mysteries my life in the community was full of. It was amazing what I didn't know, and yet they all seemed to effortlessly keep track of my movements.

I sat in the back and half listened to the boys' chatter. I still had no idea what they were saying most of the time but the language was coming back into my head. Little word by little word. Amazingly, I thought as I looked around at the boys, we'd made it through one term. Their attendance was good. I'd have to work on the girls, perhaps speak to Treasure since it was mostly her grand-kids who were skipping. But when I took everything into account we were all doing well. Lekisha's study was up to date, Caleb was working consistently and once I got through the reporting I'd have four weeks off. Patrick hadn't mentioned the case the last few times we met and it was a subject I'd learnt not to ask about. I was hoping he would let me meet his son in the holidays. We could stay at my flat in Sydney, which I really should do something about. Eddy had offered to find someone to sub lease it and I should get back to him about it, though perhaps put off finding a tenant till the end of the holidays. I wouldn't mind a bit of winter rain or seeing the sea again. I'd love some time with Patrick away from here. It would be a bit of a test. Some bush affairs never translated into anything except disappointment elsewhere once you discovered how different you were in another setting. I wound my window down. It wasn't good to get ahead of the game. One step at a time, I told myself, would do.

CHAPTER 25

It was the last day of term and we were in the schoolroom, ostensibly finishing reports. Henry was there too. We were all trying to ignore Caleb's hacking post-flu cough as we endeavoured to work out how to get everyone to the last game on the first day of the holidays. Henry's car had broken down and he was hoping to borrow one from Red Bore or see if a spare could be rustled up from Kilka. We'd left messages for Annie and Patrick and were waiting around to see what they had to say. When the phone rang I expected it to be one of them.

Henry answered it, then quickly handed it to me, looking worried. 'Ros,' he said. Mum was frantic. At first I couldn't understand a word she said.

'Slow down,' I said. 'What's wrong?'

'Have you heard the news?'

'What news?'

'The government's just announced an intervention into the Aboriginal communities of the Northern Territory. They're suspending the Racial Discrimination Act.'

'What do you mean, an intervention?' I asked. Around me, Caleb, Henry and Lekisha were sitting quietly, listening.

'They're sending in the army,' Mum said.

'The army? What for?' I felt as though the bottom of my stomach had dropped away.

'I don't know, to save people.'

'Mum, you're not making much sense.' I was starting to wonder if her depression had got worse. Perhaps it was interfering with her sense of reality.

'It's in response to the full report. You know the one,' she said. 'It's the federal minister. He thinks he can single-handedly save every community from itself, rescue every kid.'

'From who?'

'From danger. Pedophiles, neglect.'

'With the army?'

'With the army. Go and listen to the radio.'

'Is there a war coming?' Lekisha asked. Her grandfathers still told stories about watching for the Japanese.

'Not quite,' I said, perhaps too quickly.

Their faces were grave as they studied me for clues. 'What is it? Tell us what happened,' said Lekisha.

'Mum says the government is bringing in a whole lot of people, including the army, to fix things.'

'Fix what things?' Henry asked. He knew it wouldn't be his broken car, that was for sure.

'What?' Lekisha demanded, scared and angry. 'Fix what?'

I didn't know how to say the words. Pedophilia, sexual abuse, violence, neglect. It was better they heard it from the horse's mouth. 'What's the time? It will be on the news.'

'What about the car?' Henry asked.

'If you want to you can wait here in case Annie or Patrick ring back.' The car didn't seem so important to me right now, but I knew I had to stop myself marshalling people, acting like a big boss. The car business, the football, it all mattered to Henry and Caleb. It mattered to me.

'Let us know how you go,' I said as Lekisha and I left.

We listened to the news but it wasn't much help. I missed Floyd's insider position. He'd have known all the details and could have explained what was happening as Lekisha asked so many questions I couldn't answer. In the end she went home feeling bad. I gave her a packet of Tim Tams to take home to the kids. It felt like a pathetic gesture of support.

I went back to the school and called Patrick. It took ages before the line wasn't busy and I made lists of things I needed to do in the break to keep my mind off things.

I hardly got a hello when I got through. He was straight onto his custody case.

'I'm totally fucked now,' he said. 'I'll never win. Not a fucking day visit pass.'

'You don't know that,' I said.

'I feel so powerless.'

'Well imagine how the community feels. All the families.'

'Hey,' he said. 'I don't think I'm in the mood for a lecture on empathy.'

Mum had a line: words fan fire. I bit my lip.

We drove into the footy grimly in the morning. Technically it was the first day of the holidays but it didn't look like we'd be having one. Patrick was nowhere to be seen at the grounds. He was the only person missing. It seemed everyone from East camp and all the relations from everywhere had come to the grounds. There were so many town families and their kids we could have run two or three teams. All anyone was talking about was the intervention, trying to sort out what it might mean. I was pleased to see Mum had stayed away. I didn't think I could cope with her dramatics at the moment. Michael was there. He wandered around in his calm pre-sentencing mode, encouraging people to wait and see. It might not be that bad was his message.

Annie told Lekisha and me to forget about having a holiday, reminding us that the four-week break was technically not leave, but simply a stand-down from teaching. An emergency staff meeting was scheduled for the Monday and we were to front at Red Bore.

On the way home from town we talked about the game and little else. We'd won. It was the only good thing that had happened in days. So we milked it for happiness.

I expected to see him at the meeting. But Patrick didn't show there either and he hadn't answered one text I'd sent him. He hadn't answered his home phone so I wasn't sure where he was. I rang him again from Red Bore before I left because it would be easier for me to drive straight to Kilka from there and I was sure I could work something out with Lekisha about the car.

When Patrick answered his phone I felt a rush of pleasure. He sounded okay. But he didn't want me to come. He was going to Sydney the next day and had lots to do. When he could, he'd call me. I felt like I hadn't since I'd first left Floyd. Sad and miserable.

'You right,' said Annie coming back into the office.

I burst into tears.

'It's terrible. It's a bloody mess all right,' she said, 'but things will be okay in the end. They'll calm down.'

She assumed I was crying about the intervention. It made me sob more. Patrick and me. What a pair. Thinking about ourselves in all of this.

It was a crazy week. Gossip and rumours were flying, dangerous as shrapnel.

The legislation was going through at a cracking pace.

Iry was on the news, broadcast after broadcast, stating that the intervention was well overdue. The government had been neglectful in the extreme. Kids were dying, women were being mistreated. Sniffing, drinking and gunja abuse was rampant. Disfunction and anarchy reigned. Her voice was full of barely restrained hysteria. I didn't think she was lying and I did agree people needed extra support. All the health and education statistics proved it. But I felt it wasn't doing much good to tar everyone with the same dirty brush when it seemed to me most of the problems were symptoms of poverty and disempowerment. I wasn't the political animal my mother was but it all smelled a bit off to me.

Operation Outreach was rolled out with alarming haste. Army personnel were due to arrive almost immediately. The Territory was about to be full of outsiders.

'Don't be the conduit,' Annie, advised us. 'It's not our job. Stay as positive as you can—people are very scared.' Things were going to be worse at Red Bore. It was a big community and would be one of the first targeted. We were just outposts. Days after the legislation went through a frontline medical team arrived at Red Bore tasked with assessing all the kids for evidence of abuse. Six families fled into the back country, worried their kids were about to be stolen.

Annie rang the day after the army teams arrival. She was raw with rage, furious at the rude and high-handed approach. The medical team had turned up at the school and, without asking permission, copied the rolls to match against the clinic records. Health workers had been coerced into assisting intervention staff to bring kids into the clinic for examination.

'If they're serious about abuse it's a pretty fucking abusive way of going about correcting things,' Annie raved. 'Maybe instead they should be building more houses so little kids aren't sharing space with adults so closely.'

It wasn't the time to remind her of her speech about being positive. Once she started there was no stopping her. I had to half listen to her for hours while I worked out what materials I would order for the next term. Assuming we'd have one.

A day or two later, after Annie's outburst, Lekisha arrived at the school when I was trying to work and demanded I get my camera and come with her. We drove up the highway where the new signs announcing the new blanket restrictions on Aboriginal land were going up. Michael had already told me they were absolutely huge. They were costed at over ten thousand dollars each. The waste of money was enough to make a person cry. If I just did the sums in our area it was about two hundred thousand dollars and it was intended every prescribed community would have one.

When we hit the southern boundary of Red Bore I could understand why she was so mad. The sign was police blue. Clearly it had been created by a graphic designer going for the graffiti look. The symbol was clear enough. A bottle with a cross through it. A ban on all pornography.

The sign was so large that it took me a while to frame the photograph. Lekisha, mistaking my lack of skill for hesitation, was not impressed. 'Take it,' she demanded. I snapped a few of the sign and a couple of her angry face.

'Why do you want a picture of it?' I asked, as I showed them to her on the little screen. It was so offensive. So rude and unnecessary.

'Record,' she said. 'Show the kids. Keep it for Rosia and the little ones so they can see what was done. Aboriginal history.'

I let my breath out slowly. There was nothing I could say in comfort.

At Promised Land boundary we passed the holes they'd dug for our sign. Any day now, we'd be labelled drunk pornography-loving deviants, along with everyone else living on Aboriginal lands.

The trip Magdalene had wanted us to take to Iltja was never mentioned. If it had been on her radar as Mrs Press had recently mentioned, then it was no longer.

Spooked by the intervention, people seemed to want to stay as close to home as possible. I missed Patrick. I wanted company and comfort and, while he spoke to me on the phone, he was hardly in any mood to be much company. Linda had managed to get a delay on the court date and he was now in Sydney with no hearing and little access to his son. He'd had a fight with his mother, who'd told him little boys needed their mothers not their fathers. So he wasn't speaking to her. His sister was taking him away for a fortnight up the coast and the good news was that the courts were considering allowing him to take Tom for part of the holiday. When he came back he'd have some mediation with Linda. It was compulsory. I felt too far away to help, and though I would have liked him to ask me to come down, he didn't, despite the hints I made to have him invite me.

Annie was entirely preoccupied at Red Bore and there was nothing more I needed to stay at Promised Land for. But Lucy was away so there was little company in town. I wasn't sure Mum would be much fun and I decided not to test it. Four weeks was a long break, longer than other states. It was a throwback to the days when teachers were always from down south, and before commercial flying was very affordable and the government mob with their families had to drive or catch the train home. I felt lost about how to fill in the time, but without anywhere to go I stayed.

The country stayed dry as a bone. Every day was sunny, the sky always blue. Sunshine brought warmth to the middle of each day, but the air was thin and cold. Like everyone else I lit a fire most nights. I sat around mine alone most nights. My skin cracked with the dryness. If it wasn't for the fancy moisturisers Lucy had given me I was sure the skin on my face would have peeled right off. When Patrick rang one night and told me he could take Tom away but the place he was going to with Gillian had no phone service

I felt sick about how lonely I'd be without even the small contact we had.

'It's only for a few weeks,' he said.

'The weeks here are long,' I said.

'Don't I know it,' he said, 'but it is good for me. Linda can't hassle me or get in Tom's ear while we're away.'

I tried to be cheery for him. I wanted him to be happy. I just would have preferred to be happy with him.

I did think it might be good if I got away somewhere for a while. I even rang a travel agent and looked at going to Broome for a break, knowing it was just a fantasy. I might have been entirely useless as any kind of protection against the intervention but I couldn't just bail on the community. I couldn't.

Centrelink had started flying in southern staff to put people on income management agreements and Magdalene had asked me to stay close to Promised Land. I wasn't looking forward to it and neither was she. At Red Bore, Annie had to help the interpreter explain to the old men that they wouldn't be able to buy bullets for hunting unless it was on their list of essentials. Although the interpreters were explaining in language, the old men couldn't understand. What were these whitefellas saying now? That hunting wasn't essential? They'd lived long lives, mostly working as stockmen, and they thought they'd heard every crazy idea whitefellas had come up with. But it seemed they'd been wrong.

In town Mum was alone with Michael away. He had been seconded to draft a response from his organisation on the human rights issues relating to the suspension of the Racial Discrimination Act. Mum seemed to ring constantly in his absence and could tie me up for hours raving. She had an opinion on every aspect of the emergency response. If there was one immediate benefit of the intervention I could see, it was the effect it had on her. While it might have been exhausting for me it was good to see that she'd changed her tune about her own legacy. The last thirty-seven years of her life, which she'd been prepared to write off, now needed defending, and her old fire was blazing.

Mum and Mrs Press came up with a good idea to cheer people up. Magdalene agreed. Caleb was stoked. Tommy jnr, who was still a legend to our kids, was prepared to come up and run a coaching day for the football team. I'd seen him once or twice at our games and I was as flattered as the others he'd take the time to come out, drive up and spend the day with us all.

Mrs Press brought Mum and a tribe of grannys in her car. Tommy jnr followed in his. When his car doors opened more young fellows than I thought was possible piled out. The visitors had brought meat, bread and salad. Henry put himself in charge of the barbecue. I felt bad Kilka didn't manage to get over but we had a good day. Everyone came out to watch, even Magdalene pushing old Esther over, sat out of the wind in the sun for a while. Tommy jnr ran through some drills with the kids but the day was more about having fun than serious training. It was for all the kids. Even Declan toddled his way into the chaos and had a turn at kicking. After lunch, Tommy jnr organised an impromptu game. To my surprise even the old blokes joined in enthusiastically and the kids absolutely had a ball. I took lots of great action shots, then copied them onto a USB stick for Mum, along with the pictures I'd taken of the signs.

She thought she'd email the photos to Floyd in case he could find someone in his old contact book to write a positive story about our little community. I hoped he could too. We all needed more good things to be happening.

CHAPTER 26

I hadn't seen Maxine for ages. I imagined she had permanently fled into town to stay outside the scope of the intervention. People in town weren't having their money quarantined. At least not yet. I assumed Caleb might have gone to join her. After Tommy jnr's clinic I never saw him. Henry and the older fellows who'd been around seemed to disappear too. It might have been my imagination but Promised Land was feeling more and more like the hollow land. The women were left. Most were already under the pump and became even more stretched. Men might not be much help domestically, but they drove and fixed cars, shot kangaroos and, most importantly, provided protection. It seemed odd they'd leave at a time like this, with Centrelink about to arrive, and although I did try to find out where they were, I had no success.

To help out I spent a lot of time with Rosia. I loved her and it helped to distract me from worrying too much about Patrick and what might be happening for him. Sometimes, in my more anxious moments, I wondered if not inviting me south was a way of ending things. I hoped not.

The surprise tactics of the intervention were another good reason to stay close. One day, completely without any notice, the Centrelink team turned up for an information session. There were six workers and two cars. All they really did was leave us with brochures about what they'd do when they came back. The fuel and the travel allowance costs of the visit would have been enough to pay for the new bore we were waiting on and while I wondered why the government didn't just pay for that instead, if this was about helping, as they claimed was their motivation, I said nothing. If I'd learnt nothing else over the last little while, it was to be discreet with my opinions.

After the strangers had gone, Rosia and I sat on my scrap of lawn chasing the last of the sun around. Rosia was growing up but she was still a joy. Not even her obsession with pulling my hair could annoy me. Somehow she always managed to get hold of a few strands even if I tied it up.

'Eh, miss,' I said now, as she took the chance to grab my hair. 'Be kind.' I untangled her fingers and kissed her cheeks. She laughed and grabbed my hair again.

'Too clever by half,' I said. 'Auntie will get cross.' I jiggled her up and down, not cross at all, while she laughed her cute baby laughs. I had to kiss her. And tickle her some more to keep her laughing.

Lekisha had a two-week training block coming up. The trouble was she was far too worried about Treasure having so many kids to want to go now. Marjory had left to get back across the border and away from the intervention and Lekisha felt like she might have no choice except to miss the study. Family always came first. I didn't like to become too obligated to the family because the school created enough obligations on its own. But Lekisha had to keep up her study so I found myself offering to help Treasure with the kids.

As the family was still down on cars I volunteered to take Lekisha into town. At least this time her training was in Alice Springs so she could come back if it was really necessary, which made everyone feel better about the arrangement. I took Kane, Preston, Sammy, Little Mary and Rosia with me, so we could have a day out.

We all had lunch on the courthouse lawns. Sweet and sour pork, fried rice and honey chicken. All favourites. The shopping centre security would have thrown us out for the kids being barefoot if we'd tried to eat in the food court, so I ducked in and bought take-away. I was expecting to take Lekisha to the training institute after lunch but she said she had a ride to the Institute. She took herself off to meet whoever was taking her at the shopping centre. I could only assume her mysterious boyfriend was driving her in his blue Falcon.

I felt like we should do something since we were in town. I asked the kids what they felt like doing. Sammy thought swimming but it was too cold and the pool was shut anyway. Preston suggested the movies. That was a good idea. They were all keen. Yes, yes they were begging. I looked at them. It was funny but I hardly ever noticed how badly they were dressed; their hand-me-down trousers and shirts, the lack of shoes or their unbrushed hair, until we were in town.

We'd never get in the cinema without shoes. A few pairs of new shoes weren't going to send me broke; I hardly spent money and the kids didn't have expensive taste. While we were at Kmart it was just as easy to get some socks too. When the kids saw some hood-ies and asked for them too, I could see no reason to object. With everyone in flash new jumpers, bright new shoes and with their socks pulled up, a new fashion which I found most unattractive, we fronted up at the cinema, confident we wouldn't be turned away.

Preston chose. It was a pirate movie and I wondered what they'd think of it. None of them had ever seen the ocean, a boat or really knew what pirates were. But they loved it. They laughed at the sword fighting and were inspired to get up and do a bit of their own with the cinema nearly empty and I let them roll about as much as they wanted on the carpet play-acting. Rosia thought it was a great game and in the end it was her screaming with laughter that got us in trouble and nearly evicted.

At the movies the kids had convinced me to get them the monster packs of junk food. A large Coke, popcorn, ice-cream and Maltesers. It was a big mistake. As we did some food shopping afterwards Kane was very pale and quiet. On the way back to Promised Land I had to stop the car so he could vomit. By the time I dropped him home he was back to his normal self and wanting more sweets but the vomiting incident had made me decide I'd stop with the junk food altogether. Preston almost had a Tim Tam habit and it was my fault. From now on I'd give out fruit when the kids asked for food.

When I went to drop off Rosia, Treasure told me to keep her overnight, as Declan had gastro. I couldn't believe my luck. In the coming week she slept over with me most nights. Her small body was like a radiator, keeping me warm, but it was love I knew that was at the heart of the warmth.

I behaved as if I was her mother. When Treasure mentioned Rosia was due for immunisation shots I rang the clinic and made an appointment. I even took her to the clinic, consoling her when she wailed with pain. Afterwards, I bought her new clothes and toys as a reward for being so brave. While I was in the shopping centre I saw Frank coming out of the newsagent and quickly, before he could see me, I wheeled the pram into a bookshop, pretending to myself it was because I wanted the next book in the crime series Iry now had introduced me to.

Back in my little donga I added the new clothes and toys to the collection of things I'd already gathered for Rosia. I had a little basket which was filling. Things I'd decided were best for her in her life with me.

I poured all my attention into her to such an extent I didn't even notice how sulky the other kids were with me when I saw them about.

One afternoon I woke from a nap, with Rosia curled up in my arms. Her breath was warm and sweet, her lips seeking my arms as though my body might offer sustenance. I stayed as still as I could while the emotions crashed around in my body. Suddenly I saw things clearly, and a cold feeling crept through me. I didn't quite understand how I'd let the situation get to this. But I knew with certainty that what I was doing was wrong. I was running my own little intervention. More than that: I was stealing Rosia from her family. It was just as Caleb had suspected I wanted to months ago. Once I'd seen my help for what it was there could be no going back to pretending.

Without waking Rosia, I got up quickly and dressed. I gathered her things. Folded her tiny dresses, paired her socks, bagged up her toys. The new towels and packets of disposable nappies I put into the blue baby bath with all her special infant food. Rosia woke shortly afterwards and I picked her up in one arm and the bath in the other. As I made the short journey to Treasure's house I tried not to register the squeeze of her chubby legs at my waist or her singsong chatter with its mix of the makings of English and Arrernte. By the time we got to Treasure's door Rosia must have sensed my tension, and her hand held my arm tightly.

'I got to go to town,' I said as soon as Treasure had opened the door. 'She's hungry.'

'Now?' Treasure asked, puzzled. It was early. Lekisha wasn't due back for a couple of days, and she was knee deep in kids. Her house was full of everyone's kids, chaotic and full of action. Sammy and Kane were fighting over buttering bread. Preston searched the sink for a cup, clean or dirty, then gave up and drank straight from the UHT milk container, spilling it down his chin. Declan sat on the sofa, pushing off his cousins in a wild game which could only end in tears. The TV was sucking the power from the solar panels greedily and the volume was deafening. Soon Treasure'd be trying to get this lot through dinner and into bed before she was a wreck. She looked at me for an explanation, her hands clasped at her back. I was usually helpful. Compliant.

I thrust Rosia into her unwilling arms. 'Now,' I said. 'Sorry. I've got to go.'

Before I'd even stepped off the verandah I could hear Rosia start to scream.

CHAPTER 27

I pressed my foot down hard on the accelerator. I didn't care if I got a speeding fine. I just needed to get away, and I cursed Patrick for not being around and the intervention for keeping me at Promised Land. It was a big mistake not keeping up my own life. I should have taken advantage of Lucy being away, hung out in town and made myself some new friends.

I found myself driving to the hotel I'd gone to a few times with Patrick. I just couldn't cope going to Lucy's large empty house. I certainly didn't want to talk to Mum about the last few weeks. I could hardly bear thinking about what I'd done. The fantasy I'd let myself live.

I closed the heavy curtains and climbed into bed to make myself stay still. I felt like running all the way back to Sydney. I was ashamed of my behaviour and I had to think about where to from here. I couldn't leave Promised Land. I would stay. But I needed boundaries. Rosia wasn't my baby. The kids weren't my responsibility. I was the teacher and I needed to get a life of my own. I'd let what was happening in Patrick's life dominate mine as if we were in some committed relationship. We were lovers. That was all. A bush affair for now, and perhaps not destined to be much more, given he clearly didn't want me to get closer to him. I started to cry with self-pity. It was easy to give in to. I was exhausted too. Bone tired. I cried so much I thought I'd vomit. Then I slept.

When I woke it was daylight.

I went out onto the balcony. It was pale dawn. Buttery light fell down sides of the chocolaty ranges. A honeyeater landed on the balustrade. It cocked its head at me, inviting a chat. I told him I blamed over-tiredness for my dramatics. My headache was gone and I felt clear-headed. He nodded his yellow-capped head as if in agreement and flew off.

I wouldn't waste money on a rubbish hotel breakfast. I'd go see Mum and Michael. They liked the early mornings.

A song I liked was playing on the radio and it kept me sitting in the car in Mum's driveway. When she banged on the window I got quite a fright.

'Where have you been?'

'At the Sheraton,' I said, switching off the radio and getting out.

She grabbed my arm. 'At the Sheraton? Did it not occur to you to let someone know? You just ran away from Promised Land and went to a hotel?'

'I went to a hotel. It's not a crime.'

'The girl has turned up,' Michael was shouting to the Presses, sharing the information with the whole street. I had no idea why he thought this needed a public announcement.

I managed to twist out of Mum's rather desperate hold on my wrist, my face flushed red with embarrassment. I didn't think I'd felt so shamed since I was a kid and she'd gone off about me riding the flooded river in front of the whole street.

I strode angrily inside and faced them across the island bench. 'I had no idea anyone would worry about where I was. I'm a big girl. Thirty-six, actually at the end of the year.'

'We're your family, Alicia, of course we're going to worry,' Michael said, in the tone he usually saved for addressing anyone he thought was an idiot. 'You better get on the blower and call Promised Land. Treasure is beside herself.'

'Treasure? Why?' I asked.

'She said you brought Rosia back out of the blue and left her. Yesterday. She thought you must have got bad news from us. And when we assured her we were okay, she thought something must have happened with Patrick. She was really worried. I assumed you were at Lucy's and promised to get you to ring her back. But Lucy's was locked up and I couldn't find you anywhere. I even rang the cops to see if there'd been an accident.'

'Oh my god, what a carry-on!'

'She said you were proper sad,' said Mum.

'Okay, I was. But—'

Mum spoke over the top of me. 'You remember the story of Treasure's brother?'

I winced. It came back with a jolt. The year I met Floyd, Treasure's younger brother had hung himself. The recriminations had been harsh and protracted. A lot of blame was placed on Treasure because she'd been the last person to see him.

'You didn't think I'd . . .?'

'We were worried,' Michael said. 'It was quite unusual behaviour for you.'

I couldn't believe they'd think I'd ever hurt myself but Treasure's reaction now made sense. Feeling guilty, I called her immediately. She was relieved to hear from me but didn't make a fuss. I was grateful she didn't go off at me like Mum and Michael had. Lekisha got back to Promised Land that afternoon and I found out later she turned it into a big joke about fidelity. *Alicia went to a hotel without telling anyone. It's a secret who she met. By the way, Patrick was in Sydney!*

I charged my phone at Lucy's. There were a heap of messages. A lot from Michael and Mum. Some from Patrick. I was curious as he wouldn't have been able to count on me seeing them. My phone was so rarely in range or on for that matter. Perhaps he had thought I'd gone away like I'd insinuated I might the last time we'd spoken. But I was glad to see them all the same. I texted him back. Sure I'll pick you up on Saturday.

I didn't know what would happen but I did want to see him. There wasn't much time, only a night. I had to be back at Promised Land by Sunday some time. Early enough to start school on the Monday and he'd have to get organised at Kilka but it would be good to touch base and see where things stood.

Lucy came back earlier than expected, looking tanned and unhappy, and we had a quiet afternoon together. She had washing to do and unpacking while I played in her garden weeding. I read a bit. We punctuated the day with a few cups of tea and catch-up chats. I told her the Treasure story. She listened without comment and I found I could tell her about what I felt I'd done with Rosia. It wasn't something I'd gone anywhere near when talking to Mum and Michael. And wouldn't. Lucy was different. She was always the person I let in on the worst of myself, which is why I loved her so much. Because she loved me even knowing these things about me. Lucy seemed to really understand how it was easy to get caught up in being desperate without even knowing you were doing it. This was when I found out she'd actually taken some new young lover with her to Bali. I hadn't even heard about her, which Lucy explained was of course how these things went. Some part of you knew you were doing the wrong thing so you kept it under wraps. I thought about how I'd ducked into the shop that day to avoid Frank and knew she was right.

'So who is this young thing?' I asked.

'It's best you don't know. Town's too small. Though of course you may well find out,' she said. 'It was hardly her fault that when I woke up to myself I ran away. I changed my ticket, got a taxi and just left her when I realised what I was doing was just so foolish.'

'You left a note, I hope?'

'A message at the hotel reception,' she said. 'How's that for being unkind?'

She put her head in her hands and groaned.

'At least you told her,' I said, 'she's not out searching the streets of Ubud for you.'

Lucy lifted her head and made an effort at cheering up. 'I suppose that is one thing. The whole thing, it's just a shame job. I was flattered by her attention. I knew it was never going to work. Not just because she was your age. I was just desperate to try something. Being on my own into old age isn't really something I aspire to. Independence can be extremely overrated.'

I rubbed her back. I knew exactly what she meant. It was a disarmingly honest appraisal of why she'd behaved liked she had. Being desperate could make most of us lose a sense of perspective. Look what I'd just done with Rosia. At least I wasn't being blind about Patrick. We had a connection there was no doubt. He had stuff to sort. Big stuff. But if we were honest and I was realistic about what he could offer I thought it was a relationship worth keeping.

Long after Lucy was asleep I found myself on her front deck watching the stars. It was amazing, really, how much had happened to me in such a short time. I was lucky. Promised Land had given me much to be grateful for. And Lucy said Patrick and I could have the house to ourselves all day tomorrow, which added to my sense of good fortune.

I picked Patrick up at the airport. I'd been a bit scared of how I might feel when I actually saw him. It was an advantage to see him before he noticed my arrival so I had a few moments to appraise him and my feelings. He had a brown jumper on that looked new and blue jeans. His hair had been cut. He spotted me and smiled, walking towards me. I felt good. I was glad to see him. He got in and tossed his bag over the seat into the back.

'You look fantastic,' he said.

'You look cleaned up.'

'Don't worry. I'll soon be back to my scrubber ways.'

He leant over and kissed my neck as he was reaching on his seatbelt. Once he'd clicked it in he put his hand on my thigh. I wondered about this easy assumption we'd take off where we'd left and forget the prickly bits in between. For now it was okay. I talked about the football day and anything else I could think of that was upbeat, which wasn't much. He didn't mention court. His hand drifted to my knee. Our bodies had an agenda. At Lucy's we went straight to bed. When we got hungry I made cheese on toast and took it back to where he was.

At dusk we heard Lucy come home. She put music on and we got up and joined her. She offered to cook us dinner. We had no other plans and accepted the invitation. Patrick lit a fire. It roared the room warm. And over the meal with a few glasses of wine Patrick told us about his break, some more details of his court case, which now was adjourned for a few months, though he didn't dwell on the subject. He got his camera out and showed us some photos of him and Tom. His family. I stopped him at the one of the beach.

'My flat,' I said, 'is just up that street. With a new tenant hopefully reviving my three very hardy pot plants.'

'You're a hopeless gardener? I don't believe it.'

'She is,' said Lucy. 'Yesterday she weeded out all my new kale seedlings.'

I laughed, a bit embarrassed. Is that what they were? 'I'll buy you some more tomorrow.'

'No need.'

We ended the evening on a light note. Making jokes as we cleaned up, teasing each other about small faults. Like how Lucy still didn't know left from right. And Patrick had taken two weeks to learn how to text on his new phone. Perhaps this was what made it easy for Patrick to tell me once we were in bed the two very heavy things the lawyer had told him would go against him. Living at Kilka was one. If he moved back to Sydney and got a job, preferably in a good private school, his chances were much better, though he'd never get custody. Linda had a strong case about being the established primary carer, but even for access a move was advised. Secondly as he hadn't re-partnered he shouldn't at this time. Girlfriends should be kept discreet. They were very easily turned into ammunition for the other side.

I listened while my chest grew tighter. His fingers brushed across my belly. I stopped it wandering.

'You right?' he asked.

'I might brush my teeth,' I said.

I looked at my face in the bathroom mirror. Everything on the surface was unchanged. Well, girl, I said to myself, it's up to you what you want.

I dropped Patrick at the fleet yard in the morning so he could pick up his car. He kissed me goodbye and told me to be safe.

'Ah,' I said, 'Safe. Funny little concept that.'

'You're being a bit cryptic today aren't you?'

I kissed his mouth. I was in a mood. I figured I could be. Surely it was the right of every girlfriend on the side to behave as they liked.

CHAPTER 28

B ack at Promised Land I wanted to hide in my donga. I had things to do. Especially work, which might help me stop thinking about Patrick's conversation. He hadn't said he'd agreed with the lawyer. In fact, he hadn't said anything else about it. Last night by the time I'd gone back to bed he seemed almost asleep. He'd stirred and hugged me to him. I'd thought I'd toss and turn but I'd slept well too. We'd had a slow breakfast with Lucy and then hit the road. I could have waited to have him tail me up the highway but I'd chosen to drive on ahead, knowing he wouldn't pass through. It was much longer to come via Promised Land and I guessed we'd see each other at football or training if it was on.

I'd just got my papers out ready to get my head into school mode when there was a knock at the door. I knew it wouldn't be Lekisha. She'd just waltz in.

Henry and Treasure were on my deck. I was worried it might be to tell me off for scaring Treasure. Thankfully it seemed not to be.

Henry exuded a quiet excitement. The Iltja trip, which had been shelved due to the intervention, would go ahead. It would happen soon hopefully, he said, and Magdalene would talk to me about it. It could be an excursion for the kids. Something good to make everyone come back. I wasn't sure who exactly might have left. I hoped Marjory hadn't taken all her kids. We couldn't afford to lose numbers. Centrelink's quarantining of cash certainly wouldn't help us there. I'd have to check when exactly the Centrelink workers were coming. The date had shifted so often, I'd lost track. In theory people would get the same amount, only they'd have to spend it on essentials. It was a very clunky system though. They could choose Red Bore or the local shop near Mum's, which had signed agreements with the federal government. Or go all the way to Tennant Creek. Hardly any shops had come on board and I didn't want to be playing the messenger in my relationships with people. It would cost me too much.

Henry had no idea when Centrelink was coming. He didn't want to talk about it either, which suited us all. He did want to talk about the football. He'd brought Caleb back and they'd agreed Tommy jnr would help coach the football team from now on. It wasn't clear if this was some sort of disciplinary action. How it came about didn't really matter. I liked the idea. I was quietly confident Tommy jnr would help mould the Cats' raw talent into a team which might win the flag for our small community. I knew how much that would mean to them—and to me.

As I saw Henry and Treasure out, Lekisha was going past.

'Come and give us a hand,' I said. 'There's a lot to do.'

'You help me with my essay?'

'Sure, if you bring it over.'

Lekisha's study. One more headache to manage. I didn't know

why I even cared if I had a lover at all. I didn't have time for one. Part- or full-time.

It was a slow week with half of the kids still in town. Lekisha had to go in on the Wednesday and make it clear if they didn't come back, there would no football team. The boys weren't to think they'd just become part of our team's town ring-ins and she'd told them she'd personally withdraw the team from the competition if they didn't come back. On her return I was full of praise for her tough love stand. I knew she would be more effective than me but it wouldn't have been easy for her.

By Friday we had most of the boys back but we were still only up to ten in the room. I cursed the intervention. This was exactly what no-one needed. Red Bore was faring worse, though Annie did mention the silver lining in her dropping numbers was that she might have to let go of a teacher. And her Victorians had driven her mad with the way they'd whinged at having to reduce their trip to Kakadu by a week because she'd held us all back except Patrick. She couldn't wait to let one go. The other would hopefully follow. Good riddance, she had said with a laugh.

I kept half expecting Magdalene to drop in with instructions about Iltja. All week she never came. I hoped it wasn't all talk. I was keen to go somewhere. Somewhere with water sounded great. It was still cold but just to look at some would be a nice change from the dry scrub. Patrick's pictures of the beach had made me nostalgic for sea although I would happily settle for a freshwater rock pool at this stage.

Early on the Saturday Tommy jnr was waiting for us at the oval in town. I shook his hand.

'Thanks for taking on the team,' I said, as if the arrangement had something to do with me.

'No sweat.'

'Oh, and congratulations. I hear you had a boy this time. Good for you.'

'Thanks. He's going to be spoiled rotten by his sisters.' Not just by them, I imagined.

Just then Patrick arrived with the Kilka kids and I gave him a distant wave and went to get two takeaway coffees. When I came back I handed him one, but wandered away to stand well apart from the men.

Pre-game training was in full swing. Tommy jnr had, to quote Caleb, some deadly ideas. I was pleased to see that Caleb was chuffed rather than offended at his recent demotion. The signs of his recent drinking binge in town were starting to fade, and he still looked a little gaunt, but he was in good spirits.

Patrick came over and told me in an entirely unnecessary whisper that allowed him to lean in close that Tommy jnr was full of praise for the boys' skills and Caleb's work with them. I liked his breath on my neck, having him want to be so close, but I felt torn.

When the game started, I sat down on the top of the grassy hill at the side of the oval, and Patrick sat next to me. We had our coat collars turned up against the cold, and when he moved closer to me, our sides touching, I didn't move away. I wasn't sure how to play things exactly, to take what I wanted and leave what I didn't want well alone. The trouble was what I really wanted wasn't on offer.

In spite of the break and all the disruptions, the Cats played well. Our ruck had to work hard against a bigger, taller team, but we stayed on top and in the end the boys won by a solid margin. It was a relief to see that their spirits hadn't been dented by the upheaval and uncertainty of the last few weeks. Or at least their football skills.

After the game, Lekisha insisted I come along with everyone else to eat takeaway on the council lawns. I wound up sitting opposite Patrick and kept stealing glances at him. Minute to minute I seemed to change my mind about whether I should get him to clarify if he was going to keep me like his bit on the side. It wasn't so bad except it didn't suit my long-term goals for the relationship at all. He caught my eye and smiled. I glanced away worried he might be able to read my mind.

Preoccupied, it took me a while to realise that the discussion had turned to how we would celebrate if we won the flag. Patrick was suggesting we have a big lunch together and get some trophies and prizes to present to the kids. It required all the families to put in some money, something I wasn't sure they'd be able to do. Promised Land had Centrelink coming on Tuesday morning. They'd already gone to Kilka. Everyone there was now income managed, which meant they had their rent, power and food costs taken out of their payments and Red Bore was the only shop they could really realistically choose to shop at. If there was a celebration at the end of the season we'd definitely have to pay for it.

I was leaving when Patrick caught up with me falling into stride alongside. We walked together to Mum's car which I'd borrowed so I could have a bit of a freedom over the weekend. Though for what I hadn't decided.

'Do you want to catch up?' Patrick said.

I shrugged. I did and I didn't. My body was urging me to say yes. My head cautioned me against it. I thought about where we could go. A hotel or Lucy's. We could have borrowed camping gear from Mum's and gone bush but it was a lot of effort that would take energy I didn't have. I smiled apologetically. 'Another day?'

'Sure.'

He swung an arm around my shoulder and gave me a squeeze. 'Is everything okay?'

'Is it?' I asked. 'I don't know. There's a lot on.'

I didn't have to be specific. His beaten look told me he knew.

'I'm fond of you,' he said.

'And me of you.' I gave him a peck on the cheek and left, determined to try not to make a big deal of the situation.

I suddenly made an excuse to go to town to pick up supplies when the Centrelink workers arrived. I just didn't want to be a party to it. Everyone was crabby for days afterwards and if I'd been there when the agreements were signed I was fairly certain people would have been cross with me. Now everyone had to shop at Red Bore store. It was crazy. It was expensive and rubbish. And not much closer than town. There would be choices in the future, though not for months. I could hear the question in Lekisha's voice when she was telling me. When she wondered, when, would they ever get many choices? It made me question my role.

Lots of the issues I had teaching seemed to point to the same core conundrum: Schools were one more agency of colonisation.

It didn't help that I knew the official line off by heart. My job was simply to teach the kids the skills they needed for modern life, and they would have to learn for themselves how to keep a foot in both worlds. But the two worlds were like different planets. One was undeveloped, desert country which was home. And the other was imagined, a place where TV shows came from. The job of the school, it seemed, was to convince these kids—who could track goanna, see a kangaroo miles away, follow a ceremony for days— that TV land was not just better but real.

It did my head in, and some nights I'd ring Annie or Lucy and pour out my frustrations. I often wanted to ring Patrick but didn't. Things had become a little awkward between us since I'd turned him down at the beginning of term but with work and football we hadn't stopped seeing each other completely. We overlapped. And I liked him. A lot. I still found myself gravitating to him, standing too close, wanting him. But I couldn't let it go any further. I could see his position, but I found I had one too. I didn't want to meet in hotels. Or pretend I wasn't with him in public. Nor was I going to risk being something that could blow up in his face if Linda's lawyer sniffed me out. And be the one to take the blame for his loss.

If he decided not to listen to his lawyer. Then that was another matter.

As winter warmed towards spring, so did the dry weather. I longed for rain, but there were no grey clouds. Just blue skies day after day, relentless and clear.

One day in August, notification about the upcoming LAP tests came through on the fax.

'I think some of our kids could pass this test,' Lekisha announced unexpectedly. I'd assumed we'd apply for an exemption. The LAP was a national test. It stood for Language Acquisition Performance, and Annie had advised against doing it. She said the spelling and comprehension components would simply demoralise the kids with their use of culturally loaded English. 'How can a desert kid have a clue what a buoy or a unicorn might be?' she had scoffed. Having looked at the content of the LAP, I tended to agree with her. However, she said that we were free to make up our own mind about the test. Lekisha was surprisingly adamant we should do it.

'Magdalene will want us to,' she said, 'and it's only for a few of the kids. Those the right age.'

'But they won't know the words—how can they spell them?' I thought I was being sensible. Not controlling.

'Alicia, are you working for the intervention now? You the new boss for Aboriginal people?'

'No,' I said blushing. She hardly ever told me off like this.

'Good. You say lots of our words without knowing their meaning and you can spell them.'

'Like what?'

'Altyerre.'

'I know what it means, it means dreaming.'

'That's only one bit of its meaning. Simple one. Whitefella one.'

'A dictionary meaning.' That was fair enough I thought. But Lekisha didn't concede. She tried another example. 'God.'

'God?'

'Yeah, God. You don't know the meaning.'

'Yes, I do. I was confirmed, same as you, remember.'

'But you don't believe in him.'

I was finding her literal approach exasperating. 'God's not exactly a difficult word to spell anyway.'

'Try ceremony then.'

I chose not to reply. A long and uncomfortable pause fell. I hoped she'd given up the subject.

'Country, then. What's that mean, if you're so smart?'

'It means place.'

'No it doesn't. It means more than that.'

I thought about it for a while. She was right about that. I was beginning to see her point. One didn't necessarily need to know a word's meaning to spell it. It could be learnt regardless. The surface, the shape of it inked on a page.

'Sorry,' I said. 'If you want to do it, we do it. But only if you drill the kids in spelling. Take twenty minutes each day to work with them. I'll work on the reading passages, and tips to answering comprehension questions.'

'And Caleb will encourage them.'

'That's right. He can motivate them.'

We started the very next day. Lekisha came to class all prepared with copies of the old tests and a sequence of word groups, every one written neatly on large strips of card.

I was impressed. 'You're going to top your teaching class.'

'I already am.'

I grinned. A fired-up Lekisha was a beautiful sight.

She carefully explained the tests to the students and how we'd

practise hard so they would do well. 'Just remember them,' Lekisha urged, holding up the words. 'Hold their shape in your head.
The pattern in the words.' She broke the words up into their
parts, showed them the forms, the similarities. Her method was
the same as when we were out hunting, following tracks.

After ten days we were in the groove of achievement. All the
students, even the ones who often dodged spelling and writing
activities, were trying hard. I felt Caleb's analogy become real
despite all the upheaval. We were a powerful well-oiled machine,
capable of any challenge.

It was a Thursday. Like all Thursdays it was fairly quiet as people
went to shop with their pay. Now they came back with less of the
toys Centrelink didn't want them wasting money on but also less
fresh food and less in general. Red Bore was not cheap. Thursdays
every fortnight were no longer happy days.

It started raining late in the night. This was proper rain, the first
I'd seen. I padded outside in a dressing-gown. The night air hadn't
been freezing for a while, just spring cool. Rain usually came later
or earlier in the year, but I didn't care. It made me happy to watch
the water pool on the ground, to see the streams running in through
the holes in the old tin roof onto my scrappy verandah floor.

By morning the rain had softened to a light drizzle. Lekisha
turned up at school earlier than usual, her hair glistening. Honey
ants, she suggested. I didn't think for a minute about the rules.
Instead I grabbed BBQ meat and bread from the freezer, juice
boxes, a few sultana buns—all the supplies we had.

When the kids arrived we started packing them into the car. I was glad I had Mum's again so we could take whoever wanted to go. It was more and more of a habit borrowing her troopy and it was probably time I got a car of my own. Not that she ever seemed to mind. She was into walking these days and in this weather it was pleasant. When we picked up Treasure, Henry asked if I'd talked to Magdalene yet about Iltja. I shook my head. I'd started to think of Iltja as not really existing. It was like the word just had to be said, over and then forgotten.

The rain had stopped but low clouds immersed us in a strange grey gauze as we travelled east along the Kilka road. All the country's colours had shifted down a few tones. Green plants became olive, red dirt rusty. It was like travelling out into a foreign land. When we were nearly at Kilka we veered off into the scrub. The cloud had thinned and lifted. In the distance small slits of blue were opening at the horizon like eyes peering at us.

As it wasn't an authorised trip, Lekisha had rung Patrick so someone knew where we were going so I shouldn't have been surprised to see the Kilka school car parked on a hard bit of ground ahead. It looked as though he'd brought more women than kids, and they were already at work, digging.

Our kids spilled out the back and I let Lekisha deal with the chaos and politics of handing out the digging sticks and deciding who could take the one football. Digging was women's work and the boys weren't that keen, though they'd be more than happy to eat the spoils.

'So,' said Patrick, leaning in my open window. 'Are you avoiding me or are you just the busiest teacher and most dutiful daughter on the planet?'

I didn't expect this directness and didn't know how to answer. He put a hand on my neck. 'Are you right?'

'Fine,' I said, flustered by the rush of feeling his touch sparked in me. I jerked the door open, forcing him to step back, and tried not to think about the hurt that flashed across his face.

Just then the football came down from a wayward kick and bounced into his leg. He scooped it up and booted it as though he hated it, sending it into the sky. I quickly weaved my way through the scramble of boys positioning themselves to take the mark, seeking out the shelter and protection of Lekisha's company.

On most days I was fairly useless at digging, not used to the physical demands of bending and pounding the spade repeatedly into the hard earth. But today I pushed myself, wanting it to hurt and to push all thoughts of Patrick away. I dug so well Lekisha noticed and asked what had got into me.

To get ants you had to dig deep. Lekisha kept hassling different kids to come and clear away the dirt and they would for a while before they gave up and she'd have to nag another. Honey ants were a big treat. Rain made them easier to catch, as the ants were drawn out of their deep underground nests towards the surface moisture. When we'd dug far enough, Lekisha took over, following the tunnels. All the kids were happy to help at this point. Every one of them hoping Lekisha would favour them with the first honey ant.

'You mob need to read that story of the Little Red Hen, again,' I said but no-one was listening.

There were still some clouds to the west but the cover had lifted while I'd been digging and the sky was back to a pale version of its former self. Patrick had a fire lit and a billy sat on the flames. Treasure sat beside it, feeding in sticks to hurry it up. I found the salt and sauce and gave the bread a squeeze to make sure it was defrosted.

From the carry-on we could tell that the nest must have been located, and soon kids came up to the fire with their tiny treats. Preston had one crawling on his palm. It was blackish-red and carried on its back a full clear bag, filled with an amber liquid, about the size of a five-cent piece. I thought he might be planning to give it to his grandmother, but instead he pinched the ant at the head and bit off the bag.

Treasure didn't mind, but I told him that if he didn't like sharing he could wait last for a sausage. Unconcerned by my threats, he ran off to beg more honey ants from Lekisha.

Patrick spent most of the time playing football with the boys. Occasionally I'd sense him watching me but I hadn't responded. While I'd been organising lunch he wandered away. No-one called him back. Unlike me it seemed he was allowed to go off alone wherever he pleased, which I found myself resenting. Clearly they trusted him more.

Tired, Lekisha came and sat down. The kids were full of sausages already but there was still an abundance. She helped herself to one off the barbecue plate. 'Missing him?' she said, wiggling her sausage cheekily.

'Don't be stupid,' I said.

'Not me that's been stupid.'

We stared at each other like we'd do as kids in our glaring competitions. I looked away first and Lekisha gave me a conciliatory pat on my shoulder.

'Hey, any ants for me?' I asked.

The best hunter, she was always the most demanded of. I knew they were her favourite too so they were harder to get than most things. 'The kids got them all,' she said, trying to put me off.

'But I love them, you know that. I cooked your kere and dug for you.'

'They got 'em,' she said. 'All gone.'

She put the last of her second sausage in her mouth and pushed herself off the ground to go back to her digging work. I begged with my eyes.

'Please,' I whined.

'You make me weak,' she said. 'Here.' She pulled a small jar brimming with ants out from between her breasts and pressed it into my hand. 'You have them.'

I ate only three. Each a delicious sweet drop of honey. I sealed the rest back in the jar and hid it in her bag so she could have them later when there weren't so many mouths around.

I was left alone at the fire and slowly packed up the mess, trying not to resent the fact I always got the job.

An hour or so later Patrick came back as I was almost finished packing up. He put some leaves in my hand.

'For headache,' he said, 'for tension. You pound them and put them on your head. Tie them on with a bandage or something.'

'I'm not tense.'

He put a hand to mine and I pulled away.

'Don't be too hard on me,' he said, his eyes searching my face for clues. 'It's not easy for me your choice.'

I shrugged. I wasn't going to talk about it. He had to know he'd encouraged it by telling me what the lawyer had said. It was hardly a free choice.

I had a headache all the way home. Luckily I was rarely expected to drive out bush. I was disappointed in myself for handling things badly with Patrick, disappointed that even the clouds out west, where the best chance of rain came from, had gone. I wanted more water. More honey ants. More sweetness in my life.

CHAPTER 29

At the game it was clear to see the new skills the boys were learning from Tommy jnr were turning them into a tight outfit, and they won the game easily. There were only two more games until the finals and the Cats were currently at the top of the table. In spite of this, I hardly watched. I was absorbed by my own thoughts. Since I'd arrived at the oval Patrick had avoided me, and I felt unjustifiably hurt. I'd sent some photos I'd been taking for him with Caleb when he'd gone there for training in a gesture of good will. A note had come back, just two words. Thanks, Alicia. It seemed mean and cold.

As soon as the game finished I left on foot with Mum. She'd walked even though she had her car back. I wished she'd driven. Town was quite unsettled and had an edge to it I didn't like. Each week it seemed that more and more refugees from remote communities flooded into town, escaping Centrelink and the harassment of the intervention workers. The drinkers and the campers hiding near the river and in the bush on the edge of town, I saw as a steady reminder that the intervention was no great success. I made sure I didn't look too closely at the people we passed who were gathered in the dry creek. I didn't want to see Maxine among them. Her abandonment of Rosia still made me furious. I found I just couldn't be as forgiving as Lekisha and Treasure appeared. My anger was probably exacerbated because since the holidays I'd not seen Rosia much either. Treasure seemed to know not to ask me to mind her, even though I'd never told her the truth of why I'd fled that day. I knew it was for the best but it made me feel lousy all the same.

I relaxed at Mum's. Unlike Lucy it wasn't her nature to probe into my personal life, though I knew that if I did bring up the subject of me and Patrick, she would give me her thoughts at length. We split the paper and I settled myself on the shorter of the two couches. I wondered what people in the south were saying about the intervention. I would have been especially interested to hear what Floyd was thinking on the other side of the world, but given the spot I found myself in with Patrick, it seemed silly to ring while I was vulnerable. Too many other emotions would be in danger of being stirred up.

The confident, knowing tone of the experts and analysts in the paper made me tired. I only wished I could be half as sure about my own opinions on anything. What I wanted to know was what sort of job was I doing?

I folded up the paper. I needed some reassurance. 'How's my score going, Mum, my good-girl points?'

'Oh you, about a million. Remember, though, the trick isn't whether you can get them but if you can keep them.' Her grin was teasing.

'Yeah, I figured there was a catch.'

'Iltja might get you some more.'

'Has Magdalene talked to you about it?' I asked.

'No, not recently.'

'Well, she hasn't talked to me either. Henry mentioned it a few weeks back. Otherwise I'm in the dark. They better give me some lead time if they want help, otherwise they can do it themselves.'

'Good luck with that,' Mum said, and we laughed. Talking tough was easy, actually following through nigh impossible, and didn't we know it.

Michael came home late and made some pasta while Mum made a tomato sauce. It was strange seeing them working side by side in the kitchen, but I could see they were enjoying themselves. Lucy was expected to join us and she arrived in time to help me set the table.

We didn't talk politics over dinner because we knew it would get us all riled up, so we told small gossipy stories and laughed a lot. After dinner I found another bottle of wine at the back of the fridge and we all moved to the couches in the lounge. Lucy and me seemed to be putting it away. Soon enough the intervention reared its ugly head. It was an impossible subject to leave alone. Every story Lucy told seemed to have as its sub-theme the failure to seek advice from people working on the ground. Mum claimed the government actually considered long-term non-Aboriginal workers in the Aboriginal industry to be a major part of the problem. In some cases they were regarded as a bigger thorn in the government's side with respect to their plans for the future than Aboriginal people themselves.

'If this was a war,' said Mum theatrically, 'then I'd be interned for the duration.'

It wasn't very late when Lucy, who was fairly drunk, and I left in a taxi. We sat in the back, Lucy's head on my shoulder and I watched the dark shape of the ranges run beside us all the way to her place where we turned to the north and they kept running out west.

I took her hand up the stairs to help her and we stopped in the kitchen for water.

'Is it true, you're not seeing Patrick anymore?' she asked.

'I see him. We're not lovers at the moment. He's got too much on his plate.'

'Patrick's good for you. He gets you, because he understands here. You love people and country and it's your life too. Floyd never got that.' She stabbed the bench with her fingers to make the point.

'You finished?' I asked, getting us both glasses of water.

'No. One more thing. I think I might still love Annie. I might have been wrong.'

'Really,' I said, 'when you sober up you can focus on that, rather than my relationship. Okay.'

I talked straight but Lucy's drunk advice made me wonder if I shouldn't change my mind or at least be brave enought to talk to Patrick about how I felt before he also backed off and we were left with nothing except a cold space between us.

I woke early, feeling okay despite drinking too much the night before. Lucy was still asleep so I headed off on foot back to Mum's.

I was planning to go to a public meeting that morning about the intervention. Annie was going to meet me there at ten. Blossie was coming too, but I wasn't sure about Patrick or any of the mob from Promised Land.

By the time I arrived at Mum's, Michael had already gone to work even though it was a Sunday. She was still in bed, reading. I plonked myself on the bed next to her. 'Aren't you coming to the meeting about the intervention?'

'Nope.'

'Really?'

'Is Gloria going?'

'I don't know,' I said. 'Does it matter?'

'No, the meeting doesn't matter.'

She seemed to be in a grumpy mood so I hauled myself up, putting on the coffee before doing a quick reconnaissance. Mr and Mrs Press were sitting on their front verandah. Tommy jnr was there too and the yard was teeming with small children.

'Gloria's at home,' I reported back to Mum, 'but the meeting doesn't start for a bit.'

'She's not going, Alicia.'

I sat on the end of the bed and waited for an explanation. This was Ros, always in the thick of the action. But she ignored me and kept reading.

'What are you doing?' I asked finally.

'I was hoping to just lie here and get a cup of tea from my beautiful naive daughter.'

I shrugged. I poured tea for her and coffee for me, bringing them back to the room with a plate of cut orange and pear.

The pear was tart, the orange sweet. While I waited for Mum to explain herself I pulled at the threads of her bedspread in an attempt to provoke her but she simply drank her nettle tea and nibbled on pear as she read.

'Don't you believe in public action anymore?' I eventually asked.

She took off the glasses and rubbed the small red crease across the bridge of her nose. 'I'm not sure what I believe matters. Do I think the meeting will change anything? No. Do I think anyone's really interested in Aboriginal people managing their own lives? No. Do I believe I've made much difference? No. Is the intervention needed? Yes on some levels. Have they gone about it arse-up? Yes. Are my opinions contradictory? Yes. Is it complex? Oh fuck yes.'

'You finished?'

'Yes my last word.'

I didn't want to engage her in a fight but she was confusing me. Mum always knew what was right. Her opinions were fixed and hard, not questioning and wishy-washy. Without quite understanding why I wrote SORRY in big letters on her bedspread by pulling out threads while she studiously ignored me. When the word was done I curled up next to her on the bed.

'I love you,' she said. 'That I'm sure of.'

In the end I didn't go to the meeting, not out of any solidarity with Mum though her mood certainly had some effect. I didn't want to see Patrick if he did turn up now that Lucy's words, only a surface scratch last night, were under my skin. Instead I took a big trolley around the supermarket and made a good job of filling it. The shopping took so long I barely had time to drop off Mum's car

I'd borrowed and say goodbye before Annie was expected to pick me up. Mum hadn't moved out from her room.

'Bye,' I said. 'Keep up the cooking. And be kind to yourself.'

'And you too,' she said, reaching up to hug me goodbye. 'You don't have to run that school. There's always someone else. What did Ian Push say that time? "Whitefellas—they're like grains of sand on a beach: one washes away and another washes up."'

'What a stupid thing to say,' I said, releasing myself.

'Is it? Do you see the wheels falling off where I've been in the harness for thirty years?'

This was too large and dangerous a conversation for a Sunday afternoon. It was a potential bonfire, and I decided she could fire it up with Michael if she wanted, not with me. Luckily just then a car beeped outside. 'That'll be Annie. I have to go.'

'Say hello to Magdalene for me, will you?' Mum said. 'Tell her I'd like to see her.'

'I will. But she's not coming to town much. Perhaps you should visit.'

'Perhaps I will.'

'I love you,' I said.

'I love you too.'

I paused briefly at the doorway and studied her. She was still too thin and pale. I was glad it was Michael and not me who would have to deal with this latest mood swing of hers.

I was relieved when Caleb turned up for class on time on Monday morning. I'd been a little worried with Lekisha away for her last study block he'd slope off back to town and I knew that my own moodiness wasn't going to make this time without Lekisha easy. It was always hard without her steadiness but by Tuesday I knew we were in for a rough few weeks.

Not that he was a great help in the classroom. Without Lekisha's steady support I soon began to struggle. While Caleb was conscientious, his real interest wasn't study but football. He and the Cats seemed to feel caged in by the schoolroom. To alleviate the tension, I let him take the boys out for footy practice every day, thinking that without their distracted presence I had a better chance of controlling the little kids. The boys seemed to have turned the carrot and stick back on me. If I let them out of class more often, they'd behave better when they were in! So much for the 5.4 hours of instruction I was meant to be giving. By the fourth day without Lekisha I had extended the lunch hour and brought forward the end of the day a good half hour.

My management techniques were barely adequate. There were daily riots in the class and in the end I was so desperate I had to call in a reluctant Treasure to help. Class brought out a much grumpier side to her personality; I think if she'd had a ruler or a cane at her disposal she would have used it. As it was, the palm of her hand connected with plenty of young flesh, though only that of her own grandchildren. She didn't hit other people's kids because it would have started a war, but you could see she was sorely tempted.

After school on the Friday I was sitting in the schoolroom, planning lessons for the next week, when Magdalene came in and plonked herself down in a seat next to me.

'Iltja,' she said without preamble. 'We got to go there and get the rain to come.' Then she started talking in language, as if I could understand.

She was making a point, I saw that, but after the exhausting week I'd had I was in no mood for a lecture, or a command. And I had too much on my plate to be organising her precious culture trip. 'Magdalene, you know I can't follow what you say if you don't use English. And I'm too busy to talk about this break now.'

'It's not a break,' she said, switching language, her English crystal-clear. 'Your mother understands. This is a country visit. It's my father's father's country. We need to pay respect. We need to clean it up and bring the rain. Wash the country of all this rubbish. We got to make things right. Now.' She gestured out at the country and then got up and left without another word, her lips tightly drawn into a thin line. I knew when she said it's my father's father's country she actually meant that the country was her ancestor. That was how close her connection to the land was and I'd foolishly been quite the rudest I'd ever been to her.

I put my head down on my desk, regretting my behaviour. I should have been more respectful. I was tired and stressed but that wasn't a sufficient excuse. Especially with all the tension around the intervention. I needed to debrief but I couldn't ring Annie. I wasn't sure what was going on with her and Lucy. I didn't want to risk that being a topic that came up. In the end I rang Patrick, feeling he would understand and that maybe asking for help wasn't such a bad way to try to patch things up. Perhaps luckily he didn't answer; I left a short message asking him to call me on the pay phone.

When I went to leave the classroom I found Lucky shut in the schoolyard. I suspected Magdalene had left him there deliberately as payback for my disrespect. It took every ounce of courage I had to walk past him and unlatch the gate. He growled at me threateningly, but when he came at me it was only to get past, almost knocking me for six. My leg jammed into the post painfully. I hated that dog.

It was after nine when the pay phone rang. Preston, who was up late, answered it then knocked on my door.

I thought about giving him a message before I realised how slack that would seem. It was me who'd asked him to call but now it just seemed using. There was a crappy broken chair at the phone I could use but I planned to be brief.

Patrick was warm and kind, happy to talk me through my worry about the trip. He told me to think of how good it was in country. The lovely pace the days took on without all the usual jobs. He also reminded me of how I'd been wanting water. I wasn't sure if it was deliberate to remind me of the last time I'd talked about this. The last time we'd been together. I did know no matter how hard I'd tried to dismiss Lucy's little talk, she might be right about Patrick being good for me.

The next week passed in the same chaotic blur. On the Friday, Treasure didn't even turn up so I gave the kids a half-day off, went home and collapsed. The only thing that kept me going through the weekend was the knowledge that Lekisha would be back by Monday.

Chapter 30

Lekisha returned on Sunday afternoon, and I was thrilled to see her. Now she had completed all her study blocks she would be a fully qualified teacher once she had all the course work in. After my torrid week without her I really wanted her to feel good about her studies and understand how important she was to the school's success. I'd always suspected it, but now I knew for sure that she would be able to do the job with less help than I would need, no matter how long I stayed. Without language, without the solid relationships she had with the kids, I was never going to be as good a teacher as she would be. She needed some organisational and planning help but she could always get that from Annie or one of the teachers at Red Bore.

On Monday morning the temperature was notching up and the north wind was blowing its bad feeling all around us. To top things off, when I arrived at school Magdalene was waiting for me at the door, Lucky at her side. Sensing my fear, he growled. Magdalene raised her hand at him and he sullenly ambled away just far enough for me to unlock the door. He then lay down on the step and commenced licking his balls like the pig he was. When Lekisha arrived a few moments later, for my benefit she gave Lucky a boot to send him on his way.

'Iltja,' Magdalene said, apparently with no trace of resentment about our previous conversation. 'We got to go. I told your mum. We going now.'

'Sure,' I said.

'Good girl,' she said. I pulled up some chairs and listened while she explained why we had to make the visit as soon as possible.

Lekisha explained that we needed to go to Iltja so the weeds could be cleared before the rain came. I knew enough about land management to understand what she was referring to. On the plains, native plants, adapted to dry conditions, conserved energy during a drought by retreating, while introduced species often thrived. In waterholes the introduced reeds and weeds took over. It was like contact history, I mused. Once whitefellas got some good country with water they held on.

Magdalene said that when the site was ready, rain could come. After. She said nothing else about their plans. The old men who'd been before and left around the time of the intervention were back, swelling Treasure's house to bursting. I hoped they were the rain-makers. I'd heard about them. Seen rain credited to their work and I'd certainly never disbelieved some people might have this sort of power.

'Rain,' Lekisha said. 'It makes everything better. Fixes up every-thing.' She smiled at me in such a way that I imagined she might be referring to more than the country.

It was only towards the end of the conversation that the penny dropped that talking to me was the last step in organising the trip. Not the first. Not even the second. The last. Nobody was asking my permission. Certainly not Magdalene. She was telling me what they thought I needed to know so that I could do my part in the organising. It was kids' stuff as far as she was concerned. Unimportant facts. Financial matters.

'Okay,' I said. 'We'll make it a school trip. That way we can get approval to have the kids out of class. Otherwise the Department might get cranky with us and threaten to shut down the school. And our numbers are a bit shaky. Plus, if it's a school excursion, they might even be able to cover some of the costs. I'll look into that.'

Magdalene frowned at me.

'We can't go straightaway,' I said trying to keep some control. I ticked off the reasons on my fingers.

'We got the LAP test you mob wanted the kids to do. One more football game; two, hopefully, if we make the grand final. The end of term just there too.'

Magdalene bunched her hands on her skirt on the top of her thighs. Her face was grim but I suspected she wasn't as cranky as she looked. Lekisha seemed too relaxed. If Magdalene was really angry, Lekisha would have left me to face the music alone.

'We got to try and get money,' I pointed out. 'It will be expensive to take everyone, all the kids, all the families. So we got to get a lot.'

Magdalene nodded.

Encouraged, I pushed on. 'And we got to win the footy first. Caleb, Henry, Patrick, all the men are really focused on that one. And it's all the boys think about.'

'Kele,' Magdalene said. So we had a deal. She got up to leave, then stopped at the doorway. 'We got a lot of mouths to feed. But Land Council will help. We ask them. They still standing up for Aboriginal people. Only ones might be.'

I nodded in agreement. It was true that allies were getting thin on the ground.

'Because everyone's coming. Not just Promised Land. Red Bore family, Kilka too.'

'Kilka?' I wondered if Patrick had known when he talked to me.

We started class that morning a little late. But we had a plan. I didn't even mind that the wind was blowing dust everywhere. Bring it on, I thought. We had a plan to put clouds in the sky.

Over the next few days I tried to find out what sort of funding we could get. There weren't many options. Given the money pouring into the Territory it was annoyingly difficult to find any that wasn't tied to employing some white boss. The short timeframe didn't help. I knew even if I got approval the money itself would take much longer to materialise. In any case I thought I could juggle the books if I needed to. Get Mum to give me some tips.

Lekisha helped me out with the language spellings I needed for the submission I hurriedly got together. Names for plants. Lucky I'd been doing that small bit of work for Patrick and knew more place names and bird species than I did once. For a land-management-focused submission we listed all the living things at Iltja that our work would assist.

On some levels, of course, the money didn't really matter.

I might have been wrong but I had a feeling Iltja would go ahead even if we could only afford to buy flour for damper and bullets for kangaroo.

Writing wasn't really my thing but there was to be no wriggling out of it. I'd assumed Mum might be of some help editing my submissions. She was claiming that everything had changed so much she no longer knew what bureaucracy expected these days and she had no intention of learning how to jump through new hoops. She did send me a fax: Stop worrying about money. Think about what you need to do at Iltja. I shook my head in exasperation. One minute she was the Black Knight the next the Dalai Lama?

I got Lucy to look over my writing. She had a good eye and I appreciated her help. When she asked whether I'd patched things up with Patrick I told her to do something about her own love life. She told me it was all grog talk and I laughed and told her it didn't sound like that was all it was to me at all.

Before I sent the final copies of the submissions off to the various agencies I took them over for Magdalene and Henry to approve. Henry answered the door and asked me to follow him out the back where quite a group of the old men who'd come and gone mysteriously for the last few months were gathered. There would have been about ten of them sitting on the ground under the bough shelter. Magdalene and Esther were there too. Everyone looked at me as Magdalene told me to read my submissions out loud. I wished there was a way to refuse, but I didn't see how. I sat down and began to read, mortified by the sound of my sentences aloud. The expression seemed convoluted, and the requests for money weak and too sucky. By the time I'd finished, I wanted to rip the letters up. What vanity had made me think I could pull off this sort of writing and why hadn't Lekisha warned me of the scrutiny I would come under?

Before I could leave the circle, an old whiskered man I didn't know got up. Motioning me to stay, he began to address us all in language. I understood two words, whitefella and myall. I was right. He thought I was stupid. His talk went on and on, and for the first time all year I felt immensely uncomfortable to be the only non-Aboriginal person present. Magdalene was rocking back and forth, I could only assume in agreement with whatever he was saying. When the old man sat down, another got up on bandy legs that had seen a lot of horse, and made a similarly fiery speech. He was followed by a third man who spoke in the same mode.

By now I was getting scared. I'd picked up a few more words, including those for girl, intervention and army. It wasn't looking good.

Finally, Henry signalled with a nod of his head that I could now leave. When I got up, my legs were a little unsteady, and not just from being folded politely to the side for too long.

As I went around the side of the house Lekisha stepped out, to grab me, beaming.

'They all proper proud,' she said.

'Proud?'

'Yeah. They reckon that's a really good story you told the government for the trip.'

'They did?'

'Yeah.'

A flood of relief swept through my body. I felt weak.

'You right?' she asked.

I nodded. I would be. 'I thought they were mad with me. They kept pointing to their heads like they were growling at me, like proper cranky.'

Lekisha smiled broadly. 'You're mad. They were just saying the government mobs got to clean out their ears and start listening to what Aboriginal people are saying. To stories like the one you wrote down for us.'

I walked home and made a cup of tea. I drank it slowly, reflecting on how readily I'd been prepared to believe people might simply turn on me. Maybe it was a whitefella thing and I'd never get rid of it, no matter how different I thought I was to others running around in the communities. It was true I wasn't some green idiot from Sydney telling people what they could and couldn't buy with their managed funds but I didn't read people as well as I should have. And I suspected it was because on some deep level I just assumed we'd be in conflict, that it was an historical imprint. When I had a chance I might talk to someone about it, Mum or Michael or Patrick even, and see if they'd ever felt the same thing or if I was just crazy like Lekisha often insisted I was.

We made the grandfinal. Easy. Everyone was happy. Except Patrick. His hearing date was set for the week before the game.

'You'll have to organise everything yourself.'

'No I won't,' I said. My hand waved out at all the people. 'I think this mob will make sure everything happens that has too.'

'Call me if you need anything,' he said.

I laughed. 'I'm not sure what you could help with from down there.'

He did the thing with his mouth, where he searched for words and couldn't find what he was looking for.

'Good luck,' I said. 'I doubt I'll see you before you go.'

I gave him a hug. We held it longer than was necessary and I gave him a quick peck on the cheek.

'See ya,' I said.

I felt his eyes on me as I walked away and I turned and waved, a mixture of regret and hope churning inside me.

At Mum's I ate some of the homemade baba ghanoush she was keen for me to try.

'It's good,' I declared.

'Texture okay?'

'Perfect.'

'And the char, can you taste it? What about the seasoning, enough? Not too much salt?'

'Mum, can you stop sounding like a judge in a reality cooking show? You're freaking me out.'

Though her good spirits cheered me. 'What you want to talk about. Community? The Intervention? Politics?' she asked cheekily.

'Iltja.'

'Iltja?'

'Yes. Magdalene tells me the water is fed by a deep spring, that there's quite a lot, and I can't wait to get into it. I feel so dry I could crack up. Have you ever been there with her?'

'No. Not with her,' she said. 'You know it's a sacred site.'

'I figured that. It's got water. Isn't everywhere with water sacred?'

'I don't know, ask Magdalene.'

'I'm asking you.'

'Like I said, I'm not an Aboriginal person. I don't speak for them.'

'Why are you being so weird?'

'I'm not being weird.'

I made crumbs of the dry biscuit she'd made to go with her dip.

'She's asked me to come,' she said, folding her arms.

I had a feeling Magdalene might have.

'She thinks it will be good if we both go. With all the families. I expect everyone is coming.'

'Everyone,' I said. I couldn't help thinking it was a bit mean of her not to help me with the submissions when she knew she was coming.

There was a look on Mum's face I hadn't seen for years which said she had a secret she wasn't telling me. I guessed it was something about Iltja and it made me feel uncomfortable. I wasn't like her, I'd never gone as deep into Magdalene's world as she had. In all the years I'd been friends with Lekisha she'd never encouraged me to either. Perhaps it said something about different times and expectations but whatever the reason it was how it was. Suddenly I felt all the gaps in my knowledge. I wasn't sure I was ready to change that.

'Do you know what's going to happen there?' I asked, trying not to sound too anxious. 'It's all good, isn't it? Nothing too left field?'

'Alicia, has anyone else ever told you that you ask too many questions?' her tone was teasing.

'Yep—Lekisha, often.'

'Well, try listening to her,' she said more seriously.

'I am listening.' Did my mother think I was an idiot?

She closed her hands around mine. 'Don't panic. Nothing's going to happen that you need to worry about. It will be lovely. Wait and see.'

CHAPTER 31

The grand final was to be held on the second Saturday in September. In the days leading up to it, I swear we bought every bit of blue and white crepe paper there was to be had in the town. Lekisha bought cans and cans of blue hairspray, and Henry went so far as to paint his minibus the team colours. I spent hours scouring the op shops, Kmart and Target for clothes in blue and white stripes. The word was they were doing just as much at Kilka to prepare. We cut paper and made streamers for a week, any pretence of getting on with schoolwork simply discarded. I was glad we'd sat the LAP tests a couple of weeks earlier. Hopefully they'd gone okay. The tests weren't as tricky as I'd feared and the kids had applied themselves more than I'd dared hope.

A courier turned in to Promised Land with a special delivery of several parcels the night before the game. From the Geelong Football Club the parcels were all addressed to Caleb, who was in the shower. The courier insisted he sign for the delivery. Caleb, though, didn't hurry. By the time he came out there was a curious group gathered. The kids were poking the parcels and taking guesses.

Patrick's efforts to keep Geelong abreast of our progress was well rewarded. Inside the first box were large Cats stickers. They were special. They just had our names on them and the stripes were wider. Same with the jerseys in the second box. Some had Irrarnte and the others had Kilka across the front. Cats were on the back They were great. There was enough for every kid. Even Declan scored one he'd be growing into for years. The stickers were stuck everywhere. On the school door, and all the cars. I wasn't sure the Department would exactly approve of the two Preston stuck on the school troopy, but I didn't really care.

The happiness being in the grand final had brought was like nothing I'd seen in the community before, though it reminded me of my own school years, when the Magpies and Tommy jnr's daring marks and fancy footwork were all we talked about for six months of every year. The Geelong team itself was going well. They were raging favourites to win the AFL flag for the first time in fifty years. A good omen we all thought. For the old Geelong faithful it was going to be a fantastic double. Once that would have been me, but ten years with Floyd and watching his Rugby league team the Bulldogs, I barely cared any longer.

I had another reason to be feeling good. Patrick had sent a fax. Lekisha had just given it to me so I assumed she'd spread the word. It was fairly impersonal. He had an interim order for an access weekend. He was bringing Tom up to see our grandfinal.

On the morning of the big game, we had a big community breakfast, with bacon and eggs cooked on the barbecue by Henry.

I helped Lekisha butter slices of bread, while Treasure spooned out porridge with sliced banana and honey on top.

The cars from Kilka turned up exactly at nine o'clock, as agreed.

It constantly amazed me how punctual people could be if an engagement was important to them.

On our arrival at the oval I saw Mum and Michael sitting in the stands with Lucy and Frank waving at us. My stomach was churning. It was hardly anything to do with the game, although I did care if we won. I wanted it as much as everyone else. I also wanted to see Patrick and his son. I scanned the crowd as I moved to join the Promised Land and Kilka mob. They were always on the far side of the oval, away from the stands. Unlike me, they seemed relaxed. Everyone was expecting to easily beat the opposing team; we'd only lost to them once, in an early round. Ever confident, Lekisha had bet me we'd win by a margin of five goals. It was one wager I hoped she won.

The game was minutes away from a start before I caught sight of Patrick standing on the other side with Michael. A small dark-haired boy was perched on his shoulders. When Patrick saw me, he put up a hand in an enthusiastic wave and nearly toppled his son off. I waved back as the boy scrambled to grab his dad's thick curls. Even from this distance I could see the photo had not lied. They were like peas in a pod.

I switched my attention to the game. Almost immediately, the other team scored. And again. In the opening ten minutes they had three goals on us. Disconcerted, I stayed where I was. The game made me nervous. Patrick made me nervous. Lekisha reassured me so I sat down close to her. I needed her confidence and calm to rub off on me.

At the next centre bounce the lanky centre from Kilka took out one of our own players with a carelessly flung elbow and the little bloke fell to the ground. Caleb had to carry him off in his arms. Preston, who hadn't dropped a ball all season, fumbled as though he had grease on his hands. Sammy stumbled for no reason. Kicks they usually nailed through the big posts went west or east of even the little sticks. Calling and encouraging the boys seemed to make them slower, more awkward, less confident. Shocked, we fell silent. Even Rosia, sitting in Magdalene's lap, sensed the mood and stopped her babbling and clapping.

At quarter-time the supporters rushed over to Tommy jnr and the team on the side of the oval. Caught up in watching the frantic gesturing and agitated talk I didn't realise that Patrick and Tom had made their way around to me until I saw them approaching up the grassy slope. Patrick looked well and happy, his green eyes engaging me as they'd done the first time I met him.

'Tom, this is Alicia, my friend,' Patrick said, squatting down next to me.

'Your girlfriend, Mum says,' said Tom.

I gave a stupid laugh of shock.

'Mmm,' Patrick said, 'say hello to Alicia.'

'Hello, Tom,' I said.

'Hello,' he said and put his hand out formally for me to shake.

Lekisha put out her hand to the boy. He looked at it unsurely.

'My friend Lekisha,' Patrick said.

'Hello,' said Lekisha, 'Okay, you don't shake. Can you high five?'

He put up a hand hesitantly. She hit it gently with her palm before he changed his mind. 'High five,' she called, and laughed at the flash of fright on his face.

'She won't eat you if you promise not to eat her,' I said, smiling gently at the boy. He was trying hard not to be terrified. I thought his mother must be a complete arsehole.

'How about a pie?' said Patrick.

'Can I have a sausage roll?' Tom asked.

'My favourite,' said Lekisha.

'Mine too.'

'Okay,' said Patrick, 'I'll see what I can do.'

He and Tom headed off. I didn't really think they'd bring us food back. I was going to ring him and see what that nonsense was all about. His girlfriend, his squeeze, the bullets in her gun. How had that happened? I texted *What the fk GIRLFRIEND???!*

If the game had been going our way I might not have been able to put it temporarily to the back of my mind. But the game was going pear-shaped. It took all my attention. I had never wanted us to win more. I found myself bargaining in my head like I used to as a kid. If we win, I'll stay on next year if the community ask. If we win, I'll make Lekisha dinner every week. If we win, I'll never tell Caleb off for his sloppy cleaning again. In a final desperate pact I promised I'd never sleep with Patrick again if we lost. Not even if he declared he loved me.

During the half-time break Lekisha deserted me to join everyone else who was advising the team and I wandered over to see Michael and Mum. They were sitting with Mr and Mrs Press and Frank and his two sons. Lucy and Annie I noticed were having an intense chat a little apart from the group.

'Don't worry, Alicia, it's only half-time,' said Mrs Press.

'Plenty of time,' Mr Press said.

Mum shrugged as though she couldn't care less. 'It's only footy.' Mrs Press gave my mother a slap on the arm and Mum laughed. 'See how footy brings out the aggression in people?'

We ignored her. 'Why aren't you lot sitting with us?' I asked. 'Scared to be seen with community in case some bureaucrat starts managing you?'

Only Frank smiled at my little joke. 'You know why we don't sit with you. You and Lekisha make too much racket. We'll stay where it's quiet.'

'You mob can talk,' I said to no-one in particular, but they all knew I was talking about Gloria. Her carry-on at Tommy jnr's games was legendary. She'd had more than one warning for her one-eyed barracking from everyone from the refs to fellow supporters.

Patrick and Tom were coming back from the shop and we crossed paths as I was on my way to get a couple of sausage rolls myself. There was no need. Patrick already had a couple for me that he handed me, deliberately taking my hand as he did.

'Delicious,' I said to Tom, pointing to his pastry.

He nodded agreeably, sauce dripping down his hands.

I met Patrick's gaze. 'I'll call,' I said.

'I'm back to Sydney tomorrow, then back to Kilka.'

'Girlfriend?' I asked.

He smiled. 'A long story.'

'I thought it would be,' I said. 'We'll talk sometime. When there's space.'

Patrick smiled, relieved, I thought. 'Good. I'm looking forward to it.'

I felt a tiny bit more hopeful. Five minutes into the third quarter I was miserable about the game. Floyd used to say if you lost the third quarter you were sunk. I didn't know why he knew this— he wasn't even an AFL supporter but a rugby man. It seemed he might be right. At the siren at the end of the quarter we were down twenty points.

Across the oval Mum had picked up Tommy jnr's baby and was pacing about with him over her shoulder, looking worried. It seemed that maybe she did care, after all. I headed back towards the grass and Lekisha. Out of everyone Henry seemed the calmest. He strode out to the middle of the oval and walked around the boys steadily as if inspecting something invisible. Preston took his grandfather's arm and pulled him down to say something in his ear.

'Something wrong,' Lekisha said, her face scrunched up with concern.

'What?'

'Henry will fix it. Don't worry.' But of course I did worry.

Henry leant into their huddle and spoke. I wondered what he could possibly say to turn things around. Even if we played much better, victory seemed still unlikely with the scores as they were. When he'd finished, a solid cry went up from the players.

'Cats!'

The Cats came back in the last quarter more like the tigers we expected. Wrestling and leaping they took control of the game.

Our score slowly crept up. We traded our silence with the opposition for their voice, screaming and shouting at the boys to go get them. Go, Cats!

Magdalene drummed on the tin advertisements on the wire fence, her skinny legs wobbling with the effort of stamping her support. Her voice was high and screeching, cutting across the racket the rest of us women were making. The men were more circumspect and sat quietly, but we barracked loudly without shame. Magdalene was insisting on the win as I kept checking the time. With three minutes left we were still eight points behind. Then Sammy put a point on. Straight after, Preston nailed a long goal. There were barely seconds left. The centre bounce had never been so crucial. To win it had to go our way. It didn't. The other team flooded forward, surging to victory, until an overconfident player lost the ball in a daring steal by Preston. He ran away with it, weaving like a demon. One, two, three bounces and he was halfway down the field. Time was almost up. He had to take a shot and his kick fell short of the posts by about two metres. For a moment I was certain we'd lost, until I saw that due to the opposition's surge forward there was no-one in the square. Achingly slowly, Preston's ball managed to grub its way across the line for a goal just as the siren sounded.

We had it. A five-point win. We ran onto the field, screaming and waving like maniacs. All the women, the girls, the boys who were too young to play and the past-it men. We flicked our streamers at the players in our excitement. Tommy and Caleb put Preston up on their shoulders. We were drunk with success, falling all over the place and singing out excitedly.

At the presentation I sat next to Magdalene and tried to take in the whole spectacle more calmly. The players from the other team were small exhausted wrecks lying on the grass. Some were crying as their mothers did their best to console them. It was a sobering sight. It could easily have been us.

We hadn't won the national premiership, I reminded myself. It was just local footy. The teams were all children.

'It's just kids' footy,' I said, to no-one in particular. Lekisha and Magdalene looked at me as though I was an imbecile. It was a win, and wins were hard to get if you were an Aboriginal person. Especially in these times. Kilka and Promised Land would get their name on a town trophy. Families would take from it all the pleasure and joy they could. It didn't matter that it was under-fifteens. They were winners.

It took an age to get everyone organised afterwards. Leaving the grounds was utter bedlam as we sorted people into cars and drove to the council lawns. I bought buckets of chicken and boxes of chips from the takeaway and got the kids to ferry them across the road. There were enough cups of soft drink to make a dentist weep and the fried chicken oozed fat, but for once I didn't worry about delivering a warning lecture on the bad food.

Patrick turned up with Tom. He had a box with him tucked under his arm. He had a quiet word to Caleb, who stood up and then asked Tommy jnr up too. They opened the box. Tom got each small trophy out of the box and handed them on. Either Caleb or Tommy jnr read the names out. Each boy came up. It was a sweet little ceremony, out in public view. Family clapped each boy and helped the shy ones to their feet. While everyone was occupied it seemed a good time to slip away. I gave Lekisha the school car key. I had Mum's. I wanted to have some weekend for myself and I waved Patrick goodbye.

Lucy's house was cool and quiet when I let myself in. There was a smell of patchouli oil and I was wondering why it seemed so familiar when Annie wandered into the kitchen in Lucy's dressing gown. That's who wore it.

'Hello,' I said.

She jumped. 'I didn't see you.'

'Sorry, I didn't think anyone was home. Maybe I should go. I don't want to crowd anyone.'

'You're fine,' said Lucy, coming in wrapped in a sarong and putting an arm around Annie.

'We were going to go to the movies, you want to come?'

'Sure,' I said.

If they weren't making a big deal of being back together I wasn't going to. If I'd learnt nothing in the last months it was that following other people's leads was usually the best and least complicated path.

CHAPTER 32

The week after our boys' success there were two things to look forward to. The school holidays, just one week this time and the AFL grand final, which the real Cats were in. I couldn't have cared less about the grand final. I wanted a break. I wanted to see Patrick. He'd faxed me saying I could call if I wanted but he'd like to meet up to talk in person. He replied to my fax. It was the only personalised one he'd sent all year and as luck would have it Lekisha took it off the machine and read it. Out loud.

'Dear Alicia, can we meet? I think about you more than is healthy and I know you must have lots of questions. So . . .'

I snatched the paper out of Lekisha's hand. 'Dear Alicia, be nice,' she teased.

'You are lucky I am nice, what if I teased you about Mr Blue Falcon. Saw you in it the other day.'

Lekisha blushed. 'Bullshit.'

It was, in fact, but it had got the desired reaction. I folded Patrick's fax away and read the details later.

*

Patrick and I had arranged to meet at Lucy's because she'd gone to Darwin for work. He was sitting on the step when I arrived. I walked towards him feeling overly self-conscious. I'd thought I'd have time to change and get dressed before he arrived. I was in bush clothes. A skirt which had seen better days and a long sleeved shirt.

'Hey gorgeous girlfriend,' he said.

'But I'm not your girlfriend,' I said tartly. 'That's the problem.'

'Will you be?' He put his hand on his heart dramatically, his expression one of appeal.

I laughed. He blocked me on the stairs. He had the height advantage. I tilted my chin and looked up. He kissed me.

'Take my bag, will you?' I asked pulling back. 'I'll get the key from the laundry,' I swung him my little pack. 'Let's go inside. You can tell me how I got the title without any of the advantages.'

If it had happened to someone else I might have found it funny when Patrick told me what Linda'd done. I felt violated. Apparently she'd hired a private investigator. I thought they only existed in the crime novels I read. He had compiled a file on me. They had records of our night at the hotel. Details of my mother's activism arrests. They knew about my divorce. I was described as being sympathetic to communist views. I had to get a beer at that point.

'What on earth was all this for?'

'To prove the type of person I was, by proxy. Someone whose tastes ran to deviants.'

I was angry.

'So what did you say about your girlfriend?'

'I said she was smart and lovely. That we'd broken up because she didn't want to be something that could be used in the court case. I understood Linda would probably use everything she could to prove her point that the Aboriginal community I live on was toxic and the people I hung out with subhuman, both the black and the white ones.'

I couldn't take my eyes off him. Fancy having to have a fight like that. It was incredible he stayed so together.

'There are transcripts,' he offered, 'if you want to read every word.'

I didn't. At least not now. I kissed him.

'So how on earth did you win? Have you won?'

'I think I'll get very healthy access rights. The judge wasn't impressed with her vindictiveness or her racism. If she'd been less over the top she might have done better. But he gave her enough rope to submit evidence which she hung herself on. Like a photo of you with Preston, Kane, Little Mary and Rosia. Outside the cinema. I don't even know when it was taken. The kids look, well like the kids look. And she tried to say it proved you condoned poor hygiene.'

'You're joking?'

'No. I wish I was. I had a child with this woman remember.'

He was quite cut up.

'Everyone had new shoes,' I said, my voice wavering with hurt. 'We were quite flash that day.'

Those poor kids, used like that. I hugged him and he held on to me tightly, burying his head in my neck, his body shaking. I stroked his back, holding him firmly, kissing the top of his head. He wiped a hand over his face and sat back up.

'Sorry,' he said.

'Don't be,' I said. 'It's done.' We took each other in, with eyes wide open. I knew at that moment I loved him.

We dropped our clothes on the floor where we were. Finally some sweetness.

Hours later, when we lay around in the bath, I said, 'You know I want kids. That is why I left Floyd. He didn't.'

'Do you?' he said.

'I do.' I cricked my neck so I could see his response.

'How many?' he asked.

I kissed his chest. 'I'm happy to start with one.'

After the break, Iltja came into focus. I hadn't had any responses to the submissions but it seemed we were going regardless. Henry was put in charge of borrowing the big-ticket items we needed: extra cars, a trailer, some tools.

Managing the kids in this hot last term was worse than I'd feared. We'd already taken a knock before but we'd had football to pull us back. Now I was on my own. The only thing stopping me getting really depressed about it, was that according to Patrick things were going worse at Kilka.

Caleb started skipping work. I wasn't sure he was going to town to drink, but the glory conferred on him by the team's grand-final win seemed to have gone to his head. I tried to pull him into line, but just like with the kids it seemed I was on my own. Lekisha could not pull him in. I decided that I would wait till after the trip to Iltja to tackle the problems we were facing. I imagined Iltja all the time, cool freshwater pools and it dominated not only my thoughts but all my spare time. Patrick and I were both drawn into helping prepare for the trip. Everything, including spending time together, would have to wait until after the trip.

One midweek evening Lekisha dropped over with Rosia. Preston wandered in after them with his usual impeccable timing around food and joined us for dinner. He wasn't the only one, but he'd missed three days of school in a row. I waited till he'd eaten his main course before telling him I didn't think he looked very sick. It shamed him enough that he slunk home when my back was turned.

While Lekisha ate a slice of orange cake I played on the floor with Rosia. I was trying to show her how to crawl. I knew it irritated Lekisha. Like most people in the community she thought a baby should be held until it walked. She'd carried Caleb for so long he'd seemed like an extension of her body, and clearly it hadn't affected his physical development. Despite good drinking times he was still remarkably fit.

'Don't glare at me like that,' I said. 'It's good for a baby's brain. Plenty of research says a baby that crawls for a long time has better brain development. In particular, there's strong evidence it's crucial in developing the skills for reading.'

'Whitefellas got a paper on everything, don't they?'

'Yeah,' I said, 'and soon you're going to get one. A diploma in education.' I poked her with my foot. 'Not everything about us mob is bad. What's with you?'

'I'm not getting paid.'

'What do you mean?'

'Nothing since before the holiday.'

'Why didn't you say?'

'You were busy. On a romantic holiday.'

'One weekend,' I said.

'You been busy.'

'Not so busy I can't work out your pay. Don't be a duffer.'

'I haven't got the sack?'

'No, you haven't got the sack.'

'That's all right, I thought you just didn't want to tell me. I thought maybe intervention mob they cut my job.'

'No, they can't touch us.'

I'd work it out tomorrow. It would be forgotten but I'd never stop wondering why things were never straight around here. Always circle way.

I was already awake when Magdalene and her brute of a dog arrived in the early hours. Pulling on my trackpants, I joined them on the verandah. She'd taken a chair. Lucky was chewing a large bone that looked like it could have been someone's leg. He growled menacingly at me.

'Keep your shirt on, I don't want your bone,' I told the dog before asking Magdalene if she wanted tea. She did.

I threw some breakfast food together. Bread from Patrick, jam, a couple of boiled eggs, before taking a seat on the far side away from Lucky.

'You're looking strong,' Magdalene said.

'Am I? How?'

'You're like your mummy. You come here weak and you get

strong.' She reached over and patted my arm affectionately. 'It's good your mum is coming to Iltja. We can have a talk there. All together. All the womans.'

I nodded. No doubt I'd find out there what she wanted to talk about. Now I could only speculate. She peeled an egg expertly and salted up each bite.

'Patrick's a good friend to Aboriginal people,' she said out of the blue. 'He's clever too. Knows lots. Woman like you should have a husband, settle down.'

'Don't worry, I'm trying,' I assured her. 'Now you didn't come over to tell me that?'

'No. I came to tell you, Iltja, we going.'

'I know. You told me, heaps of times you told me.'

'This week we go. We got the money. After shopping we go. Take someone to help you.'

'We have money?'

'Yes. My cousin in Land Council told me.'

I gave a snort of amusement. Was there nothing she didn't know first?

I gave her a hand to get up. She was tired and old but I could see the excitement in her face and she looked less worried than she'd been. I watched her walk away, moving lightly over the earth, her savage dog slavishly following.

Inside I cleaned my little house as though I might be away for a while. I'd go see Treasure and Lekisha to help with the shopping list. There wasn't much time to get organised if we left by the end of the week as Magdalene wanted.

It felt like a hundred forms I had to complete to get permission for it to be a school excursion. Luckily Patrick had to do it too and I copied his, almost word for word. And I gave Lekisha some days out of the classroom and she and Treasure knocked the shopping on the head. Not without drama. Treasure was furious when she saw how cheap Woolies was. All I could do was to tell her I'd speak to Centrelink to see if we could shift her food allocation from the Red Bore shop. But I knew the big supermarkets wouldn't play ball with the government. They were probably waiting to be paid for the trouble and it was going to take months if not years before there was a flexible system to run the quarantining of income. The other smaller drama was having to wait till the last minute to buy all the fresh food because even with the school fridge we were pressed to store it and Lekisha and Treasure did the final shop the night before we left.

At dawn the sky was the palest opal blue. I could already tell it was going to be hot. We were four weeks short of term ending and things would only get hotter. There was a distinctive smell that accompanied proper summer heat. Strangely enough out here in the desert, it was a coastal scent. Something salty and faraway. Today I didn't care how hot it got because we were finally going to the water.

I got dressed in long linen pants to protect my legs from the scrub and pulled on boots. I stuffed a few clean clothes and a couple of cotton sarongs Lucy had brought me back from Bali into my backpack. A sarong, I'd learnt as a kid, was the best thing to take bush. It could be a rug, a shawl, a shadecloth, a skirt, a rope. Almost anything.

As I picked up my swag it hit me how funny it was I'd done virtually no camping since I'd arrived. With running to town and going to Kilka and football there'd never been time and ironically I'd probably done more the year before.

Lekisha was already at the school when I got there and we packed the cars carefully, evenly distributing the weight, piling boxed food under the bench seats in the back of the troop carrier. Slowly other people arrived to help. Treasure and Henry. Caleb who'd been fairly absent. Tissianna was sitting sullenly in the front seat of Henry's car. She must have been dragged back from town during the night. Lekisha said they'd tried to bring Maxine too. It was compassionate how they'd bothered to make sure even those young ones off the rail had a chance to come on what would be an important trip. It might not help us with allocating seats, or having quite enough food but it was admirable, the level of care they showed.

As we continued to load up the cars I thought we might have overdone the supplies, although it was probably impossible to have too much food with so many people. There were boxes of potatoes, pumpkins, tomatoes, apples and oranges, and others filled with dry and canned food including biscuits, rice and tuna. We'd bought three boxes of bread and stacks of flour. I filled jerrycans of water while Lekisha sneered.

'It's got water,' she said. 'It's lovely water there.'

I ignored her. There was no way I was going to be front-page news: School teacher and pupils die of dehydration.

Treasure and I carried the heavy containers to the cars and Henry lifted them onto roof racks with Caleb's help. When we'd finished I stuck my tongue out at Lekisha, and she immediately returned the gesture.

'You two are like little kids,' Magdalene said.

I laughed at the truth in that. I was feeling that old excitement I'd felt going on bush trips as a kid. It was a pity Mum wasn't travelling with us, but she'd head out with Red Bore family.

Finally we were ready. All the blankets and mattresses and bags of clothes were stuffed into the cavities between the food or up on top with the swags. At the last minute I checked the school vehicle's oil and water.

'That car right. You going to give it a service or what?'

I grinned at Lekisha. 'Nothing wrong with being careful.'

'Nothing wrong with keeping everyone waiting, I suppose.'

I looked around. Magically while my back was turned everyone had claimed a spot in a car. They were packed to the gills. Magdalene was on the bench seat in the front of the school car I was driving, Esther sitting next to her, taking up less room than a handful of sticks. The only space I could see anywhere was between those old ladies' bones!

Caleb was already idling one of the three cars we had on loan from Land Council and Henry was at the wheel of trayback, which was by far the most heavily loaded with gear. If it had been a boat it would have been taking in water.

'I'll just be a second,' I said, slamming the bonnet closed and running towards the schoolroom.

'What now?' Lekisha complained.

'I forgot to fax the department the list of the kids going on the excursion,' I called out.

I copied off the roll, ticked off all the names, and faxed it away.

Outside, the convoy of cars stood in a wriggly line, a bulky multicoloured caterpillar with green swags lining the roofs.

'Yeperenye,' I shouted, and fetched my camera from the bag at Magdalene's feet. Once there was a camera on the scene all the kids went silly and had to stick their heads and hands out the windows. Only a mix of threats and cajoling made it possible to get one shot where no-one was pulling a clown face or making gangster gestures. Then I got in the car and we were on our way.

The dogs ran with us all the way to the boundary fence, where they got jack of it and dropped away. All except Lucky, who stayed with us till the grid. Magdalene pointed it out, chuffed her ugly dog was clearly the top one.

In the fresh morning light the distant ranges were nothing more than a silhouette. It was hard to believe it had been eight months since the day I'd looked out at their majestic silhouettes and decided to take the job. Steadily we moved towards them, the tyres deep in a rust-red track. The scene before us looked almost staged. Rocks, trees, bushes appeared deliberately placed for maximum effect as the rising sun flooded light over the country. Russet-red became pink, grasses golden. I drove with a growing sense of excitement to be going deeper into country.

When we came to the branch road the Kilka cars were waiting as planned. There were two troopies, the school's and Patrick's. I gave a small wave, which he returned with a warm smile. Trying to ignore the way my heart leapt to see him, I focused on driving and keeping my place in the convoy.

Henry led the way. I followed. Caleb and Lekisha came next, then the Kilka cars. I was shepherded, kept safe. It wasn't a coincidence I had Magdalene and Treasure in my car. We also had Tissianna, who needed looking after, although I suspected she wasn't yet feeling as sick as she would be tomorrow or the day after. At least at Iltja she could be looked after safely as her body dried out.

It became clear that Magdalene and Treasure's main role was to judge the road conditions on my behalf and provide directions. About twenty kilometres in, the track seemed to entirely disappear and I was instructed to head left and follow Henry along a route invisible to me, but which they clearly could see.

'We go here,' Magdalene said confidently.

I shrugged and did what I was told. If I'd learnt nothing else over the years it had been that arguing was pointless and even questioning was a waste of breath. I hoped by now I did it with some if only limited grace.

CHAPTER 33

Our route I imagined must be the way people had always come into this part of the country. It was an ancient path not designed for cars. Coming in on foot seemed infinitely more sensible.

We trekked up a dry creek bed for a while and the car slid badly on the flat stones. It was like waterskiing over hard windy water and I began to worry the car might tip over, so I slowly pulled us to a stop to let some air out of the tyres.

As I explained what I was doing it was Magdalene's turn to shrug as if I worried too much. What Magdalene would have told me, if she could have thought of a polite way to do so, was that I'd been away too long and had forgotten that tyres weren't the most important thing to keep a person safe: being respectful in and to country mattered far more. But she said nothing while I stuck a stick into each valve and guessed at the right amount of air to let out, without the benefit of a gauge.

When we took off again I felt the car sat down better and the driving was easier, the flatter tyres giving us more traction. Waves of flat scree crashed against the tyres and stone chips pinged against the body of the car, making hundreds of tinny splashes. I steered the car upstream as the ground shifted, lapping at the underside, dragging us in a gritty current this way and that. My passengers sloshed against each other, uncomplaining. Slowly we made ground.

In the back the women and children were busy noting details in the landscape, their voices alive. I too felt happy. Even though we lived out bush, there were many aspects of community life that were as oppressive as suburban living. Going into country was something else again, and everyone's spirits seemed to be rising.

An hour later as we cut across country, the rough side of the range inched further into focus. Like all the hills it had two distinct faces, one smooth and young, the other old and weathered. Scientists attributed this to the shifting of tectonic plates in earlier geological ages, while Magdalene, and everyone else I was travelling with, had dreaming stories to explain this phenomenon. I didn't know much about either explanation. I only saw what was there: red-washed rocks like dinosaur bones running in ragged spines. As we continued, the ground became older, worn and jagged. Sharp splintered rocks spiked up through the earth like axe heads. No flat, smooth river stones to be seen. I was intimidated by the harshness, glad I wasn't out here by myself. We were spaced out well for safety, Patrick out of sight at the rear, but we were together.

I was concentrating so hard on the few feet of country ahead of us, watching for anything that might puncture a tyre, that it took me a while to notice that we were now moving towards a gap in the rocky face of the range. It soon became more distinct and we trundled towards it over large ridges, our bones rattling. I was glad of the steering wheel to hang on to. The car moved at a walking pace and my lower back was beginning to ache from the relentless jarring. For a minute I let my eyes wander from the track ahead. I saw tiny white paper flowers, faded with age, growing in the cracks in the earth. Minute saltbush plants offered up hard ruby-red berries. Fragile beauty was in the detail, urging us on.

Suddenly we were descending a steep slope; in the back, everyone leant back as if riding on horseback. Preston laughed with glee, as though he was on a show ride. Tissianna swore, blaming my driving, and Magdalene growled at me to veer left. I ignored her. If there had been a better way I knew Henry would have taken it, and I followed his lead without question, straining the engine in low gear, keeping us upright.

The car evened out as we approached the rocky gateway into the ranges. Passing through the gap, for the briefest moment we were in the dark shadow of the range. Their weight leant in on us threateningly before we re-emerged into the light in a hidden valley.

Magdalene started a low rhythmic singing, as if the landscape was a songbook demanding attention. Notes from time immemorial found voice, passed from one mouth to another, along a line of women. Cycles were sung. The cadence was as familiar to me as wind in mulga bush though I knew nothing of the songs' meanings, only that the words belonged to this place as surely as did the animals, the insects, the blue of the sky overhead. These were songs sacred as those sung by any choral choir or the chants from a prophet's book.

As Magdalene's song completed a cycle the women took up its threads and wove it anew, younger voices finding their way within it. Preston and the other kids listened with an intensity they rarely brought to their schoolwork.

We drove on even more slowly, now in the sand. The space between the cars had closed up, and we were almost bumper to bumper, joined again like a green and white caterpillar as we lumbered into the concealed sacred site. I could almost feel the others concentrating, trying to keep the cars pushing along, the low gears whining. Steady movement kept us from bogging in the soft sand. Finally the hills folded around us. We were where we were meant to be, coming to a stop inside the gap at the bottom of a valley.

By contrast with the faded brown shades of the open country, here water brought primary colours into play. Ficus trees hung from the cliffs. Olive-green, they shot pale spidery roots in an intricate webbing down the rock face, tying themselves down. Small white gums stood in soft openings of soil.

Following Henry's lead, I parked on an arc of stone. Old tall river red gums surrounded us, their limbs lifted towards the glorious blue of the pocket of sky. Iltja was a well-concealed sanctuary. It was hard to imagine a better spot in which to hide from the eye of intruders. The eastern face was a glorious wash of burnt brown and rust-red stone. At the very base of the rocks a scoop in the sand held a small, deep pool of old, dark water. Even neglected, the site was incredibly beautiful. The springs were invisible from here, set high in the rocky face, a water course running deep underground at the base, a dry sandy river its sign.

FROM ALICE *WITH* LOVE

I opened my door and grinned at the mob spilling out of the other cars. I heard Patrick laughing and was glad he was here, that we'd share this special place even if was unlikely we'd see other much. Let loose from the cars, the kids ran in circles like dogs who'd been caged for a week until they found the water. The pool in the river's passage must once have been wide but had now shrunk in the drought to the size of a large tank. Small but deep. It shone like polished stone. Undaunted, the kids went straight in. This was clearly permitted, so I pulled off my boots and dipped in my toes. It was cold not far under the surface.

Caleb ditched his boots too and pulled off his shirt. He dived into the water in his jeans and headed straight for the rock face on the far side, then scarpered effortlessly up the steep slope. Some of the bolder kids made after him and Caleb paused, climbing only long enough to throw a handful of small stones down at them. The boys ducked and the pebbles clattered impotently on the rock face. He threw some more stones, larger and more accurately, but even landing a blow or two had little effect. For a moment I thought to intervene but then I remembered the kids weren't my responsibility here. Patrick also had put away his duty of care. Here the kids had fathers, mothers, aunts and uncles. No matter what we had told the department, this was a family trip, not a school excursion.

Patrick and I stood side by side. It was a nice feeling having him so close, knowing we had a journey ahead of us.

Treasure approached and stood next to me. 'Lovely one,' she said softly.

It was. We stood quietly watching the water, the rock face, the boys who were getting up quite high.

Concerned, Treasure warned Caleb to look after the kids. 'Those kids are with you. Don't let anything happen to them.'

In turn Caleb yelled at the boys. 'Don't bloody fall, or else.'

I laughed.

'Else what?' Patrick sang out, amused like me by the hollowness of the threat. Just seconds later Preston's feet slipped on the sheer slope. He hung by his arms, kicking his legs dramatically. For a moment he even had me fooled. Panicked, Caleb clambered back towards the boy and when he was nearly there Preston laughed and righted himself.

We all laughed so hard Caleb had no choice but to join in.

I was keen to go up myself. As a kid I'd always been a good climber and it would put space between Patrick and me. Something I guessed Treasure was telling us to do by her rather unsubtle and unusual hovering around us.

'Can I go?' I asked.

'Sure. Be careful,' she said. 'Don't go too far or in the top water. Other-side one is okay.' She pointed up the rock face with a tilt of her chin. I was a bit confused. The only water I could see appeared to be down here in the river. How could there be water on top of the ridge?

I walked around the water to the edge where the rock face rose out of it. Close up it was steeper than I'd thought. I nearly backed out. But I did have some of my mother's pride and I didn't want to look scared. Halfway up I began to panic a little and had to calm myself before I could go on. I continued to pull myself up, placing my feet with care, conscious of the drop below me. I could hear the boys cheering me on from above. By the time I reached the top

I was utterly exhausted and my legs were shaking. Acting with a confidence I didn't feel, I turned to give the small kids below a royal wave before seeking the shelter of the inner ledges. Patrick, I was disappointed to note, was no longer there to witness my triumph.

I clambered over the rocks behind me until I came to a space where the stone was flat and expansive. I kept walking along the ridge line in a northerly direction, passing between a series of rocks like sculptures. To my delight I came across a small pool of clear water. Remembering Treasure's warning I only put a finger in. It was ice-cold. Behind it was a bigger, deeper pool shaped by hard black rock. I felt that this was sacred water and I let it alone.

After a few more minutes of walking I came out the back of the ridge. From this vantage point I could see for miles. In the distance, travelling from the direction of Red Bore, were two vehicles. They slowed once they entered a dry creek bed. Below and to my right was a single tall tree, a standout in the low scrub. It seemed to call me. Venturing down towards it I came to a point where the rock split into a valley. In a curl of stone was the other-side waterhole Treasure had referred to. I recognised it immediately as the same waterhole Mum and I had been to all those years ago. Now I knew where this beautiful place was located, I understood at last why we'd needed Magdalene's permission to come here. How amazing she'd brought us back.

I didn't want to go down the way I'd come, it was far too steep. So I walked along the ridge until I found a different and easier track which took me on a more roundabout but gentler descent. From my vantage point I saw the Red Bore cars had mysteriously beaten me to camp. I imagined the only explanation could be that there was a break in the range where the track passed through which I couldn't see.

The women's side of camp had swollen but was also gaining some order. A cooking area was set up. The swags were grouped together. Little girls ran about dragging bags, working out their spot. I had no idea how many more men might have come. I didn't dare look where the men were gathered around the corner of the river bend in their own sandy camp where I could only presume Patrick would be.

Back at camp as soon as Mum spotted me she wrapped me in a big hug. I swung my arm around her and steered her out of the chaos back to the edge of a small pool of water where I'd started my climb.

We sat on the soft sand together. Some of the little girls were playing making animals in the wet sand.

'Did you see where we camped, on the other side. From up there?'

'I did.'

'I saw it on the way in. You know there's a gap not far past it in the range. It looks like a cave and you can cut through to this side. Amazing.'

'It is amazing. I had no idea this was where we were coming. Did you?'

'No, though I half suspected it was. There aren't many spots in the country with permanent water. I hoped it was but I had no idea the place had water two sides. It's very unusual.'

'And on top.'

'Really, incredible,' she said. 'And to think they'll share it with us.'

We felt blessed.

*

For the rest of the day I hardly saw Patrick. Well before dusk, he went off with the men to shoot kangaroo for dinner, and when they came back the men worked on one side of the camp preparing kangaroo and the women on the other. I got the job of cleaning the milk guts, which I hated. It felt like squeezing lawn clippings through a hose and the smell was pungent and I had no idea how anyone could eat them let alone consider them a treat. In the meantime, the kangaroos' tails and feet were chopped off. The forearms thrown away. After singeing the fur over the flame the guts were refastened with a stick and the animals laid in the pit of coals. Their feet and tails put back with them. The women made damper and wrapped potatoes and pumpkin in foil. I'd long given up my lectures on the environmental cost of foil, which was one of the very few eco-campaigns Michael had run that I'd taken on. No-one listened anyway and I tried not to worry about it because it was incredibly useful.

Slowly the usual chaos around organisation worked itself out like a slip knot, as it always did as long as I didn't try to impose my own sense of order. And I had no right to give instructions here. I was a guest, a privileged one.

After dinner, Magdalene made sure Mum and I slept well away from the edges of the group so we could be protected by the other women from spirits. Since I was a kid I'd slept in this protective circle. I was no longer the fair-haired child, but I'd never been allowed to sleep on my own. It was hard to tell if it was because of old beliefs, Magdalene only ever talked about bad spirits, but I thought it could be a more recent practice that sprang from hiding fair kids from welfare's grasping reach.

At the darkest point of the night, I heard the low voices of men, the cars starting. The men were leaving for somewhere else and Patrick with them. It felt fine to me that he would leave. With him gone I knew I could settle into being in country with the women more easily without the distractions he brought. I was fairly sure the magic we had between us was strong. I didn't think it was growing weaker with all the distance between us. Rather, the opposite might be true.

In the morning I helped with preparations for breakfast. When Treasure's fresh damper was ready, I served some to Magdalene and Mum with cups of tea. As I passed her a cup Magdalene took my hand. 'Everything is going to be right,' she said, her face serious and yet kindly too.

I wasn't sure exactly what she was referring to—life? The LAP test result? The rain coming?

'Everything,' she reiterated.

'Thank you,' I said, and I felt fairly certain it would be. Everything.

Chapter 34

The days were hot and long. The watercourse was choked with weeds, more than I'd expected, and there seemed to be few hands available to help. The work was hard and tedious, but there was little else for me to do out here so I had plenty of time to dig and pull out the plants, slowly finding a certain meditative grace in the labour. The little kids helped when they felt like it. The women made ceremony. Mum sat with them all the time. I only joined them occasionally, when I was invited. I listened. I was out in their country and they were honouring it, claiming back their power.

By day I cared for the country and at night the women cared for me. Old soiled spirit was smoked out. I heard my mother's voice sometimes. The songs went on as they had from time immemorial. Sitting where I was instructed I closed my eyes and let the sound wash, like waves, over and over. When I was allowed to leave the circle I'd lie in my swag and fall asleep soothed. The song was like an element of nature. It had its place with wind and water. While I might not have understood a word, I did know that it was core life-affirming business the women were engaging in.

Stars rippled against the dark night. They were alight and moving. Up there spirits took shape and stories were held in the constellations.

I'd wake from hour to hour and the millions of stars would have slipped away down the dome of the night sky. Sometimes I would put a hand out to their dazzle as if I could catch their light. Nothing was certain. It was the only certain thing. Life, like day, came for a while. Dark followed it. Death came. The earth turned. Within these large cycles, smaller cycles spun. Magdalene's. Mum's. Lekisha's. Mine. And whispering, whispering through the leaves in the tall red river gums was a refrain about love, of my own invention, about how only by being true to my heart could I manifest creation.

The days were full. When I wasn't weeding I collected firewood, and kneaded damper with the young women. Tissianna grew better with each day and I was delighted to see how she softened. Rosia and the toddlers added their own light to our domestic circle. Treasure and Lekisha were kept busy with other chores it was none of my business to know. I hardly spoke to my mother but there was no need. She was on her own journey and I knew we were joined in ways more powerful than could be seen.

Day rolled smokily into night. Nights into mornings. The time slipped away.

I had no idea when the end was finally reached but one morning, five days after we'd arrived, I woke to be told the men were coming back to get us.

Mum hugged me. Her arms were stronger. Her body softer.

'You right,' she said, not a question but a statement to which I nodded in agreement.

Lekisha and I tied all the swags down on the roof racks. My hands were blistered from the weeding but I barely felt the pain. I knew it would come but at that moment I was invincible. High. We tied down twenty-six swags. Others were thrown in the back of the cars as padding for those on the bench seats. Treasure helped load provisions we had left. There wasn't much—not a tail any-where or a container of milk—though there were still unused water containers on the roof. A clean soak had been made almost as soon as we'd arrived, and the sweet spring water, brought to the sur-face had been preferred to the metallic bore water I'd insisted on bringing.

While we packed, the kids who'd stayed at the women's camp—the girls and the young boys—fought over seats in the cars. I couldn't get them to lift a finger to help. No-one else seemed to care and I found I didn't really either. I had no idea how anyone knew what the plan was. It seemed like chaos to me. But when the cars were packed we drove to the junction of three tracks and waited. When the men arrived soon after I didn't look at Patrick, yet I felt surer than ever that maybe we would make it to where I wanted us to go.

When all the cars were lined up again we set off in single file. We took a different route out and I realised that the way we had entered Iltja must be secret and rarely used. This time we went under the hills and were suddenly on the Red Bore side of the ranges travel-ling the road Mum and I had come in all those years ago. As the vehicle Mum was travelling in turned north at the junction she gave me the thumbs-up. I blew her a kiss, filled with love for her and her gift of connection to this place, and this family. Iltja, in its soft way, had taught me that to get what I want might not come by trying to push things into shape but by simply allowing things to be as they were.

Patrick and the other Kilka driver pushed on hard. They had the furthest to go and I didn't blame them for wanting to get ahead. Soon they were out of sight.

At the boundary gate to Promised Land was Lucky, looking as neglected as if he'd been there the whole time and with new compassion in my heart even I felt a bit sorry for him. Though not sorry enough to squeeze him in the back. Henry more practically put him on his tray.

Arriving into Promised Land I felt elated and light-headed; while I could have easily drifted dreamily back to my donga there was work to do. Lots. It seemed to easily unfold. Surprisingly quickly the cars were cleared of their loads. Stuff was just dumped next to cars. Mattresses, slabs of foam, canvas sheets, containers, blankets, pillows, all stained with the country. People dragged in what they needed. Henry organised the cars to be taken into town in the morning, cleaned and returned. All without me having to lift a finger. Boy was I pleased. When I asked how they'd get back he looked at Lekisha.

'My friend,' she said, 'will bring us back.'

So I thought and resisted smiling, the blue Falcon man is still around. They were almost as invisible as a couple as Patrick and I.

*

Despite all the very serious rainmaking work in and around the Iltja site, the expected rain didn't come. For two days there was lightning and a play of clouds but nothing came of it. The pay phone went down. And so did the school line. I didn't see Patrick for dust and short of driving over there was nothing I could do.

It was blindingly sunny, revoltingly hot and the kids weren't very interested in coming back into the cage they found the classroom after their time out bush. At my request Henry managed to get a signal for our satellite phone by standing on the troopy roof so I could at least ring Annie to let her know it was a ridiculous situation. Red Bore had the only working line. Kilka, us and everyone to the east was out, according to her. She reassured me she was doing what she could but I felt prickly and irritated all the same.

The sun continued to shine relentlessly and my sunny mood darkened with the struggle of motivating the kids who turned up through each long, hot day. Lekisha had study days due and while I knew she had no assignments left I didn't complain when her mysterious blue Falcon man turned up and she went with him to town. It was probably for the best. At the moment I was scared she'd go right off teaching, with our class so unmotivated, and if I could have escaped I would have.

To top things off the blisters on my hands got infected. Very quickly I grew hot and weak with fever. I had the visiting nurse from the Red Bore clinic have at look at them. Usually she'd only come if we called but Annie had sent her in case she was needed and there was quite a line-up. I was the last of her patients.

'Did you go out?' she asked. 'I heard something was going on. It was a corroboree, was it, to get rid of the army? A way of pushing back the intervention? That's what I heard.'

The bandaging job she'd done looked good and my hands did feel better. But it didn't mean I owed her an explanation of business that wasn't mine and her prying annoyed me.

'Thanks,' I said. 'You've done a great job.'

She didn't like being rebuffed. 'That infection could spread,' she speculated. 'Maybe you should have a penicillin shot rather than tablets.'

Those big needles hurt a lot, and we both knew it. 'No thanks. I'll take my chances,' I said, hopping down from the desk she'd used as her treatment bench.

The dry, hot days were driving me mad, and although I was grateful when Lekisha returned we started to have arguments about the air-conditioner. She turned the thermostat up and I turned it down. We were both sick of the small space, tripping over each other. But it mattered to try to make the end of the year a success.

We had about the same amount of kids as days to go. Twelve to be exact. The days could tick down but the number of kids had to go up or we'd be closed for sure.

The next day was the hottest it had been since February. The country, the community, every brick, wavered in the heat. Mirages of water on the ground in the distance taunted me.

We spread the word. The class was focusing entirely on Christmas activities and nothing else. There'd be colouring-in and painting. Decorations to make. Biscuits to cook. School was fun. And every kid who came every day could go to the party we planned to have with Kilka. Or would plan if only we could ever get onto them.

Caleb went to town to pick up the school supplies and got blind drunk, carted by the cops to the sobering-up shelter. Lekisha stewed angrily. I volunteered to take her to get him but she didn't want me to, and it was Henry who went to bring him back in the school troopy because no-one, as a result of quarantining, ever seemed to have money for petrol. I felt sicker about how our year was sliding downhill, and while I could have gone to town, the bother didn't seem worth it.

The next morning, Lekisha was in class before me and we went about our business as if nothing had happened. After the kids had left for the day Caleb appeared. His eyes were bloodshot and sunk deep in their sockets. A razor had been scraped clumsily over his whiskers, missing the indent of his chin. Grog clung to his skin like a ghastly cologne.

'Eh,' he said. 'Is there cleaning for me today?'

I didn't know how to respond. I felt angry and sad, conscious of Lekisha's humiliation.

'My cousins they forced me.'

I didn't say anything to this. It was an excuse. We all knew that. Caleb hung his head. 'Sorry.'

'I think you better get a bit more sleep and then come and apologise to the kids on Monday.' He turned away, his shoulders hunched, then paused and took out a large envelope from inside his t-shirt. 'Mail.'

'What's in the envelope?' I asked.

Lekisha looked. 'LAP test. I think. Got that name on it.'

'Open it.'

She smiled unsurely.

'Open it,' I insisted.

We didn't get the results we were hoping for but we hadn't done so badly either. There was nothing to be ashamed of. We weren't so far below the national benchmark. Our spelling had been all right. We were on a par there. It was the comprehension where we let ourselves down. And that would be my fault I thought. I hadn't taught them well enough so they could infer meaning.

'Next year,' Lekisha said as she left for the night. 'We'll do better.'

'Next year,' I agreed. 'You'll do better.'

CHAPTER 35

O n the Saturday the phones still weren't fixed and I went to see Patrick. Now my hands weren't so infected I felt up to it. Antibiotics were amazing. I wouldn't have wanted to live in a time when they didn't exist. As I was driving out I passed Magdalene who was sitting in the shade with Esther. Lucky beside them.

She flagged me down.

'Where you going?'

'To see Patrick at Kilka.'

'Not now, rains coming. You'll get stuck.'

The sky was a clear blue. It was hot enough to fry eggs on the bonnet of my car. Rain seemed as likely as a man falling out of the sky, but I didn't want to hurt her feelings.

'I'll be back tomorrow.'

'You're crazy,' she said.

I shrugged. What was new?

I pushed the car hard over the corrugations. My air-conditioner had packed it in and it was hot with the window up, hotter with it down. I was keen to get to Kilka fast. It seemed like a long time had passed since Patrick and I had last seen each other alone. There'd only been one time after the holidays where we'd managed to be together with everything that had been going on and I hoped things were okay between us. I wondered if I'd made a mistake hoping he'd come over to Promised Land and not making the effort myself, even though my hands had been so manky I didn't want him to see them. They certainly hadn't been up to any touching.

When I got there, Kilka was fairly deserted. Even Lekisha's grandfathers, who were usually on the verandah of their house, were gone. I undid the gate at Patrick's and let myself in. The garden was the oasis I remembered but there was no sign of him. No car. After psyching myself up to make the visit it was a deflating moment. With any luck he was just out and about collecting plant specimens or talking to the old fellas and he'd be back soon.

I turned on the reticulation and drenched myself. I picked and ate a late orange, segment by segment, touring the shady parts of the garden. The afternoon passed slowly while I kept expecting Patrick to appear. It was stupid just hanging around. He could have gone to Sydney for all I knew.

I wandered down the road to Jeanie's house. She was home. Patrick was in Red Bore, dropping off the old men at a meeting. She hadn't seen a swag on his roof so he should be back tonight. I thanked her and went back to his place.

The late afternoon sky was swept into an unusually abrupt and deep blue darkness. There was no soft twilight, no watercolour of sunset pastels. Cloud crouched on the ranges, the sky a wash of mulberry stain. It seemed I had been wrong, and Magdalene had been right. Rain was coming and it was possible Patrick might stay put, especially if he was with the men who had brought this change on. I looked for his sat phone without success before it struck me he would have it with him.

I sat on the deck and watched as lightning speared the clouds open. Thunder started the rain dance. It arrived in grey and thick sheets, blanketing every open piece of sky, tearing strips off the ground with a fierce flapping. Hail followed, stoning the roof. Like small diamonds the icicles embedded themselves in the ground.

Now I hoped Patrick stayed at Red Bore. This was dangerous to drive in.

The storm belted down and it was so noisy in the house I didn't hear Patrick arrive. He just appeared and gave me a fright.

'Hey you, what you doing driving through this rain?'

'I nearly went to Promised Land to see you but I had a feeling you'd be here.'

'Based on what?'

'The old man, you know Lekisha's grandfather on Magdalenes' side.'

'Yeah.'

'He saw you coming when we'd passed the junction, but I had to keep going to drop them off. I hoped you'd wait.'

I laughed. 'Well Jeanie told me where you'd gone. She said no swag. So I waited. You took your time.'

'Sorry. I wanted to use a phone at Red Bore and Annie opened up the school for me, so I could have some privacy when I checked with the lawyers. I was scared things might have gone awry again. Sorry it's been keeping me here, lying low.'

'Yeah, well my hands have kept me away.' I held them up so he could see the last of my sores.

'Poor thing,' he said, taking my hands in his. 'But listen to this. The decision's through. I get shared custody. All school holidays. Any time with 24 hours notice on a non-school day too. It's final.'

I hugged him to me tightly. I was glad for him. For me. It was part of seeing what the future might hold.

Patrick woke me early his fingers tracing across my lower back. I kissed him sleepily as I tried to work out just how early it was. Before dawn.

'You should go now if you're going to get back to Promised Land before the storm,' he said.

I couldn't hear any rain. It had stopped long before we had finally gone to sleep.

I laughed. 'You and Magdalene, you're like one big broken record. Storm's well over.'

Patrick wrapped a cotton blanket around me and pulled me up to look out the window. Now I could see why it was so dark. The western sky bulged with black cloud.

'I'm happy for you to stay as long as you like,' he said. 'But if you want to see out the term at Promised Land you need to go now. We might just make it over for that Christmas party we've got planned if the waters go down. I reckon you've just got time before it hammers down here. You should be right to cross the river. It wasn't flowing last night. It will take the rain from the north coming down. And the crossing is in pretty good shape after such a long dry.'

'Oh my god.' I'd hardly heard what he said, entranced by the fury of the looming front. 'That's one serious storm about to land.'

Quickly I pulled on some jeans, keeping his t-shirt on.

'Okay. Turn back if you need to,' he said anxiously. 'No heroics.'

'I don't do heroics.'

'Bullshit,' he said. 'But go if you're going, and go safely.'

He kissed me. 'You know,' he said, 'we can do anything we want now. Whatever's right for us.'

I liked it. I kissed him back hard and left.

The rain started before I hit the main crossing; soon it was bucketing down, so loud and heavy I felt as though the roof was in danger of being pushed down. The tiny creeks and small overflow channels were pooling onto the track as I churned my way through them. My tyres were still soft for dry sand, and I had to drive like a sailor, my wheel a tiller tacking this way and that on the slippery dirt.

At the first river crossing the water was already running down hard. The rain must have been falling to the north much earlier. How stupid of me not to have considered this. For a minute or two I sat in the car with the engine running and rain pelting down, drumming on the metal so loudly it was hard to think straight.

I knew I'd also have to cross the other tributary, a kilometre further on. If things went badly I could get stuck on the high ground in between. With this amount of rain who knew how long it would stay above the flood line. I'd never been out here when the water was up and I had no real idea of how this country held up in floods.

I decided to take the risk, although I would check out the track first. Being brave was one thing, being foolish another. The creek ran in a fierce bubbling rush, and a dirty skirt of foam had already built up on the banks from the churning force of the water. The only way to check if the track was still intact under the torrent was to get out and walk it. The danger was not just the rushing water but what might be hidden in it—snakes, spells, sticks. Before I got out of the car I made sure my jeans were tucked firmly into the socks at the lip of my boots. I'd been taught a long time ago that all of the local poisonous snakes struggled to get their fangs through denim and release the venom. As long as no skin was exposed I should be okay. In any case, I felt fairly invincible after my night with Patrick, and even snakes didn't scare me.

As soon as I stepped out of the car I was soaked by the heavy rain and getting into the creek couldn't make me much wetter. For shallow water it certainly had a strong current. I waded out carefully and was relieved to find that it came up no higher than my knees. Feeling my way and using a stick I was pretty sure the track was still sound, and it seemed worth the gamble to cross.

Either way, there was no time to waste; the water was getting higher by the minute. Dripping wet I jumped back in the car and put it into drive. Going slow but not too slow to stall I whined across in low gear, breathing deeply and audibly. I only made one bad mistake, fifty metres in, veering off the track briefly. For a moment I was bottoming out and I had to sharply correct, hoping the back tyres would make contact again; fortunately, they did. On the opposite bank I hit the accelerator to run up the slope, the tail of the car slipping wildly. Only when I made flat high ground did I slow down, the adrenalin receding, my breathing returning to normal. If only this wasn't the one place for miles where the river looped back across the road twice.

At the top of the rise it wasn't the height of the river that shocked me. It was Lekisha waiting on the other side with a strange four-wheel drive and a man I knew I should recognise.

I got out of the car and waved. She waved back. 'This is Mr Blue Falcon,' she yelled. 'Ronny Smith most people call him. We come to get you out. I told him I'm not the teacher yet and she can't run off to Kilka and leave me, till the school year's over. So he said we'd fetch you.'

'Who's the mad one now?' I called out, bursting with happiness.

'It's peaceful out here isn't it,' she shouted through the rain, over the rushing creek. 'In all these years I've never seen this water so high. You could wade across or we might just have to sit here till the river drops and keep each other company.'

She meant the country. The creek. The rain. And us. All together.

'Usually only takes a day or five, to go down,' Ronny called and I laughed with them. There was always the option to leave the car and walk across if we got sick of it all.

None of us moved. Like me, the torrent of rain made them happy. Right now I could only think of one thing that could make the moment more perfect. Then I heard him, shouting from the crossing behind. I waved madly as he waded his way across.

CHAPTER 36

Flying in from Sydney I saw claypans brimming from the long summer rains. Creeks were potted with fresh water, the ground rich in new grasses. There were more shades of green than I had names for.

'It doesn't look like the desert anymore,' Tom said.

'That's the desert for you, it's always full of surprises,' Patrick said.

I gave his hand a squeeze. We'd just spent the entire summer near fresh water. At Eddy's shack in the south west forest. It had a river flowing through it, a deep hole of green water in the limestone rock for swimming. It had softened us. Most of the hard edges between Tom and his Dad had been smoothed in the months of playful and unhurried living. We'd learnt a lot about each other. And Patrick had been able to work on the book so it was ready for the final checks. From our base at Red Bore where we'd job share and cover Annie for two terms he could make any final changes that were necessary.

Tom was here with us for two days. He'd go back to his Mum's but Patrick had managed to get him to come with us for the apology. The courts had thought it a worthwhile exception to the orders given Tom's personal history.

At the airport we hired a car and drove to Mum's place. I gave Mum, Michael and then Magdalene, who was visiting, big hugs.

'This is Magdalene, Alicia's grandmother,' Patrick said to Tom.

'Your nanna?' Tom asked doubtfully. 'You're different colours.'

There was a moment of awkward silence.

Magdalene looked at her arm and feigned shock. 'Hey, you're right,' she laughed.

The morning opening of the parliament and the first welcome to country in Australian federal parliament had happened while we were on the plane but Mum and Michael had recorded it for us. We would watch it tomorrow with everyone else before the broadcast of the apology to the stolen generations.

We stayed at a hotel that night, after taking Tom around to see some of the sites. The reptile centre turned out to be a bad idea. In retrospect I'd been a bit enthusiastic about him holding Olive, the python. He'd had nightmares all night. There was clearly still a lot I had to learn in my new role. When I woke at dawn Patrick and him were curled up together in the adjoining room Tom was staying in and indulgently I let myself watch them a while. There was still a part of me that found it hard to believe they now both belonged with me.

By the time I'd dressed they still hadn't woken so I set the alarm for them and a note and let them sleep. I'd promised Michael help to make mountains of scones for the expected hordes who were coming to share the event with us. Mum had already made sweet dark mulberry jam and orange marmalade, though Michael had said, with some relief, that she was staying out of the kitchen more now she'd gone back to work. She was just doing two days a week working on a placement program for young social workers, but she seemed to be enjoying it and I was glad to see them both looking so well.

Frank kindly picked up Patrick and Tom and brought them over for me. He had his boys with him and they had a football which was great. They started a game out the back. Tom picked up a turn of the ball right away and joined in. Luckily for us he wasn't a rugby kid.

It was still ridiculously early by the time the scones were in the oven. I went out to sit on the front fence and wait for the others. For the first time I could remember, Mr and Mrs Press weren't sitting on their verandah. The house was shut up, the curtains closed and the sprinkler their grandchildren loved to run under was put away, the hose coiled tight as a snake under the tap. Their floral chairs looked sad and lonely.

'Don't worry,' I told the old chairs. 'They'll be back.'

I looked up at the ranges, finding it astounding this was the same view I'd seen last February. The dry brown country had been transformed. Now the sides of the ranges truly looked like a caterpillar, covered in a strange bright green fuzz. Thick new grass spread from the riverbanks up the steep slopes, lichen coated the rocks.

For the first time in an age there wasn't a single caw from a crow. The locals had returned and were in full morning song. On the road verges there were flowers, delicate blue stars, bright white paper daisies, the round yellow heads of billy buttons, all sprung up since the rain. Beautiful.

A strange car turned in to the street, and as it slowed down I realised with disbelief that it was Floyd driving.

'I thought,' he said, unbending his long legs as he stepped out of the smallish car, 'what better day to visit than today.'

'I had no idea you were really back,' I said. 'I got your postcard saying you were coming. I thought it was a joke.'

'I came in last night via Darwin. I would have called but I was whacked. You just stay in Eddy's places, do you? You don't talk? He knew I was coming.'

'He didn't mention you coming here. He did tell me he'd heard you might be taking the job with the *Morning Times* but he wasn't sure.'

'I am.'

'What about London?'

'Too cold,' he said. He put out his arms and we hugged. I let him make his way inside to deal with everyone's surprise on his own.

Soon after Patrick came walking briskly towards me, looking unsettled.

'Did you know he was coming?'

'No,' I said, not sure how to take Patrick's jealousy. I decided it was sweet and kissed him quickly. 'Floyd was always keener on surprises than me,' I reassured him. 'And he's never shied away from making an entrance.'

Suddenly Lekisha turned into the driveway too fast, nearly taking me out with her bullbar.'

'Careful,' said Patrick.

Lekisha jumped out.

'You a mad driver,' I said.

'You mad standing in the driveway. And I'm tired. Kevin O-Seven should have thought about how early we had to get up,' she grumbled. 'I even threw water on Ronny but he wouldn't get up.'

'So you left him?' I asked.

''Course,' she said, as the back of the Promised Land troopy burst open and people poured out. 'He can fly down in his Falcon if he gets lonely.' She gave my arm a friendly squeeze 'Well, I'm hungry, how about you?'

'A little bit. Did they get that demountable over? That's working out.'

'It will, no-one's hurrying that much. Blossie's real happy in Patrick's house.'

I bet she was. It was a good arrangement though. One of the schools had to close. The new policy wasn't keen on one-teacher outfits and even though Kilka was a better set up it had lost more kids whose parents had left in the upheaval of the early days of the intervention. By the skin of its teeth and, I suspected, only because there were so many unpalatable decisions to be made, Promised Land had managed to keep the school. Blossie would drive the Kilka kids each day. Her boyfriend was coming to live with her. She did sound very happy when we'd spoken.

Lucy was walking up the driveway with a covered tray balanced on tea towels in her hands.

'What's that?' Lekisha said. 'Smells good.'

'Marinated rib bones,' Lucy said handing the tray over to Lekisha who couldn't resist having a rib as she walked the rest in.

'How could you think about bringing meat at this hour?' I said as we made our way around the side.

'That's what Annie said. She wouldn't get in the car. She said she'd throw up. Anyhow, pregnant women, they whinge a lot. It's not attractive. Don't do it when it happens to you.'

'I think I'd be too happy to complain.'

'I would have thought that might have been the case with Annie. But how quickly she seems to have forgotten how much she wanted a baby. It's all about her suffering.'

I laughed. 'God you are a mean bitch.'

'Me mean? Wait till you hear Iry on the subject. So where's the man and your new boy?'

'Inside. And guess who else is here?' I whispered. 'Floyd!'

'You're joking.'

'No, I'm not. He's in the kitchen.'

'I always thought he had plenty of spunk, that guy.'

'He's indulgent, a lush for an event,' I said, joking.

'No,' Lucy said seriously, 'he's smart. What better place to write an article than from here?'

'Here?'

'Of course. This is the place the whole country's got to start thinking about once they finish with making an apology, because if they ignore what's happening here, we are sunk. We're on a path to apartheid and destruction. Floyd can make that post-apology point. He's just the man for the job.'

'God, a bit serious for you. I thought you might be channelling Iry. Where is she?'

'Canberra, of course.'

'She's not?'

'She is. She'll probably be head of the department of families in a minute.'

I laughed. Iry with more power seemed unimaginably scary.

The crowd from the bush had settled in the backyard, all the chairs taken. Some sat on the lawn. The senior men stood. Floyd was talking to them. It was nice to see him in his Blundstones, his old country shirt I'd given him all those years ago. I made my way over to where Lekisha was sitting, under the mulberry tree.

'Off!' Lekisha tipped Declan out of a chair so I could sit down beside her. 'You sit on me,' she said before he could start crying. 'And Preston, go get us some tea.'

Preston paused just long enough to let us know he had a mind of his own, but he didn't dare linger. It was nice out of the heat in the shade of the tree, bare of fruit so late in the summer. But it had been a bumper crop. You could tell from the thick stains on the ground that Mum's manic picking hadn't been able to keep up with its bounty.

I watched as Patrick came out from the kitchen and took Tom away from his impromptu footy game, leading him towards the Kilka men, who were standing against the fence with Floyd. They all shook Tom's hand as Patrick introduced them one by one.

Tom handled himself well as he was led through the group. When he took Floyd's hand, Floyd must have made a joke. The boy threw back his head and laughed, Floyd turned back to his conversation and the boy stood there a fraction longer looking at him admiringly. Floyd sensed him and patted his head in a friendly way. He wouldn't have made a bad dad at all I didn't think. But he'd got what he wanted and so had I. Almost. Floyd caught my eye and we smiled at each other. There was no regret.

In a loud voice, Michael invited people to watch yesterday's opening of parliament. There was the usual complete chaos until everyone settled around the huge TV he'd borrowed from work and set up outside. Lekisha and I moved in closer to the other women.

Preston settled down with a plate of food nearby. He was a few inches taller than he'd been at the end of the term. I thought about how I'd probably never see him prepared to put on a sarong and be a part of a nativity play ever again. Like Sammy who had lost his puppy fat, soon they'd be men. I didn't think they'd be in next year's Christmas play at all. It reminded me I should print some of the photos and give them out. Dear sweet Rosia tumbled about on unsteady legs, everyone's pet.

'See,' Lekisha said, 'she started walking the other day, straight up. She didn't bother with crawling.'

I grinned. Fair enough.

We had just enough time to watch the welcome to country. From the moment the dancing and songs began everyone, even the smallest kids watching became quiet. At the end the prime minister was given a message stick by Ngambri-Ngunnawal elder Matilda Williams House. She rose in a magnificent possum-fur coat to explain to the gathered dignitaries and guests the role of the message stick in a ceremony of 'proper respect', but she started with a joke. A joke about Parliament House leaking, at which everyone laughed. I could have cried at her generosity, the lengths she was prepared to go to, to make people feel comfortable.

Patrick passed behind me and ruffled my hair gently. I love you, the gesture said, and I loved him.

Nobody moved as we switched to the live broadcast of the apology which was due to begin. I was suddenly overwhelmed with sadness that we even had to be doing this. Why had we behaved so badly to people? It was criminal the hurt we'd caused and I felt a rush of sadness swamp me I couldn't control. I dashed to the toilet to hide. My tears seemed rather indulgent. Like I was the one who'd been hurt. I blew my nose to stop them.

When I came back, Lekisha gave me a funny look. 'You pregnant,' she said.

I squeezed her hand. 'No. Not yet.'

'You look it, all flushed.'

That was a mad thought. That would be great. I grabbed my camera like my father would have done and protected myself with its magic.

'Photo,' I called. 'Everyone look now, for history's sake.'

Lekisha bossed the group tighter for me as I looked through the lens.

Magdalene had Rosia in her lap. Preston and Sammy were doing gangster finger poses, and getting the little kids to do it too. Treasure looking somber sat to the side, Henry at the back. On the side, the old men of Kilka stood in a half-moon behind Patrick and Tom. There was a noticeable gap where Caleb should have been but he'd got three months for drink driving. Lekisha hoped it would pull him up properly because she wanted him to get a job with the new football program that toured bush schools. Maxine apparently hadn't had a drink since Christmas when Caleb got picked up. Her reasoning was simple. She was tired of drinking. So was he. He'd have his rest inside, her out and there was a new baby on the way. Mum yelled at me to hurry up and take the picture. I set the timer and ran to join the group.

When I looked at the photo later I noticed that Lekisha's kind face was glowing and Magdalene looked like Magdalene has looked to me for all my life. Contemplative, strong, an elder. Her fingers are threaded together in her lap, her thin legs crossed. Her eyes are dark and serious as she looks intently at the camera. Her expression suggests she is looking at something beautiful. Maybe it is the good future she was always able to see and guide people towards.

As soon as the broadcast started the kids sat down and fell quiet, as they did for ceremony. They were serious, focused, present.

When the camera panned around the chamber, Magdalene spotted Gough in the crowd, which pleased her immensely. She'd met him years ago and he'd remained her favourite politician. She wanted an explanation for why he wasn't sitting with Kevin but Michael explained that only the elected party could sit on those benches, at which Magdalene sniffed indignantly. Clearly she thought this was a lame excuse.

'He's number one,' she said.

The prime minister began. It was hard not to have goose bumps, not to be fairly certain this was as important a moment as I would ever see played out on the Australian political stage.

I was glad to be here with all my families. And with my new one too. I glanced back at Patrick and Tom sitting with the blokes. I was glad Kevin was saying sorry for all of us, doing it on our behalf, but, like Lucy, I didn't think this meant a closure, an end to the troubles. It felt like a firing gun, starting a race for change.

I wasn't sure how Lekisha and Magdalene were taking the speech. Henry ate his way steadily through a burger of meat and egg, chewing slowly. Parts of the speech were long and convoluted. I assumed because Kevin had taken legal advice which got in the way of being straightforward. But no-one's attention drifted.

Lekisha and Treasure pointed out someone from mission.

'See that's old Dorothy, you remember her.' I didn't catch who she was before the camera had moved. Mr and Mrs Press were centered in the frame. The camera hovered on Mrs Press as her normally serene face crumpled with emotion. The large dress purse with the silver clasp was held tightly in her hands. Her fingers were trembling. Tears ran down her cheeks. It seemed we could see straight in through her brown eyes to the storm in her heart, the swell of relief rising over the pain. The camera zoomed in shamelessly, and Mr Press's fingers were captured taking his wife's, pressing them tight, holding her with the same loving strength they'd relied on through the past years. I started to cry and saw Mum was too. We cried with Mrs Press. For her husband. For everyone who'd been dragged from their family.

When it came time for the right of reply, Magdalene was cross that some people in the crowd turned their back on the leader of the Opposition. 'He can have a turn,' she complained.

'Well, he is, Nanna, just no-one wants to listen to him.'

Magdalene sniffed unhappily. Floyd patted her arm. 'You're right, so he can,' he said soothingly. I knew Magdalene's sense of justice would be in the story he would write. He had been flat out taking notes. Even though the entire event would be reproduced word for word on a million internet sites by now, all accompanied by images, he used his notebook to record the event as it unfolded here, on the hot verandah in Alice Springs.

When the Opposition leader's speech was over and the commentators sought reactions from the crowd, someone turned off the TV. No-one here was interested in the opinions of strangers. The kids returned to playing, and adult conversations sprang up again. I stayed sitting. History had been made but it was hard to know what to do with it. The sky was piercing blue and the birds were singing to each other in gossipy groups.

'Those poor things,' Magdalene said, her voice thick with emotion. 'I hope they feel better now.'

'I'm sure they do,' I said.

'It's really sad, their story.'

'It's awful,' Lekisha said.

'No family, poor things. That's really terrible.'

Magdalene sighed and wiped her eyes on the inside of her shirt, which she lifted from the neck.

Lekisha gave her nanna's shoulder a squeeze. 'Don't worry so much.' Magdalene's compassion tore at my heart. Mum came close for a moment and squeezed our hands tight.

Rosia came up and climbed onto my lap, a chop bone in her hand. I gave her hot hair a kiss. She'd be jumping and skipping before Caleb saw her again. While there were lots of mothers, fathers, uncles and aunts to chase her, she'd be pleased to have her father back caring for her.

Mum was looking at me and I thought I knew what she was thinking. She was right. She had got better. I had become happy. We'd been looked after well by the people who owned this country. We'd given, worked hard, there was no doubt, but what we'd got back was hard to put a price on.

Above us, the sky, bleached blue again, was open with all the possibilities offered here. As it always was.

ACKNOWLEDGEMENTS

I'd like to acknowledge the Arrernte people, those past and present, as the traditional owners of Alice Springs, Mbantua. I feel privileged to live in their country and to have grown my family up here. In particular I'd like to extend my warmest thanks to those families who were part of the Irrkerlantye Learning Centre and the Ngkarte Mikwekenhe Community who inspired this book. In particular, for teaching me many things, being generous friends and good fun, I'd like to thank MK and Amelia Turner, Felicity Hayes, and Carol Turner, who has also been the best bush foods partner I could ever have had. For being a good place to take questions and have a chat, my gratitude goes to Akeyulerre, which is dedicated to ensuring there is a place for Arrernte cultural knowledge and practices and promoting and sharing knowledge with the broader community.

I'd like to thank Arts NT and the Island Residency Program through the Tasmanian Writers' Centre for their support.

The book couldn't have been written without the support of my own family. Thanks in particular to my youngest, Poppy. And to my father, Alan, who taught me the magic of reading and writing, I'll always be indebted.

To my friends, who stick by me and give all sorts of encouragement: you're great! I'd like to especially thank Genevieve, Sophie, Jane, Kate, Julia, Sally M, Sally W, Olivia, Harriet, Gracie and Maryanne. Thanks to Louise Thurtell for taking this book on and to the Allen & Unwin team, especially Siobhán Cantrill, Angela Handley and Clara Finlay, for their editorial input. To my agent Fiona Inglis, much gratitude for believing this might be possible. And, as for you, Gerard Waterford, what can I say? You're the bomb.

Finally, while this novel draws on my experience living and working in Central Australia and I have sought advice from a variety of sources, any mistakes in this work of fiction are entirely my own.

ABOUT THE AUTHOR

Jo Dutton lives in Alice Springs with her family. She is the author of two other novels, *On the Edge of Red* and *Out of Place*. She is currently working on a new novel.